FORBIDDEN LOVE

"Juliette, dear Juliette . . ." He held his breath, praying that she would not resist. The pressure in his chest, head, and loins was so intense that his body seemed full of a throbbing red haze.

"Juliette, I love you . . . you do believe me, don't you?" His hand was at her knee where her garter marked the top of her stockings. Above that his palm slid over soft, exquisite skin.

"Oh, Juliette, I do adore you. I want . . ." He drew her closer to him, and covered her mouth with his. She remained quite still for a moment, unresponsive to his insistent passion. Then she slid her arms up around his neck, and her body sagged against his . . .

Avon Books are available at special quantity discounts for bulk purchases for sales promotions, premiums, fund raising or educational use. Special books, or book excerpts, can also be created to fit specific needs.

For details write or telephone the office of the Director of Special Markets, Avon Books, 959 8th Avenue, New York, New York 10019, 212-262-3361.

GREENSTONE

YVONNE KALMAN

AVON
PUBLISHERS OF BARD, CAMELOT, DISCUS AND FLARE BOOKS

AVON BOOKS
A division of
The Hearst Corporation
959 Eighth Avenue
New York, New York 10019

Copyright © 1981 by Yvonne Kalman
Published by arrangement with Doubleday & Company, Inc.
Library of Congress Catalog Card Number: 80-2862
ISBN: 0-380-62414-1

All rights reserved, which includes the right to
reproduce this book or portions thereof in any form
whatsoever except as provided by the U. S. Copyright Law.
For information address Doubleday & Company, Inc.,
245 Park Avenue, New York, New York 10017

First Avon Printing, August 1983

AVON TRADEMARK REG. U. S. PAT. OFF. AND IN
OTHER COUNTRIES, MARCA REGISTRADA, HECO EN U. S. A.

Printed in the U. S. A.

WFH   10 9 8 7 6 5 4 3 2 1

To the Lady Librarians of Glen Eden

CONTENTS

Map of
NEW ZEALAND
showing
EARLY SETTLEMENTS
UP TO 1850

Korororeka.
Bay of Islands

NORTH ISLAND

Aukland - Waitemata
Harbour

Waikato
District

★ New Plymouth
1841

LAKE
TAUPO

Wanganui
1840

TASMAN SEA

N
W E
S

★ Nelson
1842

★ Wellington
1840

★ Canterbury
1850

SOUTH PACIFIC
OCEAN

Land occupied by Maori tribes

★ New Zealand Land Company Settlements
and date of first shiploads of immigrants.
Most places had a few earlier settlers already.

**MIDDLE
ISLAND**

★ Otago
1848

0   MILES   100
0   KM   100

MAP BY PALACIOS

SOUTH or
STEWART ISLAND

It was not yet morning and cold with the chill of late spring. Everything was grey. No colour showed in the rose gardens, and the ancient oaks that lined the driveway to Kensington Palace whispered with dark grey leaves. The Duchess of Kent stood moodily at the window biting her lip with frustration.

At first she had refused to wake her daughter, arguing that she should be the one to break the news to her when she woke, but the Archbishop and Lord Chamberlain insisted they must speak to her at once. When Princess Victoria stumbled sleepily from the room they shared, the Duchess immediately began twittering around her, dabbing at her hair and adjusting the sash of her cashmere robe.

Victoria stopped her with a command. She would see them alone. As the Duchess gaped at the door that had been shut decisively against her she thought, There must be some mistake. Surely, now that Victoria was Queen she needed her mother's guidance more than ever before.

PART ONE

EVANGELINE

1837-1838

One

At this exact moment twelve thousand miles away on the other side of the world, six children were walking along a beach. Here in northern New Zealand the dusk was gathering like a thin damp blanket to snuff out the last warmth of a midwinter's day. The sand had dulled to grey. Shadows from bush-smothered hills stretched across the beach like a shallow tide. The beach behind the children was pockmarked with footprints and scattered with scars where they had been digging with their fingers for *pipis,* succulent clams that were heaped into two flax baskets carried by the older children. These they dumped with a clatter beside the pile of stockings and wooden-soled shoes at the edge of the sand.

Five of the children were from the family of Thomas Peridot, the trader. They ranged in age from ten to four and in colouring from dark to snow-haired, but all of them were lightly tanned with a sprinkling of freckles across their noses. While they wiped sand from between their toes and struggled with laces and buttons the sixth child ran off.

"Goodbye, Turi. I'll see you tomorrow," called seven-year-old Juliette.

"I do wish that you wouldn't encourage her. She is so vulgar and cheeky," sighed Madeline, the eldest.

"She did dig the most pipis," protested Juliette.

Young Regina began to whimper. Like the others, she was bundled into a thick knitted jacket over her ankle-length worsted dress, but she had ventured farther out and trailed her sleeves and hem carelessly in the cold water. Now her hands were numbed and white, and her cheeks streaked with sand where she had scrubbed at her tears.

"Oh, don't be such a baby," said Madeline as she snatched a shoe from Regina and shoved it roughly over the bunched stocking. "There. See if you can do it up by yourself."

"My hands won't work!" she wailed.

"She can't help it; she is only five," said Juliette, who could easily remember her own inadequacies of two years ago.

"I'm only *four* and I don't never cry," boasted Thomas.

Eight-year-old Abigail, blonde, plump, and already startlingly pretty, stood up, brushing her skirts. "Regina was born yowling and with a runny nose and she will probably spend her whole life like that," she said. "Look at that face! Ugh!"

This provoked louder sobs and stung Madeline into pointing out that while Regina was gathering pipis Abby had dallied on the sand drawing pictures with her toes.

"I don't care! Tattle to Mother if you like. I hate scrabbling in freezing sloppy muck and I'm tired to distraction of pipis for breakfast!"

"You never mind gobbling more than your fair share, I've noticed."

Abby parroted, "Mad, mad, Madeline! Who can say what she has seen!" quoting the teasing rhyme their father had invented.

She failed to rouse more than a brief frown from her sister. Madeline never relaxed her dignity. Now, with a word to Regina, she dragged at one handle of a basket, waited for young Thomas to take the other side, and began trudging up the steep slope to where their cottage was a faint shape on the clifftop. The darkness was curdling so rapidly that distant hills blended with sky. Along the track scythe-leafed *toitois* whispered and nodded fluffy white seed heads at them. A morepork bird hidden close by called suddenly.

"Morepork! Morepork!" echoed Regina, swinging on Juliette's hand.

On the other side of their basket Abby said, "I wonder if the men have gone yet?"

Juliette strained at the heavy handle, frowning. They were not supposed to mention the men in front of the youngest ones. The whole subject was something of a mystery. Men often called at Peridot's cottage. Missionaries, travellers, scientists from England, sailors from the port over the hill, friends and strangers all stopped by for a mug of tea and a wedge of sweet potato bread. It was only rarely that when a caller came Mother sent the children away on an errand with the strictest instructions not to return until it was completed. It was a kind of secret, Mother explained. Father hated secrets, so they must be very careful to say nothing indiscreet because he would be terribly angry. The vision of Thomas Peridot in the grip of an unleashed rage made Madeline and Juliette quiver with apprehension, but Abby was not afraid and loved to tease them by brandishing the secret like a flag. Juliette felt uneasy. She shook her head warningly but did not speak.

The cottage was on one small promontory that edged a short way out into the wide sweep of the bay. Squatting in a clearing, it commanded a view that often included white-sailed whaling and trading ships on the way to and from Kororareka Harbour, two miles away.

The *pa*, or village, where Turi lived was on a promontory beyond a flax swamp. It perched on a bald knoll like a lop-sided crown ringed by sharp-toothed palisades and necklaces of winding trenches. Though it was ten years since enemy canoes had been dragged up the beach, tribal defences were never allowed to become neglected, for a few prosperous years and the luxury of relaxing guard could be fatal. There was no surer way to revive a half-forgotten insult than to grow wealthy and careless, and, thanks to the trade with Thomas Peridot, Te Pahi's tribe were as rich as any. Their *pataka*, the food storehouse, was kept well stocked and a watchman roamed the walls at night. If his conch shell blasted an alarm the warriors would be ready at once.

The pa was almost lost in the darkness. Below the palisades floated a watercolouring of light smoke from the exhausted cooking fires. Someone was calling the hens in a high voice. On the edge of the sand dunes was a dark square, the cage of Hine, the madwoman. Juliette shivered and took a deep breath. The smell of the Peridots' chimney smoke mingled with the salty tang drifting inland. She

could imagine the breakfast pipis cooking, sweet and melt-
ingly plump.

"What's for supper?" she asked.

Inside the cottage Evangeline Peridot was rapidly buttoning her bodice, not helped by clumsy hands that teasingly obstructed her. She was a diminutive woman with a
handspan waist that belied the fact she had borne seven
children. Thin, dark hair hung in tendrils around her face
and neck. In this half-light she was beautiful, with eyes
like great dark smudges. In daylight the conclusion might
be that her nose was too pert, her chin undershot and there
was that tooth missing at the side. Still, most people retained that image of enormous dark blue eyes and thick
lashes and considered her to be the undisputed beauty of a
pioneer district not noted for the beauty of its women.

At the moment she was panicky and distinctly annoyed,
for all the hints she had dropped had been a waste of
breath. She held out a hand, futilely, for the return of her
lace-trimmed house cap.

"Please," she said. "You must go now."

"Not until you let us in on the secret, eh, Blue?"

Jamming the house cap over his curls, the bulkier man
nodded. "Come on, tell us. What does a pretty miss like
you want so much money for?"

"Gentlemen, I do insist. Our arrangement is completed.
You must go now."

"Insist, hey?" mocked Blue. "Just because she's got our
money don't give her no right to order us about."

A tiny chip of fear slid like ice over her skin but Evangeline ignored it, drawing anger about her like a cloak.
These were easily the roughest, rudest clients she had ever
entertained but righteous anger would drive them away.

"I am ordering you out, and I'll tell you just as plainly
not to come back. My children will be here at any minute,
so kindly return my cap, then go."

"She's right, Blue!" called the thin man from the doorway. "Here come a bunch of nippers now."

Blue stopped clowning and flung the cap on the floor.
His broad face was ugly as the firelight caught only one

side of the humped nose and crest of curls. "Whore!" he
sneered.

"We'll be back at the next leave!" called the thin man.
"Be ready to welcome us."

Evangeline shouted after them, "Don't ever come back!"
At which they laughed coarsely. She clung to the doorjamb, shuddering.

The children were emerging from the track into the
clearing. They heard the shouts and laughter but not the
words. The cottage was in darkness.

"No wonder Mother is angry! You've been playing with
the tinderbox, haven't you, Thomas? Poor Mother can't
light the lamps because she can't find it. You know what
she said about that. Tinderboxes are not to play with. One
of these days . . ." Madeline broke off with a gasp.

It gave them all a fright when the two figures seemed to
loom out of the darkness at them. Juliette almost bumped
into the smaller man; she stepped back in alarm, spilling a
scattering of pipis over the weedy ground. The man was
thin, with bony hands that grabbed at her to steady her.
There was something odd about his eyes and his laughter
had a nervous edge.

"Lookit this, Blue! I got me a nipper!"

"Douse it," commanded the other man as he jolted Abigail in passing. "Come on, Johnny, we're late as it is."

Regina's wails grew louder. Juliette tightened her grip
on the handle and hurried towards the cottage, dragging
the others in her wake. Behind them the men talked
loudly as they lumbered down the path. Juliette was seized
by an irrational but overwhelming urge to reach and touch
her mother.

Evangeline greeted each of them with a hug that helped
to smother her own unease. After he had taken off his
shoes Thomas sidled around his father's bentwood rocker
and found the tinderbox and striker.

"I forgot not to play with them," he said winsomely,
pressing them into his mother's hands.

"Who were those men?" asked Regina. "They spooked
me!"

Evangeline bent to hug Regina, who snuffled against
her apron. "Just some men going to see Te Pahi. Out

you go and help Madeline with those pipis. You go too, Thomas, and see Regina washes her face." She poked at the cooking fire, stirring the coals. Should she swear the younger ones to secrecy too?

Juliette rolled the knob to adjust the flame and replaced the tall glass chimney. The room blushed with golden light. Carefully she placed the lantern in the cradle below dangling strings of dried fish, then turned to the next lamp. She struck the steel and flint together, aiming the spark into the charred linen that packed the tinderbox. It flared long enough for her to dip an oil-tipped stick into the tiny flame and transfer it to the lamp. Shutting the box, she replaced it on the shelf beside her father's pipe rack.

The Peridots' cottage had been built in less than a day by Te Pahi's men for the sum of two axes and a small keg of nails. It was a large, simple room with corner posts so stout that Juliette could not fit her arms around them, woven sapling walls, and a flax thatch in which lived hundreds of spiders. Flax mats covered the earth floor and hung on the walls to baffle draughts. Thomas had added the timber and turf chimney later, making it large enough to walk into and fireproofing it with layers of clay. Inside, the cottage was as thriftily arranged as a ship's cabin with three long bunks for the children at one end and a box bed stuffed with dried ferns for the parents. A table was braced against the wall and flanked by benches. Barrels and kegs protected foodstuffs from pests, spare clothes were folded in two tin trunks, and everything else hung from the rafters or from wooden pegs on the walls. A cosy room, thought Juliette as she set the second lamp above the table.

Evangeline hooked an onion from the cluster above her head and set it in the coals beside the camp oven as a special treat for her husband. When it was done he would crack the blackened outer shell and scoop out the centre, eating with a relish that astounded his children, all of whom hated onions. With a forked stick Evangeline pushed the hanging pots along the rail so that the stew would stay hot while the pot containing potatoes and sea water could roll to a boil. Next to that was a small pot from which came a boiling-cotton smell that could only mean steamed jam dumplings.

Regina tugged at her mother's skirts, whining about feeling hungry. Evangeline patted her head. Regina was the most difficult of her children, though she was a willing worker if she could be coaxed. The corners of the child's mouth had turned the wrong way since birth as if she held a perpetual grudge against life itself.

"Go and play with the baby. She might reach for the teething peg if you wave it for her."

"I want something to eat."

"Then go and help Madeline count out the plates." She glanced approvingly at her eldest child, who was loading mugs and tin dishes onto a tray. What would she do without Madeline to help her? Abby thought only of preening at the mirror, and though Juliette was eager, she was such a thin little thing. Just like I was, thought Evangeline with a sigh, watching Juliette concentrate as she placed the knives and forks around the table and arranged the pewter salt and pepper dishes in the center.

"Will we need mustard?" she asked, adding hopefully, "Or sugar? Will we need sugar tonight?"

"Not when there is peach jam in the pudding," said Evangeline, then changed her mind. Why not? It was over a week since they had been extravagant and tonight there were another two golden guineas under a corner of the mattress bag waiting to be hidden with the others. "Yes, we shall have sugar this evening." She turned her head. "Abigail! Leave that Sunday dress alone and go and milk Bunty. Quickly, now! Samuel is not home, so you must do it. I know you hate goats but do it properly, please. Don't think that you can slip in a dipperful of water and imagine that I'll not notice."

Juliette lifted the sugar tin down. It was light because the cone had been worn right down to an apple-sized lump. She rubbed a stale heel of bread over both sides of the grater to polish away the rust, then began flaking layers off the sugar loaf. Swiftly she licked the tip of one finger and pressed it into the powder for a taste.

"I saw you," Madeline accused instantly.

Bending her head, Juliette grated more quickly. The sugar made a delicious sweet spot on her tongue. She tried not to swallow so that it would stay there, exquisite and undissolved.

Madeline was sitting on a tin trunk with Melina propped in her lap, feeding the baby mushed apple, most of which was oozing down her chin. Young Thomas was dawdling outside, teasing Abby. Her indignant voice sounded plainly through the thin walls. Soon she flounced in with the pail and sulkily dumped it for inspection.

"I'm starving!" she announced. "Is Father going to be late again?"

"It would seem so, dear." Evangeline lifted the basin of sow thistle, called *puha*, and heaped bunches of the vegetable over the potatoes, pressing them down with a wooden paddle. A tin plate was fitted over that to conserve the steam and wilt the puha into a bitter pulp. She smiled suddenly and said, "I'll tell you what. If you all sit up nicely I shall give you each a lump of fresh bread to tide you over. Juliette, keep away from the fire, dear. Remember what happened to poor Elsie Pickerell."

Regina's whining stopped as she scrambled onto the bench. Using a stout stick, Evangeline prodded the camp oven towards the hearth. Sacking mitts protected her hands as she lifted the lid, deflecting the scalding, fragrant air.

"Oh!" gasped Thomas in delight.

"That's such a *happy* smell," said Juliette.

"We *should* be happy," agreed Evangeline. "We have a snug home, good food, pretty clothes, and a better future to look forward to."

The loaf had a satisfyingly hollow sound when it was rapped with the knife handle. Evangeline carried it to the table shrouded in a tea cloth and cut each one a generous wedge. While they ate she softly lectured them, as she often did when they were alone.

"You children are very special. You are Peridots. That's a fine old name, and you must always be proud of it, remembering who you are and why you bear it."

"King Richard gave it to us," said Thomas. "At the Crusades!"

"Not to *us*, silly. To our great-great-great-great-great-grandfather!"

"A few more 'greats' than that, Abby," said her mother.

Madeline swallowed a warm mouthful and said primly, "King Richard named him after a precious stone, because he valued him more highly than jewels."

"Just as I value my eldest daughter," said Evangeline, and the girl's plain, square face flushed with pleasure.

"Tell us about the better future!" said Thomas.

"Yes, Mother. Do tell us about the lovely house in San Francisco that we will live in one day!" Juliette begged.

Abigail exclaimed that she could see their father coming. Scrambling off the bench, she pushed Juliette aside in her eagerness to thrust open the door and gaze through to where a bull's-eye lantern was bobbing across the beach flats. Evangeline looked thoughtfully at her daughter. At times Abby made her feel decidedly uncomfortable. She was so single-mindedly her father's angel that she sometimes seemed jealous of Evangeline herself. If anybody was going to betray her it would be Abby. But Evangeline showed nothing of her fears, glanced tenderly at them all, and bade the older girls help her dish up so that their father would have his supper ready when he came in.

While Evangeline wielded serving spoons the girls handed her tin plates for dollops of puha, potato, and fragrant pork stew. Regina tugged at her mother's sleeve and whined, to be answered by a firm "Puha is good for you," which closed the subject until the following evening. They all disliked the taste but all had to eat some; even Melina got a few spoonfuls. Anybody who argued was simply reminded that their family had never lost a child through illness, not like Mrs. Jacobson at the whaling station who had buried several and never gave them vegetables at all.

An enthusiastic burst of barking heralded the arrival of Tippy. Samuel yelled halloo as he bolted the horse into its lean-to behind the cottage, and then Thomas was there in the swinging lamplight, levering his boots off on the jack. Even after he had splashed his face and scrubbed his hands he stank of oil and fish, but the children crowded around to have cheeks pinched and hair ruffled as he stooped under the low doorway and came inside.

At first glance Thomas Peridot looked like a tall, spare old man, so white was his sun-bleached hair and so leath-

ery was his skin. Now his smile bloomed into affectionate
laughter as he whirled Abby up so that her head almost
bumped on the dinghy oars. Evangeline noticed that his
face was red from drinking but white around the eyes, a
sign of fatigue.

He misinterpreted her appraisal. "By glory, but that ale
of Mrs. Jacobson's is salty," he said. "I'll wager that she
brews it from sea water."

"That doesn't stop you from quaffing it." She smiled as
she made the observation.

"The last lot was too sweet and malty, this lot too sour
and salty. She needs to take lessons from you, dear."

"That rhymed!" cried Abby as she took her place at the
table with the others.

Thomas bowed his head while Madeline asked the blessing and then chewed thoughtfully on a mouthful of stew.
When it was gone he chanted:

"Sweet and malty,
Sour and salty,
Mrs. Jacobson's ale is faulty!"

"Oh dear," fretted Evangeline as the two younger children took up the song with glee, banging their forks on
their plates to keep time. "Mrs. Jacobson will think that I
put them up to it if that rhyme reaches her ears, and she
dislikes me enough as it is."

"She's only nip-nosed because she feels inferior," said
Thomas as he tapped the salt spoon over his food.

"She's terribly jealous, Mother," said Madeline smugly.
"Last time we were there she said in a snipey way, 'And
what colour is your mother's new dress this time?' So I told
her that you hardly ever buy new yardstuffs but that you
have such good ideas for using your old dresses over and
over, and because you are so clever at sewing we all have
such beautiful things to wear."

"What did she say then?" asked Evangeline.

"She made a snorting noise and said, 'It's all very well
for some!' I was going to tell her about the dolls but she
went inside and slammed the door."

Samuel came in late as usual, a swaggering six-year-old

replica of his father, big and strong for his age with seemingly endless stamina and enough confidence to tackle anything demanded of him. As he wriggled into his place between Abigail and Regina he said, "Have you told them about the whale yet, Father?"

"I thought you might like to do that."

"Did you catch a whale, Father?" asked Abby.

"We caught a splendid one," said Samuel. "A bull."

"Most unusual, that," said his father. "Normally only the cows and calves come close to shore."

Samuel grabbed the story back impatiently. "It was just on dark when we caught it. We had been chasing it for *ages!*" Then, in desperation because nobody grasped the implications of the "we," he said, "*I* was in the boat with the men!"

Evangeline's fork clattered. "Thomas Peridot! Your solemn word!"

"And a good word it was, too. He's come to no harm."

"But it's dangerous out in the skip boat! One flick of the beast's tail and you'd all be dashed into the sea!"

"And this lad of ours would have beaten me in a race for the shore." He pushed his cleaned plate into the centre of the table and nodded to Madeline. "This is a tasty stew. Hop up and see if there's more in the pot."

"It was such fun, Mother," Samuel reassured her, as he spread gravy over the puha in an ineffective ploy to disguise the taste. "And it all happened so suddenly. I was sitting in the boat coiling ropes into wide flat snails like Mr. Jacobson taught me when all of an instant Jacky Norris up at the lookout . . ."

"*Mister* Norris!"

"Mr. Norris yelled that there was a big one right in close. The men all dropped what they were doing and out skimmed the boat with me in it. There wasn't any danger, truly, Mother. Only two harpoons and a short ride and it was ours. Father said that it may have been ill."

"No matter; there will be first-class oil and plenty of it from that old carcass."

"It was so big that the winches couldn't beach it properly!" said Samuel. His eyes flashed in the light of the lamp that hung from a meat hook above the table. "It's enormous, Mother, really *enormous!* I'll wager that it's even bigger than a *Taniwha!*"

Evangeline's lips tightened at the mention of the mythical Maori sea monster. She did not approve of the way Thomas filled the children's heads with talk of Maori things. They might be temporarily marooned here in this wild, barbaric land, but they were of British stock and proud of it. Surely they should be learning about their own heritage? But she made no comment. Once Thomas had laughed at her hesitant suggestion that he tell the children about King Alfred and the cakes instead of regaling them with stories of the Maori war lord Hongi Hika.

"Look around you," he had urged, flinging an arm towards the bush, the hills, and the pa across the valley. "Look at that luxuriant green! This is all our children know. How could they possibly imagine the Norfolk broads or visualise the soft contours of the Pennines when they have seen nothing but this wild landscape? And why try to describe King Alfred's exploits when they are puny by comparison with events that have taken place right here in their lifetimes?"

"Not quite in their lifetimes. All that horror is over now, thank goodness."

"The wars will be over when the tribes are united under one chief and that time is a long way off. I thought old Hongi Hika was the man to do it but unfortunately he was only interested in the fun of conquest and not the responsibility of being the conqueror. But no matter. We are here in New Zealand; we must learn from the land."

Though Evangeline still disagreed passionately, she said nothing. It was not a wife's place to argue with her husband, but merely to venture protests from time to time. Privately she resolved to keep their way of life as civilised as she could and she fixed her hopes and her large blue eyes steadily on the future.

Soon the plates were clean, all but Regina's on which both stew and puha were untouched. Madeline gathered up all the plates but that one and stacked them in a basin near the fire. Her mother was using the stick to prod at the pudding basin, hooking the knot to lift it out. There was a friendly hiss of water splashing over embers. She dished pudding at the table, scooping syrupy dollops onto a ring of chipped saucers. A pitcher of goat's milk sat on the table beside the sugar.

Regina began to cry in earnest. Everybody ignored her, watching as their mother sprinkled a trace of sugar around the edge of each portion. Abby splashed hers with milk and finished it in a dozen rapid mouthfuls. Regina sobbed more miserably, her dessert out of reach beyond congealed stew and limp puha. Evangeline brewed the drinks—real tea for Thomas, corn-kernel coffee for herself, and faintly bitter *manuka* tea for the children, a medicine they preferred to a weekly purging with castor oil.

Regina knew that if she had not cleared her plate by the time her father finished his tea, then he would eat her pudding. It had happened many times before. She watched him press the muslin bag of tea leaves against the side of his mug and she could bear the agony no longer. Screwing her eyes shut, she shovelled the food into her mouth.

"I was wagering on having a second helping tonight for sure," teased Thomas as he nudged the saucer towards her.

After dinner it was quiet time. The younger two undressed for bed and the older ones who had lessons to revise for Sunday school sat at the table under Evangeline's supervision. Thomas leaned back in his rocking chair and poked at his clay pipe. While her mother was tucking Melina into the cradle, Abby sneaked over to cuddle into her father's lap. He played with her curls and said fondly, "We shall have to get an enormous *tupara*, a double-barrelled musket, to keep the young men away when you put your hair up, lass."

Juliette wistfully glanced at them as she opened the Bible to the marker. If only she were beautiful and outgoing enough to be pampered by her father the way Abby was.

"We'll be marrying them off as smartly as we can find young men foolish enough to take care of them," vowed Evangeline. "Back to your lessons, miss, or Mrs. Clerkwell will be giving you another poor report this Sunday."

The weak-spined old Bible was passed respectfully from hand to hand and each child intoned a whole chapter while the others scratched letters onto dull green slates in brave imitations of Mrs. Clerkwell's copperplate script. Samuel tried hard but his letters bulged and wavered. His reading was so full of mistakes that Thomas watched him thoughtfully and with pity. The weekly application of the Reverend's cane would never make him a scholar. It might be better to let him spend the time between church services with the blacksmith, who had special dispensation to work on repairs for the farthest-flung settlers who could not afford to visit the Mission more than once a week. Smithing would be more use to a capable lad like Samuel than any amount of scribbling on a slate. Thomas knocked his pipe bowl against the hearthstone, wincing as the boy stumbled over simple phrases. It was wrong to humiliate him in this way, having him choke over work that his mind, hands, and eyes were grossly unsuited for.

Regina, clad only in her flannel petticoat, sat up in the bunk she shared with young Thomas and played with her new doll Mary, patting the braided yarn hair and planting kisses on the china cheeks. Last winter Evangeline had bought five china faces in Oliver Jarrod's store and she was making their dolls one at a time when she found free moments from the endless demands of housework, cooking, and sewing more practical things. So far only Regina's and Juliette's were finished, but already Regina's Mary showed signs of too much affection. The scarlet dress was soiled, the lace trimming tattered, and one of the eyes had been scratched in a fierce tussle between Regina and Thomas. In her owner's eyes, though, Mary was still perfection itself. Juliette, on the other hand, had decided her doll Clarice was too beautiful to be actually played with; clad in rustling lemon silk with a ruched brown bonnet decorated with yellow roses. Her mother marvelled yet again at how different her girls were: Regina destroyed beautiful things, Juliette revered them; Madeline was indifferent and Abby craved them with a passion Evangeline recognised uncomfortably as being equal to her own.

There was no clock in this home; for the Peridots the day ended when the work was done. After prayers Thomas fastened the shutters over the open window holes and set up the folding screen around the parents' bed. Evangeline braided Abby's and Juliette's hair. Madeline helped Regina while Juliette lit the slush lamp, a dish of whale oil with a wick floating in it like a fat drowned slug. Meanwhile Samuel scouted outside with the lantern, checking for valuables, for though the Maoris were their friends, stray items had a way of travelling across the gully and into the pa—like the butcher knife which Samuel left outside after feeding Tippy one night, and which was not seen again until Turi's mother produced it to cut flax.

When Samuel came back in, Tippy was following. He threw a square of coir matting near the door and on it set the old chamber pot, decorated inside with the indignant visage of Napoleon and fun for the children to use, though they could not understand the significance of urinating in the face of England's archenemy.

Evangeline moved around the room, tucking the children in and kissing them good night. Her voice and her touch were the last things each of them felt before they slipped into sleep.

But she lay awake for a long time, gazing up at the rafters while Thomas snored beside her. The sound of the insult still echoed in her head. It frightened her, bringing back in one word all the squalor of the past. Until today she had been discreet—her clients were always gentlemen who wanted more than what the slatterns of Kororareka offered, something for which they were prepared to travel and to pay highly. Today's two were different. They smelled of violence and were coarse and overdemanding. Not for them the soul's ease of perfume, soft clean arms, and the feeling of being home again at last.

I'll not do it again, she vowed silently. Never again. It had been good while it lasted. One golden guinea for a few minutes' indignity, whereas a guinea a year plus "all found" was the best she had been offered as a skivvy in Sydney. These guineas were to help furnish the house in San Francisco; they were tangible proofs of a golden future. She allowed herself the pleasure of spending only one a year and the rest, wrapped separately in silk, lay hidden at the bottom of her wicker sewing basket. Forty-three rested there now. In her mind Evangeline counted them with drowsy satisfaction.

Thomas stirred, flinging an arm over her. The oily fish

smell smothered her senses. Turning her head away, she reminded herself that soon the whaling season would be over. He would return to bush work and then, until the autumn, she would bed down with nothing worse than his warmth and honest sweat.

"San Francisco," she whispered, smiling.

Two

Thomas Peridot saw his first Maori when he was a young and impressionable assistant to his father in the family general store in Booting, Sydney, where they sold provisions under Government contract to the penal settlements on the plains of New South Wales. He had seen pictures of Maori warriors dancing the *haka* in their bead-curtain *piu-pius,* but the two who entered his father's store were vastly more frightening with their sober demeanour, frock coats, and satin cravats. While Thomas stared from behind the counter, Arthur Peridot proceeded to find out how they could be of use to each other, ignoring the dramatic implications of who they were.

Thomas knew all about the Maoris. The Australian natives might be dismissed as a lot of superstitious stone-age dwellers but those from across the Tasman Sea had a reputation for bravery, cruelty, and arrogance. These two were tall, brawny men with dark faces overlaid with indigo patterns of whorls, stripes, and curling lines to heighten the contours of nose, cheeks, and chin. Each wore a simple earring like a green knife blade, tasselled at the ear lobe with a flare of small white feathers. As they conversed in careful English the earrings joggled, the tattoos expanded and contracted, and the blue lips widened frequently in laughter to display stained teeth and brown gums.

His father treated them with such exaggerated courtesy that Thomas inferred correctly that they had plenty of money to spend. At his bidding Thomas fetched tobacco for their long-stemmed pipes, and pots of strong tea with triple helpings of sugar, which they drank with much blowing and slurping. When they had gone, Arthur told his son that he had just met Hongi Hika, the most famous of all New Zealand chiefs, who had been on a voyage to England to meet the King and was now on the way home, selling his cargo of expensive gifts in exchange for muskets and gunpowder to arm his tribe. This Arthur Peridot was glad to help him do.

After that encounter Thomas heard many stories about Hongi Hika. With those same muskets he set himself up as the Napoleon of the South Pacific, sallying forth several times a year to wage war on tribes in all other parts of New Zealand. Trading captains brought stories of massacres, slavery, and cannibalism, and showed grisly shrunken heads to illustrate their tales. A quarter of the entire Maori population had been butchered while the missionaries stood by, unmolested but impotent in their efforts to halt Hongi Hika.

When he was twenty, Thomas left with his father's blessing to become a trading agent in the Bay of Islands, choosing that area because he considered Hongi's home ground the safest territory, and confidently approaching the chief for assistance. His venture prospered. Within a year he was doing more business than any other *pakeha* (white) trader, and soon formed a permanent arrangement with Te Pahi's tribe on the south side of the bay. They proved keen to earn iron tools, sugar, muskets, and powder, and the tobacco to which everybody old enough to suck a pipe seemed to be addicted. For these luxuries they felled trees, scraped flax, and dried the choicest fish from their catches. Periodically a ship arrived with the barter goods from Sydney, an arrangement that worked well. Thomas wisely resisted pressure to keep a supply of goods on hand, for it occurred to him that, if his cottage was stocked with bolts of cloth, axes, and treacle, it might occur to the villagers that there was an easier way of obtaining the goods than working for them. But he liked and respected his new associates with a genuine warmth they appreciated. They offered him their women and called him Paritau, their adaptation of his difficult name.

It was a lonely life, for though he was equally welcome at the prim English Mission station and the boozy, brawling town of Kororareka, he had no time to build friendships. So when a small whaling station moved shacks, try-pots, and barrels to a nearby point, he was delighted. He sold them dry branches for firewood, arranged his winter employment there, and befriended Lars Jacobson, the station boss.

Five years later he was called home when his mother was accidentally killed while running from one of the packs of wild dogs that plagued Sydney. Though not in time for the funeral, he stayed for a brief mourning period. One day he was strolling along the wharf to board the *Jane Dowd* for New Zealand when his attention was captured by a most unlikely sight. In the shade of a wharf shed, huddled on a tin trunk, a beautiful and very distressed young woman was weeping. Thomas was naturally curious about why such an exquisite creature would be bent on reddening those haunting blue eyes and staining that milky complexion with tears, so he asked if she needed any assistance.

As she sobbed out a story of an evaporated governess' position for which she had travelled from Melbourne only to be left destitute, she scrutinized him through sodden lashes. Before her was a tall young man with a squarish face, well off, judging from the cut and cloth of his black mourning suit. His thick, almost white hair was pulled back into a tidy sailor's pigtail but no tar would wear a silk cravat, pearl stickpin, or white kid gloves. When she discovered that he was unmarried and on his way to New Zealand she decided that he was just what she had been waiting for. In his eyes she saw honesty, kindness, and compassion, qualities a girl like Evangeline was starved for.

For his part he was captivated. The way that she clung to his arm with her tiny hands—as though making him her protector—touched him deeply. And he was only mildly surprised when he heard himself suggest an immediate solution to her problems.

In the next few days while she lay racked with seasickness below decks, he paced back and forth in the sharp salt air and wondered at his sudden good fortune. It was incredible that she too had fallen in love as suddenly as he had, and even more incredible that she was prepared to brave the hardships of life in New Zealand. Most young women would have been daunted by that prospect but she had merely shivered and insisted that she must get away from Sydney—"this dreadful place"—and she didn't care how. Within the hour of their meeting, they had been married by the harbour chaplain.

She had asked him no questions about himself or his life and he accepted the fanciful name she offered, Evangeline Forsythe (which she spelled carefully for the chaplain), never thinking that it was the kind of elaborate name a young lady might invent for herself. A suspicious man might have noticed too that her chapped hands and rough voice sat oddly with the governess story, and that the trunk jammed with more than a score of extravagantly ruffled, expensive gowns, bonnets, and frivolities was strange luggage indeed for a young lady travelling alone. But Thomas knew little about women; he approved of the way she was friendly to their fellow passengers and he was proud when other men obviously admired her.

He worried that she might not settle in the cottage on the cliffs. But after severe initial apprehension over the fact that Te Pahi's tribe expected her to doctor their ailments as though she was a missionary's wife, she grew to tolerate their Maori neighbours. Indeed, after hearing about how some settlers had to suffer natives roaming through their cottages, poking into things, sampling the food in the pots and bringing their children and dogs with them, Evangeline realised that she was fortunate. Thomas had well trained "his" tribe to come near the cottage only in the mornings, either to sell fish or to be dosed with cough syrup, tonic, or the mustard plasters they loved so much.

Evangeline had a tough resourcefulness that was as unexpected as it was delightful. She could cook fairly well, sew beautifully, and bore her children without complaint and with only a Maori midwife to help her. Thomas was so proud of her that it angered him when the Mission women snubbed her. Strangely, she almost seemed to expect their cold attitude and calmly joined their unwelcoming circle, listening to their conversation until gradually most of the roughness in her own speech smoothed away.

To her, this life was made bearable by the prospect of the future. When it came, Evangeline with her polished speech and carefully copied manners would be ready for it. At night when Thomas was in a receptive mood she would talk to him before he drowsed off, describing over and over again the house set against the green velvet hills of San Francisco Bay. It was red brick with a glossy slate roof and a dozen chimneys with fireplaces in every room. There would be wallpapered bedrooms with four-poster beds, a special room with a mahogany dining table, chairs with brocade seats, and a sideboard arrayed with silver and crystal. The whole family would wear satin slippers inside, and while they ate they would feed tidbits to two cream- and sherry-coloured spaniels.

Thomas had heard the story many times. At first, thinking she was crying for the moon, he had generously said, "Oh yes, yes, one day we shall have that house." But as the years passed he realised uneasily that she expected him to keep his impulsive promise. Once he jokingly protested, "I know that you have never been to San Francisco, my dear, but I could wager that you've been many times to that house!"

Her reaction astounded him. His words had come lightly but plainly hit hard. She flushed under her translucent skin and flared defensively, "I've been building that house in me mind all me life, Thomas! You promised it to me. If that was meant to be a joke, then please be saying so right now."

She had raged at him! She who was always so mild and sweet-tempered! Embarrassed, he mumbled, "Of course not, dear. I, too, look forward to the day when we will live in that house."

"You do mean to keep your word?"

"Of course," he soothed. But the glimpse of metal under the softness made him look at her with a speculative eye. One thing was certain: that house overlooking San Francisco Bay was going to be theirs if Evangeline had her way, so he might just as well make up his mind to it. He began to think of the future in slightly different terms.

Three

Juliette woke up to the sound of a baby crying. She opened her eyes to see that it was just daylight; the fire was brighter than the windows. Thomas came in with his sleeves rolled to the elbows and tossed an armload of small logs directly into the fireplace, prodding them apart with the stick. Long flames of fire poked hungry tongues over the logs, crackling as they licked at the bark.

Thomas saw she was awake and bent over her, grinning. He smelled faintly of fish but more strongly of lye soap and smoke. His fingers flexed threateningly.

"No, Father, please don't tickle!" Juliette wriggled away. In half a dozen grabs he had dislodged all the children from their cosy beds and had them darting to pull on their clothes—all but Abby, who asked to be swung out of bed and was obliged.

Juliette dragged at her stockings hastily, for it was freezing in the one-room cottage with the door standing open.

Madeline was unwrapping the baby's swaddling cloth and replacing it with a fresh dry one. Abby lingered over her dressing, picturing as she dallied a green watered silk afternoon dress. Her mother, entering with a basin and a tonic bottle, threw her an exasperated glance and chided, "Bunty is waiting for you. You'd best hurry if you want to be finished by breakfasttime."

"Bunty is Samuel's job," said Abby.

"Not any longer," replied Evangeline, drying her hands on a towel. "Toss has thrown her calf and the boys are going with Father now to look for her. We heard her crying in the night and a calf calling after her."

Abby pulled a sour face. "I hate milking Bunty!"

Thomas popped his head around the door and reached for a coil of rope. "What's the fuss about?"

"She is complaining that she does not want the job of milking the goat," said Evangeline.

He was on Abby's side at once, Juliette noticed. "Then let Juliette do it. You can manage old Bunty, can't you, Juliette?"

"Of course, Father."

Abby smiled to herself but her feeling of achievement faded abruptly.

Evangeline said calmly, "Very well, dear. You may do Juliette's tasks from now on. Please take Melina's cloth out and get the others from the bag in the stable. They need to be scrubbed with plenty of lye. Use the scrubbing brush and board, and only salt water, please. Don't waste the fresh. When they are spotless you may bring them in to me and I'll scald them with some fresh boiling water." And as Abby sulkily turned to go, her mother added, "But before you begin, finish straightening the beds. That was Juliette's chore too, you realise."

Juliette was pleased with the exchange of tasks, for washing swaddling cloths was an uncomfortable task on cold mornings, while Bunty was warm to lean against and milking was easy. Bunty had yellow eyes with vertical slits, and it gave Juliette an odd feeling when she stared into them. She put her cheek against the hairy flank, tugged at the leathery teats, and hummed to herself.

Even Regina had something to do before breakfast. With a small knife she cut puha which grew lushly all over the grassy clearing. She cut it an inch or so above the ground so that it would grow back again. A cold wind slapped at her neck and she worked quickly to fill her basket so that she would be allowed inside beside the fire.

Juliette was just going in with the pail when her father's shout turned her around. Toss skittered into view, eyes rolling, tail crooked and udder swinging. Tippy barked at her hooves, and behind him, bleating with anxiety, tottered two black and white calves. Thomas emerged from the bush on one side and from the other came the boys riding a brown horse.

"Two calves!" exclaimed Evangeline in delight.

"That Mission bull certainly did a fine job," said Thomas.

"Thomas, hush!"

"Twins! It will mean no butter for a month or so, for Toss will need all her own milk to feed them, but it will be worth it at slaughtering time."

"They're not heifers, then?" Not that it mattered, she thought. Toss and Bunty supplied all their milk needs.

"There's one of each," said Samuel, who always noticed such things.

"They're no good for anything but fattening then," said Thomas. "When there's one of each they are both invariably sterile. We'll have fine roast beef next winter now."

Abigail slipped her icy hand into her father's. "Please don't talk about killing them yet. They look so pretty!"

"There's a lot more in life than being pretty, my pet," he said, swinging her up so that skirts and pettislips ruffled out like petals. Abby giggled, sure he was teasing again. She knew that being pretty was the main thing in life.

The calves were nervous about following their mother into the split-rail pen. Everything smelled strange and upsetting, and there was that barking that confused and dizzied them. Samuel pushed. They bucked and lashed out with white hooves, straining on the gate as he tried to jam it shut. In doing so he pinched a finger on the gate catch and blood dripped from the torn skin.

Evangeline was instantly alerted. Instructing her son to follow her at once, she bunched her skirts and hurried inside to fetch down the medicine chest. It was a miniature trunk neatly compartmented with labelled bottles and jars, each in its own leather nest, and a dozen narrow drawers to hold bandages, scissors, and pins. While she dispensed syrups, tonic, and plasters extravagantly to the Maoris, this chest was used only for emergencies or for her own children. An exhausted bottle or jar might take six months to be refilled so she hoarded the supplies of medicine carefully.

Samuel did not cry—he never cried—while his mother dabbed iodine over the wound and bandaged it, splitting the ends of the white strip and tying it in a knot.

"Now, don't get that wet," she said, knowing as she spoke that an instruction like that would be futile with the irrepressible Samuel.

Even as she patted his curly head he was bursting to get away. Outside, Thomas had hooked the horse up to the sledge and the jingling of harness brass advertised that he was on his way down to the sea to replenish the sea-water barrels. The track for the sledge was not the steep path the children had climbed the night before but instead followed the gentle slope of the land in a slow curve around to the far corner of the bay. It had taken weeks of slashing and chopping to form this track but the labour was well repaid in an easily accessible supply of water. The Peridots caught their roof water on a spread of canvas and funnelled it into barrels, but they never seemed to have enough. The only nearby supply was swamp water that the pa used but it had a thick brackish taste and was ineffective for washing because it stained the clothes brown.

On the lower curve of the track they passed the large vegetable garden. There was not much there at this time of the year but some cabbages and a few rows of feathery carrot tops. In another month it would be time for the big planting of beets, spinach, turnips, and potatoes, the latter covered with cabbage leaves to stop a late frost nipping them black. Thomas maintained that the Bay of Islands had only two real frosts a year—the first when his young potatoes had shown their leaves, and the second when the replacement planting had pushed through.

They glided smoothly onto the sand with barely a bump to show where earth ended and beach began. The horse pricked up his ears and trotted faster now. As they reached the fan of incoming waves Samuel lifted the pails out of the water barrels. The horse plunged in deeper until the wagon was half floating. Then father and son began bailing to fill the barrels. It took only a few minutes of scooping and splashing before Thomas jerked on the reins, turning the horse back the way they had come.

The porridge bowls were steaming on the table, and each one was drizzled with a thin stream of honey. Over the flames the go-ashore pot bubbled, driving a tube of steam up the chimney. Evangeline shovelled scoops of pipis into this pot. By the time they finished their gruel, those would be ready, juicy and plump and tasting of the sea.

Thomas asked the blessing, then said, "I thought I'd take everyone with me to Jacobsons' today. And you too, if you'd care to visit Mrs. Jacobson."

Evangeline gave him a sharp look as she returned to the table. Her hair was arranged with a bunch of ringlets on each side above her ears and a square of lace covered her head. Thomas knew what she thought of the slatternly Mrs. Jacobson but all she said was, "Regina can stay here with me. And please leave Tippy too, in case I have trouble with Toss."

"Can we take the boat?" pleaded Samuel.

"No need to, since the young ones are staying back." Little Thomas' chest swelled to hear himself excluded from the "young ones." "Don't fret about the boat," continued his father, leaning back as the heaped tray of pipis was manoeuvred into the centre of the table and Madeline put down her salt and bread. "You shall have your fill of rowing tomorrow when we go to the Mission. Aye, your fill and more!"

Setting off soon after breakfast, he and the children crossed the damp sand for a half mile and negotiated the rocks where the track turned inland. One moment they were on the sun-washed rocks and the next in the damp darkness of the bush. As always the suddenness of it took their speech away. Underfoot the path was muddy and slippery, clogged with rotting leaves and scattered with twigs. Thomas slipped the tomahawk from his belt loop and swung it at the tree ferns that leaned rough hairy trunks above them. With a few blows he severed ten-foot-long fronds to lay across the slushiest places. Slices of sunshine hung diagonally through the treetops, and there was a clean smell of decaying vegetation.

Though the bush felt hushed and silent it was so thickly populated with birds and insects that it could never be really still. From the next valley came the rustle of wood pigeons clamouring over *miro* berries in the thicket of trees where the Maoris set their noose traps. *Tuis* perched proudly, bronzed by the shafts of light, warbling through their repertoire of songs, demanding an audience. Boldest

of all were the friendly little fantails darting close to the
children and swooping with their dainty tails as flirtatious
as the fans at a royal ball.

"This one likes me!" cried young Thomas.

"He likes the insects that you stir up as you walk
along," corrected Madeline.

"I don't see any insects."

"Fantails like tiny, tiny ones," Juliette said to reassure
him.

For all his bravado Thomas was terrified of insects. Nobody blamed him, though Samuel often had to be restrained when he found an eight-inch-long stick insect in
the *rimu* trees or an enormous centipede with a coiled,
lashing body. The bush teemed with insects of a thousand
varieties: great hard-backed *huhu* beetles which hatched
from edible yellow grubs and dashed whirring at the lamps
on summer evenings, *wetas* with sharp thorns on their an-
gular back legs, gnats that swam in front of the children as
they walked, and hit-and-run sandflies which, by the time
they were felt and swatted, had vanished, leaving a white
hard patch on the skin that itched for hours. In summer
Regina was always covered with weeping blisters and
Evangeline had to wrap her hands in mittens to stop her
scratching herself in her sleep.

At the top of the saddle was a bare place like a worn cal-
lus where rocks and clay lumped together to keep the for-
est at bay. Thomas paused here so that the children could
catch their breaths before the steep descent. The saddle offered a splendid view of the multi-inletted bay, especially
on a day like this when the sea spread flat and glistering
as silk spread out for the dressmaker's shears.

Behind them was their cottage; if they squeezed their
eyes half shut they could make out the washing flapping
on the wire line and the pen where Toss was confined with
her calves. Of the whaling station below them they could
see nothing yet, but the breeze that fluttered the toitoi
plumes at the edge of the bank also carried the odour of
blubber being rendered down.

The whale had been winched right up the beach with the
help of the night's high tide. It was as big as they had been
promised, taller than the top of Thomas' head and fully

twenty Juliette-sized paces long. One side was black and
shiny, the other was red and gashed where thick ribbons of
blubber were being carved from it. Flies clustered over the
meat. Juliette looked into the whale's dead eye and felt
sad.

Thomas was examining the whale's head speculatively,
for it was his task to carefully hack out the black baleen
without breaking or splintering it so that it would fetch
the best prices on what was now an extremely competitive
market. This whale had a fine mouthful but he was old and
the jawbones were hard and brittle. Today's work promised to be difficult.

Juliette slipped out of the way when the five barefooted,
barechested Maori workers strode down the beach with
their wicked-looking knives. She hated what they were
doing to the whale and didn't even watch as they stationed
themselves along the hulk at intervals to cut another strip
of blubber.

Samuel helped Thomas cut away the whale's lips to get
at the jaw. He was not nervous about the tattooed Maoris
and chattered away, asking innumerable questions, not in
the least put out when their only reply was, "*E aha mau?*"
which meant, "What's it to you?" or "Why should you
care?" Young Thomas had followed Abby and Madeline
out to the promontory of boulders where mussels grew
thickly.

Juliette stood by herself and gazed around indecisively.
Emily Jacobson was not with her father and the other men
who were stoking the fires and stirring the try-pots to stop
the blubber from sticking. Nor was she up at the little
lookout shelter where she often climbed the thread of rickety ladders when Jacky Norris was not on duty. She was
not allowed to go near the stacked, full barrels that rested
against the cliff, awaiting shipment to Waller Brothers in
Sydney. So she must be inside helping her mother.

There were only three buildings. Two were imperma-
nent-looking huts built just above the sand line and the
third was a long shelter with open sides and a roof twelve
feet above the ground. Under this roared the fires that
heated the pots. A great heap of firewood was kept dry under an old sail nearby.

Jacky Norris' half-caste children clustered near the doorway of their hut, fingers in mouths, staring shyly. Some wore trousers, some wore shirts; but none was fully dressed. Mrs. Norris was a very dark woman with lips and chin tattooed blue like a dribble of berry juice. She squatted outside against the *raupo* wall made of rushes and reeds, propped up on her heels, clutching a grimy blanket around her and smoking a corncob pipe. Juliette had never spoken to Mrs. Norris, who was not direct and conversational like the women at the pa. The children, too, were unfriendly and if one of the Peridots wandered within walking distance they flitted inside and stared out from under the half-raised shutters.

Emily Jacobson was swinging on the post of her verandah lean-to and grinning shyly. As soon as Juliette saw her she skipped over. Emily was her friend, but then, as Abby would sniff scornfully, Juliette would make friends with *anybody*. Turi and the other ragtag Maori children were bad enough but fancy wanting to play with *Emily*, who stank so strongly that even Mrs. Clerkwell habitually pinched her nostrils when passing Emily's place on the mat at Sunday school.

"Come inside," pleaded Emily. "Come an' see what we got."

"Is it another baby?" Juliette did not want to go inside the Jacobsons' squalid cottage. A baby was a reasonable guess: Mrs. Jacobson was frequently either producing a baby or looked as though she might at any time. She had upper arms like joints of beef and bosoms as puffed as pillows but, as she would confide to anybody who would listen, she had bad luck with her children. Three had been stillborn and were buried under the cliffs, while four in the Mission graveyard had been carried off by childhood diseases, the last two in the measles epidemic that had decimated the Maori tribes up and down the coast and had killed more than half of the children in the local pa.

"Nah. We ain't got another baby. Not while 'Arald is still suckin'," said Emily. "Come on inside an' see."

Reluctantly, and hoping that Mrs. Jacobson was in a good mood, Juliette stepped over the threshold, blinking in the dim light. It was so cold in here that she clasped her arms about herself at once.

The cottage was cluttered and stinking. On the long table that dominated the room were smoky lanterns, dirty tin plates clustered with flies, a stack of dried fish, and trails of dirty clothes. Hanging low from the ceiling was the paraphernalia needed for hunting whales: harpoons, coils of rope, even an old broken anchor. Emily led Juliette around the table, dodging the backbone segments that were used as chairs. They were from an enormous whale, one far bigger than any caught in local waters.

"Left yer manners at home, did yer?" asked Mrs. Jacobson's voice suddenly, stopping Juliette, who had not noticed her reclining on a bunk bed, propped up by what seemed to be a bundle of laundry. Harald was nuzzling at her breast.

"I'm sorry, ma'am," stumbled Juliette. "I didn't know . . ."

Mrs. Jacobson thought that she was embarrassed by the spectacle of the infant suckling and laughed nastily. "I suppose that fine mother of yours doesn't do natural things in front of you children, hey?"

Her tone was not at all flattering to Evangeline. Juliette flushed.

Mrs. Jacobson plucked the baby away from her breast as though he were a leech and sat him up on her knee while she rubbed his back, all the while surveying Juliette mockingly. One breast hung free. Juliette was reminded of their sow Blinkie, whose stomach hung in similar teats when she had thrown a litter of piglets.

Emily demanded her attention with an impatient tug of the hand. "Come an' see what we got!"

Around the table the stench was suddenly suffocating. In the corner, nestled in fouled straw and among a clutter of half-chewed bones, squirmed three fluffy puppies. Their mother, a gigantic brindle mastiff bitch, lay near the fire gnawing on a bone.

"Aren't they beautiful?" breathed Emily.

Juliette nodded. The combination of cold and stink made her feel faint.

"Do you want to cuddle one?" Emily's face was pasty but her eyes shone with eagerness. To oblige her friend Juliette reached out and patted the nearest puppy. It licked her hand with such an abrupt gesture that she could not stop herself from squealing.

The bitch was instantly up in a threatening stance, growling at Juliette.

Dimly Juliette was aware of the splutter of amusement from the bunk. Bile rose in her throat with the force of a wave. Knowing that within a minute she would be sick and there was no stopping it, she turned to run.

"No! Don't run away from her!" urged Emily in panic. She did her best to stop the dog, flinging weak arms about the animal's neck. Mrs. Jacobson belatedly realised what was about to happen and shouted angrily at the dog. Juliette heard neither of them. She scrambled for the door, aware only of the urgency pressing in her throat. As she stumbled around the end of the table the dog snatched at her fluttering dress and dragged her with a thump to the ground.

Thomas' worried face appeared in the doorway, summoned by the screams. He saw in a glance what had happened. The bitch was high on her haunches, snarling a warning. Juliette was sprawled on her face, retching feebly. Thank God she seemed to be unhurt, he noticed.

Hastily buttoning herself, Mrs. Jacobson waddled over. Her accusation was shrill and indignant. "She provoked the poor thing, she did! It's the little brat's own fault! And just look at the filthy mess she's made on the floor! Who'll clean that up, then? Hey? Who'll clean that up?"

Thomas scooped Juliette up, ignoring the dog. He did not know if his daughter had provoked the attack and made no comment. Once young Thomas had been almost bitten by the same dog in an incident that was undeniably the child's fault—he had been intercepted in the act of throwing pebbles at the animal. But the charge that Juliette had made a "filthy mess" on the floor made his lips twitch contemptuously. He permitted himself the satisfaction of gazing haughtily around at the disorder, then said, "Mrs. Jacobson, I rather fancy that in a room like this one more bit of mess would scarcely be noticed!"

He left laughing. Mrs. Jacobson was so slow-witted that

it would take her a good few minutes to sift any meaning from that remark.

Juliette leaned against her father gratefully. "I didn't mean to make that dog fierce," she explained as he set her down beside their lunch basket. "Emily took me in to see the puppies and she wanted me to cuddle one of them."

"What? One of those flea-ridden curs? You'll be scratching and searching tonight, I warrant!"

The expression drooped. "They did look so sweet, Father. And I only gave one of them one little pat, but then the smell made me feel so sick I had to run outside."

He grinned. "It never hurts to get an inkling of how other folks live. You'll appreciate your own home all the more now."

She nodded, not really understanding but treasuring this moment: her father was giving her his undivided attention. Even the nasty taste in her mouth and the discomfort of an acid-seared throat could not spoil it.

"There's a valuable lesson for you in this. Never run away from a direct threat. It's different if you see danger coming, of course, and have time to escape, but not if the threat is right in front of you like that dog was. You should have looked it right in the eye and stood your ground. Do you understand?"

"If I did that, it wouldn't have chased me?"

"Right."

"But, Father, I felt so ill I had to run outside!"

Her breath was terrible. He patted her bonnet with compassion. "Eat an apple out of the basket. Take that sick taste away."

So she sat in the sun, erasing the bile with the taste of last summer's sunshine, while her father went back to the bench at which he was scraping baleen. Behind him the flames stroked the sides of the try-pots and turned into dense black smoke. Lars Jacobson was walking past the whale carcass, deep in conversation with two men, a thin childlike man and a bulky fellow with thick gingery hair like sheep's wool. As they moved towards Juliette the sound of a reedy voice caught her attention and made her look at the two more closely.

They were arguing, pleading their case to Mr. Jacobson,

who seemed unimpressed. The thin one was talking. He had an odd way of tilting his head back which puzzled her until she noticed a wart on one eyelid that dragged that eye half shut. His companion listened morosely, turning a felt hat around in his hands, standing to one side of Juliette so that she could see his broken nose and plump cheeks, as freckled as Jacky Norris'.

Mr. Jacobson was saying he was sorry, it was too close to the end of the season to take on more workers. This whale, maybe one or two more, and that would be all for the winter.

"But we're desperate! Missed our ship an' there's no work in port right now. Just for a few days, anything! We're real keen workers, ain't we, Blue?"

Blue! So they *were* the two who had bumped into her on the clifftop in the darkness. She stared.

"I cain't help yer none," said Lars Jacobson pleasantly. He picked up a barrel top and examined it for chips and cracks, put it aside, and picked up another.

The small man refused to be dismissed. Spitting nastily in the sand, he said, "Ye're giving work to them blacks! Why should you pay them and turn us away? That ain't right!"

"Douse it," said Blue urgently.

Mr. Jacobson ignored them both and continued his work. In frustration the thin man took a swing at the whaler, thumping him on his thick forearm. Juliette was astonished. The man was waving his fists in Mr. Jacobson's face in the same kind of a paddy that Regina flew into when things were going against her. Fancy trying to fight with Mr. Jacobson, who could pick up a grown man in one hand and throw him across the beach. The others had paused at their tasks to watch what was happening. Embarrassed, the stocky stranger tried to coax his friend away but was shaken off impatiently.

Mr. Jacobson looked his attacker right in the eye and without any perceivable effort squeezed the barrel lid between his hands, bending it so that it split right across. Tossing the pieces at the man's feet, he said, "I hire who I damn well like!"

The men had long gone when Emily ran over and

plonked herself beside Juliette. She took the apple and bit into what was left of it.

"What did yer go an' toss up for?" she accused, munching. "Me ma ain't 'alf mad at you, an' at yer pa, too. Oooh, but the way 'e talked to 'er! An' she made me clean up the mess, an' all, so now I'm mad at you too!" And, clutching the apple, she ran away down the beach.

Juliette frowned. She should be feeling upset at this, but to her mild surprise she discovered that she didn't care at all what poor Emily thought. What an odd morning this had been. She tunnelled her hand into the basket and retrieved another apple. This one tasted much sweeter, she decided, chewing with enjoyment.

Four

It was Juliette's turn to sit up in the prow this Sunday and oh, the pleasure of it! For the entire long journey to the Mission and the entire long row home she could dream and sigh, floating away on visions of being a water sprite or a mermaid, or the regal figurehead of a ship. At the prow the boat seemed to glide, smooth as a sea bird skimming low enough to trace the dappled surface of the bay. Huddled in the stern, the others were having a rockier ride as the boat lunged and settled with every drag on the oars.

The rest of the ballast in the prow was provided by the picnic hamper, a tin trunk really, which was packed with the tastiest provender Evangeline's skills could provide. Thick slices of pink ham from one of Blinkie's last year's litter, apples tied in a gingham cloth, an apple pie fragrant with precious cloves, a fruitcake baked in the camp oven, and, as a very special treat, some gingerbread biscuits cooked on the griddle. Juliette had helped stamp them out with the rabbit-shaped cutter. Abby, who was artistic, decorated them with currant eyes, knife lines for whiskers, and a fine powder of sugar. Madeline had made the lemonade with their own lemons, had laced it with raisins and sparked it with the sharp tang of ginger.

The morning was clear and silver, the sun behind a grey veil. A breeze tugged at their capes and bonnets, making their eyes water and cheeks bloom.

"It's going to be a fine day," said Thomas as he leaned into the stroke.

"A fine day for a picnic," echoed Evangeline. "It is so much jollier to have luncheon under the trees. Oh, do be careful with that rope, Thomas dear. You don't want to get your dress ruined, do you?"

Thomas' baleful look showed that he would not have minded that at all. Though on six days of the week he was dressed in trousers and a shirt, on Sundays Evangeline clothed him according to the custom for little boys. Then he and Regina wore identical grey coat dresses with frilled white collars and cuffs, striped red and grey stockings, and slippers like the girls', with leather thongs that tied at the ankle. This morning his loathing of the costume had erupted into a tantrum.

"I want a proper suit like Samuel's!" he shrieked as Madeline tried to dress him.

"When you are older, dear," she promised, tying Abby's bonnet ribbons and turning to attend to Juliette's.

Thomas came in to change into his good clothes.

"What's all this?" he boomed.

Thomas' wails immediately faded to sniffles but it was too late.

"This is the Lord's day and those are your Sunday clothes," his father roared. "If you are not dressed and ready before I am," he warned, going behind the screen, "then there will be trouble."

The way he said *trouble* made all the children shiver. Juliette glanced over at the razor strop hanging on a wooden peg beside the shaving mirror. None of them had ever actually felt it but they had all vividly imagined what a whipping with it must be like.

Evangeline hung her cape about her shoulders. It was peach-coloured bombazine like her dress and trimmed with bands of navy velvet ribbon an inch wide. Her bonnet was navy silk with rows of narrow peach ruffles tucked under the brim. Her face looked like the centre of a peach chrysanthemum. She was agitated. Whenever her husband roared in anger she experienced a guilty, disturbed feeling.

"Have you got your sewing bags, girls? Your slates? Your dusters? Now, mind that you don't leave yours behind, Samuel. Mind that he doesn't, please, Madeline."

Samuel's day darkened a little, but brightened again when his father said, "Feeling strong, son? We might have

to row against a head wind this morning and I'll need all
the help you can give me."

The tide was half in. As they rounded the point they
slipped past the whale. The fires were dead; nothing was
being done today because everybody but the Norris family
had gone to the Mission. Mrs. Norris squatted outside her
hut with her pipe and blanket. Juliette waved impulsively
to her but the woman gave no sign of having noticed.

"What will happen to the whale when all the blubber
has been taken off?" Abby asked her father.

"They smoke some of the meat and use some for dog
food."

Samuel said with relish, "Then they take the carcass out
into the channel, towing it with a rope. All the sharks
come around and rip the scraps off the bones. They make
the sea look as though it's boiling."

"Can I watch?" pleaded young Thomas.

"No!" interrupted Evangeline. "Nor you, Samuel. You
are to stay on shore." She added in alarm, "How do you
know what happens? Thomas, he hasn't . . ."

"I watch from the lookout," said Samuel. "Jacky—I
mean, Mr. Norris—lets me watch through his spyglass.
The sharks look *terrifying*."

Thomas laughed at the looks on all their faces. "I don't
think your choice of conversational subject is appreciated,
son. Perhaps it is not really tactful to talk about sharks
when we are out in the boat."

Around the second point they found themselves moving
between the moored sailing ships. There were a dozen in
port today, lofty and proud, their bodies as streamlined
and elegant as sea birds. Juliette stopped pretending that
she was a pixie bobbing in a walnut-shell coracle and sat
up straight, smoothing her plaid skirts over her knees. The
notorious town of Kororareka was on one side and beyond
the ships the distant Mission station. Heaven and Hell,
people called them, Heaven and Hell on opposite sides of
the bay.

They approached a wider-bodied ship that seemed to
snuggle down into the water. It was the *Norse*, Thomas informed them. Bjorn Svenson was a townsman of Mr. Jacobson's and it was on his ship that the Jacobsons had first

come to New Zealand from Sweden. Sure enough, as they
splashed past, there was the Jacobsons' dinghy lashed to
the boarding ladder. Emily leaned over the railing above
them, pulling a face at Juliette in memory of yesterday's
falling out. Juliette wanted to make one back but could not
without the risk of her mother seeing her.

"I'd give a new sixpenny piece to watch Mrs. Jacobson
come down that ladder when the visit is over," grinned
Thomas. "Aye, but she must be a sight!"

"What ship is that?" asked Evangeline, changing the
subject.

"The *Doreen Gray* from New South Wales, here with
passengers, mail, and cargo, no doubt."

"Passengers! Who would want to come to a town like
this?"

Thomas took all criticism of New Zealand personally
and his wife's disparaging remark was no exception.
"There are quite a few decent families living in Kororareka, I'll be pleased to tell you. The Bellwoods, the Meyneys, and the Yardley family too, of course."

"Papists," sniffed Evangeline.

"Aye, and good ones, too," said Thomas. "It's said that
their church thinks so highly of them that it's sending out
a Bishop and some nuns."

"Bishop Pompallier," supplied Samuel without thinking.

His father cuffed him playfully on the ear. "You've been
listening to your betters' conversations again. If only your
lessons were so absorbing, how fine a thing that would be."
He chuckled. "Bishop Pompallier it is. So soon there will
be angels on both sides of the harbour."

Juliette stared across at the town that was nicknamed
"Hell." Not that there was much to be seen at this distance. They were making way in a direct line across to the
Mission and not going near the town at all. She saw the
lines of canoes and dinghies pulled up on the beach, the
tumble of huts, and above them the "respectable" homes
peering out over hedges of greenery. Very few people were
about. A Maori man sat alone on the jetty playing the bagpipes very badly. Then the slow tolling of the church bells
rolled across the water to meet them like a carpet. Thomas

and Samuel quickened their oar strokes. They were going to be late.

They scurried with un-Sabbathlike haste into their pew. Evangeline fumbled with her hymnal and took up the song in mid-line as soon as she guessed the tune, holding the book for her daughters and feigning that she, too, could read the words.

The Reverend Clerkwell entered the church at the end of the hymn, a black robe swirling around his ankles like a stylised thundercloud. Juliette sighed inwardly. She had so hoped that Reverend Williams would be back by now. His sermons were interesting, not interminable and mind-numbing like Reverend Clerkwell's.

Immediately after the service the older children drafted themselves into two groups for lessons while the youngsters played on the lawn under the watchful eyes of the unmarried ladies. Meanwhile, the matrons fed their infants and swapped news, gossip, and recipes in the Mission house kitchen while the gentlemen enjoyed a leisurely chat over port in the parlour.

At the call of the hand bell Juliette, Abby, and Madeline lined up with the fifteen other girls outside Mrs. Clerkwell's schoolroom while the boys filed into the church for their schooling. The Reverend's wife was a gentle-looking woman with waved grey hair and the kind of skin that looked as if it would mark if pressed with a fingertip, but her voice was hard and her sense of righteousness inflexible. Even the boys were more in terror of her than of her gaunt, bewigged husband. She greeted each girl and took their bonnets to be hung on a rack until the lesson's end as a ransom for good behaviour. Juliette settled on the flax mat and opened the Bible in her lap. When Emily Jacobson shuffled in last Juliette patted the mat invitingly but Emily swept past and sat by herself. Sitting on a wicker chair at the front with a cane long enough to tap any girl sharply on the shoulder should she become inattentive, Mrs. Clerkwell called on them in turn to read.

When Abby read, Mrs. Clerkwell said, as she did every Sunday, "What a pity it is, Abigail, that your progress in handwriting and needlework lag so deplorably behind your aptitude for reading." The girls always indulged in a muffled giggle to punctuate this observation. This puzzled Juliette. Try as she might, she could see nothing funny in that remark.

Later she stood beside the chair while Mrs. Clerkwell checked her lettering.

"Very good, Juliette." Her breath was reminiscent of the privy, for she suffered agonies with her teeth. "What a pity that your sister Abigail does not have your exquisite talent for elegant writing."

While they lunched under the *pohutukawa* trees at the beach wall Juliette sought a way to tell her father about the praise she had received in class, a way that would not sound like boasting. How she longed to have him congratulate her for her achievements.

She was astonished when Abby broke the news for her. "Mrs. Clerkwell scolded me today," she confided, brushing cake crumbs from her fingers. "She thinks that Juliette is much more talented than I am."

Juliette was thrilled. Thomas grinned, sensing that there was a story coming. "What did she say?" he asked.

Abby tossed her head so that the chin ribbons fluttered. "She said," and here she launched into an entirely creditable imitation of Mrs. Clerkwell's voice and mannerisms, " 'What a *pity* it is, Abigail, that your progress in *hand*-writing and *needle*work lag so de*plor*ably behind your *ap*titude for reading!' "

Thomas laughed; even Evangeline joined in.

Thomas said, "You're a girl after my own heart, you are. I was always quick to read but I could never draw a line if my very neck depended on it. Never mind, lass, if Juliette is neater with a pen than you are. It's not such a bad thing to take after your father now, is it?"

"Of course not, Father."

"Then never mind what Mrs. Clerkwell says." At a look from Evangeline he added, "Do your best, mind, but don't fret if you can't be best at everything." And Juliette listened in stunned disbelief as he dismissed her efforts by saying lightly, "Juliette is fortunate in that she takes after her mother." She turned her head away quickly and blinked to dispel the tears prickling behind her eyelids.

After lunch Thomas strolled away to have a word with

the blacksmith and Evangeline took herself off to the Mission green where a market was held every Sunday to enable those who had travelled to purchase items they might not otherwise have the opportunity to buy—a young pig squealing on the flax leg-line or a basket of purple-skinned sweet potatoes.

Juliette remained behind with her untouched ginger biscuit resting on a napkin beside her. She had silently railed at the unfairness of it all and had pondered whether this was what the saying, "Pride goeth before a fall," really meant, and if so, had she brought the bitter disappointment down on herself? Then she noticed Emily sitting alone on the sea wall, dangling her scuffed shoes, sifting handfuls of sand through her fingers. There was so much pathos about the dejected figure that Juliette forgot her own troubles and also forgot that Emily no longer considered herself to be her friend.

Squatting beside her, she said brightly, "Look at what I saved for you, Emily," and thrust the biscuit onto her knee. "I want you to have it so that you will feel happy again."

Emily gazed at it. The black-currant eye seemed to stare fixedly back at her. Instead of thanking her she said defiantly, "What makes you think I'm not happy?"

"You don't seem happy," she said. "Go on, eat it. Young Thomas always eats the head first because he thinks rabbits are the kind of animals that bite and he is afraid of being nipped on the tongue. Don't you think that's funny?"

Evidently she did not. "Why should you care if I'm happy? Why do you want to cheer me up?"

Juliette was far too young and unschooled to be aware of the cold hint in Emily's voice. With unsophisticated directness she said, "I feel so sorry for you," and when that elicited a gasp of rage she hastened foolishly to elaborate. "I think it's mean the way all the girls are so horrid to you. You can't help it if you don't have pretty clothes, and if you smell fishy, and . . ."

"Oh!" shrieked Emily. She flung the rabbit into the sand and jumped right on top of it, grinding it to crumbly powder with the wooden soles of her homemade shoes.

"There!" she cried angrily. "I hate your silly rabbit and I hate you!"

Juliette understood nothing. All she knew was that she had tried to be friendly; there was nobody to explain that friendship is impossible if it is based on pity. She stood up quickly, wounded and uncaring. "You are rude, ill mannered, and common," she said indignantly, unwittingly choosing the words that would most effectively penetrate the varnish of the girl who leaned sobbing against the stone wall. With a toss of her head Juliette stalked away.

The green was ringed with early-flowering cherry trees whose twigs were threaded with frilled white blossoms. Though it was winter the sun fell warmly on this sheltered place and bees from nearby hives worked the petals in a businesslike manner. Evangeline was glad of the parasol to keep her face and throat in the shade. The solitude was pleasant. She did not expect to be approached but when she lowered the parasol and stepped out from under the trees she noticed that Mr. Robert Harnod, the Mission twine spinner and lay preacher, was close beside her.

"How are you, Mrs. Peridot?" he asked in a hoarse, strained tone that distorted the polite enquiry into something more intimate.

She averted her head slightly, her annoyance rising. Because he had independent means he seemed to feel he had rights she was not willing to grant.

He sensed her displeasure. "Forgive me for speaking to you like this."

"You should know better than to approach me in public. It cannot help but attract attention."

"Evangeline . . ." It sounded like the opening bars of a love song, the way it lingered on his tongue.

"Please."

"I must see you again. No, please don't turn away. I must see you."

She looked at him but would not raise her eyes above the level of his waistcoat pocket. Absurdly he felt like dropping to one knee so that her gaze might shine on his face.

"I regret that I cannot ever receive you again, Mr. Harnod."

"Why?" he asked in disbelief. "Why? Have I in some way offended you? Are you displeased with me?"

"Only with your speaking to me like this. I cannot receive you, Mr. Harnod, because it is quite, quite wrong of us and a stop must be put to it."

"No! I tell you it is *not* wrong. What *is* wrong, and inhumanly, unbearably wrong, was the misery I suffered before the day I visited your cottage and found there the kindest, sweetest heart a man could ever hope to find in this desolate and savage country. I assure you, Mrs. Peridot, that since my poor wife died my life has been one of unrelenting anguish, except for my visits with you, and . . ."

"Please don't talk like that. My mind is made up."

Telling himself that she was only angry because he had upset her by his blunt approach, he said softly, "You could not be so cruel as to abandon me now, Evangeline." As he spoke he thought he detected a fluttering in her, a quickening of the pulse at her throat. Gently, he pressed his advantage.

"I have legitimate business to visit Te Pahi's tribe and the settlements farther down the coast. When shall I come? Surely it would not be out of place if I should stop by to pay my respects to you."

She was flustered. "It is so awkward now . . . I cannot be sure where everybody will be." Delicacy forbade her to use Thomas' name directly.

Quietly he said, "You and you alone give me all the difference between a life of misery and one of hope."

Resignedly she abandoned the struggle with her better sense and conscience. "There is some shipping business to be attended to with Mrs. Yardley. In two weeks' time on a Friday."

"I shall watch for him to arrive. Open your palm."

"I beg your pardon?"

"Open your palm," he whispered again, slipping a coin into her gloved hand and fastening her fingers over it. "A token for you, of my esteem."

After he had gone she gazed dispiritedly at the golden

guinea before sliding it into her waist fob. Even if she wanted to, there was no turning back now. She would speak very firmly to Mr. Harnod when he called. This must be the very last time.

Five

November was Evangeline's favourite time of the year. The rains of winter had cleared, the long humid days of February were still at a comfortable distance, and in the meantime they could look forward to this dry golden spell. Whenever she could steal an occasional hour alone she worked on the embroidered carry bags she was making for the girls' Christmas surprises and at other times she coaxed her husband into taking young Thomas with him for the day so that she might complete the set of gentleman-style Sunday best for him. After Christmas she would again take up work on her San Francisco hope chest, which already contained a tablecloth with a deep lace border and a dozen pillow slipcovers embroidered with daisies and forget-me-nots. Now she was trying to decide on a design for a set of velvet parlour cushions. Soon she would contrive a way to spend one of the golden guineas to buy the cloth and silks she needed.

There were now forty-eight coins in the lining of the wicker workbasket. Whenever she contemplated her failure there she was overcome with helplessness. It had been impossible to refuse Mr. Harnod, who knelt at her feet and wept, pressing his face into her lap in a manner that wrenched at her heart. And Mr. Newman from Kororareka, who desperately missed his wife in Canada; how could she refuse such pleadings? And Mr. Bank . . . generous Mr. Bank, who always added a sixpence extra for the baby. . . . How could she be firm? How could she when, in the final analysis, this was all going to be for the children anyway? Weren't they just as excited as she at the prospect of that beautiful home in San Francisco?

In fact, the children never thought about it, regarding the whole matter as something of a fairy tale. And at the moment they were enjoying the fine weather, fishing, gathering pipis and mussels, speckled birds' eggs, and spiny sea eggs from rock pools at low tide. Anywhere they wandered they were safe because Te Pahi's territory extended much farther than they could possibly walk and it was tacitly known that they had the full protection of his tribe.

Juliette spent most of her free time with Turi. It was a friendship Evangeline disliked, though on reflection preferred to the association with the Jacobson girl. If only Juliette and Abby could be friends instead of bickering. It was a pity they had so little in common.

Turi was the same age as Madeline but as old as any adult in sophistication. She had seen babies born and people die; she knew about illness and the tragedies of old age, while sex held no mysteries for her. Turi had thick, oily hair that plunged down her back like a jet waterfall. All year round she wore a red cotton smock that had been discarded by Madeline two years before but was only now beginning to fit her rather too snugly. She was always barefooted and, judging by the skin glimpsed through the rents in the fabric, wore no underclothing either. Juliette liked Turi because she was always either very happy or very angry, and never sad or still. For her part Turi considered Juliette and her sisters to be freaks of innocence and tedious company but there was a compensation that made the friendship worth while. When she was playing with Juliette she had a sterling excuse not to do her chores.

This was the busiest season for trade. If Thomas could coax or bribe them to work hard from now through the summer, the tribe could have a full load of goods ready for shipment every six to eight weeks. Already almost a whole ton of flax had been cut and prepared by the Maori women from the pa. Thomas stopped at the swamp to give them some friendly encouragement before he headed off into the bush with Samuel, young Thomas, and Tippy to supervise the hauling of a huge *kauri* log. Juliette had tagged along with them as far as the swamp. It was always fun when a shipment was due. Everybody worked fast and right through the day, meals were late in the dusky evenings and there was a carnival atmosphere with singing and high spirits.

Turi was there on the bank scraping flax, while her mother stood ankle-deep in mud, cutting the long dark leaves and throwing them over towards her. Altogether there were a dozen women at work today, three cutting and the rest scraping. A baby wrapped in a blanket lay in the shade of a bush while toddlers scrambled about getting in everybody's way. The scrapers were quick and methodical. Juliette, who had tried scraping flax and knew how difficult it was, watched Turi and admired her skill. The Maori girl made a long sloping cut on the underside of the leaf with a honed mussel shell and then scraped along the leaf, paring the flesh away from the stringy fibres. In New South Wales the fibres would be processed into rope.

"Very good," said Thomas, checking the quality of their work. "Very good indeed. There will be fine goods for you to choose from when the Richmond ship comes in. Mrs. Yardley said that there are some beautiful rugs and lengths of cloth for you this time."

A toothless old crone understood little of what he said, and croaked, "There will be *waipiro?*"

"Yes, what about the whisky?" echoed another.

"What about the *mere?*" asked Thomas quickly. There were two ceremonial clubs made from the beautiful New Zealand greenstone in the pa and Thomas would have dearly loved to own one.

The crone laughed. "*E aha mau?*" she snorted. "*E aha mau?*"

The women all laughed, thinking Thomas very witty. Just as he would never sell them whisky, they would never dream of parting with their valuable heirlooms, the mere.

Turi's mother, a fair-skinned, overweight woman reputed to be the daughter of a French sailor, said, "Our ancestors had to travel right down to the Middle Island to find the greenstone for those mere. Even when Hongi Hika himself took it into his head to want them we hid them in the bush and only two of us knew where they were."

All the talking was done in a mixture of English and Maori—mostly Maori, which Thomas spoke easily. Juliette had to strain to catch the few words she understood. Middle Island. That was reputed to be a place of fairy-tale beauty with wide yellow plains, blue and white mountains, and rivers filled with smooth pebbles.

"Didn't there used to be three mere?" asked Thomas.

"That was a long time ago when Hine was just like one of us." Turi's mother nodded, her arms akimbo. She was always ready to pause for a chat. "Nobody knows what happened but our *tohunga* said that the spirits enchanted her because she lost that precious mere and she will not be cured until it has been restored to our tribe. It is an *utu* from the ancestors, because they are so angry with Hine."

Utu. Juliette shivered. Utu meant revenge, such a special revenge that Thomas declared the Maoris had elevated getting one's own back to a high art form. Utu was the excuse for countless wars between tribes. Given time, every grievance ever caused must eventually be avenged. Hine's sin must have been terrible indeed.

Thomas was asking, "What do *you* think, Marama? Do you think Hine's madness was caused by a curse?"

"Ah!" She nodded sagely. "Many people wanted to buy that mere, for it was the finest our tribe owned. Sometimes I think how easy it would be if Hine had taken it to show somebody but was paid with a blow on the head and left in the bush like a dead person. That is how she was found, and when she woke she was as mad as she is now."

"It seems to me that your wisdom is greater than the tohunga's," Thomas flattered her.

Turi's mother laughed, wobbling her chins and loosely set stomach. "Ah, the tohunga said she lost it in the bush and he is wiser than me. Besides, he is Hine's uncle and has to keep his position safe."

"As I do," agreed Thomas. "If this flax is not ready when the *Lorendee* comes, the captain will be angry with me."

"Not with you, Paritau," cawed the crone.

Thomas enjoyed the banter. "If the flax is ready early I might be pleased enough to mix up a big go-ashore pot of stirabout."

Ugh, thought Juliette, though the Maori women laughed with pleasure at the idea. Stirabout was the translucent, sweet sludge made when a sack of flour, a sack of sugar, and a huge pot of boiling water were mixed together. Sometimes the ingredients were combined in a hollow canoe and stirred with a paddle but always the mess was consumed with enormous enjoyment.

"Come!" said Turi, dragging at Juliette's hand.

One of the women called, "Come back here, Turi, you lazy girl!" but Turi pulled an insolent face at her and towed Juliette along faster.

Juliette waited outside while Turi dived into her windowless, sweaty-smelling hut to fetch tobacco and pipe. Fowls and grunting piglets fanned out in front of them as they entered the pa by the main gate, walking under the red lintel with its carved, naked figures from Maori mythology. Beside the *hangi* pits was a smouldering fire, watched over by an old woman with a face like a withered apple. She jabbered angrily at Turi while the girl used a stalk of thatch to light her pipe, telling Turi that she should be working to help earn goods for the whole tribe. Turi did not reply.

"Come!" she said to Juliette. That was almost the limit of their conversation but it served them well enough.

They picked their way towards Hine's cage across the firmest places in the raupo swamp. Turi walked with confidence from one solid spot to another, swinging Juliette's boots, her darned stockings tied like a belt around her waist with the corncob pipe gripped in her teeth. For Juliette it was a struggle to keep her balance and hold her dimity skirts clear of the mud.

All around the cage the sand dunes rippled white as foam, prickled with quill-like rushes. The tohunga had decreed this location, hoping (in vain so far) that her madness might bear the fruits of a seer, enabling her to sense when friends or enemies might be approaching. But all poor Hine had done so far was shriek incoherently whenever anybody appeared.

The girls went only to the edge of the swamp and crouched on the warm sand. From there Juliette could see Hine's greyish tangle of hair and her hunched body. She always tore the clothing that was left for her, explained Turi in a rare burst of chatter. Ripped them up with hands and teeth in the same wild rage that made her throw excrement at the slave who delivered her flax baskets of food every evening.

At the moment, Hine was disappointingly still, gazing out over the ocean. After an interval of waiting, Turi pulled the pipe from her mouth and shouted, "Hey, Hine!"

There was no response from the cage so Turi picked up a stone from the sandy marsh and lobbed it high into the air. With a skittering noise it rolled down the grey thatch roof and plopped into the sand. This time Hine uttered a low, moaning cry like Toss calling for her calves but did not look around. Turi bent, scrabbling for another stone.

"No," said Juliette, putting a bold hand on her friend's arm.

Turi looked angry. "Why not?"

"It's cruel," she offered inadequately, thinking as she spoke, How could it be cruel? They were not doing anything but trying to catch the madwoman's attention to make her look this way, yet the thought of even disturbing her seemed wrong somehow. "We should leave her alone," she insisted.

"Ha!" said Turi contemptuously. She arced the stone even higher this time and stood up, yahooing loudly.

The reaction from the pen was frightening. Hine leaped to her feet and wrenched at the stakes, howling and spitting a garble of noise that bore no recognisable relation to speech but managed to sound like the most obscene, violent curses. She scraped up a handful of filth and hurled it so that it rained towards the girls and spattered on the sand just short of where the raupo stalks concealed them.

"Quick!" urged Turi, clearly shaken. "Come!" She darted away as rapidly as a striding bird, leaving Juliette to slip and flounder behind her as best she could. By the time she had negotiated the swamp track Turi was already racing towards the pa gates. Unabated, the hideous screaming pounded at her back so violently that she longed to press her hands over her ears and could not because she was clutching both boots and skirt. Tears of panic softened her vision.

Suddenly she stopped short. The reason for Turi's frantic haste was abruptly apparent.

Hine's clamouring had echoed up and down the bay. At

the first shriek the women working at the flax swamp had dropped knives and mussel shells and come running to investigate the cause of the uproar. They had caught Turi halfway up the slope and now while Juliette shrank back into concealment she witnessed the unhappy Turi wriggling haplessly as her arms and legs stung under the blows being dealt her by the cluster of indignant women.

"Where have you been?" asked Madeline much later.

"You were supposed to help us down at the swamps," Abby reproached her. "We gathered half a jar full of flax-blossom nectar."

"We heard the madwoman screaming. Surely you heard her?"

Abby gloated, "Turi teased her. Her mother whipped her with a manuka stick. Surely you heard that?"

Juliette set her boots on the rack just inside the door and crept in, sitting down and tucking up her feet in one swift motion so that her bare toes would not be noticed. In vain.

Madeline frowned. "Juliette! What in the world have you done with your stockings?"

Six

"Do I *have* to wear my Sunday shoes?" whined Regina. "They feel too hot and they pinch my toes!"

"No, they don't. You want to wear your others so you can play in the dirt," said Madeline, waiting with the shoehorn to help. She was ready in best starched gingham and bonnet with six inches of pantalette ruffles showing below the pin-tucked hem.

"But we are only going over to the pa and hardly anybody there wears shoes. They won't care!"

Evangeline tucked baby Melina into her carrying cradle. "It is courteous for us to dress beautifully because we are their guests of honour. Everybody in the tribe will be wearing their best things to show respect to us, so please mind your manners, all of you. No personal remarks, no matter how amused you might be about how some of them are dressed."

"Yes, Mother," came from them all.

Samuel, looking uncomfortable in his adult-style peg trousers and jacket, said wistfully, "In Kororareka they're having a real fair day for their Christmas Eve celebrations. They're going to have geese, grinning competitions through horse collars, and a dozen different kinds of races."

"Including a barmaids' race," said Thomas, wiping the lather from his razor.

"How do you know that?" asked Evangeline quickly.

"Because Jacky Norris was telling us all about it. He and the Jacobsons are going."

"If the Jacobsons are going, then no doubt I shall hear

all about it tomorrow at the Mission. Regina, please stop fussing and let Madeline do your laces up."

When her father moved away from the mirror Abby positioned herself so that she could look into it. "Wouldn't it be splendid if we could have a double helping of this evening and no tomorrow?"

"No Christmas Day? Whyever not?" asked Juliette.

"Because Christmas Day itself is so *dull*."

"I don't think so! There will be a lovely picnic lunch under the trees, and Mother is taking mince pies, and Mrs. Kenlight will be bringing three of her turkeys, and . . ."

"All you ever care about is food, Julie," observed her sister with disapproval. "Tomorrow will be dull because we always have twice as many hymns and the sermon goes on forever." She looked gloatingly at the long shelf above the table where mysterious packages were stacked. Because plain paper was so precious most of them were wrapped in other things—scraps of clean rag, fabric remnants that would later be reused in patchwork quilts, and pages of old, yellowing newspaper. Abby sighed extravagantly. "Couldn't we please have our presents a little earlier this year, while it is still daylight? It seems such a long, long time to wait until dark."

"Can't wait to see what's there for you, eh?" teased Thomas. "I think it would be better if we postponed the gift giving until tomorrow evening. What do you think, Evangeline? Then they'll have something to look forward to during the long sermon."

"Oh, *please* don't do that! Please don't, Father!"

He scooped her up and tickled her by snorting against her neck. Abby squealed with delight while Juliette watched, smiling as she tucked her hair behind her ears and fitted on her bonnet.

Though Evangeline disliked these annual expeditions to the pa she tolerated them with a good grace, realising that Te Pahi's people were her husband's livelihood and the more he prospered in his dealings with them the more rapidly it would hasten the day of their departure. Pretending that she was enjoying the treat of her life, she shook hands and rubbed noses with all the women who lined up to greet her, and pinched the babies' cheeks; because of her morn-

ing ministrations she was able to address most of them by
name. Te Pahi's tattooed mother escorted her to a flax mat
in the shade where a man's worsted overcoat was draped
over a small barrel to make her a chair. The girls sat
around her, Madeline fanning the baby's face, while
Thomas and the boys inspected the hangi pits and joked
with Te Pahi about what the contents might be. Te Pahi
was very proud of his part in the expedition to Matakitaki
fifteen years before when Hongi Hika's men had killed
over one thousand Waikato natives and had feasted there
on the slain warriors for days afterwards. As an ear orna-
ment Te Pahi still wore one of the fishhooks made from
bones brought back from the raid, and Thomas teased him
about it now, asking if the fish he caught with the hook
were as tasty as the "fish" from whose body he had taken
it. Te Pahi's laughter boomed back to where Evangeline
and her daughters sat upright, mittened hands folded,
smiling as if they were at a garden party.

The hangi, the name for the earth oven, had been prepared hours before when a fire had been set in a pit on top
of a bed of hard river stones. When the fire had died down,
the embers were raked away and joints of meat, fish, and
kumara (sweet potatoes), all wrapped in leaves, were
placed directly on top of the hot stones. More layers of
leaves went in, then several gourdfuls of sea water were
splashed over that. As the steam gushed up, earth was
shovelled over the leaves until not so much as a whisper of
steam could escape. Cooked in its own juice, hangi food had
a distinctive, faintly smoky taste that all of the Peridot
children relished. Thomas preferred the Maori favourites—dishes that made Evangeline shudder—of raw mussels and onions chopped together and *kina*, the spiny sea
eggs, eaten fresh from the sea and scooped dripping and
yellow from their shells. Thomas would try anything, even
the fat huhu grubs, which were roasted over an open fire
and which tasted of butter.

Evangeline's taste was strictly English. When the flax
food baskets were brought around, Te Pahi's mother saw
to it that hers contained a generous portion of spit-roasted
pigeon and a small kumara. "*E kapai, Matua Paritau?*"

she asked, to which Evangeline replied warmly, "Yes, it is fine. And thank you, Mrs. Te Pahi."

Before the children were permitted to eat, a long prayer in Maori was intoned by one of the tohungas. Juliette's mouth watered as she sat, legs uncomfortably straight out in front of her, holding the steaming basket in her lap. The tender pork seemed to dissolve on her tongue and the kumara tasted so sweet that Juliette wondered how she could ever enjoy them boiled. There were steamed pipis and tiny scarlet *kura*, fresh-water crayfish. Like everybody else, she ate with her hands, licking her fingers and daintily tearing shreds from her chunk of pork. Turi, who was helping to look after the toddlers under a shade tree some distance away, waved a chicken drumstick at her and Juliette waved a kura in reply.

"Isn't this fun?" she asked her mother.

Evangeline smiled down at the frail-looking girl who reminded her of herself as a child. Though she tried never to favour any one of them, in her heart she acknowledged that quiet Juliette was the sweetest of her daughters.

"Are you enjoying yourself, Mother?"

"I certainly am."

Juliette confided, "I'm so looking forward to this evening. I do hope that you like our present. We all helped with it, even . . ."

"Julie!" hissed Madeline. "You'll spoil the secret."

Juliette bit her lip as her mother said, "It's time for gift giving now. Pay attention to the speeches, girls. Your father has a cask of treacle and an enormous tin of tobacco for the tribe to share. They gave him so much trade this year that he has made the gift especially generous. Isn't that wonderful?"

The girls murmured non-committally. Treacle and tobacco were equally unattractive to them. Obediently they sat, listening to the incomprehensible oratory, and because they were so well practised in polite attention it was not a real hardship to listen now. By contrast most of the Maori children in the assembly quickly grew bored and unobtrusively slipped away. Samuel and young Thomas went with them. Madeline saw Thomas' red jacket disappearing around the side of the palisades in the midst of a

group of brown, scantily clad children. She poked her
mother's knee to attract her notice, but Evangeline merely
shook her head warningly and placed a finger to her lips.

It was not until the speeches were over and the women
were assembling to perform their traditional action songs
that Madeline was able to make her report.

"Don't worry about him, dear. He'll not come to any
harm," said Evangeline. "If he is not back by the time the
concert is over you may all go together and look for him
while your father and I have a cup of tea with the chiefs."

Juliette knew many of the songs from Turi, though she
did not understand the words except that they all told
stories about things that had happened to the tribe long
ago. Softly she added her voice to the harmony, watching
in admiration as the women swayed and stamped their
feet, waving their hands until their fingers looked like
water rippling. Their flax piu-pius clashed and swung as
they danced. Then they unlooped flax *pois*—soft balls on
long strings—from their waistbands and began to twirl
these in time to the music. When it was all over Juliette
clapped harder than anyone else in the appreciative audience. She wished that they would sing the haunting songs
again and make the pois flash rhythmically in the sunshine.

"Off you go now, girls, and remember to keep together,"
instructed Evangeline, knowing that the way to prevent
trouble was to keep them busy looking after each other.

Following the path in the direction the boys had taken,
they soon stood near the edge of the sea cliff. Now they
could see the remaining sweep of the bay. Directly below
them was an inlet where a stream from the hills met the
rocks at the foot of the cliffs and there the water, though
deep, was slow-flowing and free from dangerous currents,
a perfect swimming hole.

"Look!" cried Juliette in delight. "Samuel is swinging
on the *maori!*"

Nobody knew why it was called a maori; that seemed an
odd name for something that was a cross between a maypole and a swing. It stood on the bank close to the edge of
the deepest part of the swimming hole, a stout pole some
fifteen feet high. Around the top was suspended a hoop of

twisted vines and from this ring hung a half dozen long flax ropes. In turn the naked boys ran down a short slope, grabbed the end of a rope, dashed along the bank, then sailed out and over the water until the arc reached its farthest point, where they let go with a shout and dropped into the water.

"I can't see Samuel," said Abby.

"There he is, just climbing out of the water," Juliette pointed out. "Oh, he's taken *all* his clothes off."

All stared at his shiny white body as he raced to join the line again. For the Peridots nudity was forbidden.

"I suppose he could hardly risk getting his underdrawers wet," observed Juliette practically. "If they were still wet when it was time to put his suit back on he would make his trousers damp and Mother might be cross."

"Should we call him home?" asked Abby.

"It's Thomas we want," Juliette reminded her. "I do hope he's not on the maori too. He keeps claiming he can swim but he can't really. Wait. Can you hear his voice?"

Regina spoke up. "That's Thomas and he's crying! He's crying like anything!"

The older girls looked at each other, then all pressed on quickly along the track; Madeline held Regina's hand to keep her from straying towards the dangerous clifftop. When they reached the first bend Thomas' crying grew louder, and at the second bend, louder still. At the third they found him surrounded by a swarm of bigger children. He was sitting in the middle of the track, sopping wet, his clothes making a puddle in the dust.

"Oh, gracious me," said Evangeline later when he staggered bawling towards her. She tried unsuccessfully not to laugh. "Come along home and we'll find you some dry clothes. It's time we said our thank yous and our goodbyes anyway."

That evening the children played quoits while their parents sipped glasses of Spanish wine, bought by Thomas for one shilling the bottle for special occasions. It was not quite dusk, the sky still pink and the sea gunmetal grey.

"I think I shall plant some pelargoniums along here," said Evangeline as they strolled across the clearing. "They will lean against the wall as they grow. Mrs. Williams' are doing so splendidly that she has offered cuttings to anybody who wants them. I rather fancy that I might take advantage of the offer."

"It's my turn! It *is* my turn!" shouted Regina from the game.

Thomas stopped and placed a hand on his wife's arm. "Look at that!" he urged in a low voice. To the children he called in the same undertone, telling them to leave what they were doing and come quietly. When they clustered around him he pointed to the upper branches of a nearby *kowhai*. There, trembling on a twig barely thick enough to take its weight, perched a shy bird with long trailing tail feathers. Its brown plumage was freckled with chestnut and it wore an immaculate striped white waistcoat. As the Peridots stared at the stranger it surveyed them in return.

"The *koekoea*," breathed Thomas with as much pride in his voice as if he had personally set the bird on the twig. "That little long-tailed cuckoo is the reason that there are Maoris living in New Zealand. Did you know that? Remember me telling you the story about Kupe, the great Polynesian navigator?"

"I remember," said Samuel. "You told me on the way to the bush camp once."

"Kupe lived on a tiny island hundreds and hundreds of miles away. He was an observant fellow, and as he watched the skies to see what the fishing weather might be he noticed this little chap. After several years of watching he noticed something else. At one part of the year the birds were always travelling north, and six months later they were all travelling south. From watching this bird he realised that there must be land here somewhere, and that inspired him to bring the Great Fleet to these shores."

"How do you know all that?"

"From the songs you listened to today, Madeline. One of them was all about the koekoea and its long journey over the ocean."

Juliette said, "But it's so little to fly so far. Can it rest on the sea when it becomes tired?"

"No, it cannot. For hundreds of miles it flies without a place to land and rest, without eating or drinking."

"But that's marvellous," whispered Juliette.

"Aren't we fortunate to live here and have such miraculous things to see?" asked Thomas.

Evangeline felt uncomfortable. The story of the cuckoo was one more thread in the net that held them here. It was a relief when Abby interrupted.

"Why can't we open our gifts now?" she wanted to know. "Why do we have to wait until it's dark?"

"Because then it seems more like Christmas to me. When I was a little girl, Christmastime was in the winter. The seasons are upside down in England; it is snowing there now, and when we have cold rainy days it is summer in England."

"Aye, with cold, rainy days too," teased Thomas.

Because Evangeline spoke so seldom about her childhood even Thomas lent an attentive ear as she gathered the family around her while Juliette lit the lamps. It was still not really dark but with the shutters closed they could pretend, and with Evangeline's descriptions of frost and hail they could almost ignore the heat inside the cottage.

"I was the only girl in our family, so it was my chore to scrub the laundry. In winter it was so cold that when one sheet was pegged to the rack it would be frozen hard as glass by the time the next was ready to go out. Most Christmases I recall we had steaming clothes hanging all around the fireplace."

"Tell us about your naughty brothers!" begged young Thomas, wriggling with excitement.

"Oh, but they *were* naughty, too. Terribly naughty. One Christmas they crept out early and painted all the windows on the cottage next door. Painted them over with pitch, they did, and when the poor old couple next door woke up, they thought it was nighttime and went back to sleep again. And when they woke up again, they . . ."

"Thought it was nighttime!" cried the children gleefully.

"And they got a whipping!" cried young Thomas, racing to the end of the story.

"Indeed they did," laughed Evangeline, giving him a hug. "My, what a miserable Christmas Day they had, scrubbing up the pitch and wailing all the while. Everybody in the street turned out to cheer them on. Well, now.

Juliette has finished the lamps. Can anybody think of what we might like to do now?"

"Open the gifts!"

"What do you think, Thomas? Shall we?"

"We could wait until tomorrow, of course . . ." but the rest of his sentence was drowned in a howl of protest.

This year the gifts were particularly lavish. Each of the children received new clothes, all sewn in secret. The girls had paisley printed roundabouts, or cotton smocks, cut from a single piece of cloth from Sydney; this was a special treat, for it meant that none of the other Mission children would appear in "their" pattern. Thomas received two new shirts and from the children a tobacco cutter that Evangeline had purchased. Young Thomas and Samuel both were given suits of clothes—a thrill for Thomas, for it meant the end of his baby era. In addition to all that sewing Evangeline had somehow contrived to find the time to make the girls each a calico carry bag with appliquéd designs—hearts and ribbons for Madeline, doves for Abigail, ferns for Juliette, and for Regina, butterflies. And best of all, each of the children received a shiny penny wrapped in red silk, a penny to be taken to Oliver Jarrod's Kororareka store and exchanged for whatever kind of sweets they found most irresistible.

To Juliette the best was saved for last, when Mother received her gifts. The children had spent months working on a collage picture built up from shells, strands of cotton, and tiny shreds of fabric. Abigail had copied an engraving of an English cottage onto a board and everyone had helped glue and fill in the scratched outline. All the love and effort were repaid when Madeline and Abby carried it from its hiding place in the lean-to. Evangeline gasped, and her face lit up with such genuine pleasure that the children laughed and hugged each other.

"We were so afraid you might not like it," said Juliette.

"How could I not love it? What a lot of hard work there is here. Oh, my goodness. Even the bricks on the wall are made of broken pipi shells . . ."

"Samuel smashed dozens and dozens with a mallet to make enough pieces the right size," explained Madeline.

"And I found the tiny shells for the hollyhock flowers!" cried Regina.

"Am I not the most fortunate lady in the whole of New Zealand?" she asked. "Ten shillings and a box of lilac powder from dear Thomas, this magnificent picture to look at, and the most precious family anybody could ever hope to have."

She was counting her blessings the next day in the very different kind of atmosphere at the Mission. Today there were no lessons for the children; they played blindman's buff and tug of war while their mothers gathered on the Clerkwells' verandah to toast the health of the new Queen with a glass or two of the best Canary that Mission funds could provide. Even the teetotal Mr. Busby joined in the ceremony.

A garlanded picture of the Queen was set on a small table for the group to admire.

"Poor dear lass, so young and such an awesome responsibility," sniffed Mrs. Clerkwell in a rare burst of sentiment.

"Pretty, too," said another woman.

"I wonder whom she will marry?"

"I hear tell that she's vowed not to wed. That she will stay a virgin like her predecessor, Elizabeth the First," declared one of the out-of-town ladies.

Mrs. Heaslip glanced around to see if any of the men was within earshot. "At least then she'll avoid the terrible fate of poor Princess Charlotte. That was a sad thing. They say she was *two weeks* in labour and then they had to . . ."

The other women inclined their heads to catch the details.

"If she doesn't marry, she'll be much safer," agreed Mrs. Clerkwell.

"Not if she has inherited her uncles' bad blood," said Mrs. Heaslip. "They say it would be impossible to fit the children they've sired all into one room, or even into a whole suite of rooms! And for all that there's only the one properly married."

"Have any of you ladies been over to Mr. Jarrod's emporium lately?" asked Mrs. Webber, who was deaf and had missed most of the conversation. "He has just received the most glorious shipment of new dress goods . . . sateens, cashmeres, velvets . . . and the hat trimmings are unbelievable. He has some little gilt buckles . . ."

Evangeline listened avidly.

Later that week Thomas left her at the Kororareka jetty with Madeline, Samuel, and the baby, a list of goods to be purchased, two enormous flax kits, and Tippy dragging dejectedly at the end of a leather string.

"Will you be all right while I visit Mrs. Yardley?" he asked, concerned with good reason, for against the town's lawlessness two children were scant protection.

"No harm has ever come to us before," she said firmly.

Oliver Jarrod's stone shop was the only really solid building in the beach-front part of Kororareka, and the only respectable one too. The crammed town contained five skittle alleys, three billiard saloons, a half dozen brothels which obligingly ferried girls out to the ships for orgies, two bawdy theatres, grogshops, doss houses, and trading rooms where stolen goods changed hands. Oliver Jarrod's place stood alone, respectable because it sold a variety of goods used in homes, untainted food, gardening tools, household effects, and clothing of guaranteed quality. It was also respectable because no spitting, no swearing, no credit, no drunkenness, and no fighting were tolerated on the premises. Some even whispered that Oliver Jarrod was the prime moving force behind the newly formed Vigilants society.

Evangeline stepped over the door mat with a sense of anticipation while Thomas and the other children turned towards the hills and began the dusty trudge to the Yardleys' house. Each child had brought his penny and after the visit they would have the fun of choosing sweets from the jars on Oliver Jarrod's counter. By the time they had puffed to the top of the rise Juliette's penny was a hot wet disc in her palm under her embroidered mitten.

Maire Yardley was a widow, the owner of the Richmond Shipping Line, whose ships were used by Thomas for the transport of his cargo. Her house was suitably impressive, large and wooden and actually painted white, a rare thing in New Zealand where wooden houses generally cracked and warped from the sun. Thomas rang the doorbell while the children gazed about them in wondering silence.

More surprises were in store. The door was opened by a Maori girl of about twelve dressed in a long black gown with a white starched apron bibbed in front and with a wide crisp bow at the back and a white cap pinned primly over her braids. They followed her obediently as if she had been an angel materialised through a gloom that smelled of flowers and dust.

Juliette poked Abby and whispered, "Look at that!"

They paused at a half-open door and stared into a large, dim room with a polished floor, heavy velvet furniture, and a spindle-legged table in the corner below a milk-glass hanging lamp. The entire corner, wall, and table top were draped in swags of dull black crepe around a statue of Jesus on the cross and a gold-framed portrait of an elderly gentleman in a frock coat and side whiskers.

The Maori girl glared at them. "Mrs. Yardley, she's waiting in the morning room," she said, jolting them into an awareness that it was ill mannered to stare into other people's rooms. They now followed along with apprehension mixed with awe. There was something sinister about that shrine in the parlour and something chilling about the whole atmosphere of the house. Juliette recalled her mother's scornful comments about "papists" and wondered for the first time what ominous meanings lay behind that word.

Mrs. Yardley greeted them from a chair with arms like lion's paws and a buttoned velvet back. She acknowledged them with a small curl of her lips and an inclination of her splendid head. She wore black silk tight at the bodice but with sleeves that flared at the upper arms and gripped closely along the forearms. Mrs. Yardley's skin was as white as the frontispiece of a Bible and her hair was as black as the leather cover. She wore it drawn tightly back off her face so that it lifted her eyebrows up at the corners, giving her a slant-eyed, rather languid appearance.

"So this is your brood, Thomas?" Her voice was clear and lilting with a faint accent.

"Only some of them." To the children's astonishment, he called her by her first name, which sounded like

"Maree" as he bent over to kiss the hand she raised graciously to him. "The other children are shopping with their mother."

"Ah, your wife." The tone cooled. "And she is in good health, I trust?"

Regina was already fidgeting. Juliette took her hand and squeezed it reassuringly.

Maire Yardley was saying, "We shall take tea now, thank you, Mary. But first show the children out into the garden. They may look at the goldfish." To indicate that Thomas should sit opposite her she moved her head slightly, a gesture that might have gone unnoticed by someone not used to her mannerisms.

Thomas was used to her but far from comfortable in her presence. Even after these past three years since her husband died her immaculate presence still contrived to make him feel scruffy, poorly dressed, and acutely conscious of the sweat generated in the hour of hard rowing. It was odd to consider that every Sunday he arrived at the Mission in these clothes and in this condition but never once felt grubby or ill at ease.

Maire was aware of his discomfort. She could smell it as clearly as the scent of his lye soap. While it generally amused her to make a man feel inferior, Thomas' unease annoyed her. He was a fine man with a sympathetic understanding of the Maoris which was pitiably rare in this district, and though he held strong views he did not feel compelled to force them onto others. He had no cause to feel inferior to anyone . . . unless she was misreading him and it was in fact *she* who made him so jumpy. Could it be that he was attracted to her? Despite the ten-year age difference and the beauty of his wife? Perhaps he was unhappy. She had heard rumours about Evangeline Peridot and though she had paid no attention, realising that in this climate rumour flourished like mould in a damp cupboard, perhaps she should listen and consider. It was a piquant thought, one to turn over in her mind as she asked him how strong he would like his tea.

"Light, please." He was so used to their own watery reused tea leaves that even the light was unaccustomedly strong to his palate. He watched with pleasure as she warmed the teapot and emptied it into a silver bowl, then measured out black leaves from three porcelain caddies, Indian, Chinese, and Ceylonese. The tea came with fresh cow's milk and pikelets with raspberry jam and thick cream melting into their warm surfaces. She served him herself with detached grace.

"Trade is moving along so smoothly now," said Maire. "Some say that it is too good to last."

"It won't, of course, but it may get better."

"How do you mean that?"

"I mean that New Zealand is in a trough at the moment, neither one thing nor the other. If Britain makes up her mind to annex us, then a wave of trade will follow the settlers who are certain to come here."

"Some say France will annex us," she said lightly.

"Naturally. Your Bishop is French, and of course speculation has inevitably risen since he settled here. But I doubt if it will come to anything."

"A pity." She smiled, setting her cup aside.

Changing the drift of their conversation, she continued, "Stephen wants a trial shipment of vegetables for the penal colony later this week. He is home at the moment but the *Lorendee* still has her cargo aboard . . . some problem about extracting compensation, I believe . . . These tradespeople are so unreliable, but Stephen would not be so foolish as to let one single barrel ashore unless it was paid for. Stephen thinks that vegetables will make a profitable cargo and that it was an excellent idea of yours."

"We can pack cabbages, carrots, and maize for puddings. In a month the peaches in the valley will be ready for early picking. They should travel well."

"Hone Heke's tribe has a magnificent planting of melons this year, or so I have been told. Do you think it might be worth a visit to him to see if he wishes to negotiate an export sale?"

Thomas smiled broadly. Hone Heke was the nephew of the late Hongi Hika, a splendid hulk of a man but notoriously quick-tempered and unreliable.

"What is so amusing? Have I mispronounced his name?"

"You pronounced it beautifully. I smiled because I have tried to do business with Hone Heke in the past. It was not

a success. His memory is faultless when it comes to recalling payments due to him but very doubtful over the
matter of what goods he has or has not supplied in return.
He's a rascal!"

"You sound as if you like him!" Her hand hovered over
the teapot.

"Oh, I do." He passed his cup over to be refilled.

"Do you think he is in any way like his uncle?"

"Will he wage war?" He shrugged. "I honestly don't
know. I think that Hone Heke likes it here and is content
with the status quo. Hongi Hika on the other hand was literally a destructive child with an exclusive toy. He was the
only one with muskets and they were no fun unless he
used them. Things are different now. Everybody has muskets."

"Everybody but us," and she shivered delicately.

"Now then, Maire," he said masterfully, "we shall have
no alarmist talk like that."

She lowered her lids and regarded him thoughtfully.
Without warning she pictured him, very clearly, in a frock
coat and brocade waistcoat standing beside her bed. Startled, she shook her head to clear the vision.

"I think that we should discuss business details," she
said.

Behind the house was a flat lawn which claimed the
whole area between vine-screened verandah and a hillside
crusted with terraced rock gardens. On the lawn four
young people played with hoops. All were dressed in cream
and all wore hats, the three girls capote bonnets and the
boy a flat cap with a peak that shaded his face.

Juliette suddenly felt very shy. She thought the three
girls looked so ethereal and the boy positively grand. Abby
decided at once that they were dull. She was more impressed by the people at the swing under the pohutukawa
tree by the cliff, two brightly dressed girls of fifteen or sixteen and an older youth who was dressed stylishly with a
wing-collared shirt and blue silk cravat. Abby thought
him exceedingly handsome and sighed as he grinned down
at the two girls, who squealed flirtatiously as he pushed at
the swing ropes.

The boy with the cap stared as the Peridot children came down the steps like ducklings following their mother. "What's this, Mary? Have you been out collecting riffraff off the streets?"

Juliette said quickly, "We are visiting with our father."

"Hoity-toity, eh?" laughed the boy, advancing towards them mock threateningly and waving his hoop stick about his head.

One of the girls cried, "It's your turn now, Leigh."

The oldest player, a girl of about fourteen, called, "Oh, do be sensible, Leigh. If you let go of that stick it could hit any of us or even break a window. Mama would be so cross. It takes years to replace the glass!"

Leigh grinned cheekily and then pulled a horrid face at the Peridot children, tweaking Abby's long ringlets and tugging the brim of Regina's bonnet. When he planted himself in front of Juliette she stared frankly back at him with interest. He was a pleasant-looking boy with soft features, full lips, and large white teeth which he bared threateningly at her.

She giggled delightedly. "You look like Tippy!"

"That sounds like a dog's name."

"Oh, it is! Tippy is our dog."

"And I resent being compared to a dog!" With that he nipped her ear lobe between finger and thumb.

It did not hurt very much but Juliette, who was accustomed to dealing with the impudent Maori boys from the pa, reacted at once by slapping Leigh sharply across the side of the head, quite forgetting that her palm concealed a penny.

Leigh squawked angrily and clapped a hand over his ear. His sisters arched their necks and laughed softly in approval.

One said, "I have warned you, dear brother, that if you tease you are likely to be paid in coin."

"What did you do?" asked Leigh, ignoring his sister. "That really stung!"

Nervously Juliette thrust her hand behind her back, but he dragged it forward and pressed his thumb into her palm. "I thought so," he muttered as he tore at her mitten, popping off the two wrist buttons.

His sisters glided up behind him. There was a strong family likeness of black hair, greenish-brown eyes, and clear pale skin. Their concerned expressions relaxed when Leigh held up the penny.

"There! I told you so, Leigh. She truly *did* pay you in coin for your teasing."

Juliette was the only one not laughing. She wanted to apologise—she had not meant to hit him so hard but then he *had* hurt her first. Before she could speak he was glaring around at the ring of mirthful faces, his face scarlet with embarrassment and his eyes bright with the suspicion of tears. Jamming the coin into the fob of his cream waistcoat, he dashed towards the house.

"He's got my penny!" said Juliette helplessly.

"Leigh!" shouted the oldest girl. "You must give it back!"

The verandah door slapped shut. Regina began to cry. One of the Yardley girls bent to comfort her while another placed a consoling hand on Juliette's arm. This girl was not as pretty as her sisters, for her nose had been broken at one time and badly set, which had ruined her looks. But her voice was kind as she explained that Leigh could not really help his outburst because he detested being laughed at.

"It would be futile to ask Mama's assistance," said the older girl. "She always takes Leigh's side, no matter what the provocation."

Juliette bowed her head swiftly and stared at the ground, hot tears brimming under her lids. Her penny! It would be a whole year before she would get another to spend and no use appealing to Father. He would say it was her responsibility to take good care of her things. Dumbly she accepted the buttons that young Thomas had retrieved for her. She must not cry in front of these elegant girls, no matter how wretched she felt.

"What in the name of Jove is going on here?" asked a cheerful voice, and suddenly Juliette felt strong fingers under her chin and was blinking up into the tanned, smiling face of the young man who had been pushing the swing. Sunlight danced on black curls and indulgence gleamed in his eyes.

"Oh dear," he said with mock seriousness. "Promise me that you are not going to cry."

Juliette shook her head bashfully.

"Good. If you are crying it makes everything much more difficult to put right."

"You will be able to help us, won't you, Stephen? Please?" asked one of his sisters.

"Leigh took her money and ran away."

"How much cash did this grab-and-run robber manage to escape with, miss?" asked Stephen.

"A penny," she confessed. "It was my Christmas spending money."

"Oh?" His eyebrows rose. "Well, we cannot have a sweet young lass losing her Christmas treat, can we? I shall play the stern father to Leigh once more but in the meantime, young lady, please have this." He probed into his waistcoat pocket and edged out another penny which he placed solemnly in her sore palm.

"Oh, sir, I could not accept *your* money! That would not be right!"

He laughed. "Do not worry about it. I shall recover the other penny from my recalcitrant brother's rather too generous allowance. Justice will be done." He smiled at Juliette, thinking, What an enchanting child. She looks like a fragile fair Italian child, all innocence and radiance.

She regarded him gravely, folded the coin in her thin fingers, and said, "Thank you for your kindness, but please do not punish your brother. I did provoke him with a whack across the ear."

"And he richly deserved it!" put in the prettier of the younger two girls.

The one with the misshapen nose said chidingly, "Leigh has missed Papa terribly since he died . . ."

Stephen interrupted, smiling. "It is all this feminine company. Poor Leigh feels positively stifled, as no doubt I would!"

Abby had been unusually quiet so far but now she spoke up with a coy glance towards the girls who waited near the swing. "You do surprise me, Mr. Yardley. I thought you enjoyed feminine company!"

In the name of Jove, she's flirting with me, he realised. And her all of eight or ten years old?

"If I might enquire, just who are you young people?"

"We are here with our father, Mr. Thomas Peridot."

"Ah. The children who caper on the beach near Te Pahi's pa? I am Stephen, and please allow me to present my sisters: Jane, who is fourteen and growing up rapidly, and Sarah and Rose, who are twins."

"Stephen!" came the plaintive cry from behind them.

"I would present Leigh but he has done that in his own inimitable way."

"Stephen!"

He grinned wickedly. "Please excuse me, but beauty should never be kept waiting."

Juliette gazed after him. Inexperienced as she was, she knew that there was something special about a grown-up young man who would leave his guests to sooth an upset child. She felt touched and grateful.

She wondered aloud, "Is that Captain Yardley from the *Lorendee?*"

"Yes," said Jane. "Stephen has been at sea since he was seven years old. He has been a Captain since Papa died. We all adore Stephen but seldom see him. He is away at sea most of the time and when he is at home . . ." Shrugging eloquently, she allowed the sentence to drop.

"Who are those ladies he is talking to?" asked Abby.

"The Bellwood girls," sighed Jane. "They have no time for us but whenever Stephen is home they come over on the slightest pretext. It is odd that Georgina Meyney has not accompanied them today. They all think Stephen almost divine."

"I cannot wonder at that," said Juliette.

Sarah smiled at her with an understanding that transformed her face and made Juliette warm to her at once. "Stephen is charming but he is quite his own man," she said quietly.

Later, when they trooped down the dusty street with their father, Juliette saw Leigh sitting on the horse-mounting platforms swinging his feet and munching on an enormous pink sticky sugar bun which he waved in an impudent gesture at the girls as they passed. Juliette wanted to turn her head for another look but Regina claimed her attention and the moment of crossing the scarred threshold passed without an opportunity.

Inside Jarrod's the floor was covered with dirty sawdust, the shelves and barrels were thick with dust, and the sunlight had to filter through windows covered by bars, cobwebs, and grime. Yet the place was such a rich treasure trove that Juliette's breath snagged excitedly in her throat as she stood in the centre of the cluttered room and gazed about. Evangeline was seated on a high wooden stool at one end of the counter drinking a cup of weak coffee. Unwrapped purchases filled the hamper beside her. Oliver Jarrod came forward to greet them, speaking in a low rumble that sounded like an engine running. He wore a striped butcher's apron and continually rubbed his hands on it as though his palms itched. He chattered to Thomas while the children gravely inspected the tall, smudged candy jars on the counter top. While the others chose quickly Juliette hung back, staring at the lumpy fudge, the glossy shards of toffee, and the gaudy boiled sweets.

"Come on, Julie," Thomas hurried her.

She glanced up at him, an idea forming in her mind. Pushing her penny over the counter, she said, "Could I please buy a penny's worth of Negro's Head?"

" 'Baccy? You want 'baccy? a sweet wee lass like you?" but he reached on the shelf behind him for the red-labelled tin.

"What do you want that for, Julie?" asked Thomas.

She was confused, and wanted to tell him to go away while she completed the purchase, but she whispered, "I want to get you a present."

He swung her up in the air, laughing at her embarrassment. "I don't want a present from you," he said as he set her on her feet. "That is your money. You must spend it on yourself."

He meant it kindly but to her it sounded like a rejection. She dropped her head quickly, fearing for the second time that day that she might cry.

"What will it be, then?" prompted Mr. Jarrod, and, stammering, she blurted out that she would have fudge.

Oliver Jarrod could see that she was upset and he could also guess why.

"Here, I'm going to ask a favour of you," he said confidentially, opening one of the jars and nipping off a small taste of the chunky white candy inside. He popped the piece into her mouth. "I'll ask you to try this one before you make your mind up. It's called Irish rock and it will make you feel that you are eating clouds dusted with sugar."

"Mr. Jarrod, it tastes *beautiful!*"

"So you fancy a penny's worth of this one then?"

She nodded wordlessly and he broke off bigger chunks of it than he had given the others, chatting to them all as he heaped them onto a square of coarse paper and drew the corners together and fastened them in a twist.

"Mrs. Yardley makes some of my sweets and this is a new one we are trying. That lady has a fine sweet tooth and a true appreciation of flavours." He paused and cocked his head. "Listen! Can you hear that music?"

"A drum and bagpipes, is it?" wondered Thomas.

"A drum and a fife," corrected Oliver, adding smugly, "If I'm not mistaken, they'll be the farewell party marching two rogues out of town. They were caught red-handed and guilty as you please crawling through a window at Meyney's house last night. I was one who had the satisfaction of helping to confine them myself."

"In gaol?" asked Samuel, big-eyed.

"Gracious, no, son. We've no gaol in Kororareka, nor police neither, though there's a crying need for both. These rascals were crammed into tin trunks and left locked up. We was hoping to tar and feather them but tar supplies are a bit low. After baking in the trunks today they'll not be in a hurry to come back here." He rounded the counter and picked up one of Evangeline's baskets. "I'll ask you to be so good as to come out now so I can shut up the store and watch the fun as they go past."

Thomas said, "We'll be hurrying on our way. I doubt that a drumming is a fit sight for children's eyes."

"*Please* can we stay and watch?" asked Samuel.

"You're a bloodthirsty little tyke," said his father, ruffling his hair. "I'll make a bargain with you. If you help me row home so quickly that we arrive before the shadow of the house reaches the top of the cliff, then next time Te Pahi's tribe wages war I shall let you go along with them."

They were out from the beach and skimming along the point when the drumming party came into view from behind a cluster of tumble-down boat sheds. A small group of men playing instruments marched with high-stepping feet. Behind them two grey-clad men limped and stumbled and fell as they hurried to keep ahead of the long bamboo canes swished by some in the jeering crowd that followed.

"They're quite close!" cried Samuel in delight.

"Don't look, girls," instructed Evangeline, a directive that nobody obeyed, for the noise and the tumult were irresistible and they had to peek to see what was happening. Even Evangeline's bonnet swivelled when she was unable to contain her curiosity.

A big black dog barrelled from the crowd and nipped at the men's heels, barking nastily. Tippy wriggled out from under the dinghy seat and began barking too.

"This town gets worse every year," said Thomas in disgust.

Juliette was staring at the men. One was thickset with gingery hair and the other was slight as a boy with a wizened old face. They were the men who had called at the cottage and then had quarrelled with Mr. Jacobson the next day. She leaned forward to ask her father if he recognised them when something made her glance up at her mother's face. Evangeline was sitting with her hands folded in her lap but her face was as white as a bone and her eyes were full of terror.

"Gosh! I'd hate to be treated like that," said Samuel as he leaned into a stroke.

"Then mind that you stay out of trouble when you grow up," advised Thomas. "Worse things than that happen to men who break the law."

Seven

On a day in February when heat blistered the surface of the bay, Madeline, Abby, and Juliette sat under a tree near the cottage brushing the tangles from their freshly washed hair. On bushes all around them hung clothes and bedding which they had laundered that morning, now half dry and gently steaming.

"Do you think there will be a storm soon?" asked Juliette.

"Be careful with that brush," said Abby over her shoulder.

"It's so still. If you listen carefully you'll notice that there are no birds singing," said Juliette. "Isn't that a sign that a storm is coming?"

Madeline said, "I think they probably feel too tired to sing. And so do I after all that washing."

"I'll wager that Mrs. Jacobson never *ever* boils any of her laundry," said Abby bitterly. "She wouldn't make Emily scrub and scour for hours on end nor stand by a hot fire choking in the smoke."

"We should be grateful, I suppose, that we don't have to break the ice on the water barrel like Mother did when she was a child," said Madeline. "England must be a cold place."

"I wonder what the weather is like in San Francisco?" mused Abby.

"Do you know what I wish?" said Juliette, resting the brush handle against her chin. "I wish that I could snip a piece of this hot day and hide it away so that it wouldn't spoil, then bring it out on a grey rainy day in winter. Wouldn't that be splendid?"

Evangeline came to the doorway. Hair straggled over her damp brow and her eyes were puffy from inadequate sleep. Both Regina and young Thomas had been crying fitfully all night and now the baby was feverish too.

"All finished, girls?" She sounded strained.

"Yes, Mother."

"I'd like you to go and pick the last of the peaches for me now. If they are left any longer the birds will peck at them and then they will be no good for drying. Take a basket each and do try not to bruise the fruit or it will rot on the drying racks."

Abby pouted. "You promised that today you would alter the sleeves on my poplin dress to make them gigot style like Madeline's."

Evangeline sighed, too weary to argue. "Be a good girl," she urged, "and I shall attend to your dress as soon as the children are better."

When she had disappeared Abby complained, "It isn't fair that your dress should have been ready three Sundays ago and mine is still all in pieces!"

"And I don't think that you are being very fair to Mother!" Madeline protested. "The only reason my dress was ready was that I helped her with it. If you made an effort to improve your needlework, then your dresses could be any style you wish. Even Regina can turn a seam and knit, but you still expect *me* to make your stockings for you!"

"I shall marry a wealthy gentleman and then it will not matter if I can neither sew nor mend," decided Abby later.

They were in the speckled shade of the peach trees now, where the silky grass reached to their waists. The air was perfumed with the smell of decaying fruit.

"It will not matter then that you cannot cook nor bake nor tend a garden nor care for a baby," said Madeline tartly. "Nor do laundry properly nor scrub potatoes and get all the dirt off, nor . . ."

"Why are you always so crabby?" interrupted Abby, effectively silencing her.

The peaches dropped into their palms at a touch and the ripest burst with juice as they bit into them. Sweetness flooded their mouths.

The baskets were half full when Tippy's barking and Samuel's whistling heralded their approach as they came along the track from the bush camp. His sisters called to him from where they perched up among the leaves, their aprons bunched around their knees. When Abby threw a peach pit to Tippy he snapped at it, thinking it was a snack, but spat it out quickly and would not be tricked again.

Samuel had come to fetch more flour and salt to take back to the camp.

"Stay and help us for a while," begged Abby. "You are so fast at picking and can climb among the branches much better than we can."

He caught the peach Juliette tossed him and bit into it. "Sorry, girls, but I'm needed back there. They are felling a difficult tree."

"He talks like one of the men," said Abby resentfully when he had gone. "Anybody would think that he did something useful instead of getting in the way all the time. I'll wager that they sent him on an errand just to keep him away in case that tree falls on him!"

She repeated this theory to Samuel when he returned. The baskets were all heaped and the girls lay resting. Juliette thought that the crushed grass smelled of summer and earth and bread. She twirled a long stalk between her teeth. Peach juice stained her chin.

Samuel took the ribbing good-naturedly. "Of course I don't do anything to help at the lumber camp," he agreed cheerfully. "But it is a splendid way to avoid having to do any work around the house. I can leave it all to you."

Abby shrugged. She noticed that he had two baskets. One contained a bag of flour but the other was empty. "You have time to pick peaches now? Well, bad luck, old man! We've picked all the easy-to-reach ones."

Samuel's mouth twitched. "Mother said that I could leave this for you to fill and take one of the full ones."

"No!" cried Abby furiously. "We worked hard to pick those peaches!"

Madeline looked exasperated. "Stop it, you two," she said. "Take this basket, Samuel. But be careful not to drop it or the peaches will all squash to a pulp."

"Thanks. Come on, Tippy!" His amused gaze lingered for a last moment on Abby's flushed face.

"I'm not going to help," she announced, when he had gone.

"Do you ever?"

Juliette said drowsily, "At least Mother doesn't want us home in a hurry, so we can laze here for as long as we like. Isn't it a lovely day?"

"I think I shall have a nap before we fill the last basket," sighed Madeline. "That crying kept me awake most of the night."

"Mmm," said Juliette.

When they woke the glare of the day had faded. Madeline sat up with a jolt.

"Oh, gracious! Mother will be worried!"

"The sun is still quite high," said Abby.

"Let's be quick and fill this last basket," Madeline urged. "Mother will need us to help her and we are late already."

But as Abby had said, all the easier peaches had been picked, and their progress was slow. Finally Madeline decided to take the full basket and return home to help prepare the dinner. She left the others to finish.

"Don't be too long," she said.

"We won't," Juliette assured her.

"My mouth tastes funny," Abby complained. "I hope I'm not getting a fever too."

Evangeline had just given Melina a small dose of weak manuka tea and had tucked her back into her crib when she heard a noise outside. Samuel, she thought. He must have forgotten something. It was not like him to be inefficient but in this hot weather everybody's thinking processes seemed muddled.

"What is it, dear?" she called. But as she opened the door she realised that it couldn't be Samuel. Tippy always barked furiously as they neared the house.

Johnny and Blue stood there, blocking her view of the world outside.

Evangeline was shocked; she had not seen these two since the day of the drumming weeks before. She had imagined that they would have long since quit the country and had put all thought of them from her mind. Without speaking she pushed the door shut but Blue simply put his foot in the jamb and leaned against it.

They were inside with the door fixed tight behind them before Evangeline spoke. When she did it was with anger and fatigue. "Go away, please. I told you before that you were not welcome here. Just because I was . . . kind to you once gives you no right to come back against my wishes."

"Now, that ain't much of a welcome, wouldn't yer say, Blue? Here we come all this way on a blazin' hot day an' she don't so much as offer us a drink."

"I shall offer you nothing," said Evangeline firmly. Men had worked around her good resolutions so often in the past but these two were boors and not deserving of any hospitality.

The thin one rubbed at his jaw where fine stubbles softened the creases. "When we heard yer call out 'dear' we thought maybe yer was feelin' more sociable."

"Just look around you," said Evangeline in desperation as they settled themselves, Johnny in the rocking chair and Blue at the table with his boots set arrogantly on the bench. "Please don't put your feet there! Just look around you and you will see that I am too busy to even pass the time of day with you. I have three sick children here. Now, please take yourselves off." She looked from one to the other, cajoling them now.

Johnny kicked at the floor and set the rocking chair in motion. His faded felt hat was low over his narrow brow.

"Yer really ought ter know somethin', lady . . ."

"Lady!" snorted the other.

"We jest ain't goin' nowhere. We come a long way ter see you an' we ain't goin' out that door until we got what we came fer."

"No!" Her indignation rose. How dare they? "It's impossible . . . you must see that!"

"I don't see nothing!" said Blue loudly.

His voice woke Regina, who had been dozing fitfully. She began to whimper.

"Oh, look at what you've done!" Evangeline glared at him as she stepped towards the bunks.

He reached out a hand and grabbed her slender arm, drawing her up short. She thought, idiotically, that there was something in his manner that reminded her of Tippy pouncing on a rat. Impatiently she jerked at the grip and felt a jolt of dismay as his hand tightened.

"Leave the nipper be," he ordered. "Like Johnny says, we came to talk."

"How *dare* you order me about in my own home! How *dare* you! Let go of my arm!"

"Douse it!" And, as he spoke, he twisted her arm.

The unexpected hurt made her breath catch in her throat. Wrenching herself free, she backed away from him.

"That's better," said Johnny. "Now hush yer mouth and listen ter what we have to say. We came all this way, not for a taste of yer company but because yer got somethin' we want."

"What?"

"Don't need ter look at me like that. Blue an' me, we got ourselves in a bit of trouble."

"I know." She rubbed at her arm.

"Oh, yer do?"

"I saw you being escorted out of town."

"Bastards," rumbled Blue.

"We got ourselves a problem, now. That town don't want us an' now the Mission farm don't want us so we have ter hie ourselves off to somewhere we ain't known, if you see what I mean."

Evangeline looked at them with loathing. How could she ever have been such a fool as to entertain these men? She must have been mad. Coldly she said, "I fail to see how I can help you."

"Oh, but you can." Johnny smiled. "No ship will take us on as crew, at least not to any place but Sydney, an' we cain't show up there. What we need is the payment fer a passage ter somewhere where we can walk about without fear of bein' recognised. If we don't have that, then our only other hope is ter start walkin' south, an' that could be mighty dangerous even fer us, what with some of these fierce tribes that live inland."

"You wouldn't be harmed," she assured them, beginning to drift with the meaning of their visit. "Most Maori

tribes respect white people and want their help in trading."

"You don't say?" Johnny smiled. "But it so happens that
we ain't so fond of them Maoris an' it seems a better idea
ter buy ourselves a passage ter Canada or Alaska or somewhere where there's scope fer two enterprisin' fellows like
us. O' course, fer that we need money."

Their faces were both fixed so expectantly on her that
she said dully, "So you came here hoping to rob me."

"She's quick," said Blue.

Evangeline flared, "Well, I'm sorry but your journey
was wasted. I have no money, none left, that is."

"Ye're lyin'," said Johnny.

"There's no money here. It's all gone to the Richmond
Shipping Line to secure our passages to San Francisco. We
are leaving next month."

Johnny was confident she was bluffing. "Yer ain't such
a fool ye're goin' ter bring that money out in front o' yer
husband. That's one thing we do know about yer. He ain't
got the dash of an idea what's goin' on here. So stop yer
flappin' an' give it us."

"I haven't got any." Damn them! That money had taken
patient years of accumulation and she'd be damned if she
was going to hand it over to a pair of petty, cowardly thugs.

"Then we'll have ter find it," sighed Johnny resignedly.
"Find it, Blue."

He lay back negligently while Blue went eagerly to
work. The first thing to be searched was the precious and
meagre collection of chinaware. An ornamental teapot
shattered on the floor. Then a tea caddy, then the porcelain
tobacco pot and the porcelain pipe rack. Blue's fingers fastened around a figurine of a lady in a slim pink gown.

"Stop it!" cried Evangeline.

Regina wailed. Young Thomas woke and sleepily began
to struggle to sit up.

"Yer better stop now, Blue, so the lady can tell us where
it's hid."

Evangeline paused, biting her lip. It occurred to her that
forty-eight sovereigns could buy more ornaments and porcelain than the whole cottage could contain. She shook her

head, declaring, "I've told you all there is to know. Now stop that at once and go before my husband comes home."

Johnny shook his head. "And him in the bush camp an' not due home until after dark? Try the dolls, Blue. Sometimes people hide money in dolls. Rip them open an' see."

Regina was wide awake and sitting up now. She watched, riveted with horror, as this strange, horrid man took Madeline's beautiful new doll down from the shelf and stabbed it right in the middle of the back with a knife. Rag stuffing tumbled out as it was flung to the floor. Abby's doll was next, and Regina flinched as the beautiful violet bonnet was dragged off and the violet gown slashed up the back. That too was cast aside and the man reached for Regina's Mary.

"No!" Her anxiety propelled her out of bed and she bumped her way past the baby's crib and lunged at Blue's arm. "No!" she shrieked. "You leave my doll alone!"

"That must be the one," drawled Johnny, swiftly easing himself up and seizing Evangeline to stop her from interfering.

"No!" screamed Regina as the knife descended. She struggled furiously and fastened herself to the hand that held the weapon. Blue swore and shook at her but she was as tenacious and stubborn as a dog. With both feet she kicked at him as she swung with all her weight on his arms in a desperate attempt to save her only toy. He shook her again, cursing, and took a step forward to try to dislodge her but he stumbled over Madeline's doll and tripped. He took another blind step to save himself. His knees struck the crib and he was off balance completely, going down on top of the tipped crib and the baby with Regina, the doll, and the knife—all into one heap of bodies and splintering wood.

"My baby!" cried Evangeline, and even Johnny's bony fingers digging into her shoulders could not stop her frantic dash around the table.

Blue was lumbering to his feet; he saw the baby at the same moment as her horrified gaze fell on it, the neck gashed and spurting, the black knife handle protruding like an exclamation mark.

"I didn't mean . . ." he began clumsily.

Evangeline did not hear him, nor did she hear the wails as young Thomas and Regina clung together in fright. Her eyes moved from Melina's body up to Blue's face, rising unseeingly. They were enormous, dark blue with great black centres. As though in a nightmare her mouth opened and she screamed—loudly, one long, shrill, endless scream.

"Shut her up!" cried Johnny urgently. "Quickly, or we'll have half the tribe here in no time. Hurry!" He rounded the table and glimpsed the baby's body. "Oh, Christ in heaven! You've really done it now!"

Belligerently, he said, "It were an accident! An accident, I tell you."

"Never mind. Just shut her up, and the children, too. Hurry!"

And just outside the door they met Madeline, running towards the screams she'd heard and struggling with the overflowing basket of peaches.

The girls at the old orchard had not heard their mother's cries but they heard Madeline's harrowing shriek and recognised the abruptly stilled voice as hers. They stopped and stared fearfully at each other. Juliette was in the tree and Abby down below was trying to catch the fruit in her cupped apron as her sister shook the branches.

"She stopped," whispered Abby.

"Yes," said Juliette, thinking that the silence was far more frightening than the scream had been.

"What do you think has happened?" asked Abby.

"She must have fallen and hurt herself." Juliette scrambled down and dusted her hands of bits of bark.

"It sounded *terrible!*"

"You know how Madeline screeches," Juliette reminded her. "Remember the noise she made the other day when there was that huhu beetle caught in the spider's web? It probably isn't anything, but we'd better go see."

They left the peaches and were part of the way up the long, sloping path to the cottage when the unmistakable noise of running filtered along towards them. There was a thudding of feet, the sound of arguing, and the noise of branches bending and slapping back. Juliette scurried off

the track and crouched behind some flax bushes. Abigail
plunged in behind her and lay down, breathing hard.

"Ssh," warned Juliette. The thudding came closer and
mingled with the pounding of blood in her ears.

"Not them nippers," protested a panting voice. "We
should-a left them nippers."

"An' have them tell everybody? Yer mad? Yer want to
get strung?" The voice was reedy and vaguely familiar.

"I don't like to hurt nobody but especially not nippers."

"Ah, shut up, Blue. Stupid doxy should-a told us where
the money was hid."

Arguing, the two men burst into view and then were
past. It was all in the space of a few footfalls but they
might have stood still for an hour, for in that brief time Juliette recognised them both. They were the men she'd met
in the dark, then had seen at the whaling station and later
still had watched as they were drummed out of Kororareka.

When they had gone the girls stood nervously on the
path.

"Who was it?" asked Abby, smoothing her crushed
dress.

Juliette looked back down towards the peach trees. "I'm
frightened," she said.

There was not a sound from the cottage. Nothing. Juliette took one step, then another—and stopped. All around
the cottage door, scattered like great pink hailstones, were
Madeline's peaches. There was the basket lying on its side
and there, right against the house with one arm stretched
up against the wall as if she was reaching for something,
was Madeline herself.

Her sisters rushed to her. She was lying face down in the
parsley bed, her bonnet was stained red at the back.

"She's been hurt!" cried Abby, turning her onto her side.

Madeline flopped over and her eyes stared at the sky.
The skin of her face was crosshatched with little white
ridges where she had pressed against the parsley stalks.
Her chin was muddy. Abby dabbed at it with the corner of
her apron but when she touched her sister a bubble of
blood bright as a cherry appeared at the corner of her
mouth.

"I'll fetch Mother," said Juliette and dashed straight into the cottage. She was already tense and frightened and what she saw now was so foreign to her that it took a full minute for her to realise what she was looking at: that the red and white bundle sprawled back over the table was her mother, that those bundles on the floor were her sisters and her brother. There was clutter everywhere, things smashed, bedding and torn cloth scattered. But despite this the scene printed itself on her mind and her terrified eyes took in every appalling detail: the bone sticking pink and jagged from her mother's butchered neck, the mass of sodden purple flesh that had been young Thomas' temple, smashed with such ugly force that one eye bulged partly out of a socket, the grotesque disarray of Regina's limbs and the blood that ran in a bright, wide ribbon right across her brow. And Melina . . .

Mercifully Juliette's mind collapsed. She turned blindly and fled from the house. As she ran she sucked great gasps of air into her lungs.

"Julie!" called Abby, and abandoning the hopeless task of trying to rouse Madeline, she raced after her.

Halfway along the beach she caught up to her and together they ran to the pa for help. Although Abby had seen far less of what had happened, it was she who had to tell the tribal elders what was back at the cottage and to ask them to send someone for their father. Though she had not seen the men it was she who in the end tried to describe the footsteps and voices. Juliette merely sat on the ground shivering and hugging her arms tightly about her knees. When questioned, she looked blank and shook her head. Later in the lanternlight, when Thomas' haggard voice pressed question after question on her, she pleaded that she did not understand. Why were they here at the pa when it was so late? And could they go home now? Mother would be waiting supper for them. Mother always worried if they were not home at dusk.

PART TWO

THE
CLERKWELLS

1838-1840

Eight

Even a shark drawn to the threshings of a hurt creature could not have travelled to the scene as swiftly as Mrs. Jacobson. She was at the pa just after dark with one of Jacky Norris' children to hold the lantern for her.

"What a fine check they got, not letting me go near your house!" she complained as she settled herself awkwardly on the matting near Thomas. "I can't imagine that I could have disturbed anything, but they told me I had to keep away."

Thomas closed his eyes.

"I've not come to be in the way," she said briskly. "I'll collect the girls and be gone." She made no move to rise. "It's a queer thing that the murderers got away so easy. All these Maoris and them so very clever at finding things in the bush. The murderers should have been caught just like that!" She snapped her fingers and leaned forward. Sour sweat seemed to steam off her. "I wonder if they tried very hard."

Thomas looked at her blankly. Her gaze was fastened on his face as though her gossip-greedy soul could draw nourishment from it. She wanted to have been there, to have seen it all. Even he had been spared that. By the time he had arrived undertakers had done everything—tohungas they were, men whose work made them so *tapu* they had to be fed morsels of food on the end of pointed sticks. The bodies, wrapped like rolls of matting, were lying in the clearing amongst a scattering of peaches. He would never be able to eat a peach again. Two big bundles, two smaller, and then the baby. Melina's name meant "honey sweet." Evangeline had heard the name at the Mission and seized it. Evangeline. She had been the sweetest wife, the most devoted mother. Why couldn't he feel anything? Why couldn't he mourn? Why did he have this dreadful sensation as if his head was packed tightly with straw?

Mrs. Jacobson confided, "You do know what I mean, don't you? These Maoris are deep. They must know more than they say. They always only let on a little and keep a lot to themselves."

"There's virtue in that," said Thomas, longing for her to go away.

"It must have been some of these Maoris, from this tribe, who did it," she continued relentlessly. "Why else would the girls be so upset when I tried to talk to them just now? They both broke down and cried, they were so glad to see a white face!"

Thomas had stopped listening. One of the young chiefs had returned from the cottage with a bottle and glass which Thomas had sent him to fetch. A few strong swallows of whisky scorched his throat but did not clear his head as he had hoped. Bemused, he noticed that those few swallows had taken a whole glassful. He poured another.

"The girls can stay with me just as long as they like. No need for you to worry about them. You can come and stay, too, and Samuel, of course."

"We'll stay here tonight. Tomorrow, after the house is burned, we'll go to the Mission for the funeral."

"Burned?"

Her face looked blurry in the light. He was very tired and had eaten nothing for hours, but the whisky fired him. His hands wavered as he poured a third glassful.

"Have you ever heard of *muru*, Mrs. Jacobson?" he asked with unsteady earnestness. "No? Well, muru is a Maori custom. When someone has had an unfortunate or tragic experience, he"—he tried to point at himself and splashed a little of the drink on his shirt—"is relieved of his possessions by the local tribe. Tomorrow morning they will go in there and take everything . . . everything! And then the house will be burned down."

"Everything!" She was shocked and more than a little disappointed. Evangeline had some very nice porcelain and if nobody else was wanting it, surely it should go to her rather than in the direction of the pa! Discretion, however, forbade her to come right out with it, so she fumed in silence.

"I've rescued a few things, a doll, a workbasket, my tools, a few of the pots, things like that. As for the rest, they can have them. Turi and her mother sorted out the girls' dresses . . . and Samuel's things. But what would I do with Evangeline's hats . . . and dresses . . . Evangeline's pretty dresses!"

Mrs. Jacobson watched him cry without the least sense of embarrassment or shame. Those tears were as much whisky as grief, she was a witness to that! Real grief she would have respected, but he had to down almost half a bottle of spirits before even one tear had fallen. She had always suspected that there was something very odd about the Peridots. So, rather righteously, she stared at him until his shoulders stilled. Then she said querulously, "*I* should have been very glad of Evangeline's dresses and bonnets to make over for myself and Emily! Really, Mr. Peridot, you might have spared us a thought!" Indignantly she waddled away to collect the girls and was offended when, instead of falling into her arms as she had imagined, they both wept and cried and refused to go with her.

As she puffed back over the track behind the boy with the lantern she pondered at length, recalling the many scraps of gossip and innuendo she had heard about Evangeline over the years. By the time she reached home she had almost convinced herself that the killings had been a divine retribution for wickedness.

"As we sow, so shall we reap," she misquoted, untying her grease-spotted bonnet and hanging it up behind the door.

Mrs. Jacobson's help was the first proffered but not the only one. In a time of crisis all the European families allied themselves, conscious of their isolation and vulnerability in this tiny embroidery of civilisation on one corner of a vast blanket of savage wilderness. The vicious killings had chilled them all; the fact that days after the deed (despite several organised searches from Kororareka and the Mission) no culprits had been apprehended struck fear into those living in lonely outposts. Women and children flocked into the bay for protection from their own terror. And at the focus of this crisis Thomas and the Peridot children were showered with gifts, food, and offers of hospitality. He was deeply affected and mistook it to mean that, despite the myriad subtle snubs, Evangeline had been well regarded after all.

He decided that he and Samuel should continue to work and now live together wherever the work took them, basing themselves in Kororareka itself and staying when necessary at the pa or the bush camp. Such a life was patently unsuitable for the girls, and Juliette especially needed sympathetic care. So he accepted Mrs. Clerkwell's offer to foster them. The Clerkwells were childless and able to care for the girls; they understood children and already knew his daughters. And the Mission was within easy reach of Kororareka without being under its influence. Though Abby shrieked when she was separated from her father, he was firm and did not look back until he had pushed the dinghy out from the shore and was settled at the oars.

Juliette was thoroughly bewildered by this upheaval in her life. She had been told that her mother and the other children had "died" but knew from comments and hastily ended conversations that there was much more to it than the outbreak of a swift and sudden fever. It was not long before she knew the whole truth, but the most puzzling thing of all was that she was supposed to hold the key to this mystery. In those first days she was questioned over and over, asked how many people she saw running down the track, had she ever seen them before, what had they been saying, and was there more than one person as Abby said, or was it just the one man? To all these questions Juliette shook her head, mystified. No matter how hard she concentrated or how many clues Abby gave her she was unable to remember anything about that afternoon except the walk up to the house with the sun hot on her back and her shoes scuffing in the dust until finally there were peaches spilled on the ground. There the memory snapped.

"Please, Julie," her father pleaded. "Please think as hard as you can." But though she tried until her head ached she was unable to dredge up anything new.

On the night of the funerals she had her first nightmare.
She and Abby were walking along a winding path in the
late afternoon, eating peaches and laughing, when suddenly the sky darkened. Footsteps pounded around her
and the peaches were flung from their hands so violently
that they splattered on the ground. She woke up to find she
had jerked upright in bed. She was freezing cold and yet
breathing with great deep gasps like someone overheated
from running. In the first instant she awoke her eyes
snapped open in the darkness and she whimpered aloud;
then she realised that she was in the Clerkwells' box room
on a makeshift bed and Abby was there with her.

"Are you all right?" whispered her sister. "You cried
out."

"I had a nasty dream . . . a horrid, horrid dream."

"What was it about?"

"I don't know." Juliette shivered. "I don't know at all.
There were peaches, and I felt dreadfully hot and then suddenly terribly cold. Please, Abby, please come and cuddle
in with me."

"Hush!" said Abby. "Mrs. Clerkwell's coming. You've
gone and woken her up too."

The door swung open to reveal the missionary's wife, her
face grazed by the angle of the guttering candlelight. Her
hair was tufted with rags and though it was a sweltering
night her gown was buttoned to the neck for modesty.

"It is fortunate that I had to leave my bed to take a small
dose of laudanum for my tooth because otherwise I might
have been unaware of this lapse in behaviour. I presume
that there is some explanation for this noise?"

"I had a bad dream."

Abby said, "She woke me up, Mrs. Clerkwell. She cried
out. It must have been a *terrible* dream. Now I feel frightened too."

"Hm." She looked at them thoughtfully and went away,
returning with the purple laudanum bottle, a glass of
water, and a spoon. It tasted so bitter that Juliette gagged
as she forced it down.

The bad dream was reported to Thomas, who in turn
consulted the ship's surgeon from the H.M.S. *Resolve,*
which was in port. In the parlour at the Clerkwells',

Thomas, the surgeon, and Mrs. Clerkwell discussed the matter of Juliette's health.

"It was sensible of you to dose the child with laudanum," the surgeon said. "It would be a good thing to continue this for three or four weeks, keeping the dosage small, of course."

"Of course."

"What troubles me most is her state of mind," he continued. "She has witnessed something terrible and it would seem that if she could be made to remember certain details then the criminals could be apprehended."

"If only she *would* remember!"

"It is natural for you, her father, to feel strongly about this, but here I must appeal to you for caution. The mind is a brittle thing, and the mind of a child even more so, for it is still not fully formed. If she is agitated or placed under too much pressure her mind could give way and madness may strike her down. May I speak frankly, Mr. Peridot?"

"Please do."

"I realise that the loss is so fresh that it is impertinent to the point of rudeness for me to say this, but I may not see you later, and therefore I shall say what I think. Though you could not have made a finer choice than to place them in the capable and sympathetic care of Mrs. Clerkwell, Juliette does need you, her natural father. I would suggest that, as soon as you feel able, you prepare to remarry so that the girls can go to you."

"Well!" said Mrs. Clerkwell, pleased at the compliment but horrified at the suggestion . . . and poor Mr. Peridot with his wife just buried and the ground still raw!

"I understand," said Thomas, but his jaw was tight and he did not trust himself to look up from where his fists were clenched on his knees. "But can I also take it that if there were some way of making Juliette remember, then her mental condition would also clear itself?"

"Yes, I'm certain it would, Mr. Peridot. But such a process could be exceedingly dangerous. I must ask you to promise not to push the child into trying to remember."

Thomas tried to be fair, but the killings had overwhelmed him too. Every time he saw Juliette he longed to shake her until she screamed out the truth; the frustration of being able to do nothing gnawed at his nerves until even the sight of her and her resemblance to her mother made his senses flare as though scalded. Through all his torment he said nothing, visited the Mission faithfully for a weekly duty call, and allowed Abby's bubbling affections to ease his spirits.

One evening as the girls waited at the sea wall they saw Thomas bring Evangeline's huge wicker sewing basket out of the dinghy. While Tippy frisked enthusiastically around them he set it on the grass and opened it.

"Clarice!" said Juliette in wonder, for she had forgotten her doll and now here she was, even prettier than ever. Her brown silk bonnet still wore the yellow rose and her skirts still rustled when Juliette tenderly picked her up and cradled her gently.

Abby was staring indignantly into the basket. "Where's *my* doll?" she wanted to know.

Quickly Thomas said, "This is the only one that wasn't broken. I didn't know whose it was, but since there was just the one left I thought that one of you could have it and the other could have your mother's sewing basket. She treasured it, you know."

"Clarice," breathed Juliette, her face glowing as she touched the china cheeks.

Abby scowled. "Do you mean that I have to have the nasty old workbasket and Juliette keeps the doll?"

"It is hers, so that would seem fair."

"It's *not* fair!" shouted Abby, her face reddening. "I hate sewing! I hate it! Juliette loves sewing. She should be the one to have the workbasket."

Timidly Juliette held Clarice tight against her chest.

Abby squeezed out huge tears, appealing desperately to her father.

"Perhaps you might make yourself a doll, pet," he suggested helplessly. "There is another china face in there."

"I couldn't, you *know* I couldn't! My sewing is far too messy!" Sobbing, with shiny wet cheeks, she begged, "Please, Father! Juliette could easily make herself a doll! She easily could because she can sew so perfectly! You ask Mrs. Clerkwell if you don't believe me!"

Juliette trembled.

Thomas was worn down. He did coax Juliette with an apologetic smile as he prised her beloved Clarice from between her hands and he did have the grace to look concerned when she too shed tears, but once the deed was done it was final. Abby snatched the doll and ran away while Juliette stared numbly at the workbasket.

"What a brave girl you are," Thomas said.

With a gulp Juliette wound her thin arms around his neck and snuggled close for a few minutes with her eyes closed and the scents of sea salt and tobacco strong in her nose. For those few minutes it seemed to her that she had received the best of the bargain.

Living in the Mission was a vastly different existence for them. Though they had the company of the dozen or so Mission children, there was no more of the romping, loving atmosphere that the girls had grown up in. The Reverend and Mrs. Clerkwell did try but the only time the girls were really happy was when their father arrived for his weekly visit. On Sundays the four of them grouped in the pew that once was crammed full; it was a sight that plucked at the hearts of the congregation.

But life at the Mission was full of interest and if the girls were not actually happy they were not unhappy either. Because they were told repeatedly by Thomas that this was temporary, that one day they would all live together again, Juliette and Abby were able to look on their stay as a visit rather than a life sentence. The Peridots had been forced by geography to do most things for themselves but in this community work was shared and the burden lightened so that there was more time for daily prayer services and evening hymn singings. While Evangeline used to bake her bread each evening, here at the Mission was a baker with a cavernous oven. When shoes were to be replaced or mended there was a shoemaker to tend to them. And at Mrs. Clerkwell's suggestion Thomas took Samuel to the Mission tailor to be fitted for a new black suit. The girls had each been plunged into mourning and all their pretty clothes taken away and dyed a muddy, greyish hue. Abby took this very hard and wailed over the loss of her powder-blue poplin and her sprigged pink muslin.

Juliette tried to understand the depth of her sister's

longings but she honestly did not mind being in mourning because it showed respect to their mother. She did not even prickle in rage when the Mission boys called:

"Ape, ape,
Dressed in crape!"

after her. So she found it difficult to appreciate Abby's despair. Didn't her sister have Clarice, and wasn't Clarice the most beautiful thing in all the world? Surely Clarice was compensation enough for having to wear mourning?

But Abby's discontent grew.

One day when Juliette was putting her embroidery away in the workbasket she noticed a scrap of lace poking out from under a bundle of sock-darning wool. She pulled it out and stared at it in dismay. It was Mrs. Clerkwell's lace handkerchief which she had received from her mother in England only yesterday. Fortunately Mrs. Clerkwell was in the parlour giving a piano lesson to one of the older Mission girls so Juliette could take the opportunity to slip into her bedroom and drop in onto the floor beside the washstand, hoping that the incident would escape comment.

A fortnight later another handkerchief appeared in the workbasket. This time, after tucking it behind a parlour cushion, Juliette attempted to speak to Abby about the thefts. Her sister rounded on her with such hostile abuse that Juliette dropped the whole subject at once. Perhaps she was wrong. Perhaps it was one of the Maori girls who took the things. There were two of them, bright, quick, and swift to acquire the skills they were there to learn; but they resented Abby and Juliette, treated them as interlopers, and talked about them in Maori, obviously rudely, if the Clerkwells were not present. Juliette was in awe of them because they were so self-confident, and a little afraid of them because they were both tall, strong girls and quick to pinch or shove if she got in their way. They didn't seem devious (and she knew that Abby was) but she supposed that it was possible that they had secreted the stolen handkerchiefs in the sewing basket hoping that she might be blamed for the theft.

One winter afternoon the Clerkwells were out visiting young Mr. Harnod and his new bride. Juliette had just finished embroidering the last rosebud on a little bonnet for a Maori baby and was folding the silky ribbons neatly inside it when she heard a crash from the parlour—the unmistakable noise of china breaking.

The Maori girls had their day off and at first Juliette thought there might be an intruder. A dull fear weighted her body, but then came the sound of muffled weeping and she realised what must have happened.

Abby was sitting on one of the best brown plush chairs with her apron twisted in anguish in her lap. At her feet was a shattered heap of eggshell-fine, rose-coloured crockery. Among the jagged pieces was a clearly recognisable spout and a snapped-off handle with tiny rose leaves daintily painted on it.

"Oh, *Abby!*" cried Juliette. "The best teapot! How did that happen?"

In distress she sobbed, "I was pretending . . . pretending to have a tea party, and . . . and the pot slipped out of my hand!"

There were the teacups set out on the occasional table, each cup and saucer with a matching plate tucked underneath. A tea strainer rested on the brim of its own exquisitely decorated slop bowl. Creamer and sugar bowl stood ready and the tongs had been carefully placed on a little dish of their own. Juliette looked at the lovingly arranged tea set and her heart ached for her clumsy sister.

"What will Mrs. Clerkwell say?" whispered Abby, and the two girls stared at each other.

They had returned most of the crockery to the cupboard when the front door clicked to announce the Clerkwells' return. With frantic haste Juliette collected the brittle shards into her hands in an effort to get them out of sight, but when she looked up she realised that it was already too late. Mrs. Clerkwell blocked the doorway, grimly holding Abby by an upper arm. Abby looked sulky.

"Well," said Mrs. Clerkwell. "I turned from hanging up my cape only to see that mischief has been wrought in my absence. You girls both know that this room is not for children, unless they have been specifically invited."

"I just went in there now," said Abby quickly. "*I* didn't do it."

"Well, we shall see what you were doing then," and she stepped into the room. Juliette stood up miserably with the ruined teapot cradled in her hands. Mutely she held out the pieces, offering them to Mrs. Clerkwell, who flinched as if struck. Letting go of Abby's arm, she advanced purposefully towards Juliette and cuffed her soundly across the side of the head. Scraps of crockery dashed over tiny booted feet but her anger was such that she could not think clearly enough to stop and see if the teapot was worth mending and some of the pieces crushed under her heels as she cuffed Juliette again and again until the Reverend heard her and came in.

"My dear!" he exclaimed, shocked.

"Oh, look what she's done!" and in frustration she turned to her husband and beat her small fists helplessly against his chest. "Look at what she's done! My beautiful, beautiful teapot."

"I shall buy you another," he soothed.

"Where?" she snapped. "Where can one buy a teapot in this savage wilderness? Where can one buy anything at all worth having in a place like this?"

"Mrs. Clerkwell!" he reproached her. "I have never heard you speak like this before! We are here to do the Lord's work. I shall send away to England for another teapot exactly like this, and I am quite confident that Mr. Peridot will recompense us for it. He undertook to do so if the girls lost or damaged anything. It was part of the agreement, and I know he will honour it. So let us be having no more of the matter."

It was never mentioned again in front of the girls. Thomas arranged through contacts in Sydney to replace not only the teapot but also the hot water jug, which had been broken in the journey from England. The only comment he made was to tell Juliette gently that he was disappointed in her and had not thought she was the kind of child who would make free with other people's possessions. Juliette flushed at the bitter injustice but she realised that vindication would prove to be a hollow victory so she said nothing. Towards Abby, however, her feelings changed.

She had never felt a very warm love towards her sister but
now that cooled completely. Abby had let her take all the
blame as though she were a stranger and this frightened
Juliette. On whom could she depend if her own sister gave
her no loyalty? She felt herself to be so friendless that
when her nightmare recurred she lay morbidly staring at
the grey square of window, comfortless. And when Mrs.
Clerkwell looked hard at her with her pale, flat gaze, Juliette longed to tell her the truth. But still she said nothing.

In truth, Mrs. Clerkwell suspected that Juliette was not
entirely to blame for the mishap. She had a high opinion of
the child, finding her to be polite, industrious, and cheerful; and Mrs. Clerkwell prided herself on her clear-sighted
reading of young character. But most of all Mrs. Clerkwell
liked Juliette because the grave little girl took the trouble
to be interested in those around her. She seemed to know
when Mrs. Clerkwell was caught in another embroilment
with toothache and would ask after her health, offering to
find her some *kawakawa* leaves to chew to relieve the pain,
and once even imparting the unwelcome information that
sometimes Maori people committed suicide rather than
put up with the torture of inflamed teeth.

"It really isn't so bad, dear," she would say, though Juliette knew from her malodorous breath and the glimpse of
brown, pitted teeth that they were worse than any in Te
Pahi's pa.

Though she was the only one who suffered the pain, the
Reverend did the complaining. She disturbed him when
she arose in the middle of the night to sip at the laudanum,
she disturbed him in the evening when he was writing sermons or translating the scriptures into Maori for new
books of texts. How could he concentrate?

As it happened, one of their house guests provided the
answer. Scientists of one persuasion or another often
stayed with the Clerkwells, who had more room to spare
and were always glad of the company. During one of Mrs.
Clerkwell's most severe attacks they were giving hospitality to an ornithologist, a Mr. William Wren, whose name
(they knew a little about English birds from a picture
book), sharp nose, bright eyes, and thin, clawlike hands

gave the girls a lot of repressed amusement. Mr. Wren boasted that he had suffered from toothache many times and he assured Mrs. Clerkwell that the only thing to do was to visit a surgeon and have the infected tooth pulled.

"Please! I cannot go to our surgeon. He is clumsy and rough, and I could not bear to even contemplate the prospect of consulting him. No, let us leave the matter."

"Ah, but will it leave you?" asked Mr. Wren.

A week later when Mr. Wren's ship was sailing he persuaded both the Clerkwells to come out in the rowboat to look over the ship and to see him off. They returned in the dusk, singing with an unsteady exuberance. Inside the house they leaned against the passage wall and laughed.

"They've been *drinking!*" hissed Abby, putting Clarice down and going to look while Juliette set out mugs for their supper of tea and bread.

"It seems that we were lured onto the ship under false pretences," said the Reverend, taking up his steaming mug. "Mr. Wren took us out there so that the ship's surgeon could look at Mrs. Clerkwell's teeth."

"He pulled three," she reported happily. "Three teeth, and it doesn't hurt at all!"

"You were insensible," the Reverend reminded her.

"I most certainly was," she agreed. To the girls' astonishment she actually giggled.

Once a month Thomas and Samuel stayed on after the Sunday services to take dinner with the Clerkwells. Knowing that they had a room at one of the less disreputable of Kororareka's doss houses and probably ate the stalest of meals, Mrs. Clerkwell always put herself out to contrive as delicious a dinner as she could. She was a poor cook; her meat tended to be stringy and tasteless, her vegetables soggy and puddings sticky. But when the remnants of the Peridot family gathered together under her roof she made sure that there was always a soup or a morsel of fresh fish to begin the meal, a slab of cheese and a glass of porter to end it, and great heaping platefuls of food in between.

The first visits had been awkward. The Reverend had to restrain himself from offering words of comfort that might grate instead of soothe. He had never met anybody who had been as devastated as Thomas Peridot was and he felt unable to help. Mrs. Clerkwell prattled on, talking far more than usual to cover up the holes of silence, and Thomas thought as he ate that well-meaning people could be the most boring on earth. Especially well-meaning *Christian* people. Privately he thought the Clerkwells typical of the worst of the missionary type, those who interfered with the Maoris' lives, causing untold damage, all so that they might secure themselves a passage to the next world. He thought that until one evening over the mussel soup he said almost facetiously, "What brings an educated man like you out to a life of toil amongst ignorant and barbaric heathens? Do you not find it an insult to your intelligence?"

It was a throwaway question. He prepared to half listen, for he had heard the answer so often before, parsimonious nonsense about "enriching the soul," and "devotion to one's fellow man no matter what colour," et cetera.

To his real amazement the Reverend glanced at him mildly and laid down his soup spoon in order to give his full attention to the answer.

"Sir, I am neither intelligent nor particularly well educated." He spread an upturned hand modestly. "Of course, I do try to live up to the qualities expected from a missionary. We are told that we must be 'practical, patient, pious, and prudent.' " His eyes glinted with unaccustomed merriment. "Though not 'pompous' as many of the local wits would have it believed. But I find your question astonishing, you who have lived so long with the Maori people. Of course I do not find them ignorant or barbaric; whether they are 'heathen' could be the subject for a lengthy debate! No, sir, I do not find them an insult to my intelligence but a challenge."

"In what way?"

He propped knobbly forefingers under his chin to consider, then asked, "Has it ever occurred to you, Mr. Peridot, that the Maoris have a fascinating parallel in history?"

"Yes, indeed," said Thomas. "I have observed many of their customs and in almost every instance I have felt that there is something oddly familiar about them. Even the cannibalism has an eerily familiar echo. . . ."

The Reverend intoned, "He that eateth my flesh and drinketh my blood dwelleth in me and I in him."

Jesus said that, thought Juliette. She remembered suddenly her father trying to expound these strange ideas about the Maoris and Jesus to her mother, but Mother put her hands over her ears and said that she would not listen to blasphemy. She could see them all around the table, young Thomas, Regina pouting over the puha, Madeline fetching second helpings of stew, and Melina gurgling in the cradle, and a sickening wave of longing and nostalgia engulfed her. Why can't we go back? she wanted to cry. Why?

"The Maoris think that," her father was saying with an eagerness that seemed heartless to Juliette in her present homesick mood, "they really believe that if they eat part of their slain enemy all his finest qualities are absorbed into their own bodies. His strength, bravery, intelligence . . ."

"Just as Christ meant, I'm sure," agreed the Reverend. "Wouldn't He have meant that the taking of the Body and the Blood should lead to taking Him as an example for one's life?"

"You're absolutely right, though I hadn't thought of it quite that way," said Thomas. "But it is the little things that puzzle me. Why do the Maori mourners cut themselves so that blood streams from their arms and faces and breasts just as the ancient Hebrews did?"

"And all the harrowing crying and loud wailing," put in Mrs. Clerkwell as she removed her husband's untouched soup plate. "When I hear a Maori *tangi* I am always put in mind of the story of Lazarus." She set the roast before her husband.

"So you think that the Maoris somehow, at some time, have had knowledge of the Bible too?" asked Thomas excitedly.

"I think more than that," said the Reverend as he laid a thick slab of meat on the top plate and waited for his wife to remove the plate and dish the vegetables around it. "It is my firm opinion that the Maoris are the lost tribe of Israel."

Thomas frowned. "You would go so far as to say that?"

"I most certainly would!" His gaunt face had become illuminated in the glow of his enthusiasm. "Refresh your memory if you will with Deuteronomy, Chapter 20, where Moses is exhorting the soldiers to be brave and valiant when they go into battle. I read a translation of the very words to a group of our local chiefs and their astonishment was so great that for a whole minute not one of them was able to talk! And you, sir, must know what fervent orators they are! The words were almost identical to those the tohunga uses to exhort his warriors to show courage and daring. The very same! And read Leviticus, Chapter 24, where revenge is mooted, an eye for an eye and a tooth for a tooth! If that is not an identical concept of Maori utu, then what is?"

"Yes, the Maoris' preoccupation with utu is worthy of the Old Testament," said Thomas soberly. "And utu here is a sacred obligation of a strength to be envied by any organised religion. If the person who has the power to exact it fails to do so, then that person is haunted day and night until the revenge has been exacted. Dreams plague them incessantly until they are driven to perform the utu and so break the curse."

"A primitive concept but arguably a biblical one," nodded the Reverend.

Mrs. Clerkwell felt uncomfortable. This was tactless, considering that poor Juliette had been suffering in exactly the way her father described. The moment the laudanum was stopped, her nightmares returned. She seldom cried out, but next morning her dark-rimmed eyes told an eloquent enough story. Now the good lady intervened. "Would you care to postpone the remainder of this topic until after-dinner porter?"

Juliette's face burned with excitement as she stared at her plate. That's what is happening to me! she thought. I saw what happened the day Mother was killed. I don't remember it but these horrible dreams are a way of trying to force me to remember. Oh, if only it would come back to me, then the murderers might be caught and my bad dreams would stop. If only I could remember.

Nine

Though Victoria's coronation took place in June 1838, it was almost Christmas before the accounts of the ceremony finally reached the antipodes. Maire Yardley was seated at the dining table with copies of English and Australian newspapers spread over the crocheted cloth when Thomas called.

"Aye, but Evangeline would have lapped this up," he said as he scanned the descriptions in the London *Times*. "She loved talk of clothes and jewellery, what the duchesses and countesses wore. Mind, I had to read it to her because she never did seem to get the hang of reading. Made her dizzy, she said."

Maire was taken aback because he had mentioned his wife so casually. Then, impatient with herself for such a foolish reaction, she said, "Your wife was always very colourfully dressed herself, I believe."

"Very clever, she was," and he went on to describe some of the things Evangeline had made for the children. He spoke with a detached enthusiasm that Maire considered favourable. It was taking a long time but he was definitely beginning to get over it. She felt so encouraged that before he left she took four brightly wrapped packages from the mantel.

"These are for the children," she said in a brisk, cool tone that brooked no argument. "A trinket each for Christmas. And there's a token for yourself, besides."

Thomas flushed. "But . . . but I can't . . ."

"And good day to you, Mr. Peridot," she said firmly.

In the Clerkwell household it was Juliette's task to unwrap the bundles of English newspapers, iron them, and arrange them in exact chronological order in a cupboard in the parlour. It was difficult to press the badly crumpled ones without crimping in sharper creases and she had to work quickly because the newspaper scorched easily if the irons had been allowed to get too hot.

After dinner she unwrapped the bundles delivered from the *Lorendee* while Mrs. Clerkwell sat at the other end of the kitchen table, showing Abby yet again how to sew feather stitches.

"Do try to concentrate, Abigail! It is called feather stitch because it should be light and dainty as the feathers of a tiny bird. These stitches look more like hen's feet!"

Abby gurgled, and hastily swallowed her laughter when Mrs. Clerkwell fixed her with a sharp look.

"This is a serious matter, Abigail."

"Oh," cried Juliette, gasping.

"What is it, child?" Mrs. Clerkwell half rose but Juliette rushed to her chair and thrust a crumpled newspaper in front of her.

"This is all about the Queen's coronation! It is one of the most recent newspapers in the bundle! Please do read it to us!"

Mrs. Clerkwell's voice softened as she read.

"They spent two hundred thousand pounds on the festivities," she said. "Gracious me! I cannot even imagine such a sum. Even two hundred seems a fortune!"

"What did they spend it on?" asked Abby, sewing as slowly as possible.

"Decorations, processions, bands, balloons, and a two-day fair in Hyde Park. It says here that the grand procession alone cost twenty-six thousand pounds. Oh, what a sight it must have been. How I would adore to have been there!" She paused as her husband came into the room. "I hope that you do not mind, Reverend, but we have purloined one of your newspapers to read about the coronation."

"Ah, the news is here? Splendid. Do look them all through and remove the newspapers that have special news of our Queen. I shall read them first."

"Are you quite certain? You are so particular about having your news arranged in the order in which things happened. I thought . . ."

"Never mind, Mrs. Clerkwell," he said, sitting down near her. He unfolded a letter written on thick paper and said, "It appears that we are to have guests again soon. In two months' time, to be exact."

"Who is it to be? How exciting!"

"My nephew and niece, Garland and Asia Clerkwell."

She was silent for a time before saying without enthusiasm, "I remember them well. He has a lisp and she is yet unmarried."

"That is correct. Yes, Asia must be almost thirty now." He smiled and scratched the back of his neck up under the dull brown wig. "I rather fancy that she is being sent out here in the hopes that we might find her a husband."

Mrs. Clerkwell's face was impassive. "Mr. Harnod is safely married and I cannot think of anybody else who might be suitable."

The Reverend's gaze drifted from Abigail to Juliette and back again. "It would be fortuitous if we could help to arrange a match," he said.

In their every spare moment Juliette, Abigail, and Mrs. Clerkwell made baby clothing. It had fallen to Mrs. Clerkwell to continue a custom begun by the earliest missionaries in the days when infanticide was practised widely by the Maoris. Babies had often been smothered at birth for the slightest of reasons: if there were too many babies in the pa at that time, if one was not perfect, or even if it was a girl. Despite the horror expressed by the missionaries and all their efforts to stop the ghastly custom, it continued. Then Catherine Leigh, a missionary's wife, found that the Maori mothers adored European baby clothes. She told the mothers to be that if they brought the baby to her after it was twenty days old she would present it with an embroidered layette. After spreading that word as thickly as she could she returned home to sew and pray. It worked. By refusing to consider any baby until it was clearly past the newborn stage she ensured that a bond had time to develop between mother and child. So one barbaric custom gave way to a new, entrancing one.

In modern times the clothes were given as a christening gift, making them in effect a double incentive. Juliette loved making the dainty white bonnets and jackets, each embroidered with tiny rosebuds where the ribbon ties were anchored. Mrs. Clerkwell was near despair over Abigail's efforts—or lack of efforts, to describe them more honestly. The two girls simply could not be more different: Abigail so very like her father, blonde, round-cheeked, and sturdy, while Juliette was so thin and wraithlike despite the weekly dosing of castor oil she was forced to swallow. As she watched the two girls, Mrs. Clerkwell realised that it was imperative that their father marry someone with a loving heart. And before too long, too, she hoped. Surely he could see the need for urgency himself.

Because her mother was seldom mentioned Abby allowed the memory of her to diminish until Evangeline was as insubstantial as the faded rectangles on the wallpaper where pictures had once hung. Samuel was least affected by the deaths; he was used to being with his father, accustomed to the rough life of bush camps and whaling stations, and did not mind the stench and unappetising food of the doss houses. Juliette missed her mother fiercely, thinking about her in the daytime when she hung back watching the other Mission children play together, and crying for her in the empty hours of darkness after she had woken shaking from a nightmare of peaches and a hot sun.

But it was Thomas whose life had been upended by the tragedy. No sooner was the worst of his mourning over than the reality of his loss translated itself into daily terms and slapped itself down in front of him like an account to be settled. His bed was hard and lousy, clothes unmended and poorly laundered, and the diet appalling. Even after a year he could not control feelings of disgust as he fished a fly out of the sour gravy.

The cook snorted at his complaints and blew her nose on a bunch of her filthy gown.

"If yer don't like it 'ere yer kin go," was her standard reply to everything. He would have gone, too, except that all the other doss houses were worse. Hospitable families had offered lodgings for his stays in Kororareka but Thomas shied politely away. The proximity of married happiness would have been unendurable. This was no existence for young Samuel but he let him stay. The boy's company was part of his life, soothing as a familiar blanket.

As the year passed and his domestic discomforts increased, he began to think about the surgeon's advice more frequently. At first the idea was dismissed the instant it flicked into his mind but later he found himself looking at it, turning it over, and examining it. Evangeline could not be replaced but perhaps there could be another, different kind of marriage.

There were half a dozen unattached females at the Mission (three virgins and three widows), while two respectable spinsters also lived with their families on the outskirts of Kororareka. All had noticed him favourably, all were aware of what a considerate and devoted husband he had proved to be, and none had failed to calculate that Mr. Peridot must have a very tidy sum put by.

Maire Yardley soon realised that the community was catching Thomas up in an eddy to swirl him around the eligible young ladies until he was netted and landed. Nobody liked to see young women alone when there were fine men available; all felt that it was an honourable duty to bring two people together in marriage, for families enriched the community while spinsters and bachelors could cause problems. Maire decided that if she wanted him she had best begin. Accordingly she invited him to dinner regularly, once a fortnight. Each time he praised the rich desserts she acknowledged with the proper touch of modesty that they were her creations. Intricate needlepoint was left on a chair so that it could be picked up and commented on before Thomas could be seated.

Thomas was impressed; he could not help but be. He already thought her handsome, elegant, and businesslike, and now he was being made to realise that the span of her accomplishments was broader than he had thought. However, though his admiration increased, he came no closer to thinking of her as an attainable, desirable woman. She still made him feel awkward, uncouth, unwashed. He wondered about the fact that most women made no impact on him at all, yet the impression of Mrs. Yardley was as strong as acid. It was decidedly not what she might have hoped for but she noticed only that he was again back to blushing and believed that she was making progress.

Mrs. Clerkwell disapproved strongly of this friendship. When she learned that Thomas was making frequent calls to the Yardley home she knew instantly what was in the wind. It was well known that Mrs. Yardley had never experienced an unselfish feeling in her life, and if she felt the need to offer Thomas hospitality it would not be out of compassion but rather with the thought that she would benefit from her hospitality.

"I shudder to think of what may happen, Reverend," she confessed one night. "An Irish papist! It could not be worse."

He pointed out gently, "Ah, Mrs. Clerkwell, it could be much worse. Mrs. Yardley's husband was an Englishman, and she herself came from a fine Protestant family. Yes, it could be worse."

"But she's a convert, and they are so much more . . . rabid! Oh, what would happen to these poor girls if they suddenly found themselves under her care? Anybody would be better for him than Mrs. Yardley! And the girls need a kind, motherly woman to care for them. Mrs. Yardley would be most unsuitable. They say she's as cold as a headstone."

"Don't fret, Mrs. Clerkwell. Miss Asia Clerkwell will be here before too long and we must see what we can do."

"What?" Mrs. Clerkwell sat up in bed. "Do you mean to pair Mr. Peridot off with your unfortunate niece?"

"Why not? I'm sure that even you must admit that she would be better than a converted papist."

At that, Mrs. Clerkwell lapsed into a long, thoughtful silence.

Miss Asia Clerkwell arrived at the Mission several months later than expected, alone and wearing crape.

The Reverend was ferried out in a canoe to fetch her ashore and as a special treat Mrs. Clerkwell allowed the girls to accompany him. Dressed in black taffeta smocks with black bonnets, they squeezed together on a plank seat and counted the smooth bites the Maori boys' paddles made in the water. It was an exciting morning for them.

The Reverend's niece had been referred to so mysteriously that a romance clung about her name like moss. They imagined her to be like Mrs. Yardley: regal, distant, and cool.

She was none of those things. While the girls watched in astonishment, a plump woman with a large nose and jutting jaw bustled across the deck and flung herself into the Reverend's scrawny arms with a sudden, violent outpouring of grief, pushing him back against the rigging so abruptly that his wig was wrenched askew. Ignoring his protests, she straightened it for him while Captain Bjorn Svenson guffawed at the Reverend's embarrassment.

"It's a good thing that I did not greet you with more enthusiasm!" she boomed. "A suitor of mine was rowing out once and his wig tumbled right into the water among the swans. They took it to be a morsel of food and had worried it to shreds before they discovered their mistake. Poor Mr. Wentfort had to complete the journey with his kerchief tied about his head for fear he would catch sunstroke. I could not look at him without dissolving into merriment." She turned to the Captain. "You have been splendidly kind to me, sir. The journey from Sydney has seemed too short."

While Juliette gaped and the Reverend hemmed and hawed, Captain Svenson clasped her black-gloved hands in his and bowed over them. Miss Asia looked impatient until he straightened up, whereupon she leaned clumsily towards him and pressed a kiss into the bearded cheek.

"There!" she declared in satisfaction. "You have impressed me most favourably, Captain." With that she proceeded to heft herself over the railing where the rope ladder was tied. Both the Reverend and the bemused Captain sprang to her aid, though she clearly had no need of it.

Juliette was fascinated. As she listened to the stream of prattle knotted with small outbursts of sobs or laughter she thought that never had she met a lady more sure of herself and less self-effacing than Miss Clerkwell. It was going to be fun having her around. She was dismayed then as they crossed the lawn and were out of earshot of the Maori lads to hear the Reverend rebuke his niece.

"I must protest in the strongest terms about your behaviour," he said pompously.

"Why, Uncle, what do you mean?" Tears stood in her prominent blue eyes, a leftover from her last reference to "poor dear Garland."

"I refer to the way you took your leave from Captain Svenson. If you display such familiarity towards strange men here at the Mission you will find yourself an object of speculation with dismaying rapidity."

Miss Asia tossed back a head crowned with an extravagantly ruffled black bonnet. Her laughter flung up to the wide autumn skies.

"*Dear* Uncle, this life in the wilderness has not changed you one single *particle!* You always were a stuffy moralist and, alas, you still are. Have the savages taught you nothing at all of life?"

At that the Reverend's neck grew as dark red as a turkey's and he strode ahead of the others up the shell-strewn path and into the house.

She saved her story until dinner. Tears splashed onto her pickled pork and sweet potatoes as she recounted how on the voyage from London brother Garland had forged a friendship with a retired banker, a man of charm and educated tastes. The banker was only interested in travelling as far as Sydney, so it seemed natural that Garland and Asia should spend some time there as his guests before making the final stage of their journey.

"There, I was left entirely on my own," she told her fascinated audience. "I had no interest in accompanying Garland and his friend. Mr. Elsberg's tastes were for adventure of a rougher nature than appeals to me." This was said with a wink directed at her shocked uncle. "I was free to amuse myself while they spent a month-long journey up the coast, or down the coast, to hunt crocodiles. Garland returned with five large hides which he tried to present to me—unsuccessfully, I might add. He was greatly altered by his adventure, brown as a native and almost as free with his speech. Mr. Elsberg thought it a splendid joke and was quite ridiculously proud of having made a man of him but I felt bereft. Since poor dear Mama died Garland has been totally dependent on me. His defection was most upsetting. I seriously considered leaving

Sydney and, by taking passage here, hoped to force Garland to think sensibly about this friendship and to come with me. Alas, I could not find the courage, and so off they went again, this time to trek through the desert."

"What happened to him, child?"

"Oh, Aunt, it was terrible. Poor Garland! On the edge of the desert he trod on a poisonous snake and was killed."

"Oh, my dear! And you had nobody to turn to?"

"Only Mr. Elsberg, and he seemed more distressed than I. He positively haunted the undertaker's parlour. Such devotion is rare indeed!"

"Very rare," agreed her uncle in a tone that caused Mrs. Clerkwell to glance sharply at him.

"But God's will be done," Miss Asia sighed. "I am here safely after a pleasant voyage. Captain Svenson was so kind. He is a cultured gentleman, quite superior in manners to most of the passengers. I have asked him to come calling on me when next the *Norse* is in port."

Dismayed, Mrs. Clerkwell blurted out, "I really do not think that a sea captain is quite suitable as a companion for you, dear. Besides, your uncle and I have someone in mind for you to meet."

"A dreary widower, no doubt, with a log cabin and a tribe of half-wild children! No, thank you, Aunt! You may enjoy the rigours of primitive colonial life but I view it with nothing but horror."

"Oh dear," fretted Mrs. Clerkwell later. "I do hope that Miss Asia is not going to live up to her reputation for being difficult!"

Her fears were speedily realised. Though she got on famously with the girls and—surprisingly—with Thomas, who enjoyed her company and roared appreciatively over jokes that no lady would dream of recounting in mixed company, thought Mrs. Clerkwell, horrified—it was soon obvious that the Mission was no place for anybody who was not willing to shoulder a fair portion of the communal burden. Miss Asia had no idea that anything but the pleasure of her society was expected in return for the hospitality extended to her. Though she spent the major part of every day resting with her slippered feet up on the parlour settle, she arrived promptly at the table for each meal and

managed to find the time to go visiting around the Mission
most afternoons. With what remained of her time she sat
at the mirror dressing her hair. It was long, thick, and reddish and she was extremely proud of it. Juliette watched
her sometimes as she rolled it into two long fat sausages,
one at the back in a curve around her nape and the other
right across her forehead.

"Hair is a lady's crowning glory," she proclaimed authoritatively as she clucked over Juliette's thin curls and
urged her to rub olive oil into her scalp to thicken them.
Abby's blonde waves were also criticised for being "without liveliness," a condition for which Miss Asia prescribed
eau de cologne sprinkled on a scrap of silk that was tied
around a hairbrush.

One afternoon she paused on the verandah to examine
the girls' handiwork. Miss Asia leaned her large nose over
towards Abby's work, then Juliette's, and said, "Why
should young girls make baby clothes? You should be sewing trinkets for yourselves or for your dolls."

"This is the only doll we have," Abby told her pertly.
"She used to belong to Julie but now she's mine."

Juliette frowned. Reminders of the loss of Clarice still
hurt like a dash of hot water on a burn.

"I have Mother's sewing basket instead," she explained.

"But no doll?" said Miss Asia in her loud, droning voice.
"Every little girl should have a doll of her own. I have just
had a splendid idea. I will make you a doll with my very
own hands. Would you like that?"

Juliette's eyes shone. "Oh, yes," she breathed. "Yes,
please, Miss Asia."

She heaved her bulky figure up out of the chair and
dusted down her skirts. "Then it is as good as done!" she
declared. "When I have finished writing my letters home I
shall begin directly on the most beautiful doll you have
ever seen!"

But Miss Asia's letters must have been extremely time-
consuming to compose, for the weather turned from cloudy
to showery and then to rainy as winter settled in and no
sign of a doll's creation materialised. Juliette longed to remind her of her promise but said nothing.

Mrs. Clerkwell was not so tolerant of her niece's laziness. After two months of growing irritation she marched into the parlour where Miss Asia was resting and informed her that her period of mourning was at an end and from now on she could earn her keep.

"Of course, Aunt," agreed the lady at once. "Anything you say. You must know that I came here with the attitude that I am only too anxious to help, and that anything you ask of me I shall be only too happy to do."

Taken aback, Mrs. Clerkwell said hesitantly, "Mrs. Williams needs some assistance with the sick. Every morning there are queues of ill Maoris waiting to have medicine dispensed to them. She will be so grateful for your help."

"I would love to do that, Aunt," Miss Asia assured her. "However, my physician in England told me that because of my own delicate health I must not ever have the slightest contact with sick people. If it was not for that strict directive, then I would be eager to start at once."

Mrs. Clerkwell stared at her will ill-concealed disbelief. "Then you may care to assist me by taking over my classes of girls," she said briskly. "If you do that I shall be free to cope with other chores."

"Oh, please tell me what the other chores are, and I shall do those," begged Miss Asia. "I fear I would be hopeless as a schoolmistress, for my own reading and writing are pitifully inadequate."

"That niece of yours is . . . is insufferable!" sputtered Mrs. Clerkwell when she was alone with her husband that night. She held his shirt by the shoulders as he pulled his arms out of the sleeves, then unbuttoned both collar and cuffs for laundering. "She will not do anything to help though she swears that she longs to be of service to the community. No matter what is proposed she wriggles out of it with a marvellous excuse."

"Do elaborate, Mrs. Clerkwell," he said dryly, not wanting to listen to her complaints but knowing from experience that there was no way out but to listen through to the end.

"I suggested that she visit the pa and help the Maori women learn their prayers and hymns by heart, but she informs me that her delicate sensibilities would be injured by proximity to cannibals and nothing I say can persuade her that she has nothing to be afraid of. She declines to help the Mission ladies with their babies, for she has no experience. She shrinks from my suggestion that she spend some time learning Maori so that she might take up a little of the heavy task of translating the Scriptures. Languages are her *bête noire*, she says, and she has no ear for them. And as for humble housework! Well, Reverend, there I must say I admire her inventiveness. She has escaped very neatly by assuring me that the heat of cooking brings on fainting spells and dust provokes sneezing fits so she cannot sweep or tidy."

"Is there nothing at all to be found to occupy her?"

"Oh, she assures me constantly that she is eager to work."

"Has she suggested anything, Mrs. Clerkwell?"

"Yes," she said grimly. "She fancies that she might have the task of arranging the flowers in the church. I can imagine what Mrs. Williams would say to that and I shall not even waste my breath suggesting the idea. But, Reverend, arranging flowers is not work and it is work that she must do for our community and for her own soul!"

"I agree, and I shall talk to her," he promised. With his cream flannel nightgown flapping about his bony ankles he climbed into bed and opened up his Bible.

Next afternoon Miss Asia left the interview with her uncle and sat moodily on the verandah where the girls quietly sewed baby clothes. She picked up Clarice and idly plucked at her silk skirts while Juliette held her breath, hoping for some word about her promised doll.

"What would he know?" she asked them suddenly. "My uncle knows nothing of the glories of civilised life. Do you realise that every year poor Garland and I used to summer in Viareggio and travel to Baden Baden for the season? Our names have been mentioned in the social columns of the *Figaro* so many times that it became a bore in the end."

The girls looked at her uncomprehendingly.

She raised her head with a sniff and turned to look out at

the bay. "I cannot imagine why I ever wanted to come to New Zealand," she announced. "Only people who are insensitive, coarse, and with no appreciation of beauty should ever think of coming here to live in such primitive conditions."

Her nose was very pink and it quivered slightly as she talked. Juliette wondered if she had been crying, and wanted to comfort her.

She heard herself say, "I do wish that you could marry Father and be our mother," and was utterly mortified when Miss Asia clapped her hands onto her knees and roared with laughter.

"What, me? Become a settler's wife and live here permanently?" Then she glimpsed Juliette's stricken face and added hastily, "Your father has more sense than to ask me, more's the pity."

Juliette bent her head over her stitches; her cheeks were scarlet.

It was not long after that day that Miss Asia quietly disappeared. She had gone to Kororareka with two of the Mission women for the purpose of buying some yard goods to make smocks for the Maori schoolgirls. When they arrived at Oliver Jarrod's store they found him entertaining Captain Svenson from the *Norse*, which was ready to sail that afternoon. The Mission ladies turned their attention to the bolts of cloth at one end of the counter while Captain Svenson completed his business. Shortly after he had gone they noticed Miss Asia had gone too, but they thought nothing of it, assuming that she had stepped outside for a few moments. As she had not returned when their purchases were ready they sent a young Maori assistant out to look for her. Within a minute he had come back, urging them to follow him and see for themselves. There in a tiny rowboat was Miss Asia, her face hidden by the bonnet rim that was turned towards the looming side of the *Norse*. Very faintly they could hear Captain Svenson laughing as he dragged at the oars.

Mrs. Clerkwell said nothing. Silently she packed all of her niece's things away in her trunk.

Juliette cried. She had loved Miss Asia and that love had been squandered. It was weeks before the hurt faded, though the promise of the doll had already been forgotten.

Ten

In 1839 there was no such thing as "law" in New Zealand. In Kororareka anything still went despite the efforts of the Vigilants to keep the worst troublemakers out. In contrast, the Mission was too sternly self-governed, with a hundred and more petty rules at which even the most pious of its residents chafed. But a "law" for everybody simply did not exist.

The main trouble was that Britain could not decide whether it wanted to be bothered with a few scraps of far-flung territory, which promised to be a far more expensive worry than they were worth, and took the attitude that anybody who came to settle must do so at his own risk. When the New Zealand Land Company was formed in England in 1839 with the sole aim of organised settlement, the government was angry and tried to hinder it.

It took the interest of the French to make them change their minds. Though the establishment of Bishop Pompallier and his nuns in the Bay of Islands, and the arrival of the self-styled "King" Baron de Thierry, who settled with his retinue of some ninety officials on three hundred acres of land nearby, were generally ignored by the local population, the British Government sat up and took a great deal of notice. They decided that the balance had finally accumulated enough to tip the scales in favour of official colonisation. Britain arranged to send Captain William Hobson, R.N., to put a proposition to the native chiefs. In return for protection from exploitation by the influx of visitors they must cede all sovereignty of their lands to the Queen. It was impossible to offer protection unless they were willing to acknowledge the Queen as their ruler. This seemed to be the simplest answer to the complex array of problems.

At the Mission everybody was delighted but in Kororareka the mood was turbulent as rumors fought each other for credibility. The fact that the missionaries supported the proposed treaty was reason enough for suspicion. True, the treaty would ensure protection in the event of Maori uprisings and would guarantee that New Zealand would never become, like the neighbouring New South Wales, a dumping ground for convicts, but there would be a price in the form of taxes and enforced law and order.

"Some people would like to have the world running for their exclusive benefit," said Maire as she poured Darjeeling tea into a gold-rimmed cup.

Thomas smiled. "There's not one of us alive who wouldn't do that if he could!"

She regarded him speculatively as she handed a plate of cookies. "I doubt that you would. I perceive you to be a man of honour, who would set the needs of others above his own and who would stand by his word no matter what the strain."

He selected a ginger raisin cookie. "You judge me too highly, I think."

"Not at all. In many ways you remind me of my late husband. Such a fine man he was, too. We miss him very deeply, especially Leigh, I'm afraid. I do so worry about him, Thomas. He needs a man's influence, a gentleman's influence. He has taken to wandering abroad in the town when I am busy with business concerns and he has acquired a motley gaggle of acquaintances, all unsuitable companions for a boy his age. He needs someone like you to show him a good example."

Despite Samuel's protests, the next time Thomas visited the Mission Leigh accompanied them, and he did so on the frequent subsequent trips too until Samuel finally stopped complaining. It was not Leigh's fault that he was such a curious mixture of arrogance and timidity, of sophistication and naïveté, of kindness and callousness. Samuel pitied him. Leigh had no father and everybody knew that to a boy a father was more important than a mother: a father taught his son all the really important things in life.

When they arrived at the Mission the first time Juliette was on the path with a basket, picking dead flower heads from the plants in the border gardens. Suddenly Abby dashed past her, calling out and waving a polishing rag. Juliette stared, saw the dinghy approaching, dropped the basket, and followed.

Abby had reached the shore as her father was dragging the boat above the high-water mark. She wriggled between his arms and fastened her hands behind his neck. Laughing, he held her with one arm while with his spare hand he tossed out the anchor. The boys were already racing towards the stone steps.

Juliette hung back uncertainly, recognising Leigh with an uncomfortable prickle of anxiety. He had grown taller and broader in the two years since she had last seen him but his face retained the soft, unprotected look she remembered so clearly. Her eyes grew enormous as she regarded him, shyly standing her ground and hoping desperately that he would not tease her as he had on their last disastrous meeting.

He paused in front of her, panting. Juliette stared at his feet, quaking.

"Hello there!" he said pleasantly. "I'm Leigh Yardley."

Her eyes rose to meet his. He was smiling at her, actually smiling.

"Pleased to meet you," she whispered.

"Come on, Leigh!" called Samuel impatiently.

"Goodbye, then!" he shouted as he dashed after Samuel.

"Goodbye," whispered Juliette. She was still standing there, staring after the boys, when Thomas and Abby walked up across the lawn.

Everybody at the Mission set to with vigour to prepare for the treaty ceremonies. There was an element of righteousness in their enthusiasm that rankled with outsiders. Annexation to Britain would reinforce the missionaries' authority and many thought their influence with the natives too strong already.

In mid-January school was dismissed until the festivities were over but this did not mean a holiday, for every pair of hands was needed to help with the complicated preparations. Juliette sorted vegetables, trimming beans of leaves and stalks, washing and then lightly salting them in layers in wooden kegs. More beans and other vegetables had to be planted for the winter food larder, so the boys were kept busy in the freshly ploughed fields out on the hill slopes. Watermelons were rolled into the shade where they would ripen slowly and be cool and crisp when cracked open. All the early fruit was packed into straw-cushioned trays and the cool shed behind the church smelled tantalisingly of peaches, apples, and small sweet cherries. For weeks now the fish nets had been dragged through the river mouth at every tide and growing lines of smoked fish hung like drying tobacco leaves above the flour barrels in the bakehouse.

The ladies of the district had each been issued a sack of flour, a scoop of soda, and a basket of lemons together with a cone of sugar. These ingredients were to be processed into Madeira cakes with the addition of the plentiful eggs from the Mission flocks. When Mrs. Clerkwell's allocation had been delivered she recruited both girls to help her with the grating. The baker lent three iron graters; a coarse grater produced brewer's crystals for mixing in the dough batter, the medium grater made caster sugar and was also used to grate the lemon rind for flavouring, while the finest grater produced soft cloud drifts of icing sugar. Abby began the job of grating sugar; Juliette squeezed and grated lemons, while Mrs. Clerkwell stirred the cake batter and beat eggs to a pale fluff.

The results were poor. Either the cakes had split raggedly on top or else they sagged in the centre, but they smelled delicious. Juliette made a large bowl of icing sugar and whipped it with lemon juice for frosting.

As the great day approached the Mission began to fill. Flotillas of canoes glided like silent sea birds across the harbour and striped the sand under the sea wall with rows of smooth, long hulls. It was rumoured that over a hundred chiefs were coming, each with scores of relatives, supporters, and warriors who were trained, armed, and ready in case treachery should slip in amongst the overt good feelings. The chiefs were as easy to recognise as roosters in a flock of hens, so splendid was their attire. Many wore full

European dress topped by gorgeous *kiwi*-feather or dog-skin cloaks, rare white-tipped *huia* feathers in their hair, and all carried the finest meres that their tribes owned.

Though the Mission soon filled, more people kept arriving. The grass on the village green was packed with bodies. Food in kits lay everywhere and Mrs. Clerkwell declared that there could not possibly be a single fly left in Kororareka, there was such a grand time for them on this side of the bay. Some food came live and squealing on trotters, some squawking and shedding feathers or peering through gaps in flax baskets. Eel traps were set in nearby creeks and men returned festooned with slimy black bodies as thick as Juliette's neck. The Clerkwells' back door was kept locked from the inside for fear that everything they owned would be pillaged by Maori children. No washing could be done now, as laundry hanging out to dry would be an irresistible temptation to the visitors. Juliette had forgotten how much the Maoris smoked. Even toddlers seemed to have pipes stuck jauntily in their mouths and old, head-scarved women squatted gossiping in the sun without bothering to remove the pipe stems held between their teeth. Juliette and Abby were badgered by children no bigger than themselves. "You get me tobacco, eh?" was the constant demand in tones of various shades from friendly to menacing.

That night Juliette woke in terror. The room was stiflingly hot with the shutters closed. Her heartbeat drummed in her ears, loud as sinister footfalls. She pressed her thin face into the mattress cover and wept hopelessly.

The gathering crowds had brought the tragedy home for Thomas, too. He had never ceased patiently questioning people who might know something about the killers. He hoped one day to seize on some fact, some insignificant remark or an incident that did not fit in with everything else he knew. So far he had built up a comprehensive picture of what everybody in the district was doing at the time but learned nothing that might be of any value to him. From habit he still questioned people but now he could see pity in their eyes.

"Thomas, old friend," said Jacky Norris frankly, "do leave it be. It's a terrible thing, there ain't no denyin' that, but thems what done it got clean away, an' sour though the thought might be there ain't no fixin' ter change it. No matter what yer do."

"He be right," agreed Lars Jacobson, who was also in at the Mission helping to set up the huge ship's spars that would provide the backbone for the sailing-canvas marquee being erected. They were lunching under the pohutukawa trees.

"I know I'm attempting the impossible and I feel in my soul that I will never know what happened . . . but if you knew what an empty feeling that is, you would understand."

"I know too well," said Jacky. "You remember when one of our nippers jest up an' vanished? That were terrible, not knowin' what befell 'im. Were 'e drowned, or taken by Maoris, or wandered off in the bush an' lost? We never knew, an' by the 'ell it's a sick feelin' all right."

"Yer need another wife," observed Lars, wiping his mouth with the back of his hand. "Arrh, but that ale's too sweet. No quenching in it. Aye, Thomas, it's another wife you need. Yer time of respect's up and done." He winked slyly. "I hear the widder Yardley could do with cheerin' up, too. Might be summat there worth the askin' for."

"Mrs. Yardley?" He laughed, flattered that he should be paired off with her even by these two but seeing the impossibility of it. "Mrs. Yardley wants class, not a rough layabout like me! Come on, let's be getting the last post up if we want old Busby to put his hand into his pocket for us. I wonder how he likes the way he's been given the shove? He did all the work to organise this treaty, and to thank him the British Government boots him out. I think that the Queen is taking us on reluctantly, that's what I think."

"Yer could be right," said Lars gloomily. "Don't see why we needed this nonsense meself. We was gettin' on pretty fine, wasn't we, Jacky?"

"Aye," said Jacky. "That we was."

Most people in the Mission felt sorry for Mr. Busby yet excited about the new governor, Captain Hobson, who seemed to be a very important man indeed. Thomas rowed

Juliette and Abby around the H.M.S. *Herald* when it lay at anchor in the bay. The sides of the ship were riddled with gun ports and cannon poked through gaps in the deck railings. Juliette decided that what made a man powerful was all the soldiers and guns he had to back up his orders, and when she expressed this opinion to her father he said that he couldn't have put it better himself, which made her glow with pride. Sailors in blue and white uniforms leaned over the side and when they saw two little girls in the rowboat, demure in black dresses and bonnets but with white mittens and white stockings (Christmas gifts from Mrs. Yardley), one of the sailors tossed a folded paper into the boat. It contained three twists of barley sugar, one each for them and one for Samuel. Juliette ate hers very slowly in snapped-off bites, holding each piece in her mouth until it had slowly melted away.

Thomas exchanged chat with the sailors, who bemoaned having to have a Christmas summer, while Samuel was sufficiently emboldened by the gift of candy to call out cheekily, "Where's the Guv'nor?" to which they replied with a grin and the shake of their heads.

Nobody saw the Governor until treaty morning. Though he had been besieged by invitations, all had been refused. He was not a well man, Mr. Harnod gravely informed the Clerkwells when he brought a welcome petition for them to sign.

"Ill, my eye!" snorted the Reverend with uncharacteristic sarcasm. "He's merely ill at the prospect of his distasteful position. I'll warrant that poor Mr. Busby will be glad to be out of it. Scant support Britain has given him, I must say."

"He's writing the treaty, did you know that?"

"There! That proves what I've been saying! Did you hear that, Mrs. Clerkwell? The Governor is reluctant to come ashore, reluctant to meet the chiefs, and now reluctant to draft the treaty. His heart's not in this appointment at all!"

Mrs. Clerkwell said in a low voice, "We heard that he had actually invited the Roman Catholic Bishop to tomorrow's service, but of course we couldn't believe *that!*"

"I'm afraid it is true, Mrs. Clerkwell. He has invited all the clergy."

"Well!" she exclaimed after he had gone with their grudgingly given signatures. "All our work, all our hopes! And as if there were not enough troubles to torment us, I fear that another toothache is developing."

"We shall see," said the Reverend, staring out of the window at the huge marquee along the bay. "We shall see what happens tomorrow."

What did happen dismayed her so that her jaw throbbed with hot pulses of pain. At a little after eight when Mrs. Clerkwell was fussing with Abby's bonnet, there was a thumping at the front door and Thomas' voice calling out to see if they were ready.

"Please, Reverend, do let them in," she said irritably, resolving to take a little tonic wine herself before she left the house, just to see her through the day. Her tooth hurt so badly that every time she opened her mouth the slight draught of air sang shrilly along her nerves. The Reverend disappeared and did not come back, as expected, with Thomas.

"There, girls." She patted their shoulders and as soon as their boots clattered in the corridor she dosed herself with the wine, downing it with a shudder. Taking up her basket of embroidery in case she found a comfortable place to sit, talk, and work, she followed the others, wondering why the Reverend had not been his usual hospitable self and asked Thomas in for a cup of coffee before they all set out. As she stepped into the wedge of glaring sunshine at the door she discovered the reason. Thomas was not alone. For some unfathomable reason he had seen fit to bring Mrs. Yardley and her younger children with him.

The Reverend stammered, "Mr. Peridot has brought a guest with him, dear."

"I met Mrs. Yardley once at Oliver Harrod's emporium," said Mrs. Clerkwell coldly.

Mrs. Yardley's lips twitched slightly but she nodded her black bonnet gravely in Mrs. Clerkwell's direction and then went through the ritual of presenting each of her daughters formally as if at a ball. In turn the girls curtseyed, one gloved hand holding the side of the silk gown, the other clasping the stem of a lace parasol.

"What enchanting young ladies," said the Reverend. Like a bouquet drifting on a lazy stream, they moved together across the lawn.

Mrs. Yardley talked continuously, unaware that the lilting sound of her voice grated on Mrs. Clerkwell's senses. If only we could think of some excuse to divert our steps, she thought, glaring at her husband, who plainly did not mind being seen in such company. To arrive at the ceremony with papists! It was going to cause a scandal.

"I would have expected you to come with the Bishop," she said suddenly.

"Dear me, no! Bishop Pompallier is our spiritual guide but he is not a personal friend. I was planning to be escorted by my son Stephen, but the *Lorendee* must have been delayed. It was so generous of Mr. Peridot to escort us here so that we could show our support."

"How very public-spirited of you," intoned the Reverend. "Have you seen the Governor yet, Mr. Peridot?"

"He came ashore an hour ago," Thomas told them. "We went directly to the Residency, thinking that you would surely be there, and lingered there long enough to see the Governor rowed ashore."

"Oh, but he looked so grand!" said Jane.

"Our Governor is a master of the dramatic first impression," agreed Thomas. "He stood amidships in the stern of the longboat, dressed in braided uniform with a cockaded hat, and his bearing was everything the Queen could wish from her representative."

"I was greatly admiring the portrait of the Queen which you have so patriotically displayed on your verandah," said Mrs. Yardley as they turned into the path that led through an archway of flowering wattle trees to the Residency itself. "My, how pretty it is here! I have never visited this side of the bay before, though Leigh has told me a little about it."

"It is pretty, especially on such a glorious day," agreed the Reverend in a tone so agreeable that Mrs. Clerkwell almost gagged. *He* who spent hours at a time fulminating against the Bishop and against papists generally, ranting

on about the harm they were doing to the Mission's cause
by setting up in opposition and confusing the natives . . .

When they reached the Residency where the gardens
were misty blue with forget-me-nots, Mrs. Clerkwell's
faith in the justice of life was vindicated. There on the verandah stood Mr. Harnod, shepherding guests in to speak
privately with the Governor. When he saw the Clerkwells'
companions his eyebrows knitted but he beckoned to them.
In her haste to be rid of the Yardley entourage, Mrs. Clerkwell jerked at her husband's arm and steered him towards
the steps. Her back stiffened as she stepped through the
door, leaving her unwanted companions behind.

Mrs. Yardley fluttered a black fan at her chin in a feminine gesture that accented the severe styling of the black
gown. Jet trimming glistened like wet coal at the wrists
and high collar.

"We have places reserved in the marquee," Thomas
said. "Let's have a look around first. I shall show you those
magnificent war canoes near the river mouth."

Juliette stared around with interest. There was so much
to be absorbed, so many fascinating things to stare at, from
the rows of sailors "on guard" everywhere to the lofty
white canvas clouds that swelled gently as the breeze filled
the tent. Garlands of flowers drooped in the heat, though
the marquee had been left open to the view of the bay and
distant Kororareka, wavering in the summer haze.

They met the Jacobsons as they strolled out onto the
strip of lawn between tent and sea wall. Here the ground
was covered with fallen pohutukawa-blossom needles
which clotted in the grass like blood. Clusters of people
spread mats and settled in the shade. Mrs. Jacobson
bulged under a thin print dress and her hair straggled
from under a battered-looking bonnet. Emily glared at Juliette. Since the day of their bitter quarrel they had never
resumed their friendship.

At the tide edge Samuel and Leigh tossed pebbles into
strings of splashes while Tippy barked and made brave
little dashes into the shallow water.

"Come on, boys!" called Thomas.

The boys scrambled up the bank, panting. Leigh wiped
his hands on his trousers and grinned at Abby. He reached

out to tug at her ringlets but she jerked her head back in time. Juliette was no longer nervous of Leigh—in fact, she decided that she liked him and wanted to have him notice her. But it was Abby he gave his arm to in a parody of gentlemanliness. She laughingly took it and they led the way around the end of the marquee to where they had started.

"Here he is!" said Thomas. "Look, Abby. Look, Julie, this man is our new Governor."

Juliette held her breath. The icing of white feathers on the imperial hat shone as he stepped into the sunlight. A small rattle of applause rolled ahead of him, bursting into a roar as he walked towards the marquee. Juliette was close enough to reach out a timid finger to touch one of the splendid, ornate, gold-encrusted epaulettes.

"Juliette!"

But Captain Hobson turned and smiled at the thin girl with the huge, liquid eyes, who jumped and thrust her hands abruptly behind her back.

The local missionaries were arranging themselves in order on the dais beside the Governor, Mr. Busby, and the Captain of the *Herald*. All the missionaries were dressed plainly in black as befitted the men of God. Bishop Pompallier had other ideas about correct dress, ideas that drew a gasp from the crowd as he strode behind the others in a purple and gold gown, Bishop's hat and flashing jewels on his fingers and a heavy crucifix around his neck. With imperious confidence he mounted the dais and seated himself in the chair next to the Governor.

The northern Mission party hissed on a collective intake of breath. "The utter, colossal cheek of it!" said one of the wives. "Did you see the way he pushed the Reverend out of the way?"

"The Governor doesn't seem surprised. What they are saying must be true."

"This is really too bad. First we have to endure the wishy-washy Mr. Busby for the best part of a decade and now they send us somebody whom we can't even trust to support the Missions. What will the chiefs think?"

Juliette learned two things from the portion of the ceremony that followed. Speeches, especially speeches that are read aloud, can be stupefyingly boring; and from the translations that followed each bracket of sentences she found that she understood a great deal more of the Maori language than she had suspected. It was so easy to follow as the Reverend Henry Williams spoke it.

The hours droned by. Governor Hobson spoke so softly that it was inevitable that the words would drift over the children's heads unheard. After each translation there was earnest discussion among the chiefs, and the Governor had to wait until that faded before he could proceed. When the Queen's message and the treaty had been read, the chiefs argued it in turn, striding up and down before the dais, urging the other chiefs to listen to them. This was more interesting to watch, for some of the chiefs were talented actors and used exaggerated movements of arms and head to emphasise their arguments. At first the chiefs seemed to speak against the treaty, saying that they wanted the pakeha to pack up and leave New Zealand, while others tried to persuade fellow chiefs that to put one's mark on the treaty paper was tantamount to agreeing to become one of Queen "Wiktoria's" slaves. With stretched but still intact patience the Reverend Williams explained yet again what the treaty meant. The day inched on.

Out behind the Residency, on a piece of level waste ground, shelters had been set up and pits dug for earth ovens to roast dozens of pigs, scores of baskets of kumaras, fish, and eels, and over two hundred chickens. Young men dug out the mats that covered the packed food and gushes of fragrant steam escaped. Delicious aromas drifted from the shelters where baskets of meat and vegetables were being served to queues of hungry people. Over fires children tended trays of roasting shellfish, pipis, and mussels, deftly removing them as the shells popped open. Juliette and Abby wanted to buy a flax dish from one of the young hawkers so that they could join the queue of diners but Mrs. Yardley explained that a meal awaited all of them back at her house.

Stephen was waiting on the verandah. "I was intending to come and observe some of the festivities," he said, raising a glass to them in a toast. "However, by the time we had the holds secured and instructions given to the crew there were clear signs that the party was breaking up. How has it been, Mr. Peridot? Did the matter resolve itself?"

"It was interesting," said Jane.

"It was boring," contradicted Leigh.

"Run out to the kitchen and ask Mary to pour you each a drink of lemonade," instructed Maire as she busied herself with glasses and water jug at the tray stand. "Whisky and water, Mr. Peridot?"

"Thank you. No, Stephen, the matter has not quite resolved itself. We shall have to wait and see what the chiefs decide, but there is far more opposition than I expected. A great deal more."

"I'm not surprised. Did you know that Tarrance Ballin's ship took a whole cargo of tobacco up to the northern tribes a month ago? A small token of esteem it was, from the Kororareka 'businessmen.' And I heard tell that a similar gift found its way south too."

Maire said, "It is perfectly understandable that the local businessmen wish to keep the status quo, for after all they have more to lose out of this than anybody."

"And I think that we should try to give the Maoris credit for having enough intelligence to see through crass bribery. Though they are often as not referred to as 'savages' they are certainly not stupid."

"Ah, but it is greed that the businessmen are pandering to, and there is plenty of that in any community."

"True," said Thomas with a smile. Every time he saw this lively, intelligent young man he liked him more.

"What I do not understand," continued Stephen, "is why dear Britain is going to such an enormous amount of trouble. As someone of Irish descent, I can vouch for the fact that Britain usually colonises by the simple process of going in with soldiers and shooting anyone who has the temerity to object."

Maire said dryly, "You are an incorrigible cynic, Stephen, and it is sad in one so young. Don't you think that the new Queen might have something to do with this more democratic way of acquiring a colony?"

Stephen laughed. "And you are an incorrigible royalist.

But I don't mind how it's done, only that it is. The minute that treaty is ratified we'll begin organising our own ship-loads of settlers. This business will do great things for the Richmond Line, taxes or no taxes." He nodded to them both. "If you'll excuse me, there are some matters that cannot wait until morning."

"What a fine boy he is," said Thomas. "He is a credit to you." Glancing at her, he noticed with compassion that she looked drawn and tired by the unaccustomed day in the fresh air. To cheer her he said kindly, "What a picture you looked today with your daughters. People were admiring you, did you realise that?"

She was feeling weary and knew perfectly well that at the moment she showed every one of her fifty years, but Thomas had paid her a personal, unsolicited compliment. This would have to be the time to ask him.

Her voice was serene with only a trace of huskiness to reveal her nervousness as she boldly put her case to him.

Thomas and Maire walked slowly with the crowd to the jetty when the ceremonies were over. Together they waited for the Governor to walk over the carefully spread matting to his longboat to be rowed back over the water to the *Herald*. Two chiefs who had helped sway the others to sign the treaty had been invited back for a celebration din-ner on board. Patuone was already in the longboat, stand-ing in the prow and waving the fine greenstone mere that was presented to the Governor to be given to Queen "Wiktoria." Thomas watched longingly as the thin emer-ald blade sliced through the afternoon sunlight.

"Aye, but there's little I'd not do to own one of those," he confided.

"Perhaps you will, one day." Her black-gloved fingers rested lightly on his arm in a proprietary gesture.

He placed a hand over hers for a second. "There's not much chance of my ever owning one of those magnifi-cent things. Even Captain Cook himself could not man-age to persuade the chiefs to part with one. What chance have I?"

The Governor walked slowly down the stone steps, nod-ding right and left. His face was drawn with exhaustion but he held himself as erect as if he were corseted. The crowd pressed close behind the double-range guard of sailors, cheering and waving, for now that the treaty was signed and therefore a fact most people's doubts had disappeared. *Faits accomplis* never make people apprehensive in the way that possibilities do.

As Captain Hobson was stepping into the longboat a commotion boiled up in the throng jostling behind him. As abruptly as a peach stone spat from puckered lips a wizened Maori tohunga sprang forward and thrust himself in the Governor's way.

"*Aue he horoheke! E koro e roa kua mate!*" he screamed at the Governor's face.

Captain Hobson smiled a grimace of fatigue. His eyelids twitched. Plainly he did not understand and he saw no significance in the horrified murmurings which washed an echo over the incomprehensible remarks.

Maire's hand tightened on Thomas' arm. "What did he say?"

Thomas shook his head.

"Please tell me. It sounded positively frightening."

"It was." Thomas paused. "He said, 'Alas, an old man! Soon he will be dead!' "

Maire shuddered, then pushed the information away. "It must be a case of resentment. Of sour grapes, perhaps. Yes, it must be. That fellow did not want the treaty and now his anger is coming out because the majority decision went against him." She lowered her voice. "Will you come home to dinner again, Thomas?"

"Yes, I should like that." He smiled into her eyes, still not able to understand his good fortune. "But not the girls. Mrs. Clerkwell was quite ferocious when I returned them so late last night. I must not antagonise her. She has been very good to them."

"Have you told them yet?"

"I shall do so now, if you will be so kind as to excuse me. Then I will return them to Mrs. Clerkwell and meet you back at the boat."

She smiled. Her face seemed to light with a soft incandescence when she looked at him.

* * *

Something important to tell them, thought Juliette in bemusement as they followed their father to a spot under a rose arbour beside the house. Her blood chilled suddenly. Perhaps they had found Mother's killers.

Abby swung on her father's arm. "I know what it is," she sang. "You have found a home where we can be together."

"Something like that," he said.

"Oh, Father! That's wonderful! I have been begging for this every night, in my prayers!" She shot a look at Juliette, who was in a position to deny it—very seldom did Abby ever bother to say her prayers. "Isn't that true, Julie?"

Thomas took his younger daughter's hand and gave it an affectionate pat, to make her look up at him. What a grave, silent little creature she was, not like Abby, whose nature was like the sunny weather passing over the earth.

Abby accidentally bumped Juliette and tried to climb into her father's arms.

"Do tell me about it, Father. Have you managed to find a housekeeper? What is her name? I do hope she's not a Maori lady."

He set her on her feet. She was really far too big to be climbing all over him. "We *are* going to be a family again, but it will not be just the four of us . . ."

"What do you mean?"

"Easy on, there. Don't be upset. I mean that there will be other people, not just us."

"A housekeeper?"

"Not a housekeeper."

Juliette said blankly, "You are getting married again?"

"I know already," said Samuel, smug but plainly disinterested.

Juliette was too stunned to speak. She had loved Miss Asia enough to want her as part of the family, but the thought that Father could think of marrying a stranger was indigestible. The idea sat like a stone in the centre of her mind.

"Mrs. Yardley will make a good mother to you girls."

Abby gasped and shrieked, "I *hate* Mrs. Yardley!"

"Of course you don't," Thomas said wearily. "You have

only met her twice. She is a kind, noble woman and she is willing to include us in her family. I for one am grateful and I would have expected you to be grateful too. Now, come on, Abby, don't start sulking. Think about it and I'm sure you will be pleased. We shall be getting married in a few weeks' time, and by then I expect you to have accepted the fact and decided to be happy about it."

"How can I be happy about it?" wailed Abby.

Juliette felt like crying too. She wanted to tell her father that he had ruined the dream that one day they would be together again, just the four of them, happy with each other and not needing any outsiders. But what would be the point of saying this? Obviously Father did not share that dream, he *did* need someone else. But what would this new life be like?

They would all be going to live in Mrs. Yardley's fine, big house. That would be exciting. And she would have sisters and Stephen and Leigh for brothers. A cold thrill climbed her back at the thought. Would Leigh accept her or was he reacting to the marriage in the same way as Abby was? In many ways their positions as the favourite were the same, and both had a lot of attention to lose. How terrible it would be if Leigh resented her through no fault of her own.

The girls would be kind. Juliette felt confidently sure of that. It would be fun to have big sisters, and it might have unexpected advantages, too. Jane excelled at needlework; perhaps she could sew a beautiful doll so that Juliette could trade it and get Clarice back again.

She looked up at her father. "I am happy about it," she told him solemnly.

PART THREE

MAIRE

1841-1846

Eleven

Thomas and Maire were married at a simple service in the Bishop's parlour. Nuns attended Maire and Stephen was the only other family member present. Nobody from the Mission attended.

Thomas had hoped to invite Lars Jacobson to be his best man but when Maire ventured her caustic opinion he immediately forgot the idea. Thomas had never needed the reassurance of friends, so he left the wedding arrangements to Maire. The fact that it was to be a papist ceremony did not worry him, though he did experience a twinge that might have been conscience. Evangeline would be shuddering in her grave if she knew.

For their mother's sake he tried to insist on one thing: his children must be able to make up their own minds about religion; they must not be coerced into anything.

Maire regarded this request with cool amusement. She had no intention of letting them be anything but Catholic.

"Why, Thomas! How can anybody be coerced along the path of true faith?"

To which Thomas had no answer. In truth, he didn't care if the children were raised to be Buddhists. His views on God were nebulous; on humanity, deeply sympathetic; and on organised religion, almost contemptuous. He held the opinion that Protestant-Catholic squabbles had always been politically based and therefore were not worth a dab of salt. He was satisfied that he was bringing the girls into a good, moral household. It was all that could be hoped for.

The Clerkwells did not share his complacency and told Thomas so in the most forceful terms that their religious training would permit. Abby and Juliette listened through the thin wall and might have been forgiven for thinking that Thomas proposed to marry a Hottentot whose customs would thrust the defenceless girls into mortal and spiritual danger.

"Catholics can't be that bad, surely?" Juliette leaned away from the wall. "Jane and the twins are perfectly nice girls, don't you think?"

"Shush!" Abby listened, then sighed. "They've stopped talking. They probably heard your voice."

"I was only whispering, and I don't see how they could hear. Abby, what is so terrible about being a Catholic?"

"It's nothing you can actually see, but they won't go to a proper heaven like ours. Catholics can't help it because they don't know any better."

"Mrs. Clerkwell was saying that you and I will be Catholics when Father marries Mrs. Yardley."

"Even if they whip me, I shan't be one," said Abby.

But perhaps it isn't something so *very* terrible, thought Juliette. She asked Mrs. Clerkwell for details, but all she received by way of reply was extravagant weeping and a suffocating hug. The good woman wailed that the girls were lost souls, but packed their bags briskly enough when the time came.

To Juliette the most exciting aspect of the move was the prospect of living in the elegant house on the hill, and she was disappointed to learn that it would be only a temporary home.

Governor Hobson had thus far spent less than five consecutive days in the Bay of Islands, but he had already decided to move the site of the capital to the Waitemata harbour, two hundred miles away to the south. There all the important Maori tribes were within easy communication distance. This announcement took everybody by surprise, for the Governor had suffered a stroke on the schooner *Trent* while on an expedition to collect signatures for the treaty; the stroke was a disquieting reminder of the Maori prophecy of a few months earlier. When he was taken ill most people expected him to slink back into the Residency to recuperate, and to mind his own business while things went on as usual in Kororareka, but Governor Hobson was a man of stronger will than health. He or-

dered five consignments of sawn timber from Thomas with
the instruction that they be shipped to the Waitemata for
resale as building materials. The new town, named Auckland, needed them. The Mission's disbelief soured to dismay. Why go so far away and strike a new town on virgin
soil when every facility a town needed was already right
here? Their cry was taken up by Kororareka, who could
see lean times ahead. How could the town survive if the
new capital drained its lifeblood away?

The Governor was both deaf and unyielding; he refused
to discuss the matter. Inevitably, there were rumours that
the grand new Governor cared as little for the Mission as
for the squalid town across the bay.

As the Reverend Clerkwell put it, "Forsaking both
Heaven and Hell, be betook himself to a new, unsullied
place!"

These decisions vitally affected the Richmond Shipping
Line and their three ships: the *Lorendee*, the *Marjoree*, and
the recently acquired clipper, the *Sarendee*. In Stephen's
opinion the Peridot-Yardley family should waste no time
moving to the new capital. The *Sarendee* could take a load
of timber to England and return with a load of settlers.
There would be so many opportunities for business in
Auckland that it was preferable for the family to be based
there too. Maire agreed and easily persuaded Thomas to
establish a trading emporium there. After all, the first
firms in any new district flourished and grew, free from
any competition. And Thomas, with his intimate knowledge of the Maori language and customs, was in an un-
equalled position to win the confidence of the Waitemata
tribes, and perhaps even to become their exclusive trading
agent. Thomas found his wife's enthusiasm infectious and
gratifying, especially after so many years when Evangeline regarded his business as a dreary, distasteful chore.

There was another reason Maire wanted them to move,
one she wisely left unspoken. While they lived in Kororareka, there was always the shadow of Evangeline's killers.
Maire knew that Thomas still hoped to find them, and she
knew what a hopeless ambition that was. And hopeless
ambitions thwart achievable ones. She wanted to help rid
her husband of the phantom that haunted him; the shift to

Auckland would surely do this. A new scene would clear away the past and allow a fresh start.

The Governor's commissions kept Thomas extremely busy in the months following the wedding. He would come home for a few days and then be gone to the bush camps for a fortnight. Abby complained that she saw less of him than she had before, for now when he was at home he was shut away with Maire for so much of the time. All the sisters had of him now was the occasional sound of his voice, punctuating Maire's low, lilting laughter.

"I hate her," said Abby one afternoon.

"Who?" asked Juliette. They were on the verandah, where a winter vine-skeleton made a stark pattern of shadows on her face.

"Her, of course. She's stolen Father."

"Aunt Maire?" Juliette pronounced it "Maree" as they had been told by Maire herself.

"I shall call her Aunt Mare," said Abby spitefully. "A mare is a mother horse, isn't it? Well, that's what she reminds me of with her long nose and her black mane."

"She is kind to us!" Juliette protested. She was shocked that Abby would talk about her stepmother that way.

"She is *not* kind!"

"She took us out of mourning, didn't she? I would have thought you would be delighted to be rid of those horrid black dresses."

"I don't feel *that* grateful. I was so looking forward to being out of mourning that I could hardly wait. I had planned to choose material for a new gown from the bolts of dress goods on Oliver Jarrod's shelves . . . you remember how Mother used to let us pick the colour we liked? I had planned on that pretty cerise muslin. And some black ribbons for trimming . . . no, some white ribbons, for I won't wear anything black ever again, not even as a trim! Oh, Julie, I had set my heart on it."

Juliette soothed her. "You can't help it if you are so close to the twins in size that their castoff gowns fit you. But some of them are very pretty."

"They're so insipid. All the girls' clothes are such horrid colours. It's not a bit fair! And you, because you're so small, you get to have new ones made! No wonder you think Aunt *Mare* is so kind!"

Juliette leaned her face close to the fretwork of vine stems and gazed through to the goldfish pond.

"I'm happy here," she decided. As she spoke she knew in her heart that she was even happier than if their dream had been realised and there were just the four of them living together. True, she had a small part of her father's time; but she had far less of Abby's company, and Abby was so disagreeable lately that the less of her company Juliette had the more pleasantly the time passed.

The Yardley girls had warmly welcomed Juliette and Abby, even though the increase in the household meant that Jane had been obliged to relinquish her single room to the newcomers and squeeze into the already cramped room that the twins shared. This arrangement lasted only until the girls decided that Jane could "adopt" Abigail and the twins would share Juliette. So Jane had moved back into her old room and Juliette now had the trundle bed in Sarah's and Rose's room.

Abby adored Jane, a young lady at that exquisitely painful age in which nature and society conspire malevolently, that limbo between childhood and maturity. Jane's main yearning (which would be instantly replaced by another of equal intensity as soon as this one was fulfilled) was to be able to put her skirts down and her hair up. Her mother had ruled that this would not happen until she was at least eighteen . . . an interminable age away. Whenever Maire was busy and not likely to come in and disturb them, Abby would guard the door watching admiringly while Jane spent long hours combing and arranging her hair before the bedroom mirror.

"Jane's a hundred times more interesting than the twins!" Abby declared. "A thousand times more interesting."

"What is?" asked Leigh, coming suddenly along the verandah. He had a slice of cake in his hand and his chin was dusted with powdered sugar.

"Nothing!" said Abby haughtily.

Though the twins shared Jane's pale cream and bitter chocolate colouring, they were so very different from her and from each other in personality that Juliette's life changed the moment they took charge of her. They were fifteen now, a year older than Leigh, but still coltish and ungainly. They were identical in looks except for Rose's broken nose.

One afternoon when they were alone on the back lawn shelling a basinful of early peas for dinner, Sarah confided to Juliette how it had happened. It was an accident that had happened five years ago. The girls and Leigh and some other children were playing tag one summer evening. When it was Leigh's turn to be "it" he fished a weta from where he had hidden it near the old pohutukawa tree. Brandishing it like a weapon, he chased the girls, laughing like a maniac and threatening to thrust the beast under their bonnets or up under the loose sleeves of their gowns. They had fled shrieking in terror, especially Rose, who detested insects. She had scuttled to the verandah with Leigh in pursuit, waving the weta, which was flexing its legs as though preparing to spring. Rose had rushed up the steps and turned her head back for one last glance. When she turned back again to dash inside to safety, she had run right into the doorjamb.

"Oh, what a fuss there was!" said Sarah. "You should have seen the blood! It was splashing about like holy water at a christening, and the accusations were flying around too."

"Was Leigh punished?" Juliette asked, hoping that he had not been. After all, it had been an accident.

"Leigh has not known the meaning of the word 'punishment' since Papa died. Stephen tries to discipline him for his own sake. He's been so good to us all, and he works so hard. Stephen is the best one out of all of the children—barring me, of course!" And she grinned and popped a row of peas into her mouth.

"Who was blamed for Rose's accident?"

"Oh, Leigh was. But he carried on so, crying and clinging to Mama's apron, that you'd think it was him who was wounded! Poor Rose!" She thoughtfully popped another pea into her mouth. "Her face was pulverised! All swollen, and black and blue. She looked terrible for weeks and weeks. Yet when Stephen came home he didn't say a word.

It must have given him a real shock because he hadn't known about the accident, yet he greeted Rose and gave her a gift as he always does and never said a thing. She never minded it after that. He carried the act off so well that she thought her disfigurement was scarcely noticeable."

"That was kind of him," said Juliette.

"It helped, but Rose is still sensitive, and she does get upset if somebody mentions it. You'd expect children to be the tactless ones but it's always the grownups who comment. Stephen gets angry and says that they would soon think twice before making personal remarks if young folks were permitted to make a few in return. Can you imagine telling old Mrs. Meyney that her voice is so loud that they can hear it in Heaven; or telling Mr. Bellwood that his ears stick out and his fingers are a good deal too friendly?" She laughed. "They would deserve it. Both of them have been quite mean to poor Rose."

Juliette liked both twins equally and for different reasons. Sarah was undoubtedly more amusing and entertaining. She and Juliette enjoyed games of skittles and hilarious rounds of snap, but it was to Rose that Juliette found herself returning more often when she was feeling lost and homesick. Though Mrs. Clerkwell had been dry and strict she had given the girls a lot of time; whereas Maire's household ran itself and the children seldom had anything to do with her. Juliette missed the security of having some sympathetic person to talk to, and it was not long before Rose found herself filling that role. Rose seemed to understand that this delicate eleven-year-old needed mothering. So she listened to Juliette and talked to her, then sat her on one end of the long piano stool while she rippled out a lullaby. Juliette had no idea what the tune was—the only songs she could recognise were Mission hymns and none of *them* was likely to be played under this roof. But the tune was pretty and peaceful; it made her eyelids droop and the corners of her mouth turn up.

"That was lovely!" she said when Rose rested. "Can I learn to do that?"

Rose was doubtful, then she reconsidered. "I cannot see

why not, for your hands are so very clever with a needle. But it will mean hours of dedicated practising."

"I'm willing to try. Oh, Rose, will you teach me? Please?"

"If you like," she said.

It was not a success: Juliette did not have the right touch for music at all. After days of solitary practice and five laboured lessons, each less successful than the one before, Juliette declared that it was no use. When Rose could not deny the truth of this but simply sat biting her lip and unhappily staring at the piano's candle brackets, the younger girl glanced at her briefly and burst into a storm of tears.

"What's the matter? I heard sobbing." Sarah's concerned voice came from the doorway.

Rose told her.

"Why, you daffy gosling! How can you expect to learn something which we have had drilled into us for years!"

"At least ten years," added Rose.

"You must not cry about that! It takes years and years to become adept at the piano."

"Whereas we, for all our schooling, are not nearly as clever as you are at sewing. Not even Jane can sew as beautifully as you."

"Of course!" said Sarah. "You must try to concentrate on your own skills. You excel at sewing, so why don't you make yourself something really splendid?"

"A doll," said Juliette slowly. And she told the story of her beloved Clarice and the sewing box.

"Clarice?" said Sarah. "Do you mean to say that you are mooning over that bedraggled, grubby doll that Abby drags everywhere?"

"Clarice wasn't always grubby," said Juliette indignantly. Her tears were completely forgotten. "She only got that way after Abby had her."

"You can make yourself a much prettier doll than Clarice." Sarah confidently perched on the end of the piano, cream morocco slippers swinging carelessly. "You are clever enough to do it."

"But I have no fabric."

"That's easily obtained," said Rose. "And I'll help you with the pattern, if you like."

"And I shall 'borrow' Clarice so that we can copy how to do it." Sarah grinned wickedly.

"We can even dress her in the same colour as Clarice, only more beautifully, of course," put in Rose. "I feel certain that there is some daffodil-coloured silk left over from our summer gowns, tucked away in a corner of the old blanket box. It will suffice for a gown, pettislips, and a bonnet." She paused, frowning. "What about the face? Shall we ask Mary to draw one on silk? She is so talented at drawing faces. Then it could be embroidered."

Sarah giggled. "Mary might draw a Maori face, with a chin tattoo. A *moko*."

"I have a spare doll's face in the sewing basket," said Juliette. The mood was beginning to infect her: she, too, could see the beautiful finished doll. "The face is identical to Clarice's, for Mother bought faces enough for all of us girls. But their dolls were broken and she hadn't yet made Melina's doll because she was so little, and it didn't seem to matter leaving hers until last. . . ."

The twins looked at each other uncomfortably. This was a decidedly taboo conversation and neither of them wanted to encourage Juliette.

"That's why there is one left over," concluded Juliette. She was a little troubled but not shaken by the subject line she had just crossed. She smiled at the twins. "There is some pretty trimming in the basket, too. Only scraps, because I used up quite a bit making bonnets for the Maori babies at the Mission . . . for their baptismal clothes."

"Bribes," said Sarah.

Juliette laughed at this daring criticism. "That's what Miss Asia used to say! She said that it was bribery and corruption because if there was no baptism there were no beautiful new baby clothes."

"Mrs. Clerkwell would be horrified if she could hear you!"

"She would be even more horrified if she could see me taking lessons from Sister Concepta!" Juliette pointed out. "Oh, what a fuss about nothing!"

It was not going to be as easy as they had first thought,

the girls decided after carefully examining Abby's doll.
Joining legs and arms to the body posed the most problems, but despite patient sewing and unpicking, the doll
was almost finished by the time the household was disrupted by the chaos of packing for the journey to Auckland. Now the twins were busy all day and Juliette could
only find rare moments when she could take Clarissa (as
Sarah had dubbed the new doll) from her hiding place in
the sewing basket, unwrap her, and secretively add two or
three perfectly neat stitches to the pink calico torso.

She was seated on the grass under the pohutukawa tree
one late afternoon utterly absorbed in her work. She had
been left behind when Maire took the others out to choose
fabric for their new travelling clothes, because all of her
clothes were new. Abby was ecstatic. After so much complaining, she had finally worn her father down to the point
where he had agreed to talk to Maire about getting her
some new gowns. Maire was displeased; she saw no reason
why anybody, even her attractive husband, should tell her
how to bring up girls. When Maire looked at Abby now it
was with dislike. On the occasions when it was necessary
to speak to her, there was coldness in Maire's voice. Abby
was not sensitive enough to realise this. All she knew was
that she had scored a victory and soon she would be
gowned, trimmed, and beribboned in the finest new frip-
peries to be had in Kororareka.

Juliette had one final seam to complete and then
Clarissa would be ready to dress. At the moment she
looked strange and very bare with long, pink sausages for
arms, longer ones for legs, and a peculiar pillow-shaped
body that stiffly supported her large head. But her face
was lovely and the hair something of a miracle of good fortune. Old Mrs. Meyney had a passion for false curls which
she wore pinned under the front of her bonnets to make
glossy fringes; they deceived nobody but looked satisfactory to her. When a bundle of old clothing came from her to
be distributed to the Catholic Mission poor, it was given to
Sarah to be sorted out. There, tucked in an old bonnet, was
a cluster of auburn curls. When the tangles were teased
straight and Mrs. Meyney's lavender scent rinsed out, the
curls were sewn to Clarissa's pink calico scalp. The web-

bing stretched neatly over it, hiding the ridge where the
china face was secured. With gentle brushing and coaxing
Juliette had drawn the curls into two bunches of ringlets,
one above each ear, in Evangeline's favourite style.

She finished the last seam and carefully fed the cotton
end back along the line of stitches to neaten it off. She
stabbed the needle away in the leaf-shaped pincushion and
held Clarissa out at arm's length to admire her work. She
would never have believed it possible but with the twins'
help she had actually made herself a really beautiful doll.
She could begin on the pettislip and perhaps, with luck,
even finish everything by the time they reached Auckland.

A shadow fell across her.

"What have you done to Clarice?" asked Samuel. He
and Leigh flopped onto the grass beside her, and Leigh casually snatched the doll from her grasp.

"It isn't Clarice," said Juliette. She did not take her eyes
off the doll. Leigh was squinting at it through half-closed
eyes. He was browned and lean after weeks in the bush
with Thomas and Samuel, but his face had not changed; it
was still the face of an indulged child.

"It looks like Clarice. But quite indecent, don't you
think, Samuel? Don't you think it should have some
clothes on?"

Juliette tried unsuccessfully to snatch it back. "It's *my*
doll, and I made it. Oh, please give her back to me!" She
tried again to grab it but Leigh held it further out of reach.
"You won't hurt her, will you, Mr. Leigh?"

He laughed and swung Clarissa around by her plump
arms so that her head and feet twirled and the arms
twisted up like corkscrews.

"Oh, please don't!"

The doll paused upside down. He tugged at the pink
hands and Clarissa began giddily spinning the other way.

"She's a circus doll!" cried Leigh. "Do you know what a
circus is, Juliette?"

"Come on," said Samuel disinterestedly. "Let's go and
see if Tawa will get us something to eat."

Leigh started towards the kitchen but paused to smooth
the doll's limbs and to restore her to Juliette. He was set-

tling Clarissa in her arms, bending over her and smiling, when the pony trap clattered up the drive. Glancing past Leigh's shoulder, Juliette saw her stepmother's head turn in their direction. The trap stopped.

"Leigh! Come here at once!" Maire's voice had a sharp edge. "Come and help carry the packages. And you, Juliette. Why are you dawdling out there when I instructed you to dust the parlour furniture?"

"I finished it, Aunt Maire."

"Then you should have asked Mary for another task. Help me down please, Leigh."

Later that evening Leigh crept into his mother's bedroom and laid his head on Maire's shoulder as she sat at the dresser brushing her long black hair. She paused in mid-stroke, laid her brush down, and placed a hand on his brow. He looks so tired, she thought with a squeeze of conscience. I should not have sent him away with Thomas. Bush life is too rigorous for him.

"You should be in bed," she said gently.

"I wish that I could sleep with you. Like I used to after Papa died. Why did you marry Uncle Thomas?" he whined, picking up the silver-backed hand mirror. "They've spoiled everything!"

"I thought you liked the Peridot children?"

He pulled a sour face. "Samuel is always trying to order me about. Can you imagine it, and he's only ten! And Abby is so silly!"

"*Abigail*, dear. Nicknames are vulgar."

"So is she. Did you know that she and Jane have been reading those soppy love stories, those twopenny novelettes that the Bellwood girls leave lying about?"

"What about Juliette?"

There was something in the way her eyes fixed on his face in the mirror that made his gaze slide guiltily away. "I don't like her at all," he said.

Maire smiled. "I'm so glad that you are being sensible, dear. It would not do to become too friendly with those children. They are not like you and your sisters; they have not had the benefits you have received. In fact, the details of their upbringing would make one shudder!" She placed her palms one on each side of his face and waited until he was looking into her eyes. "If young Samuel is bullying you, then you do not need to go into the bush camps with him any more. I promise you that you will never have to do anything you don't want to do."

"I know," said Leigh with satisfaction. "Here, Mama. Let me brush your hair like I used to."

The Yardley homestead had been brought from England in prefabricated sections that were assembled on the site. Thomas persuaded Maire that, as she would never recover the cost of it by selling, it would be best to have it dismantled and reassembled in Auckland. Though she had had her heart set on a new home, the thought of losing money was enough to prompt her into making a compromise. The homestead would become a future renting proposition and the family could live in tents, if need be, while waiting for her dream home to be built. Thomas laughed at her tenacity and told her how much he admired her astute business sense. She thanked him coolly. His compliments were always so disappointingly impersonal.

Stephen leaned smilingly over the railing of the *Lorendee* and proudly hoisted his womenfolk over the side of his ship, something that rarely happened; the indignity discouraged all but the most enthusiastic ladies from scrambling aboard for a mere social visit. As he grasped them at wrist and upper arm to steady them, it amused Stephen to notice how differently each made this last, awkward step of the ascent. Maire was supremely self-possessed; one would think that she was doing nothing more difficult than stepping daintily up a flight of carpeted stairs. Rose thanked him for his assistance and added an admiring comment about the craft, while Sarah teasingly accused him of squeezing her arm "much harder than necessity decreed." Young Abigail almost bounded aboard, full of confidence, and skipped over to attach herself to her father, who was supervising the loading of their luggage. Finally there was little Juliette, standing forlornly in the rocking boat and gazing in fear at the ladder that slapped against the side.

The Maori youth who stood beside her heaved up the square wicker workbasket. Stephen caught it easily but groaned to entertain her.

"What have you hidden in here? Pirate treasure?"

Large, shy eyes turned up to him. "Everything I own is in there, Mr. Stephen."

"Then you had best come right up before I begin to rifle it," he joked, adding in concern because she did not smile, "Miss Olivine, are you all right? Would you like me to come down and carry you up?"

At that she shook her head quickly and grasped the hard, tarred ropes. What would Leigh say if he saw her being carried on board? He might scoff at her. Biting her lip and concentrating as hard as she could on placing her feet properly, she made her way up in little, careful lunges, not letting go with one clinging hand until she had secured a tight grip with the other. Her shoulders hurt from the tension and her knuckles bumped and scraped on the ship's rough timber. A voice immediately above her head shouted, "It's *kapai* now, Manu! It's all right. She's safe." The shout gave her such a sudden fright that her breath blocked in her throat and she almost let go; she would have, except that a brown, lean hand fastened over her wrist and gently pulled. In a smooth unbroken movement she found herself stepping onto the top rail and swinging up and over into Stephen's arms. Her hands were clinging in panic to the shoulders of his dark blue brass-buttoned jacket.

"There!" He set her down on a barrel. "Now, don't tell me that you were afraid! Not sweet Olivine!"

The name did make her smile this time. She had a pure smile and even white teeth, clear peach-coloured skin, and those enormous, shining eyes that made him smile at her despite his attempts to be mock serious.

"I was nervous!"

"There is absolutely nothing on the *Lorendee* to make a young lady nervous. I can assure you of that."

She was instantly confused, saying, "I didn't mean to sound ungrateful, Mr. Stephen! I feel certain that this is a very good ship, and Father says fine things about it. It is just that I have never been on anything but a rowboat before, and I feel nervous about the journey."

"You will find this rather a new experience."

Her voice lowered earnestly. "Is it so very, very terrible to be seasick?"

"What a question! We have not thought of hauling the anchor yet."

"Is it so terrible?"

"What makes you think such a thing?"

"Leigh told us that everybody is seasick on their first voyage and that it is worse than being dead. He said that often people try to fling themselves overboard to end the torture, and they have to be restrained, even tied to their bunks." As she spoke her eyes grew bigger. "Please tell me. Is it really so bad, or can't you remember so very long ago to your first voyage?"

He tried not to laugh. So very long ago! How ancient did he appear to those dark blue eyes that brimmed with such solemn secrets? He was on the point of asking, but he restrained himself with the thought of what her innocently frank answer might be.

"My dear Miss Olivine, seasickness is not mandatory, despite what Leigh has told you. The weather promised me that it would behave itself and remain excellent, while the sea has vowed to do its best to resemble this harbour on a fine day. Leigh cannot help teasing, and I think that the fact that you asked me for a second opinion shows that you are beginning to sum him up with splendid accuracy. Do you want to know a special recipe? Take a pinch of salt for every tale he tells you."

"A pinch of salt?"

"More if his stories sound too frightening." He could see that she was a little puzzled but before she could ask in detail about pinches of salt he lifted her down off her uncomfortable perch and chucked her under the chin. "Off you go now, Miss Olivine. I have more young ladies to help aboard. It seems that I am to be blessed with feminine company this afternoon."

And feminine giggles, and feminine squeals, noticed Juliette later as the Bellwood girls and Miss Georgina Meyney fluttered around Stephen.

"Are they coming with us?" she whispered to Sarah.

"They would stow away if they could," she said flatly. "They have come to bid Stephen goodbye. They did not get a proper opportunity yesterday morning when they visited, nor yesterday afternoon when Mama shooed them away. Honestly! Mama told me that she would lock us up in a convent rather than allow us to throw ourselves at a young man like that!"

"I feel sorry for them," said Rose. "When you stop to consider the matter, can you think of any really nice eligible young men here in Kororareka?"

"I desperately hope that Auckland will be better," sighed Jane. She had already surveyed their fellow passengers and had been disappointed in her quest for attractive young men.

"Stephen said that there were royal soldiers in Auckland."

"What? The military? Oh, do tell me what he said!"

Sarah shook off the fingers that dug into her arm. "Hush! Mama may hear you!"

Juliette was still watching the three young ladies around Stephen. It was clear to her that they were all competing with one another for scraps of his attention, and that while he certainly seemed to enjoy the fuss, he did not pay special notice to any particular one. There was merriment in his eyes but no real warmth as he answered their flirtatious remarks and smiled at them all.

Suddenly Juliette announced, "When I am courting I fancy that I shall choose a young man who will be willing to give me his exclusive attention!"

She spoke out loudly enough for the twins and Jane to hear; she hadn't bargained that Stephen, standing with his back quite close to her, might hear her as well. To her consternation she found herself whisked back onto the barrel and into the centre of the group, hearing Stephen say, "This young lady has the right approach . . . Do go on, Miss Olivine, tell these ladies what you have decided to do."

The Bellwood girls and Miss Meyney looked at Juliette with ill-concealed annoyance. There were only a few precious minutes of Stephen's company left, and the last thing they wanted was a child to fritter any of the time away. Aware of the resentment, Juliette wriggled uncomfortably.

"Please, Mr. Stephen, let me down."

Georgina Meyney had an unfortunately heavy square jaw and thick eyebrows which gave her a slightly menacing aspect. She stared at Juliette.

"Why are you indulging in silly names?" she demanded, in her shrill voice. "Why this 'Mr. Stephen,' for mercy's sake? And why are you calling the child 'Olive'? Her name is Juliette, isn't it?"

"Not Olive, but Olivine. Miss Olivine, sweet Miss Olivine, is what I call her."

"And whatever kind of nonsense is that?"

"Ah," said Stephen, suddenly so cool and sober that the vague resemblance to his mother showed in his face. "Peridot is a precious jewel, and olivine another name for the same stone. Don't you agree that she is like a jewel, petite, pretty, and perfect?"

There was a snort from Miss Meyney, who was far from being either petite, pretty, or perfect. The Bellwood girls looked at each other and shrugged. In embarrassment Juliette scrambled down and fled to where Thomas and Maire were watching the handling of their crates of precious chinaware.

On a packing crate close by huddled Mary and Tawa, the Maori servants. Smartly dressed in dark grey gowns, capes, and bonnets, they put their heads together and cried in abject misery.

From time to time Maire tried to soothe them, but now she was growing exasperated.

"Girls, I shall be terribly cross with both of you if this foolishness continues for much longer. Of course we are not taking you to the Waitemata to sell you as slaves! Of course you will not be abandoned to the Auckland tribes, nor will you end up in anybody's cooking ovens! Of course you will see your families again! Your chief wants you to come with us, and if he is satisfied that no harm will befall you, then don't you think that you should trust us to look after you?" She appealed to Thomas. "I do declare that if it were not so impossibly difficult to train new servants I should leave these two behind directly, and select new ones when we arrive."

Mary caught that last remark and interpreted it as a threat. She looked up imploringly, eyes reddened, brown cheeks grimed with tears, and pleaded, "Oh, please, Mrs. Yardley, don' send me an' Tawa back to the pa!"

Maire replied crisply, "My name is Mrs. Peridot and it has been Mrs. Peridot for six months. No, I shall not send you home unless you persist in this ridiculous wailing."

Thomas said, "Is it so very difficult to train servants? In my experience the Maoris have been exceptionally quick to learn skills in bush work. Are the women less intelligent, perhaps?"

Maire consulted her list and ticked off another two items as a barrel and an oblong crate were carried past. Then she turned back to her husband.

"Oh, I have tried having houseboys as we did in Singapore, but not once the girls had reached an impressionable age." Quite careless of the fact that Mary and her sister were within earshot, she elaborated. "It is the subtleties which make training girls so difficult. Once I asked Mary to wash a piece of fish before cooking it because it was gritty with sand, and to my enormous surprise I shortly thereafter found her scrubbing it with soap and hot water! It was quite inedible, of course!"

"It seems like a language difficulty more than one of intelligence," said Thomas.

"Young English girls are no better, believe me! On another occasion . . ."

Juliette did not wait to hear any more. She had noticed Leigh and Samuel down at the end of this deck, where steps ascended to a higher level. Plucking up the determination that she always needed to approach Leigh, she skipped along as nonchalantly as she could. The boys were leaning over a packing crate that had been tied down to pegs protruding from the decking. When she drew close she could see that inside the crate, cowering unhappily on a whiskery nest of rough straw, was Tippy, his nose and eyes faint gleams in the narrow gaps between the boards.

"But why is he in there?" asked Juliette.

Leigh informed her loftily, "Stephen had him put in

there to be safe. If he is running about loose one of the sailors could well take it into his head to throw him overboard."

She felt her face growing tight. "Throw him overboard?"

"Sure!" said Leigh happily. "On the last trip from Sydney somebody had a pet dog which used to run about and was always getting in the way of the sailors, tripping them up and nipping at their heels when they were trying to do their work. One day when the dog was being a particular nuisance, one of the men noticed a shark sliding along in the water beside the boat, so . . ."

"Stop it!" cried Juliette, clapping her hands over the sides of her black bonnet. She gazed at the black nose and white muzzle, picturing the shark's head, water surging over the rows of teeth, and Tippy's paws flailing up a foam, his eyes huge with fear. "How could anybody . . ." she whispered.

"They do that quite easily," said Leigh. "Mother said that some of the Maoris don't have feelings like us."

"And a lot of pakehas don't neither," said Samuel. "We saw a show in Kororareka where they had dogs fighting against big ships' rats in a pit. I hate rats but I felt sorry for them there. Father says there's cruel people of all colours. And what about the men who killed Mother and the children? Father said he's willing to wager his life that no Maori would do a thing like that. Not for no reason."

Leigh did not like to be contradicted but he had found from experience that he was certain to lose any fight picked with Samuel.

"Come and see the bullock team your father has bought," he told Juliette. "He is going to use them to drag timber out of the bush near the new town." He tipped his cap down so that the peak almost hid his eyebrows. "Come on, Samuel."

"You go on," Samuel said. "I'll stay a while longer with Tippy. He's still frightened and he doesn't know what is happening."

"Oh, very well." Obviously disgruntled, Leigh grabbed at Juliette's hand and dragged her along after him. She did not really want to go, especially not when he was in an uncertain mood; yet she did so sincerely long to be friends.

Down they went, around a sharply turning flight of narrow steps, and onto a lower deck. She was panting and blinking in the gloom when he stopped abruptly and thrust her around the corner of a solid wooden fence.

"Oh," she cried in fright.

Leigh laughed. "Give you a shock then, did they?"

They certainly had, especially the nearest beast, which she had almost bumped into. But now that her eyes had adjusted she could see a whole long row of great red oxen, all chained nose to timber, the nearest ones staring at her with white rolling eyes. All had blunt white horns and flat red curls pressed to their foreheads. There were flecks of froth on their broad white noses.

"What a lot of them!"

"Eighteen altogether, and Stephen is trying to buy ten more."

"Are these oxen from the Mission farm?" Vaguely she recalled something being said about the oxen there being superfluous now that a team of Clydesdales had been bred. That was it; Thomas had joked that the people at the Mission would be weary of chewing tough beef by the time they had finished eating their oxen teams.

"No. These are just young ones, from New South Wales. I say there, those bullocks bite! Don't go too close."

He was watching her carefully for her reaction and it occurred to her that, like the story about the sailors and the dog, this was probably a lie. Perhaps a "pinch of salt" meant a dash of scepticism! So she deliberately reached out a small hand and patted the nearest bullock on its rough nose.

"Aren't you scared?" asked Leigh in disappointment.

"Nothing frightens me." The words quavered slightly but she had managed to inject some airy casualness into the tone.

"I'll wager some things do."

"Nothing!" Though even as she spoke a thudding echoed in her ears to mock the remark. Footsteps. Running, pounding footsteps. She shook her head.

Leigh leaned over her, leering horribly, making claws with his fingers, a growl gargling in his throat.

She stared at him as calmly as she could, smothering the

strong urge to duck under his arm and bolt for the stairs. Instinctively she knew that to run away would earn nothing but contempt, so she decided that when he pulled her hair (as she was sure he would), she would slap him just as she had done before. She braced herself, but to her astonishment his head bent swiftly towards hers, and his cushiony lips pressed for a few seconds on her mouth. It seemed like a long, long moment. Of their own accord her eyes closed and she was conscious only of the pressure and the tingly, prickly feeling around her lips. It was a tense, unbearable sensation but at the same time oddly delicious.

Then the pressure lifted and with it the warmth of his skin. Cool air laid a hand on her upturned face, and when she opened her eyes Leigh was striding away fast up the stairs, his cream velvet jacket flapping.

She stood at the railing as the *Lorendee* moved slowly up the harbour, sail bulging awkwardly in the slight breeze. Behind them the Mission was like a sketch on a map border. The trees and buildings seemed cramped and tiny below enormous billows of cumulus clouds that were whiter than the canvas sails. Three canoes cut clean lines across the harbour, drawing slanting wakes, like Mrs. Clerkwell's knife gliding over icing to make a feather pattern. Gulls perched on the thick mast beams, squabbling rowdily over the best positions; while passengers felt the ship's gliding movement and came up from below, crowding the railings to catch a last picture of Kororareka, looking sleepy and deceptively innocent under the open skies. A rowboat bobbed near the jetty. The Maori boy rested at the oars while three bright parasols fluttered as the young ladies waved their farewells to Stephen.

Maire's attention was fixed on the roof of her house. Sunshine burned like a torch at the front windows above the dark hedge of trees.

"I do hope that it transports safely," she said, a light frown showing her anxiety. She had doubts about the wisdom of going away and leaving it to be dismantled later.

"No harm will come to it. Old Mr. Meyney will keep an eye on it until the work begins and he is perfectly capable of supervising that. And if the move does damage it slightly, what of it? No matter what happens we shall do well for ourselves."

"Yes, between us we shall do well." She noticed that people were casting glances at them. This invariably happened when they appeared in public together, and it was understandable: the wealthy shipping widow and the well-known trader. But Maire was also aware that many of the curious looks were directed their way because of the halo of tragedy that still surrounded Thomas. This irritated her. Maire hoped that in Auckland they would be respected solely for what they were, a handsome pair of successful business people who would be an asset to the very top level of society. Yes, it would be a relief to get away from this place where "society" had been exclusive to the resident British agent and his circle at the Mission. Governor Hobson would set a different style—had he not proved this by inviting the Bishop to the treaty signing and then seating him at his right hand?

"I beg your pardon?" she said, startled. Thomas had spoken to her: her mind was so firmly fixed on the future while the past slipped silently away before her eyes that she had not heard a word of what he was saying.

He took her arm. "I was saying that this is yet another change for the girls, the third in as many years. I do hope that they settle happily in Auckland."

Oh, the girls again. She stifled a yawn. The girls meant that insufferable Abigail, of course, for the other seldom came into his sphere of attention.

"The girls are perfectly happy," she assured him with only a trace of impatience in her musical voice.

"I am anxious that their education should not be too disrupted. . . ."

"My girls are working wonders with them," she put in deftly. It was the truth. "Jane hears Abigail with her reading and the twins take turns with Juliette." She did not mention Sister Concepta's regular visits. It was not a matter she was actually keeping from him, merely a subject she overlooked as not worth troubling him about. After all, she was paying all the fees for those lessons, and if he broached the subject she would say that naturally she assumed Abigail would keep him fully informed; she seemed to keep him informed about anything else that did not suit her.

"I know that the girls are in good hands," said Thomas. "Truly, you have so many praiseworthy qualities."

Her mouth tightened a little. Why must he always mention her practical qualities? Still, in all fairness, Richmond had been little better in that way. And he certainly didn't measure up to Thomas in other, far more important ways. And though Richmond had been an outwardly charming man, he harboured such a deep distrust of the Maoris that without Thomas' support it was probable that the Richmond Shipping Line would have foundered. She had a great deal to thank Thomas for. Maire's lips relaxed in a hint of a smile as she dwelt on some of her blessings.

The Mission was far, far away now and even the church spire was lost into the blue smudge of hills beyond. Juliette propped her chin on the sun-warmed railing and wondered what the Clerkwells were doing now. Would they still be taking classes; the Reverend in the church with a group of boys and Mrs. Clerkwell in her little raupo hut with the thatched roof and the mats on the floor for seating? She wondered whether she would ever see either of them again, and the thought gave her a lumpy, sad feeling. Mrs. Clerkwell had not been very motherly but she was kind in a brisk, no-nonsense sort of way. With Rose's help she had composed a short thank-you letter which had been sent to the Mission a fortnight ago. But no answer had returned, nor had there been any reply to the card she had sent at Christmas. Juliette wondered if Mrs. Clerkwell had cut the girls out of her thoughts the way she had done with Miss Asia when that lady ran away with the Scandinavian captain. If so, it wasn't fair. She and Abby had been taken away; they had not fled without a word of gratitude.

The sails rounded as the *Lorendee* moved majestically past the harbour and began to pick up speed, skimming along at a smarter pace. The crowd on deck had thinned out but Juliette remained where she was, shoulders hunched against the breeze and watching the coastline fall behind. Strips of sandy beach melted into the blue water, and trees on hill slopes faded into flat, dark green. As they moved along the coast, familiar bays folded and unfolded with a speed that made a joke of the Peridots' laborious progress through these same waters every Sunday for so many years.

The crew, mostly Maori men, busied themselves putting up and taking in sails in a ritual which they had practised so many times that communication and orders were unnecessary. Juliette noted and admired the way they clambered up rope ladders and balanced precariously in the rigging; but then her gaze turned back to the land. Would she ever come this way again?

I'm like those bullocks, she told herself. They have no power over what happens to them or where they go. Somebody got them onto the ship somehow and here they are. And Mary and Tawa; they are going away from their home and their families—everything they have ever known—for the trivial reason that it is difficult and inconvenient to train new servants! But us, too. We are all off to a strange new place simply because our new Governor doesn't think that the Bay of Islands is a fitting place for a capital! Nobody cares what any of us think, or what we want . . . off we go with no more to say about it than those great red oxen.

And then her heart stopped. While she was musing, the ship had glided through the deep-water inlet that washed up to the promontory where Lars Jacobson's whaling station leaned against the tall, sandy cliffs. One moment she had been gazing at raggedy bush-clad hills, and the next moment the whaling station was right before her eyes. Then before she had time to stare and seek out the details she remembered, the scene was swiftly rushing past, while a capering bunch of Jacky Norris' half-caste children raced along the beach. Their voices screamed like distant gulls' calls.

And now they were opposite Te Pahi's bay. Juliette's chest was crushed with an unexpected pain as her eyes dumbly sought the knoll on which their cottage had stood. She could not find it at first: they were such a distance out, and the bay curved back sharply from the whaling station so that perspectives flattened. Ridges, gullies, and hills appeared in quite different shapes from those she remembered. The pa she recognised immediately and the cage where Hine the madwoman was confined stood out surprisingly well. Working back from there, Juliette found the dark flax thickets in the swamp, so just up from there must be . . .

Her eyes rested on the place in disbelief. That had to be it, that bare patch. Was that where they had lived for so many happy years? Could it be? There was the scrape of track leading up like a tail from the long body of sand hills; there were the clumps of broom bravely waving a yellow beacon to catch her attention. Father had planted those shrubs as a surprise for Mother. They had been spikey little bushes when he smuggled them home, wrapped in sacking. Evangeline hadn't noticed them there on the edge of the bank until they had suddenly run up their hundreds of little golden flags. The children had found her kneeling in front of them one morning, pressing the branches to her face, weeping as though her homesick heart would break from joy.

Stephen found Juliette chilled through and crying quietly, clinging to the railing. Bay of Islands was far behind; land was now vague, grey spray-washed hills with foam-soaked feet. The sea had rumbled into an eiderdown of dark blue over which the ship ploughed, pointing up, then down.

"Are you seasick, sweet Olivine?"

The bonnet shook. She did not look at him.

He reached down and picked her up easily, freeing her grip from the rail. Submissively she leaned against his shoulder.

He gazed at her. "Not sick at all?"

"No."

"Then what is it?" Something warned him what the trouble might be, but he said, "You can tell me anything you want to, and if there is any way I can help, or anything I can do to make the trouble go away, then I shall do it."

Her eyes lowered and she fiddled with his cravat. Her little fingers were icy against his neck.

"Let me take you below, where it's warmer. We can't

have our sweetest young lady catching a chill now, can we?"

The kindness in his tone dissolved the hard knot of pain in her throat. With a sob she pressed her face into his neck; her body shook and trembled. Stephen carried her back a few paces and leaned against the mast for support, folding her close against the shelter of his jacket.

"What is it?" he asked gently.

"I want my mother!" she confessed with a fresh rush of tears. "I want her so very, very much that it hurts. I know that I'll never see her again, nor Madeline, nor Thomas, nor Regina, and darling little Melina . . . she was just the most perfect little baby . . . It hurts so that I can't see any of them ever again . . . so sore and empty. There's nowhere to go back to. Our old cottage is gone . . . there's only a bare place there on the hill. Everything is gone, and I do so want to go back."

Sympathy almost choked him. He twisted his face and kissed the wet cheek. She did not seem to notice the gesture, but her arms clung tightly around his neck.

"Everything is gone. Mr. Stephen, I am sorry to burden you with my troubles, because it all sounds so silly. But it hurts so much. . . ."

With his free hand he stroked her numb cheeks. Emotion threatened to overcome him, too. "I do understand, dear little girl. Believe me, I understand."

He swung her down and sat her on a hatch cover beside him, his arm protectively around her thin shoulders. Though she still cried softly he talked to her—not in a light way that would belittle her grief, but seriously. He told her about the fear of the unknown that affects people all through their lives, and of the longing for safe, familiar things and happy times that they have known in the past. He told her a little about his father, who had helped him and taken him everywhere in the same way Thomas had elected to bring Samuel up, and how he missed his father when he died. And then, because he had been there twice and could tell her about it, he described the Waitemata and the raw, new town: the fern-covered hills dotted with makeshift tents and Maori-style *whares*; the newcomers from England dazed by the starkness of it all as they tried to cope with setting up homes, scratching out gardens, and carrying out the daily chores of washing, cooking, and just getting to know each other in that strange new environment.

Juliette finally tipped her serious little face up to him and said, "Mr. Stephen, you make this sound like an adventure, a real, proper adventure!"

He smiled. It was safe now to be less serious. "Hasn't anybody ever told you what life is all about? Adventuring! That's right. If you are not planning an adventure, you might as well not be alive at all. And you, my pretty Miss Olivine, are about to embark on one of the most exciting adventures there could be. You are going to be a real, true pioneer. How do you feel about that then, hey?"

"I feel terribly giddy," she confessed.

Suddenly he noticed that she had grown extremely pale. Her lips were bloodless and dark circles ringed her eyes.

"Oh dear," he said. "I think you are going to find out exactly what it feels like to be seasick!"

And she promptly did.

Twelve

Stephen often likened the landscape of the Waitemata to "the moon covered in scruffy brown fur," and nobody ever disagreed with this observation. Though clothed with a shabby blanket of fern, the contours of land were bleak, slashed into gullies and twisted up into blistered cones with scooped-out craters. Last night a scientist visiting Thomas had declared that in his view the capital was planted in a veritable hotbed of volcanoes, the last having erupted a mere two thousand years ago and the next eruption due at any time at all—information that the listening Juliette found highly disturbing. She recognised from the terraces carved into their sides that several of these brooding cones had been pa sites long ago. Why had the Maoris deserted them? Had something frightened them away? Why had they sold such a huge tract of land so eagerly?

Today the ragged tent town seemed to bake on this hard, brown hearth, and there was something sinister about the seven cones that Juliette could see from the top of the rise. It was ten o'clock in the morning and promised to be sweltering by noon, and unbearable by three. Juliette's thin cotton dress and pettislip stuck to her back and dragged at her legs. Like the other girls, she carried utensils to bring drinking water for their little camp and, like the others, she was thirsty, irritable, and pink-faced.

Jane led the reluctant procession. They all stopped at the crest of the rise to rest. Around them waist-high ferns crinkled dryly in all directions; the expanse was broken only by an occasional tent with its corrugated iron cooking shed prudently set in a wide clearing.

Jane dropped her empty buckets and sighed. "This is

scarcely what I visualised us doing when Mama told us that we would soon be living in the new capital town. I had imagined balls, outings, a smart pony trap, and dozens of friends!"

"I thought that at least we would be enjoying ourselves as much as we did at home!" said Sarah.

"Oh, do cheer up," said Rose. "Unless we use a lot of water we only have to make one journey each day, and it really isn't so far. And it does give us something to do and see. I think life is rather pleasant here."

"Nothing but a dizzy round of fun," said Sarah dryly.

"But this is servants' work," complained Jane. "I think that Mary and that lazy Tawa should be the ones to carry our water."

Nobody commented on that. Mary and Tawa were being kept so busy that the two Maori girls had not even had time to nourish their fear of the local tribes, and they didn't even try to hide now when the Maori hawkers called each morning and evening with flax kits of vegetables, luscious peaches, plums, fish, hens, and plump pork on the trotter. Mary and Tawa were finding this life very tiring, for it is not easy to cook, wash, and housekeep when home is a tent, and dust and flies abound. Washing hung out to dry was soon covered with a film of red grit. The firewood sold by the hawkers was often so green that sap ran out of it and the flames spluttered and died, marooning the half-cooked dinner. Scavenging Maori dogs came sniffling around the cookhouse the second backs were turned; they could whisk a chunk of bacon away or overturn a bowl of eggs and escape into the endless fern, all within moments. The servants' lives were so hemmed in by tedious tasks that they had no time to carry water.

"If only it wasn't so far from our tent to the well! We could have just as easily settled down here, or over there on that rise. We didn't have to live practically in the Governor's lap."

"I don't see that it matters for now, Sarah," said Jane. "After all, we have to wait for the land sale before we can be finally settled, and we may not be able to secure land there. We may find that we do have to live closer to town after all."

"Closer to the barracks, you mean," laughed Sarah slyly. "You would like that, wouldn't you, Jane?"

"Hold your tongue." Picking up her buckets with an air of righteousness, Jane marched ahead again, with Abby skipping smartly to catch up.

Juliette snatched off her bonnet and used it to fan her scorching face. Her hair was wet with perspiration.

"Hurry up!" called Rose, so she jammed the bonnet on again and forced her feet to walk faster, ducking her head as the taller fern fronds swung back towards her.

Their way to the well led over three undulating rises and down through a grove of pohutukawa trees to the flat land that spread like a muddy apron below the Point Britomart cliffs. High above, on the cliffs themselves, an ever growing stone-wall crown encircled the cluster of barracks buildings. As the girls moved down towards the grove they had a fine view of the parade ground, which was, as usual, dotted with soldiers and horses exercising.

Jane's footsteps slowed.

"Come along, Jane," teased Sarah. "You remember what Mama said about staring at soldiers?"

Jane tossed her head. "Those are officers there with the horses, and for your information there is an eternity of difference between soldiers and officers."

"Yes." Sarah giggled. "Officers wouldn't look at you twice. They like beautiful women."

The well was lined with wood like an enormous barrel, to stop salt-water seepage. It was sunk right against the cliff in the spot where a fresh-water spring had been discovered. Nearby, on the water edge of the apron, was a heaping mass of rocks, brought there by barge from around the harbour. Teams of soldiers worked in turn to trundle these rocks in small wooden barrows up a steep path to the top of the hill where they were gradually added to the wall. The soldiers wore what they called "undress" or working clothes: dark blue trousers, red shell jackets cropped at the waist, and dark blue forage caps, all of which were dusted with a fine, grey powder from the stone.

Directly beyond this scene was the town proper, a collection of tents, Maori-style huts, and patchwork cottages. None had even a hint of permanence, for everybody was, at this stage, squatting on the land, waiting with impatience for the land sales still several weeks away. Two buildings, however, gave the impression of being there to stay. One was the dark stone Government store on the waterfront; the other, a mere hundred yards beyond and also on the shore, was the Peridot Trading Emporium. It was already labelled with an ornately painted sign in black and red, a compliment to the soldiers, who had already reciprocated by spending much of their shilling-a-day wages on the goods offered there. Juliette thought the building looked smart at this distance and that the regimental colours showed up well, but up close even she could tell that it had been hurriedly erected by inexperienced men (the *Lorendee's* crew) from unseasoned timber that was already beginning to warp and crack.

As the well came into view Sarah perked up. "I see the soldiers are working today—that will please our Jane!"

She had meant it lightly, but they all paused in mid-stride when they saw Abby and Jane already at the well: helping them with the dipper bucket and pulley was one of the soldiers. He was leaning close, very close, to Jane, and seemed to be whispering something to her. Jane was laughing in a rather giddy way as she looked up at him.

"These pretty lassies have got to be your sisters," the soldier said. "The same lovely eyes and the same delightful faces. But what about these young ones, then? Are they cousins of yours, Miss Yardley?"

Miss Yardley! He had certainly wasted no time.

One of the soldiers called, "Hey there, Potter! You'd best be looking lively or the sergeant might catch you and give you a right good wigging!"

"What's a wigging?" asked Abby.

"A scolding, and nowt to worry about." He grinned. He was thin and tanned with very white, slightly uneven teeth. "If they talk about a touching over, well, that's a different thing again. I would look lively at the threat of that. Now, what were we discussing before my friend so rudely interrupted us?"

"You were telling us about Yarmouth," said Jane with an arch smile. "Mr. Potter comes from Yarmouth, in England."

"Fascinating," said Sarah. "But we had best be going now, Jane, just as soon as we get these water pails filled."

They expected Mr. Potter to rise to that suggestion and help them as he had assisted Jane; but instead of moving to do so, he drew Jane aside with a bold touch on her wrist and began to speak to her in an earnest, low voice. Juliette watched them while she waited her turn at the dipper bucket. Jane was not smiling now. Once or twice she shook her head and spoke rapidly and passionately in an undertone. Abby stood beside them, openly listening to every word.

Rose splashed water into Juliette's pots, saying, "There you are, little sister," in her affectionate way.

She was stooping to grasp the handles when Sarah said, "Look out!" It sounded urgent. Juliette glanced up.

Galloping towards them were two horses. Leigh rode the second one; but in front, and almost upon the girls, was Maire, erect and elegant in a black riding habit. She was perched sidesaddle, but riding with such grace that she seemed almost part of the black horse itself. It was too late to warn Jane. The tip of Maire's plaited leather riding crop had sliced through the air and stung her sharply across the shoulders before the girl even realised what was happening.

Potter dropped Jane's hands and stepped back, his face flushing with anger as he opened his mouth to protest.

Maire patted the neck of her restive horse to calm it after the excitement of the gallop. She wheeled it about so that she was alongside her eldest daughter and looked down at her with contempt through the swathe of black veiling that draped the brim of her smart black riding hat. Ignoring Potter's furious babble, she addressed herself coolly to Jane.

"It seems that I cannot trust you," she said.

"Mr. Potter was only helping us, Mama."

"But not Sarah, or Rose, I noticed. It seems more likely that he was helping himself, as common soldiers are wont to do."

"I'll not stand here and be insulted," burst Potter but nobody listened to him. Only Abby's eyes followed him sadly as he strode away to resume his work amid a flurry of saucy comments from his friends.

"Dismount, please, Leigh. Jane is coming home with me," said Maire curtly.

"But, Mama! That horse has no sidesaddle. I cannot ride it."

"You shall ride it as best you can," snapped Maire.

And Jane, who had borne the humiliations of being struck and of being reprimanded in front of the others without any signs other than a whitening of her pale skin, now began to sob. Immediately Rose rushed to her and put a comforting arm about her waist.

"Mount up, please," said Maire. "Leave her alone, Rose."

"What will happen to her?" asked Juliette as they walked slowly up the rise through the grove of trees.

"She'll get a whipping, of course," Leigh said cheerfully. Jane's pail swung lightly in his hands. "It serves her right. Mama told her not to talk to the soldiers. They have frightfully bad reputations, you know."

"You don't even know what that means!" challenged Sarah.

Leigh's face darkened and Juliette hoped that he would not lose his temper. He had let the others walk a pace or two ahead and had chosen to stroll beside her. It had given her a little thrill of happiness when he did this, for she had so few chances to talk to him these days. Maire took him everywhere with her, and when his mother was about he ignored the girls so deliberately that Juliette had begun to wonder whether her stepmother had forbidden him to talk to them. She looked at him quickly, remembering the warm, tingling feeling when he had kissed her.

"Sarah doesn't mean anything," she said.

"Sarah doesn't know anything," he amended, and laughed at his own wit.

"You have your nose in a knot because you have to carry water with us instead of acting like the duke on horseback," Sarah taunted. "Well, perhaps this little chore might liven up your life. It must be excruciatingly dull riding about and doing nothing all day."

"Oh, just look at that," said Rose, who had been longing to change the subject. "Do look at that magnificent tui!"

The large, glossy bird was perched on a stem of flax flowers, probing the tubular red blossoms with its long beak. In the glaze of sunlight its feathers shone bluish green and the tuft of white under the throat gave it a jaunty appearance.

"Isn't it beautiful!" said Juliette.

The bird flapped to another flower stalk, taking no notice of them. Its wings rustled like taffeta.

"Watch this." Leigh's fingers scrabbled at the hard ground until he had loosened a sharp-edged pebble. Crooking his arm to take aim, he moved suddenly and the stone whirred towards the bird. Juliette cried out in the same instant, startling the tui. It flapped away, disappearing between the trees which fringed the cliff edge.

"You spoiled my shot!"

"And a good thing, too!" said Sarah.

Leigh looked so angry that Juliette's courage shrank, but she faced up to him with what assurance she could muster. "I know that you weren't trying to hit that tui, were you, Mr. Leigh?"

He was so astonished that he couldn't help laughing.

"And what is so funny?" she asked gravely.

"You are! I think that all girls are silly, but you must be the silliest of them all." Moving quickly, he reached behind her and tweaked one of her chestnut braids, then dashed away over the rise towards home before she had time to react.

"Leigh, you've forgotten your water buckets!" called Sarah.

"You bring them, since you're so clever," he shouted back.

Sarah sighed with exasperation, but Rose said, "Leigh didn't get as angry as I thought he would. He must like you, Juliette."

"But he said I was silly," said Juliette uncertainly. "And he pulled my hair."

"He got out of the way smartly afterwards, too." Sarah laughed. "Do you remember that time when you slapped

him and you had the penny in your mitten? I rather think
that he has had a healthy respect for you ever since."

"That's nonsense!" said Abby at once. "It's always me
that Leigh pays attention to. He even told me I was pretty
once."

"Perhaps you were pretty . . . once," said Sarah, at
which Abby flounced off indignantly, her water pails
sloshing.

"There is no need to look so thunderstruck, my girl,"
said Maire briskly as she glanced up from the list of trading goods she was checking. "You must realise that, if you
are seen chattering to common soldiers out in a public
place, then you will be considered fast, and nobody respectable will have anything to do with you. And because you
chose to disobey my directives, I think it best that you do
not come to the Governor's little musical soiree."

"But, Mama, you promised . . . once I turned eighteen I
could put up my hair and let down my skirts . . . you promised . . . and my birthday was weeks ago."

"That was before you chose to make a spectacle of yourself. As it is now, I consider it best that you keep out of
sight until anybody who saw you that day will have forgotten who you are." She glanced up again. "Do I make myself clear?"

"Yes, Mama."

"Then off you go. Stephen will be wanting these lists tomorrow. Goodness, he will have to bring more candles; we
never seem to be able to keep up with the demand. And I
must cancel the rope order. For some unfathomable reason
nobody seems to need that. Ah, well . . ."

Abby was waiting out of the line of vision through the
back tent flap. Seeing Jane's miserable expression, she
hastened to offer comfort.

"Never mind if you have to stay here with us. We shall
have a splendid time here all on our own. Just think of it!
We will be able to do whatever we choose."

"Not if Sister Amy is coming to keep us company," said
Jane gloomily. "She is always cross and hates the tiniest
amount of noise."

"Those whiskery warts on her chin!" said Abby. "I can never concentrate on the Gospel; I keep staring at them."

But it was the dumpy little Irish nun, Sarah's friend Sister Moya, who came to sit with them. She arrived on foot from the tiny temporary convent building in the town, carrying a gift in her basket of five melons from the nuns' own garden. Juliette thought it amazing how she always managed to look as immaculate as a black and white plumed bird. Her neat black boots shone like liquorice. Sister Moya had a round, sallow face with the hint of humour behind steel-rimmed glasses; and her breath was scented with oil of peppermint, which she sprinkled frequently on her tongue to ease the torments of bad teeth.

"I dinna understand why it is that I should be so cursed," she had once confided to Maire, whose own teeth were beautifully straight and white. "Sure an' I have a sweet tooth, but so have you, Mrs. Peridot. An' yet you say you've never had a moment's trouble!"

"Ah, but I don't often indulge my sweet tooth. Sweets should be kept as treats for special occasions."

"That I couldn't bear," said Sister Moya frankly. "I love my sweets so dearly that it's not a day I'd be able to exist without them."

So when Maire saw which of the nuns had come she measured out some coarsely grated sugar and set it on a dish, saying, "You may use that, Sister, and no more. Yes, I'm well aware that there will be candies brewing as soon as Mr. Peridot and I have ridden over the hill."

Leigh and Samuel raced with Tippy after the horses; they ran with the wind catching in their lungs and Tippy's excited barks slapping at their ears. They stopped on the edge of the cliff where the path wound down and along to the plateau on which the temporary Government House sat marooned in fern.

Leigh was panting. "I don't understand Uncle Thomas. He's a real man, and yet he's all dressed up like a baron of beef just to be polite to stupid ladies, and he'll have to sit still for hours listening to dreary music. Ugh! I'll not bother with that palaver."

Samuel's breathing was steady because he was so fit

from bush life. He was already strikingly like his father, with the same straw-white hair, tanned skin, and even the beginnings of squint marks which deepened as he took his usual pause before replying.

"Father says that people often have to do all kinds of things they ain't fussed about. I figure that being sociable with ladies is just one of them."

"I'll not," decided Leigh, kicking at the ferns. "Ladies smell sickly sweet and giggle all the time."

"Not Juliette," said Samuel. "She's always kind and she never complains."

"She's not a *lady!*"

"She will be one day," said Samuel, adding slyly, "You might not have to worry about ladies. You might be like Stephen and have them all swarming round like flies over a dead dog." He broke off, disappointed that Leigh did not rise to the bait, but Leigh was standing still, staring out into the harbour where the shapes of two ships were dark grey blots in the dusk.

"Hey, that's the *Sarendee,* and it was leaving her berth earlier, remember?"

Samuel nodded. They had climbed back up the cliff path to sneak the spyglass but Maire was in the tent so they were unable to get it.

"Something must be wrong," continued Leigh. "She should be out past the islands by now. Say, wouldn't it be a pickle if the harbour-master has run her onto a sand bar as he did the *Duchess of Argyle*? And what's that other ship? It looks like the *Lorendee*."

"Could be," said Samuel disinterestedly. "Father was saying he hoped to see Stephen before we go back to the timber camp tomorrow afternoon." He moved towards the cooking shed where Tawa and Mary lay on flax mats in the evening cool, puffing on the clay pipes they could enjoy in uninterrupted luxury since Maire was gone for the evening. "Look at the way Tippy is smooching up to those two!" he exclaimed in disgust. "Anybody would think that he's trying to cadge a puff from them pipes! Come on, Leigh. There's no sand bars there. Stephen says that part of the harbour is as deep as a woman's motives."

* * *

At the moment Stephen was saying a great many things and none of them droll or witty. A half hour before, the two ships had met. Stephen had taken one look at the *Sarendee's* spread of sail and had issued hasty orders to his own crew while running up a signal flag to Captain Corringham. Within minutes both ships had glided to an uneasy halt and, despite the protests of the "common" pilot, Stephen was soon being ferried by gig to the side of the clipper.

Captain Corringham had never seen Stephen so angry.

"I couldn't believe my eyes when I saw those topgallants! The same, exactly the same, as when I inspected them in Sydney. Not a patch on them, not a panel replaced. Tell me, Captain Corringham, are they or are they not the same sails I declared unfit for another long voyage?"

The Captain nodded. He had a tobacco-coloured face with the creases and expression of a gloomy basset hound.

"I suppose the Royals and the skysails are also the same? Why?" Stephen strode over to the foreshrouds and tugged at one of the ropes. "This isn't new. I ordered the ratlines replaced. Every inch of it. This rigging won't stand a gale-force wind and you know it, sir!"

"I'm not happy about it either, Captain Yardley."

"Then why, when I gave you written orders to obtain everything you needed from my yards? When we replaced the big sails I prepared for this and the sails are made and measured. There's plenty of rope fresh from the spinner sitting in the shed all ready to be fitted. So why are you setting out in this sloppy state?"

"I think you might hazard a guess at the reason, sir. All due respect, o' course, but Mrs. Peridot came down herself and looked it over. And when she asked if this rigging would last another normal voyage I had to say, well, yes, so long as the weather was favourable and we didn't get no twenty-footers."

"But you don't allow for favourable conditions. You prepare for the worst ones. You taught me that yourself, years ago when I was your second mate!"

"So I recall, sir. But Mrs. Peridot . . ." He shrugged.

"You might as well tell me what she said. Everything she said. Then you can have Mr. Rough guide you back to the wharf. You'll set out when you're ready. And don't worry about what Mama might say. I'll fill her ears with so many horror stories about storms at sea that she'll not quibble over such matters again. But tell me, Captain. What reason did she give for countermanding the orders? Did she accuse me of profiteering again? If so, I hope you quoted those prices from the Sydney chandlers."

"I did indeed, Captain Yardley; but if you'll pardon me, sir, for interrupting, I think that your bosun is trying to attract your attention." He pointed to the ridge above Government House. Smoke and the flicker of blinking yellow flames were feathering along the hilltop. "Captain Yardley, isn't that your mother's home there? That looks like quite a fire."

Fire was the one thing to be dreaded above all else but, as Thomas said later, the accident could not have been better timed. If the wind had been blowing in the other direction or if the ship had not been there, so close, then a real tragedy could have ensued.

From what they could ascertain, the fire had started when Rose upset the pot of toffee she had been stirring, causing the fire to flare up suddenly. Startled by her shrieks, Juliette had grabbed the pot. But in the process of flinging it away from the cooking shed, she had badly burned her hand. Instead of immediately smothering the pot, everybody had rushed to help Juliette; so by the time they turned their attention to the pot and its burning contents, the flames had rippled along the short dry grass like swarming yellow bees. Before they could do anything the fern had caught ablaze. Quite a considerable area had been consumed by the time the sailors from the *Lorendee* arrived, armed with soaking wet sacks to smack out the flames; but when Thomas and Maire rode up to the scene soon after there was nothing to do but survey the smoking, black-bristled earth and the sight of a distressed Juliette tearfully clinging to Leigh, who was doing his awkward best to comfort her.

"I see," said Maire when Sister Moya tried to explain how the conflagration began. "It is Juliette's rash carelessness we have to thank for this. It's a mercy that all our belongings weren't burnt to a crisp."

"Oh no, Mama," Rose hastened to assure her. "It was my fault, really. I screamed and Juliette rushed to help me. I think that, if she had not done so, then the cookhouse would have surely burned down."

Maire ignored her. "Leigh, come here, please, and help me down. Juliette, will you go to the tent at once. I shall speak with you directly."

That night Juliette slept poorly, troubled as she was by the pain in her bandaged hand and the blame that had been unfairly levelled at her. She had lain awake for a long time breathing the sour smell of smoke that clung to her bedclothes. Outside she could hear Stephen conversing with one of the sailors who was helping him keep watch over the burn in case it should flare up again. His voice lulled her.

Presently the choking scent of scorched fern changed into the syrupy aroma of ripe peaches, and the voices changed rhythm and became footsteps drumming closer and closer over the hard summer ground. The sun was hot on her back. Dizziness swamped her. She wanted to run, but peaches lay so thickly on the ground that there was not a single clear space into which she could tread.

"Olivine, wake up!" said Stephen urgently. "Hush, hush, now. There's no need to cry out. I'm here."

"Stephen? Mr. Stephen?"

"It's me." He scooped her up and carried her past the sleeping girls to the moonlit night outside. Settling her on a tarpaulin-covered crate of household goods, he said, "Well, now, little one, was that another of those nightmares?"

She nodded sleepily against his serge jacket. "But I'm *not* a little one. I'm twelve now."

"Indeed?" In the wash of moonlight she could see his lips twist into a wry smile. "So young and so brave, too."

"Do you think it was my fault, Mr. Stephen?"

"The fire?"

She nodded again. "Aunt Maire blamed me, and when I tried to tell what happened Father got cross and told me not to argue. But I thought Rose was in danger of being burned, you see, so I picked up the pot and threw it away. I realise it was a silly thing to do, but . . ."

With his rough sailor's fingers he tipped her chin up towards him. "It wasn't silly, Juliette. It was brave. An extremely brave act. Instead of running away from danger you looked it right in the face. That takes real courage."

"Father said I should never run away from danger, unless I was absolutely certain I could escape. But today was different. I was afraid that Rose would be hurt. So I wasn't being brave at all, really."

"More than brave." He noticed that she was shivering despite the warm night air so he tucked the blanket around her. "Is that what woke you in such an unhappy mood? Dreams about the fire?"

She answered matter-of-factly. The dreams were becoming a part of her life, harrowing to experience but less frightening to look back on. "It's always the same, Mr. Stephen. I was really terrified when I was dreaming it, but as soon as I heard your voice, I felt safe."

"I'm glad of that." His arm tightened around her thin shoulders. "I'd hate to think of you being unhappy."

"Oh, but I'm not!" she said. "I have so much to be thankful for. Rose and Sarah are wonderful to me, and so is Leigh when he's not away with Aunt Maire."

The hard ripple of jealousy astonished him, but he recognised it at once. Jealous of his sixteen-year-old brother over the attentions of a twelve-year-old child? Impossible! But he had to struggle to keep his tone casual as he asked, "So Leigh is kind to you, is he?"

"He's perfectly charming," she said happily.

And you are a perfect fool, thought Stephen to himself.

Thirteen

Jack Bennington was no taller than Juliette, though he made himself appear larger than life by the subterfuges that diminutive men seem driven to employ: loud voices, thick-soled shoes, tall-crowned hats, and a strongly authoritative manner. He was seated on a hard-backed dining chair in the sitting room of the old Kororareka house, now on its new site next to the store. The five Peridot and Yardley girls clustered demurely on and around the long sofa. Maire sat a little apart in an armchair, as regal as Jack remembered her; and Leigh stood behind his mother, arms behind his back like an army guard, staring openly at the young man who sat awkwardly on a footstool beside Jack. This was Tim Bragg; a thin-faced, sandy, and nondescript young man whom Jack Bennington had introduced as his sister's boy. Jack was discussing him now.

"So things are different out here, hey?" And he clapped the young man on the back, causing him to lurch slightly forward. "So Jack is as good as his master out in this New Zealand. Or should it be *Tim* is as good as his master?"

They all laughed politely, chiming in with Jack Bennington's guffaws. Jane felt sorry for the nephew. He looked decidedly uncomfortable, holding his shapeless felt hat at the chest of his shiny pin-striped suit like a shield to protect himself from his uncle's remarks.

"Did you have a comfortable journey, Mr. Bragg?" asked Jane as she took his cup to pour him a second cup of tea. Her wrists were slender and lace ruffles drooped as she performed the graceful ritual.

"Of course he did!" boomed Mr. Bennington. "I was there to look after him and teach him all the airs and

graces. He knows how to crook his little finger when he
sups and how to kiss a lady's hand. He's going to be my
foreman, he is, and when we've a new one trained he's
going to manage my saddle shop for me. You'd not think it
to look at him, but he can turn leather into poetry with
those hands."

Tim Bragg flushed and ducked his head, and Jane
thought indignantly, Why, he's talking about his nephew
as though he were a horse up for sale!

Sweetly she said, "Are you bonded over to work for your
uncle then, Mr. Bragg?"

Jack Bennington looked startled and Maire was obviously shocked by the impertinent directness of the question but Tim spoke out frankly, saying, "Aye, I'm bound
over for a long time. Cabin passages cost real money and
Uncle Jack here wouldn't let me travel steerage with the
other lads, so I'm bound to work until I can save up the fare
. . . and the interest too, of course. . . ."

Jack interjected quickly, "But you're a good man and
you deserved the best. What does it matter if you are
bonded? You'd not find better wages than what I'm offering."

"Two and sixpence a day is what the going rate is here,"
said Leigh. "The soldiers are all envious. They only get a
shilling."

Jack swallowed, then tried to smile. "Prices are rising
everywhere, aren't they? My, my. But why should we be
talking business when it's such a long time since I saw my
dear friend Mrs. Yardley?"

"Mrs. Peridot."

"Of course! Now doesn't that in itself go to prove that it
has been far too long? My dear, you do look ravishing. If
that bounder Peridot hadn't swept you off your feet I swear
to you that I'd have married you myself the minute my
boot soles slapped down on the dock timbers! We opportun-
ists should always stick together, my dear, don't you
agree?"

Maire had been permitting herself a smile at the touch
of her old friend's compliment but the warmth dropped out
of it at the word "opportunist," and her back lengthened

perceptibly. There was a brief prickly silence which was broken by the clanging of a bell.

"Well, bless my soul! Is that a fire? Not an attack by these here Maoris, is it? I've heard that they are fearsome fellows."

"Nothing like that," said Jane. "It is merely a signal that fresh bread has come out of the ovens at the bakery. Mama, might I please be excused to collect some? We do need fresh at home."

Tim Bragg was on his feet immediately, bowing formally to Maire.

"Might I beg leave of you too, ma'am? I'll be seein' she comes to no harm."

"Certainly," said Maire, but she waved her fingertips to the other girls to indicate that they should follow too.

Jack Bennington was gazing around the room with interest, considering everything he had been told about the history of the house.

"It doesn't seem right for us to be taking this fine dwelling while you folks all cram into a tent," he said. "Surely it should be the other way around?"

Maire did not like to admit that she wanted to supervise every nail and every plank of their new home. "We are tired of life under canvas but we want to treat you well. I want a good job done and what better way to ensure that than to see to your comfort?"

"But if we lived on the site, then you could be here close to your stores . . ."

"Gracious me," said Maire, flicking open a jet-coloured fan. "The emporiums are my little hobby—no more than that. Mr. Brook manages them very well for me, while I spend much of my time socialising. The Governor is a very dear friend, but so are many other of the newcomers. There is an extremely nice class of people here and all the little formalities are properly observed despite the conditions. Can you imagine my silver visiting-card tray in our tent? Well, it is, and from necessity too. . . ."

"Are you sure there isn't more to it than that? Why stay on there when I am perfectly willing to live in the tent?"

Maire fanned her neck, causing the ruffles of black lace

to flutter becomingly. She saw that he was staring at her
with a shrewd expression.

"When we left Kororareka I resolved that my daughters
would come into contact only with young men who are
suitable prospects for them. Here in the town we have the
unfortunate proximity of the military establishment. It is
bad enough that Leigh seeks the company of soldiers, but
he at least knows the difference between a common lout
and an officer and cannot come to much harm. But the
girls . . . one cannot be too rigorous. . . . I hope you understand why I am not anxious to move into this area, even for
a few weeks." She folded the fan with a clack. "No doubt
you are anxious to see the land I bought for you? I am so
pleased with my success at the land auctions. We secured
our house lot, and this piece with the house and shop, the
sites for a further dozen stores, and a large section on the
hillside overlooking town which can be subdivided into
half a dozen house plots. Leigh and Stephen will each have
a fraction of that but you and I can come to an agreement
about the remainder."

"That sounds most suitable," he said, faintly shocked by
the blunt way she was speaking out. He knew she had a
good head for business but to show it so brazenly without
even a hint of disguise seemed most unladylike.

"I think you will agree that I have done well for you,"
she continued. "You will hear many complaints from people who have been unable to buy land at all. The Governor
has set high prices, you see, and has made it unlawful to
deal with the Maori tribes directly."

"If they own the land and we want to buy it, surely it is
practical and sensible to deal directly with them?"

"It is the *law*," she explained as though that reason
could not be argued with. "Personally I agree with it. People used to be able to buy land for ridiculously tiny
amounts . . . axes, muskets, kegs of nails and such things.
You can imagine what riffraff would soon surround us if
such a situation were allowed to continue."

"All the more trade for us, though, hey?" He tugged a
handkerchief out of his fob pocket and mopped his damp
face.

"Had you ever been to Kororareka you would under-

stand perfectly, but let me illustrate what I mean by saying that it is better to have five hundred customers who
are able to pay than five thousand who cannot."

"True, true. So everybody is pressuring the Governor,
hey?"

"Yes, poor man. And him so ill, too. A section of the
settlers—squatters they are, really, for they as yet hold no
land titles—a group of them have banded together to
hound poor Governor Hobson. They attack him in person,
circulate scurrilous pamphlets, and are so bold in their
spite that they even made up a petition calling for his
removal—and then forced him to send it to the Home Government in London! What do you think of that?"

"Terrible!" said Jack Bennington, thinking wistfully of
all the land he might have been able to buy for a few axes
and kegs of nails.

The young people strolled towards the open-sided timber
tower that housed the baker's bell. It stood beside a house
at the far end of the road, near the wall. A young Maori boy
clad in a pair of red knickerbocker trousers swung on the
bell rope. From here they could hear his yelps of laughter
and see the sunshine polishing his bare chest.

Leigh was already across the road and heading for the
hotel, a two-storeyed unpainted structure with a wide verandah stretching out over the footpath. In the shade soldiers tossed dice. A couple of them called to Leigh when
he approached. Juliette heard the shouted greeting and
turned to see where it had come from. A sad feeling pushed
some of the contentment out of her mind, for she had hoped
that Leigh would come to the baker's too.

"The baker's oven is around at the back of the house,"
Jane was saying. "It is a huge clay oven with an iron roof
over the top. We get so much rain here in Auckland town
that there is a danger that the oven might collapse if it
gets too wet, so they made a roof over it to keep it dry."
Gracious, she thought, I'm prattling like Abby when she
gets excited. She began again. "What made you decide to
leave London, Mr. Bragg?"

He laughed, a fresh, healthy sound. Jane liked it.

"Is my question so amusing?"

"I could have wagered the last pound in my pocket that you were going to ask me what I thought of your town."

"You are perfectly correct. I was going to."

He looked at her with a new interest. Most young ladies would have denied such a thing.

"What is your name, Miss Yardley?"

"Jane. Plain Jane."

"Not plain at all."

It was more than a polite refutal and from it she gleaned that he liked her too. Her chin rose a fraction and the corners of her mouth twitched. Abby snickered and Jane pinched her arm.

"You have not answered my question yet, Mr. Bragg."

"It may be tediously dull for the likes of you, livin' in such an excitin' place. My pa and ma was killed in a fire where they worked. A linen factory, it were. Forty-nine folks was killed and a lot of orphans made that day."

"Oh, I am sorry! I should never have asked if I had known."

He smiled reassuringly. "It were a long time ago. Me and me brothers were in the workhouse for years, but when I were fourteen Uncle Jack heard I were a likely lad to work and he got me out. I already knew a fair bit about leather, so he had me apprenticed to a saddler an' I spent me spare time workin' for him, learnin' the carpentry business too."

"What about your brothers? Were they rescued too?"

"They was already left the workhouse. I were the only one there."

They walked on awhile in silence, Tim still looking around with interest. Carriages and open wagons rumbled past. Goats browsed on weeds at the roadside. Tim laughed at a cow with a bell around its neck and was incredulous when Jane explained how cows, goats, and pigs roamed about quite freely and were real pests.

"They can lean against the stoutest wall and make a way through to the vegetable garden. We were all awakened one morning before daylight by an astonishing noise, a loud crunching. Mama put on a wrap and hurried outside to find two cows chewing up our cabbages. Have you ever seen a cabbage with one enormous bite taken out of it, Mr. Bragg?"

"I must confess I ain't."

Jane said suddenly, "Where was your Uncle Jack all those years when you and your brothers were in the workhouse?"

Tim looked uncomfortable. "I'm truly grateful to him for what he's done for me," he said evasively.

Jane nodded. She felt that the question had been answered.

Five months later Fintona was completed, a beautiful house, if a trifle showy. It was far more elegant than Government House next door, which had been sent, prefabricated, and which was reputed to be an exact replica of Napoleon's house at St. Helena. The Peridot home had wide roofs clad with wooden shingles, a peak in the centre and more gently sloped roofs skirting all around to shade the verandahs that bordered the house on all sides and would eventually be trimmed with deep borders of lacy woodwork. The rooms were generous, airy, and cool, but prominent fireplaces would ensure that it was cosy and dry in the wet winters.

"From the harbour this place looks like a Chinese pagoda," said Stephen, stretching out long booted legs to the warmth of a log fire.

Maire's chin raised haughtily. "I fail to see why it should resemble anything Chinese."

"It does, though. Probably the verandahs and the pointed roof. All it needs are ropes of bells and lanterns strung from the corners to be really authentic."

Maire set down the gloves she was mending. "If you do not approve of this house, Stephen, you are under no obligation to stay here. Really, the seamstress' work these days is so shoddy. Only twice these gloves have been worn and already the seams are disintegrating." She glanced sharply at her husband, who was dozing gently on the other side of the fireplace in the wing chair that matched the one Stephen occupied. He looked exhausted but she wanted to wake him so that he could back her up in what she was going to say to Stephen. She tapped her slippered foot on the Turkish carpet and sighed with impatience.

"I gather that you have problems, Mama," said Stephen with polite disinterest.

"Yes, I do," she said swiftly. "I am far from satisfied with the way you are countermanding my orders. The *Lorendee* is your business, but the other two—really, Stephen, you cannot go overriding my instructions the way you are doing. The captains listen to you instead of me as they are bound to, and where does that place me? In a laughable situation with no authority, no voice, and no command over the Richmond Line. Stephen, I do wish that you would look at me when I am talking to you. I have the most distinct feeling that you are not listening to me."

He stared into the fire. "I am listening to you, but I do not agree with what I hear."

"Of course you do not agree! If you did, then I would have no cause to speak to you like this!"

"Mama, you can trust me to run the shipping line in a way that will profit us best in the long run—yes, in the long run. I cannot agree with your policy of short-term profits no matter what the harm done to us or our name . . ."

"Please be specific, Stephen, if you wish to speak against my decisions."

Thomas' eyes opened and he slid a look at Stephen, who was now standing with his back to the fireplace, angrily facing his mother.

"Very well, then, if you want specifics you shall have them," Stephen was saying. "This commission you arranged for the *Sarendee* to transport out a load of Parkhurst prison boys, for example. Have you any idea of the ill feeling that will cause when they disembark? The Treaty of Wantangi specifically prohibits bringing convicts here. There will be a stain on our name through this, Mama."

She picked up the glove and sewed intently. "They are apprentices, Stephen, and all their passages were paid in good money, in advance."

"Not good enough to clear our name, I fear. It is partly because of that business that I have assumed control." His tone modified and he said cajolingly, "Come now, Mama.

What can it matter to you if I take full responsibility for the shipping line? You are so busy here with your two stores, your boardinghouse, so surely this will be simply one less worry for you?"

"I'm sorry, Stephen," she said after a long pause. "I cannot allow it. You have control of your shares and Leigh's but with my thirty per cent and the girls' blocks of ten per cent each I do hold the majority and I insist on my rights."

Stephen stared at her for a long moment, then turned and strode out through the french doors. They slapped shut behind him.

"He is right, you know," said Thomas from the depths of his chair.

"I don't care!" said Maire with such petulance that he could tell she was really upset. "I don't care what people think!"

"Ah, but you do, my dear. The society that means so much to you is made up of people. If you offend them, they will cast you out."

Maire was silent. She stitched stubbornly.

"I don't mind, you know," said Thomas. "I care nothing for balls and parties, and I have no compulsion to see Abigail and Juliette married off to some ne'er-do-well ninth son of an obscure Duke. It would not matter to me if we were snubbed by this snobbish crowd you hold so dear. I have a satisfying life with my workmen and the visits to the Waitemata and Waikato tribes for trading."

"You are almost a Maori yourself in some ways," said Maire coldly. She was still crushed by the helpless anger of one who knows she is in the wrong and is unable to manoeuvre herself out of the corner.

"I know I am," said Thomas mildly. "The Governor said so when I visited his sickbed. He seemed to think it a quality of great value. I cannot imagine why."

Stephen sat on the verandah steps looking up at Juliette, who was perched on the top step, sunflower gingham skirts spread over her knees, a brown felt jacket laced at the neck against the cold, and a brown felt bonnet with gold ribbons. Stephen thought she looked almost as enchanting as Clarissa, who sat in her lap in a foam of yellow silk and lace.

"Do look at the lorgnette pouch I made for Clarissa. See, it hangs at her waist just as Aunt Maire's does."

"So it does. That's very clever; you embroidered it beautifully. And what do you do all day, Miss Olivine, while I am away at sea?"

"I help Magree, the new cook. She's funny, I can't understand her Irish accent, but she teaches me to bake and stew and make preserves and puddings. I hope she stays longer than all the other servants do. Did you enjoy that chocolate and hazlenut pudding which we had for dessert last night? I made that."

"Is that why you served it?" He noticed that the bows on her laced-up shoes were flopping undone, so he loosened the cords and retied them for her as she replied.

"I often wait on the table. So does Abby. It was my turn last night. It's quite fun, and so is cooking, but I do hate the messy jobs, the vegetables, plucking hens and doing dishes. When I'm doing those I try to think of something else."

"What about your lessons?"

"Sister Moya coached us for our first communion but there have been no lessons since. Aunt Maire says it's not necessary. I wish there were, because I enjoyed lessons and there is so much I don't know that I feel positively ignorant. But Abby thinks it is lovely not having to worry about reading or writing, so she is happy, at least." She pulled a little face and then said, "Oh dear, I honestly intended to try and amuse you, Mr. Stephen, and I am having no success at all, am I? You came out here with such an angry face that I was at once determined to try to cheer you up."

"Did I look so very angry?"

"If the sky were as black I would know that we were in for a terrible storm." She clapped her hands. "There! You did smile."

"Of course." He had smiled to oblige her but inwardly he seethed more angrily against his mother. On previous visits he had noticed that Maire cared nothing for her stepchildren. She was naturally undemonstrative—he could

forgive that. However, to cheat them out of an education
and to have them working about the house as unpaid servants was despicable. He resolved to discuss the matter
with Thomas before the *Lorendee* sailed with tomorrow's
tide.

A door slammed noisily on the verandah. Juliette looked
up to see Leigh standing behind her holding a bridle

"Come and join us, Leigh," she said.

Leigh shrugged and said scornfully, "And play with
dolls? No, thank you. Dolls are babyish."

"We're not playing with dolls. We're talking."

But Leigh took no notice, he simply strode away swinging the brass and leather bridle as though she had not spoken.

Stephen saw her bright expression fade and thought,
She still has that idiotic crush on him. The realisation
gave him a small stab of pain; suddenly he experienced an
overwhelming and totally impractical desire to shield her
from all and any kind of hurt. Her air of fragility disturbed
him.

Thomas had few conflicts with his wife. He was clear
sighted enough to see her for what she was and he had a
far more accurate picture of her than the one Stephen
viewed through the angry haze of thwarted ambitions.
With patient courtesy he listened to Stephen's concerned
comments about the children, then explained that the
girls would have finished their education anyway by this
time and that they would have had to work much harder at
domestic chores in their old life and even at the Mission.
Stephen protested that the family was well to do, the girls
had a right to something better; but when he finally gave
up it was with the distinct feeling that he and Thomas had
been speaking different languages. In a sense they were.
Stephen had been raised with the ideals of ladies and gentlemen, common folk and servants, but Thomas saw nothing demeaning about honest toil. On the contrary, he
thought that cooperative effort was one of the finest princi-
ples in life. Stephen's heart beat to the English word but
the voice in Thomas' mind was Maori.

Thomas was speaking Maori now, calling first to one

friend, then to another, to somebody's brother and someone else's cousin. He knew them all by sight but the names
were too many to hope to remember. He and Maire were
sitting soberly in their high-wheeled buggy, a vehicle that
carted goods from ship to shore and that they used whenever it could traverse the path they had to travel. At the
moment it was stopped at the side of the road outside the
green, white-fenced burial ground. The single horse had
black bows on its harness and a black ribbon around its
nose. It kept shaking its head to dislodge the ribbon, and
its mane fluttered in the breeze.

Maire sat perfectly still, her features muted behind the
swathe of black veil. Beside her Thomas was calling out
warm greetings, leaning out of the buggy to rub noses in
the Maori kiss with especially dear friends. Even when the
buggy rocked as some young scamp climbed up to hug
Thomas, she barely noticed. Her heart was bleak, her
mind empty. The Maori women flowed past and on into the
cemetery, following the flag-draped coffin. All the women
wore white-spangled wreaths of clematis in their hair. The
men, following, carried tins and sticks, which they beat in
a slow, maddening pulse, or muskets, which they waved
above their heads. Some of the pakeha mourners looked
apprehensively at the size of the vast, swelling crowd and
at the violence implicit in musket waving. But Maire
didn't see a single weeping face or hear a moment of
wailing. She was numb.

The Governor's death was blamed on many things.
Some blamed a servant who had inadvertently given him
the wrong medicine to drink. Maire knew what was at root
to blame. Governor Hobson had been harassed, tormented,
ill used, and libelled by many of the people who had the
gall to openly attend his funeral service and to pretend
grief. Maire had almost left the church in disgust, which
would have made the special dispensation she had received to attend a Protestant ceremony unnecessary. But
whatever the reason for his death, one thing was certain.
For the time, at least, their social gaiety was suspended.
The deputy Governor loathed Maire and made no secret of
it. He had gone so far as to ask Governor Hobson if they
could not raise the tone of gatherings by excluding trades-

people; he had come right out with this while she and the Governor were enjoying a pleasant tête-à-tête at a late afternoon garden party. She had ignored the jibe and had snubbed the nasty man at every opportunity, especially when she floated past on the Governor's arm. The Governor was her entree into everything worth going to—hers, Jane's, and soon Rose's and Sarah's. Already Jane was attracting some gratifying attention from some interesting quarters. Nothing to hold one's breath about yet, but the potential was definitely there for an excellent match.

And now the Governor was dead.

Fourteen

"It's not right, I say," said Jack Bennington, who was sharing news and letters from England with the Peridots. "That German Prince is far too cocky, too big for his boots by far. What he is doing is degrading the throne."

"I will not allow it," chided Maire. "You are not to speak out against the Queen or against her dear Albert. They have done us the greatest service and we should be so grateful that no critical thoughts can find room in our minds."

"Which favour is this, my dear?" Thomas handed her a whisky and took Jack's glass to be refilled.

"Why, I should have thought that would have been obvious. The Queen and her Prince have delivered us from this insufferable deputy Governor and sent us a real one. A favour worth toasting, don't you agree?"

"Wait and see," warned Thomas gently. "The new Governor's views may be similar to the ones we have suffered under this past year. Religious and class prejudices are not exclusive to the few."

Jack Bennington had his back to them. While he sipped at his drink he studied their tree, an uprooted young rimu by the looks of it, gussied and tinselled to the point of grotesqueness after the ugly German manner. When Windsor Palace Christmases and the popular new custom of decorated trees were described in the press there was nothing for it but that Auckland must have them too.

"I see you are admiring our Christmas tree," said Maire. "Isn't it beautiful?"

Thankfully he was saved from answering by Abby, who dashed in with her face alive with excitement and her bon-

net becomingly awry. She clung to Thomas' arm and
tugged him towards the door.

"Do come outside, Father. And you too, Mr. Bennington.
There is an enormous bonfire outside the barracks wall. It
looks as though they have a man burning to death on the
very top of it. Do come and see it!"

"Might that be that Parkhurst boy that nobody was
game to flog?" said Jack.

"That poor lad was wrongly accused," said Maire,
who was sensitive to any references to the controversial
youths. "Those boys were a hand-picked group of fine lads
despite what ill-informed people might have said about
them. Mind you, we have had such a magnificent trade in
locks, bolts, and window bars since they arrived that we
really should not complain."

"Do come and look, Father!"

She gets worse each year, thought Maire, regarding
Abby with distaste. It did not escape her notice that Jack,
too, was gazing fondly at the lively, pleading face. She was
pretty, there was no denying that, but so pushy, so strident, and so demandingly selfish that her mere presence
made Maire's nerves jangle. What a pity she was too
young to be married off.

The girls leaned over the verandah rail, gazing out
through the curdling dusk. Though it was two promontories away, the bonfire raged so hotly that the flames burnished their faces with orange light.

Thomas stared at the distant scene. Shouts, yahoos, and
pistol shots slid across the water. Great leaping flames,
black figures packed tightly back by the intense heat,
madness.

"It's an effigy of our Acting Governor!" cried Jack in delight. "Look at it—the frock coat, the top hat!"

"That's who it will be, all right," said Thomas.

"A toast to the end of his stay in office," suggested
Maire. "And a toast to our re-entry into society."

In many ways the time of virtual exile for the tradespeople had been advantageous. Instinctively they had banded together into a substrata of Auckland town society,
forming a strong bond. This bond was helping them

weather out a small but sharp depression the young colony
was suffering. The Peridots felt no ill effects from the trade
decline that sent many smaller traders bankrupt. Thomas'
net of contacts spread so widely that, if the timber price
dropped, the flax deals compensated, and if the price for
rope was poor at the moment, he could call on tribes to provide extra vegetables or dried fish for the lucrative Sydney
market. Meanwhile the three Peridot stores flourished;
some commented bitterly that their success actually
caused the death of   ny competitive shops. Maire's reply, when she bothered to say anything, was that they
were able to offer goods at the lowest prices because of the
shipping line—if it was a crime to offer people bargains,
then that was news to her. The customers never complained.

Auckland was expanding like a rising loaf. The Richmond Line was so busy bringing loads of immigrants and
goods that often Stephen had no time to come ashore,
much to the disappointment of the young ladies who invented excuses to visit the Yardley girls whenever the
Lorendee was in harbour. Jack Bennington's team of car-
penters worked long hours Mondays to Saturdays building
houses to cope with the never ending demand. Often new
settlers had to camp in the courthouse or town hall until
somewhere could be found for them; and on rare occasions
when the thick-walled gaol was empty, that was pressed
into use as a hostel too, much to the amusement of the children, who peered through the barred windows and took
turns at pretending to be in the stocks that stood ready for
drunks in the street out the back. The new settlers all wore
a bemused look for the first few weeks; their introduction
to the new land began when Mr. Rough, the harbourmaster, donned his white gloves and climbed aboard their ship
to guide them into safe anchorage, and ended with them
sitting dazed on their heaped possessions in cramped, temporary accommodations. Juliette met dozens of newcomers
in the course of her work as a counter girl in the main emporium and soon learned to paste a bright smile over her
irritation as she forced herself to listen to the same repeated complaints.

"Eee! The flies 'ere are summat terrible! No sooner yer get meat home an' it's swarmin' maggots."

"I put a flour dough all around my meat ter keep it from the flies, an' mice nibbled it away in the night. Bold as brass, they were."

"Have yer got any spiced sausage? Me family are so sick o' pork they say they'll throw it at me if I give it ter them again. That much? Ee! I think we'll stick ter plain pork an' like it—at least the price is right."

"Pork, pork, pork! Never thought I'd ever say I were sick to me stomach of the stuff. Back home it were a luxury, but oh, what I'd give now fer a nice piece o' good roast beef."

But worst of all were the remarks from the Maori haters.

"Me 'ubby got slapped inter gaol last night," said a fat woman whose face shone with indignation. "Mebbe he did have one or two pots o' ale too many, an' mebbe he does turn a mite quarrelsome when he's in 'is cups, but 'e were dragged off ter gaol by a nigger! Now, I tell you," and she waved a grimy gloved finger under Juliette's nose, "I tell you that we didn't sail right round the world ter be molested by no black, smelly niggers!"

"Do you mean Maoris, madam?" asked Juliette, forcing politeness.

"I mean niggers! Nasty, smelly things they are! What I want ter know is, why are they allowed ter roam about as though they own the place? They ought ter be rounded up an' driven back inter the hills, right away from us decent folks!"

Juliette's feet hurt. "Madam, they do own the place," she said. "This is their country and we should be grateful that they permit us the use of some of it."

"What? Us be grateful to those dirty, uneducated, ignorant niggers? Yer must be mad, child!"

Juliette's temper snapped. "Madam," she said evenly, "I think you should know that there are thousands of Maoris here in Auckland town who can read and write. They are so keen to learn that they come here pleading for employment simply in return for education. Have you ever felt like that? Can you read and write?" The last thrust was deliberate. This customer could only recognise products she had used before and had asked Juliette to tell her what several other clearly marked items were. It was obvious that the woman was completely illiterate.

"The cheek of it!" The fat woman snatched her purchases from the counter and wheeled around in a quiver of rage. She almost knocked over Maire, who had just entered, the hem of her black riding costume looped over one wrist, her riding crop under her arm as she began stripping off her long leather gloves. The bump took her quite by surprise.

"I do beg your pardon," she said, then, lifting her veil, asked, "I do hope that nothing in this establishment has upset you. . . ."

"Upset? That ain't the half of it! That uppity young wench yer got serving there! She don't know 'er place an' that's the truth of it! Cheek o' the devil, she has!"

Maire looked faintly but genuinely shocked. Her eyes flicked a cold, brief glance in Juliette's direction.

"Are you accusing one of my assistants of insolence?"

"Call it any fancy name yer like, but I call it common cheek, takin' the side o' them dirty niggers against a respectable Englishwoman!"

Behind the counter cowered two of the young Maori people who worked in the store, dusting shelves and making deliveries of grocery packages that were too heavy for the ladies to carry home by themselves. They were only vaguely aware of what this fuss was about. In Auckland town it was taken for granted that the Maoris and settlers shared a friendly, loose relationship, each helping the other and both gaining in the process. The word "nigger" was still an unfamiliar one.

Jane opened the music-room door. "Do any of you know where Leigh might be, please? Mama is looking for him and she is distinctly annoyed. He promised that he would be home for dinner."

"I'm sorry, but I have not seen him," said Rose.

"No doubt he is amusing himself with the soldiers at the Rising Sun again. Is that not where he usually is?" Sarah held her breath as she carefully placed another card on top of the tower. "There! I was certain that would topple them but the structure still stands as firm as a Scotsman's jaw. Your turn, Sister Moya."

"Perhaps you'll be telling me what it is that young Leigh does in such a place," asked the nun as she considered her move.

Sarah propped her elbows on the table. "Gambling, I think. I do know that whenever Stephen comes home Leigh asks him for money. He's obliged to give it to him against Leigh's share dividends."

"Gives him money for gambling?"

"He has to. The money is his by right. Leigh wouldn't get a penny of Stephen's own money. All he cares about is his ship and he'd not sacrifice a plank of the one he's planning to buy, no matter how desperately Leigh pleaded."

"Is Mrs. Peridot knowing where he's spending his time? And is it ale he's supping there with his soldier friends?"

"Don't worry. Mama isn't stupid and she would guess if he had been drinking, for she always bids him to kiss her when he comes in. . . ."

"What Rose is saying in her genteel way is that Mama sniffs at his breath," put in Sarah with a laugh. "If she discovered he had been drinking ale she would give him a terrible whipping."

"Mama has never given Leigh a whipping," said Rose, signalling with her eyes toward Juliette's bent head. A little frown emphasised that further discussions about whippings might be tactless.

Juliette glanced up, eyes still red from weeping. "I do hope that Leigh is all right. There have been so many knock-down-and-grab attacks lately by these poor unemployed newcomers that it isn't safe to be out so late."

"He is big enough and ugly enough to look after himself," said Sarah.

"He is *not* ugly."

"Anybody might be forgiven for suspecting that you are secretly in love with him," said Sarah, but she promptly amended that by saying, "No, you cannot be. Jane hints constantly that she is in love and she acts as though she had a mysterious stomach-ache."

"Jane has always been 'romantic.' "

"It's a fine, devout young lady she is," said Sister Moya.
"And while we're speaking of devout young ladies, I'm
wondering about those Bible readings of yours for the
church tea on Saturday. The Bishop himself said to me
that he's looking forward to hearing them."

This was a subject Sarah wished to avoid, so she adroitly
changed it. "We are looking forward to the tea too. Jane
has a new lemon-coloured dress to match her disposition.
Mama had it made to impress that young man who calls
here almost every day—the one who looks like a hen."

Sister Moya threw back her head to laugh and the lamplight turned her lenses into two flat pebbles.

"Well, he *does* look like a hen!"

"Do you mean the Honourable Simon Whytnorth?"

"Yes, Rose. Think about his beaky nose and the way his
Adam's apple bobs about like a hen's wattle. I must point
out the likeness to Jane."

"You *are* mean!" But Rose laughed too.

"Do you think she loves him, Sister?"

"If it's in love she is, then it might just as well be with
him. But it's not me you should be asking about love."

Juliette said nothing. Since Sarah's wild accusation she
had been still and thoughtful. Was Sarah right? Could it
be that she was in love with Leigh?

In Auckland society people had to make their own fun,
so any excuse was seized upon for celebration. The arrival
of Governor FitzRoy provided a more valid excuse than
many. Wags said that the citizens of New Zealand were
temperamentally unable to find good in their Governors,
and this was a good thing because they derived as much
pleasure from farewelling an unpopular Governor as they
did from greeting a yet untried one.

The main public welcoming festivity was a race day at
Epsom Race Park. Horse racing was now such a passion in
Auckland town that there were two such parks (yet only
half the children of the town had schools to attend). At
Epsom there were avenues of imported flowering cherry
trees and two large, vast-roofed grandstands. Flower beds
bright with petunias ringed a white and gold band rotunda
where the brass band of the 80th played during intermis-
sions

After today's races there was to be a special cold colla-
tion and champagne dinner to which the entire Peridot
family had been invited. An honour indeed, for only five
hundred invitations had been issued and many aspiring
society couples were nursing trampled feelings.

"This is our chance to make a truly memorable impression of grace and dignity," said Maire, handing Samuel a
brand-new suit of clothes to try. "Come now, go and put
them on. The size was taken from your working clothes, so
they should be an excellent fit."

"Do I have to go?" he asked his father.

"Becoming a gentleman is not something that happens
naturally," Maire answered.

Samuel's face plainly said that he cared nothing for the
idea of becoming a gentleman. Thomas laughed and rum-
pled the thick blond hair.

"Do as your Aunt Maire says and see if you can't steal
more hearts than Stephen!"

The girls were uniformly dressed in cream lace dresses
with ruffled sleeves and gathered skirts that draped softly
to the ankle, showing cream silk stockings and cream-
coloured shoes. Cream or white were the only suitable colours for young ladies "on show," insisted Maire.

"It is extremely important to lodge the correct first impression in young gentlemen's minds."

"And if we are all dressed in uniform it is easy for Mama
to see us in the crowd," whispered Sarah, adding in a normal tone, "It would matter not a scrap what colour I was
dressed in, Mama, for I am quite resolved on becoming a
nun, like Sister Moya."

Maire pretended not to hear.

Sarah's ambition puzzled Juliette, especially when she
saw the two together in earnest conversation: beautiful
lively Sarah and the dumpy, round-faced nun. Rose, with
her gentle manner and ruined face, would be better in a
cloistered life than the entrancing Sarah. Sarah was the
one to attract all the admiring stares whenever they were
out. But Rose was the one who spoke longingly of being
married and having children of her own. It was so unfair
that one's outer shell was so important, thought Juliette.
It seemed that all the glorious prizes in life were awarded

to those with the most beautiful faces and the most contrived outward charm.

Like Abby, who was now a strikingly beautiful young woman. Her hair had mellowed to the colour of sugar syrup and her skin glowed with health. She was tall, slender-waisted, but with a short neck and chubbiness of shoulders and arms that hinted of ample proportions in later life. Jane had coached her well in the arts of flirting. There wasn't a trick with the twirl of a parasol or the flutter of dark gold eyelashes that she could not employ to coax someone into giving her her own way. Tomorrow was to be her fifteenth birthday, and Thomas had been furnished with a long list of suitable gifts. Abby was no fool and had discovered long ago that the more she asked for the more she was likely to receive.

The girls were in the morning room trimming their cream satin bonnets with velvet ribbons of different colours, Maire's one concession to individuality. The crunch of carriage wheels and Tippy's frantic barking could be heard from the driveway. Presently Tawa tapped at the morning-room door and looked in.

"Mr. Bennington has arrived."

"Come in!" called Jane disinterestedly, but Abby was already alert with interest and opened the door herself to greet him. He entered bearing a large striped box which he ceremoniously set on one corner of the cluttered occasional table. "Just stopped by to offer some of you a ride to the races in my new carriage. Got delivery of it yesterday and it rides like a dream. But you shall soon decide that for yourselves, hey?"

"That is most kind of you, Mr. Bennington," said Abby, eyeing the package.

"Should be a good day today. Two of my best horses running to win. Miss Winsome should beat all the others in her line-up, too, if I say so myself. It was a lucky thing, naming her after the most winsome lassie I know, hey?" and he winked at Abby.

Juliette watched scornfully. She thought Jack Bennington loud and vulgar. Maire liked him and Stephen and Father both thought him amusing company. There was ways laughter at the dining table whenever he stayed for supper.

Maire greeted him pleasantly now as she swept in, gowned in a dark grey silk and a grey silk bonnet with a curl of white feathers around the crown. Juliette stared at her: she had never seen her stepmother in any colour but black before. The grey made her look no less elegant or handsome, but softer, somehow.

"Thank you, Mr. Bennington," she was saying with a smile. "Yes, our Governor is the reason for such celebration that I thought a personal gesture might not go amiss. And what have you there?"

"With your permission, a birthday gift for Abigail."

A touch of tartness crept in as she said, "How did you know it was the child's birthday?" She noted that Abby had at least the grace to blush. "Very well, but I hope that you have not been too extravagant."

The string came off the box in a trice, and out came the most beautiful sky-blue silk bonnet Juliette had ever seen. It was tiny, a mere confection, but decorated all over with blue flowers made of sateen and edged with a trim of dark green silk leaves.

"It's gorgeous!" exclaimed Abby.

"And there's a cape in there to match," said Jack expansively. "We can't have those pretty shoulders getting freckled now, can we?"

"Mr. Bennington, how can I thank you?"

"You will bring me good fortune, I know," beamed Jack with pleasure. "Now, are we all ready to go?"

"Come with me, Jane," said Maire. "You will ride with us. Now don't forget those parasols, girls. The sun is hot today."

They rode with the top down, keeping a smart pace ahead of the Peridots' fashionable buggy. Jack and Thomas drove, flicking at the horses to urge them along. The men were close in age and there was a good-natured rivalry between them.

The race park was thronged with what must surely be the entire population of Auckland town. It was late morning, and already hundreds of small groups were settled in premier positions on the sunny slopes ready to watch the arrival of the Governor and his procession around the track. A woman with a cluster of youngsters around her doled out a favourite treat to her brood—chunks of bread dipped in melted pork fat. Two Maori girls sold lemons and apples at the gate, and all around the split-rail fence other goods were for sale: pies, sandwiches, chunks of white cheese, slices of roast pork, and apples that had been dipped in crunchy yellow toffee. Everybody stared at Jack Bennington, with his black coat, bright gold shirt, and black and white striped cravat. He beamed and nodded to the familiar cries of "Hey there, Flash Jack!" which greeted him at every revolution of the wagon wheels.

Thomas, in the following buggy, was being hailed by the Maoris, some in blankets, some in English dress, which looked odd with tattooed faces; but most of the Maoris they saw were concentrating on another matter and did not notice the Peridots' buggy pass by. A fresh copy of the free publication, the *Maori Messenger*, had been printed this morning to coincide with the influx of natives. In groups they pored over the paper, taking turns reading the news items aloud, then venturing opinions of what had happened, why it had happened, and what should be done about it. Of particular interest were items about other Maoris. Reports of drunkenness or other unlawful behaviour were a cause for deep shame. The Waitemata Maoris prided themselves on their good citizenship.

In the centre of the track below the largest grandstand the regimental band of the 80th played stirring English folk songs. The girls hummed the tunes as they gazed about with interest. There were many new faces here today; Auckland town was growing so fast that it was difficult to keep up with all the new arrivals. Jack Bennington's hat was being constantly doffed but he had time to toss a few remarks over his shoulder at the girls behind him, pointing out the horse pens where Miss Winsome and his other horse, Coalblack, shared stalls with the collection of other hopefuls, including a dozen horses recently imported from Chile.

"They're calling one of the races the Valparaiso Stakes in their honour," he told them. "Some say they've got real steam legs and can go like the furies themselves, but they'll have to be something special to outdo that beauty of mine!"

"Will there be a race for the Maoris and their horses to-day, do you think?" asked Juliette.

"Always is. The last race is always for the darkies, hey? I rather think that today the prize is to be something by way of a joke . . . a fifty-pound loaf of bread to be shared with the whole tribe. That and the money, of course."

"We must make certain that we are close by when Mrs. FitzRoy is called upon to present that prize," said Sarah. "Oh, look! There she is, and she teased me that the Bishop would not let her come. Sister Moya! Here we are!"

They descended in a scramble of bobbing parasols and flashing cream shoes. Maori boys led the carriage away and Jack held out his arm for Abby.

"Now, my pretty lassie, let us promenade and let them all see how bonny you are, hey?"

The Governor and his wife rode majestically around the track in an open coach pulled by two white horses with jingling brass harnesses. Everybody cheered and waved handkerchiefs and even the strings of colourful bunting fluttered obligingly.

Jane sat at a small table with Thomas, Maire, and the Honourable Simon Whytnorth. He looked even less appetising to her now that she had heard Sarah laughing about his unfortunate profile. As often as she could she turned her head away, her eyes searching the crowd. Tim had said that he would try to come but his Uncle Jack wanted some cupboards finished and as he still owed Uncle Jack six pounds of the fare money . . . Bother Jack Bennington, she thought angrily. Bother them all!

"I say there, Miss Yardley," the Honourable Simon said in a hurt voice. "I do believe that you did not hear my joke!"

Under the table, Maire's toe struck warningly against her ankle. Yes, Mama, she thought wearily.

Leigh had escaped his mother's eye, something he did at every opportunity. He was in the shade of the grandstand, playing at rolling dice with some of his soldier friends, when the girls drifted along.

"Where's your granddad?" he called to Abby.

"*Mr. Bennington* is readying one of his horses for the next race," she told him.

At the sound of her voice the soldiers looked up, and Leigh could see how their eyes lit up in appreciation. Leigh sought instantly to make an impression on them. He strolled out until he blocked Abby's way, then said loudly, "Here is a little something for your birthday," and with that gave her a kiss full on the lips. The soldiers clapped and whistled. Abby blushed becomingly and pushed Leigh in the chest.

"Don't you be quizzing me, for I'll have none of your sauce!" she said. Leigh laughed.

I don't care, thought Juliette, who had seen and heard it all. I don't care about the gifts, because I'd rather go without a bonnet at all than have to simper up to Mr. Bennington to get one. And I'd rather not have gifts from Father than be openly begging for them. And Leigh only kissed her to amuse the soldiers. I know he did, and what kind of reason is that? I don't care! She raised her chin and squared her shoulders but hurt shone bright in her eyes.

Jane's neck was beginning to feel stiff from constantly twisting to speak first to one and then the other of the Bellwood girls. One of them was married and the other engaged, both to junior Government officials. It was the only way to achieve any kind of security in these uncertain times, they told Jane seriously. Maire was openly eavesdropping and permitted herself a smile. In one week of trading the Peridots could buy any Government official for the equivalent of his whole year's wages.

"Why are times uncertain?" asked Jane.

"Don't you know that there is frightening talk of war up in Kororareka? Mama and Papa are so alarmed that they are making arrangements to come to Auckland."

Maire's eyebrows rose.

"And what is this talk of war?" She beckoned to

Thomas, who was a few yards away talking to the Governor's secretary.

"It is Mr. Hone Heke," said Susannah Bellwood. "He is making so many threats against the Government and against the settlers that it is said even the people at the Mission are beginning to feel quite nervous."

Thomas said, "Please don't be too alarmed by anything he does, ladies. He is a blustering bully and a rascal, but no more than that."

"Mr. Peridot, he chopped down the flagpole!" said Susannah.

"He did what?"

"Chopped down the flagpole, the one that stands on the hill overlooking the harbour. The Bishop said that it was because he thought it was magical, and that it was stopping all the ships from coming in. The Maoris up in the Bay of Islands are very angry that there is no trade with the whaling ships as there used to be, and Hone Heke wants the Government to put everything back the way it was before the treaty."

"When did this happen?"

"Two days ago. Our ship left the same afternoon that it happened. It caused such a stir up there!"

"I can imagine," said Maire.

"It is such a worry, with Mama and Papa still left there, with such a threat of danger hanging over their poor heads. If only something could be done!"

Thomas rubbed at his sandpapery jaw. He didn't like the sound of this news, but then Heke had a right to feel aggrieved after doing all he could to see that the treaty was signed. But war? Heke was unpredictable but Thomas doubted that he would want to take on Her Majesty's forces in open confrontation. No, he'd not be that stupid.

"Set your minds at rest," he said reassuringly. "Hone Heke is getting rid of some anger and frustration with a session of wholesome, healthy exercise."

"I doubt that the Governor will see it that way!" observed Maire.

"And what will the Governor see?" asked the Honourable Simon, returning with champagne glasses of fruit cup for Jane and Maire.

"Nothing," said Jane. She was so bored that her jaw ached from the strain of not yawning.

Juliette stood under the rose arbour near the clifftop in the growing dusk. Behind her moths drummed on the lighted window where Rose and Sarah tinkled out a galloping duet on the piano, and far below sighed the sound of the sea.

She turned her head towards the spangled lights of the town when a soft laugh came to her ears. Curious, she strained her eyes until she found the source of the noise. It was Jane, twenty yards away beyond the young hydrangea bushes. Standing very close to her was someone she recognised as young Tim Bragg. They spoke in low voices only punctuated occasionally with more smothered laughter.

Juliette felt as though she were spying. She was going inside when suddenly Jane put her hand on Tim's shoulder. There was something desperate about the gesture that struck a chord in Juliette's mind and riveted her attention. Tim captured the hand in both of his, and then, while Juliette held her breath, he turned it over and undid the pearl buttons at her wrist. Slowly he peeled the glove from Jane's hand and pressed a kiss into her palm. It was the most sensual thing that Juliette could imagine. Trembling, she crossed her hands at her throat and closed her eyes.

A rustling noise made them open again. Jane was hurrying past across the lawn. Through a wreath of rose leaves Juliette saw that one gloved hand held the bonnet and the other, naked, was pressed into a fold of her skirt. She did not glance in Juliette's direction but walked quickly up towards the house and stepped silently onto the verandah.

Juliette followed, her mind brimming with the romance of what she had witnessed. She climbed the verandah steps and stood for a moment pressing her cheek against the white painted post.

This time she was startled by the creak of the floor boards. Abby stood in front of her, furious.

"You sneaking . . . sneaking . . ." She gave up, unable

to find names bad enough to call her sister. "How *dare* you sneak after Jane, spying on her, watching when she is having a private conversation with a friend? How dare you! What a low, sneaking creature you are!"

For a long moment Juliette was sure that Abby was going to slap her, but Abby turned with a sudden movement of unutterable disgust and strode off into the darkness. The relief of not being hit was almost as sudden and painful as the blow would have been.

Because she was still shaking when she went to bed, Juliette counted her rosary beads three times, concentrating fiercely on the prayers as she whispered them. Perhaps these holy incantations could wipe her mind so clean of evil that the dreams would not return. But again she woke in the still hours of darkness. The footsteps continued to haunt her.

Fifteen

The morning sky was a pale dove grey brushed with fluffs of the same peach as Jane's new feather boa. The silver harbour was scored by threads of wakes that followed the red canoes sliding towards the beach from Fintona. Across the harbour the land was still sleeping, a cluster of silent humps.

Jane, Stephen, and Juliette stood together on the verandah. They had risen early for various reasons: Jane because she was troubled, Stephen because the stillness of land always disturbed his rest, and Juliette because she was so excited. Today was the day of the great Maori feast and Father had promised to take everybody who wanted to go.

"There must be a thousand of them down there already," said Jane nervously.

Stephen held out a hand to her. "Come. Let's go on down the cliff path and see what is going on there."

She drew back instinctively. "Go in amongst all those Maoris? Never!"

"They won't hurt you, will they, Juliette? Juliette should know how safe it is."

"Should she?" said Jane in a voice that spoke volumes. Jane subscribed to the theory that it was the Maoris from Te Pahi's pa who killed Evangeline and the children.

Juliette twirled around on her tiptoes. A lemon-coloured feather boa trailed along her outstretched arms and then down from her fingertips, brushing the floor.

"These are beautiful, Stephen! It was so good of you to bring them home for us."

"They were all the style in Sydney, and I can't have my

girls out of fashion now, can I? What about you, then, Juliette? Will you come down to the beach with me?"

"I would love to! Do come with us, Jane. It will be so interesting down there, and so many things to see!"

"I'm sorry, both of you. I am well used to Mary and Tawa, but with that frightening talk about Hone Heke, and that dreadful massacre in the South Island, people are saying that these Maoris are only pretending to be having a friendly party. Why have it here, Stephen? Why have it right in amongst us if they are only planning something peaceful?"

"Are you really upset about this?" He stared at her quizzically. "But you are! Oh, Jane dear . . ." and he put his arms about her, drawing her head down to his shoulder. "Truly it isn't serious. Thomas knows the Maoris and he is planning to attend. So is the Governor and who knows who else! And our friend 'Flash Jack' himself . . . and he is hardly a Maori sympathiser. If he is going, can't you please allow yourself to be persuaded that we are safe and will all be alive and well this evening?"

Jane fished for a handkerchief from her sleeve and blew her nose. "It's not only that, Stephen."

Juliette had ceased her twirling and dancing, her eyes growing large with compassion. Now she wondered if there had been a lovers' quarrel of the type described in Abby's and Jane's beloved penny novelettes.

"Can you tell me about it?" asked Stephen gently.

Juliette said, "I shall wait over by the top of the path for you, Stephen." Wrapping the boa around her neck and flinging one end extravagantly over her shoulder, she strode out over the damp grass.

Jane looked up at her brother.

"Can I do something to help you?" he asked her.

"Yes, you can, Stephen, and I pray you will. I want you to buy my shares in the Richmond Line. It's important, Stephen!" She hurried on, speaking rapidly in a voice so low that he had to bend his head to catch the words. "Tim Bragg and I love each other . . . we really do . . . and I want to marry him but he is so very poor. Jack Bennington is only paying him half of what he could get elsewhere and he must stay and work for him until he has paid back all the money for his passage out. If we had a hundred pounds or so we could buy a house and some land and Tim could start up his own business of saddle making. There is almost no competition and I know he could do very well for himself . . . and . . ."

"You and he have had long discussions about this, then?" asked Stephen, watching her closely.

"Oh, no! He doesn't know that some of Papa's shares were willed to me." She smiled. "I told him that if we eloped I should have no money and no ability to earn any and he has maintained he wants to marry me in any event." She looked so bashfully proud of her little deception that Stephen knew she was telling the truth, and admired her for it.

She misunderstood his silence. "Please, Stephen! I am twenty-one now and quite old enough to know what I want! I shall sell you the shares cheaply if you like, because . . ."

"You'll sell me them at the proper market price," he told her, his green eyes solemn. "And we shall have a lawyer draw up the deed correctly."

"There is no need for that!"

"Isn't there?" A glint of mischief came into his expression. "Can you imagine what dear Mama is going to say when she finds out?"

Jane giggled. "It will be far worse than you think. Tim is a Methodist! Oh, don't look so shocked. I am to keep my faith and any children we have will be brought up according to our ways."

"So you have thought this out to the end?" He smiled. "Quite the secretive type, aren't you?"

"It has been great fun," she said.

"It is a pity that Jane is so nervous of the Maoris," said Juliette as she followed Stephen down the steep path, allowing him to help her down the awkward parts. She did not really need him to assist her: she had scampered up and down these cliffs a thousand times. But this morning, elegant in her feather boa, she felt quite the lady and an outstretched, guiding hand seemed appropriate.

"It is a pity," Stephen agreed.

"One evening last week she was playing the piano with

the curtains drawn back at the windows. When she turned around there were a dozen dark faces pressed to the glass peering in at her. You know how they love piano music; they will stand outside for hours to listen. Jane screamed and screamed when she saw them and we all came running, guessing a mouse! The poor Maoris fled in disarray, their scruffy curs following with tails clapped down behind. It looked so funny but Jane was so terribly upset and has Abby stand guard for her now. With the curtains pulled tight, of course. Oh my, but there *are* a lot of Maoris here!"

Some had arrived in the night and were camped on the beach in the sand above the high-water mark. Fern, which had been cut for springy bedding, was piled roughly into the numerous three-cornered tents made from the canoes' sails and oars. Some groups were having their morning devotionals: prayers were uttered loudly and dramatically, or hymns sung with haunting plaintive harmony that sent shivers down Juliette's spine. She felt for a moment that if she shut her eyes she could be back on the knoll outside the old cottage, with the wind blowing from the south and the strains of early morning hymns borne faintly from Te Pahi's pa.

"There's quite a few out there gathering breakfast," said Stephen, pointing. Women and children were bent over, scrabbling in the shallow water for pipis. Other groups already had their food cooking. Blackened iron pots squatted from gypsy tripods and steam carried the aromas of fish, potatoes, and the wet-blanket odour of boiling pork.

"And here is this evening's meal," joked Stephen as he almost tripped over a rope that linked a noisily foraging pig to a stake hammered into the ground.

"Poor thing!" said Juliette. "It has hardly had any happiness at all and now they are going to eat it. Why does life have to be so cruel, Stephen?"

"What a funny little creature you are, Olivine. Life is not always cruel."

"It is a lot of the time," she said earnestly. "Why is that, do you think?"

"I do believe that you asked me that riddle once before and I am no closer to a solution now. See that old woman there? I think she wants you to go over to talk to her. She has been trying to get your attention."

The old woman had a crinkled face, blue moko, and cataracted eyes. She offered Juliette a flax string of plump silvery fish. Their gills were red and the bodies were crumbed with sand.

Juliette's Maori was hesitant but she found the words to say that she had no money with her. At the sound of her speech the old woman exclaimed with delight to hear the Maori tongue spoken by a pretty young pakeha girl. She pressed the heavy string into Juliette's hand, rubbing noses with her in the traditional native greeting.

Shyly Juliette thanked her for the fish, then, because she felt that something else was called for, she scratched up sufficient Maori to ask, "Is Te Pahi's tribe here? Has anybody from the far north come for the feast? Anybody at all?"

The woman shook her head and pulled an exaggeratedly sour face as she began to relate a long story of the "bad troubles" that were stirring people in the Bay of Islands. She spoke too quickly for Juliette to do much more than snatch at one word here and another there, but Stephen understood her easily. Interrupting at will, he questioned her shrewdly and closely, and now and then challenged her information by asking her to name her sources. She answered him obligingly. A pakeha who had taken the trouble to learn Maori so well earned her ungrudging respect. She spoke on and on while Stephen listened intently, occasionally running a hand through his dark curls in a gesture of agitation. Juliette watched silently.

"That was something bad, wasn't it, Stephen?"

"Nothing that should worry you, sweet Olivine."

"Is Hone Heke causing trouble?"

"A little. Here, let me carry those fish."

She stopped where she was on the stony cliff path and waited until he had given her his full attention.

"If there is something bad to worry about, then please tell me, because if it is really bad, then I should be concerned, don't you think? But if it is not very bad, could you please tell me about it after the Great Feast? I do so want

to have a lovely day and the news of something bad but not
very bad might spoil it."

"Juliette, don't ever change. Promise me that, will
you?"

"Why not?"

"You are exquisite the way you are." For some inexplicable reason this observation saddened him.

Juliette did not notice the subtle change of mood. She
persisted. "You do understand my feelings, don't you, Stephen?"

"I think so, but not one word of your instructions!"
Bending swiftly, he kissed her soft warm cheek. "Here, let
me carry those fish."

Fear of impending hostilities had worried many people
other than Jane, for although there was an open invitation
to the townspeople to attend the festivities, there were
fewer than a hundred white faces there among the crowd
of over four thousand Maoris all come to enjoy the week of
fellowship and hospitality offered by the Waikato chiefs
from the south. Thomas, Samuel, Stephen, Juliette, and
the twins watched the proceedings from the slope of a hill
beside the crowded field.

"The *Marjoree* brought in a load of eleven hundred blankets ordered by the Waikato tribes," said Stephen. "Te
Whero Wher wanted them to give as gifts to his guests.
Mighty generous, I must say. One would have imagined
the feasting to be quite enough."

Thomas handed a cylindrical match tin to Samuel and
began stuffing his pipe.

"His *mana* depends on his hospitality," he said. "It
would never do for a paramount chief to appear stingy. His
great-great-grandchildren would never be permitted to forget it. Right, Samuel, are you ready with that match?"

Samuel folded the piece of sandpaper in two and then
with a swift movement drew the head of the lucifer match
through between the rough surfaces. Instantly it flared up
with a bright yellow burst which he cupped in his hands
and held carefully while his father drew the flame through
the packed tobacco.

"Thank you, son," he said. Samuel shrugged an acknowledgement. He was already bored and half wished he had stayed behind with Leigh and perhaps borrowed a canoe to go fishing. Waiting for things to happen was no fun at all; Samuel liked to be doing.

"I wish we could have brought Tippy," he said.

"Not with all these other thousands of mangy scraps of canines around," said Stephen. "He'd be in a fight before you could say 'Samuel Peridot' . . . and speaking of Samuel Peridot, you're growing into such a fine, handsome lad that soon you'll be swatting the lassies away like honeybees."

Samuel hung his head. He liked and admired Stephen but detested personal remarks. Trying not to appear ill-mannered, he shuffled off to a place some distance along the bank and kicked at a clump of thistles.

"But what about you, Stephen? No sign of a serious romance yet?" asked Thomas.

Stephen laughed. "Dear Mama has taken to cornering me at every opportunity and hinting in the broadest possible terms that it is time I considered getting married. I fear that she thinks I have far too much of my life and interests twined up in the Richmond Line and, as you know, we are clashing with dreary regularity on how different decisions should be made."

"And Maire thinks that if you have a wife and family you will not be too concerned about how things are run . . . that you will let her have her head, as it were?"

"Exactly."

"Maire is a clever and intelligent woman," said Thomas with a smile and a slow pull on his pipe.

"Not to mention a damnably devious one."

Thomas' eyes twinkled but he did not reply.

"Anyway, I rather fancy that I might have stoppered her hints about marriage," reported Stephen with relish. "I announced to her in all best mock seriousness that there is a Maori lass in Kororareka who has captured my interest. Tangiamata, the famous Maata's young sister."

"Not *the* Maata?"

Stephen nodded, grinning. Maata was notorious in the Bay of Islands as an ambitious and totally uninhibited "madam" of a group of Maori whores who used to row out to visiting ships and offer to service the crews. On one scandalous (and memorable) occasion she had found out that the Reverend Williams was bringing a group of visiting missionaries over to see the degeneration of the town for themselves, so she and her girls put on a free entertainment with a host of enthusiastic volunteers. The missionaries fled in horrified disbelief and it was said that the place was named Hell from that day on.

"Oh, I did assure Mama that Tangiamata is not in the least like her older sister, and that I'm sure that once Mama has a chance to get to know her she will have the same regard and affection for her that I do." Stephen suddenly roared and slapped his thigh in mirth. "Oh, but you should have seen her face! I doubt that she'll press me again on the subject of marriage!"

"Did you bring up the subject of the boatyard with her?"

"Frankly I didn't think it a good time to, and then on reflection I changed my mind. I'd rather ask you to oversee it if you are willing."

"I told you that it is not in my line."

"Nor is it Mama's."

"Surely she would be better at overseeing English staff? I feel less confident at ordering Englishmen about, but Maire could have them working at a brisk pace."

"Ha! With all due respect, she would; but only until they decided they had endured enough and would walk off the job. Look at how long she keeps English housemaids or cooks! I think the record must be a month and that was in Kororareka when I had paid a girl's passage from Sydney so she stayed long enough to discharge the debt. No, Mama can make people work hard, true enough. But she has not the lucky knack of making them happy in their work. Besides, she and I are not getting along too well at the moment." He paused. "If only I could persuade Mama to sell me her Richmond Line shares. I could well afford it—I've over ten years' wages saved. Let's face it, Thomas, those shops are more than enough to occupy her. They are doing well, too. She doesn't need to be worrying about the shipping business. But when I broach the subject she says that it is her 'sacred duty' to keep the shares Papa willed to her. She's preached that attitude to the others too, because under the terms of the will she's not allowed to buy their shares, though they revert to her if any of us die."

"That sounds like an unusual arrangement."

"It certainly is. Leigh and I both have a twenty per cent share, but I have full control over his and he can never sell to anybody but me. The girls may sell to me or to each other, but not to Mama or to Leigh. Though Papa gave Mama thirty per cent and the voting rights to the girls' shares, in effect he was making sure that I eventually have control."

"Your father was no fool," said Thomas. "He planned it so that by the time you could afford to buy the others out you would be old and sensible enough to run the show. The safety factor is a cunning one. If you'd frittered your money away you'd never be in charge. As it is now, perhaps the girls might sell to you?"

"Perhaps," Stephen said, glancing sharply at him, wondering how much he knew or guessed.

"I can imagine that the will hardly delighted your mother."

"She was thunderstruck. Actually, I've only ever seen her cry once, and lose her temper—really lose it—once. She cried when Papa died and raged the evening after the will was read. I often wonder if she would have done either if she had known ahead of time what Papa had planned."

"She is a fine, proud woman," said Thomas quietly.

"You are capable of matching her, I think."

"I never try to," said Thomas matter-of-factly. The pipe seemed to have gone out. He drew a long, flat-headed pin from his lapel and prodded into the bowl. "No, Stephen, I never cross her and she knows that I do not listen to unsolicited advice. We appreciate each other. When I consider how easily I might have wed a fussy little homebody who nagged and whined whenever I went off to bush camp or down the Waikato, why, I shudder at the narrow escape I've had. I've been fortunate with my womenfolk."

"Yes," said Stephen doubtfully, for he had heard quite a few intriguing little stories about Evangeline Peridot. "Yes, you have. But what about those other two womenfolk of yours, Juliette and Abigail? They are blossoming into beautiful young ladies, don't you think?"

"Aye, Abby is a beauty. Got all the looks in the family, she did. I'm right proud of her. Fine, bright spirit, too."

"And Juliette?"

"Oh, not her. Too quiet, she is. Has her head in the clouds all the time. She's nothing like her sister."

Stephen glanced over to where Juliette was dancing on the spot and trying to repress her excitement. The ceremonies were about to begin. Line upon line of bare-chested warriors were shuffling into position ready to perform the first haka of welcome.

"Does Juliette still have nightmares?" he asked.

"I don't know."

Only with effort was Stephen able to control his voice. "You don't *know*?"

"I never ask her," said Thomas. "The navy surgeon said that we mustn't upset her unduly."

"But that was six years ago!"

"Can't be too sure," said Thomas. "Best let it be."

That's the easiest way by far, thought Stephen angrily. It would be overstepping the bounds of friendship by a mile to imply that a little loving concern would not go amiss, and besides, Stephen knew that anything he said would be futile. Over the years the stronger and more dominant Abigail had edged Juliette aside until now she had all the sunshine to herself and her sister stayed quietly in the shade. Or had it always been that way? He looked over at the girls again, this time with real sympathy.

Juliette would have been surprised to learn of Stephen's feelings, for at the moment she was having a wonderful time. This was so entrancing, so breath-taking! Or so she kept saying, skipping onto tiptoes and clasping her hands rapturously under her chin.

"I'm glad you feel that way," said Sarah apprehensively. "I counted the warriors in that first row there at one side. There are fifty there, and as far as I can see almost thirty rows just like that one. That makes, oh . . ."

"One thousand five hundred warriors!" supplied Rose. "Oh dear."

"Yes, frightening, isn't it?"

Juliette shook her head emphatically. The dark chestnut ringlets rippled below the rim of her apple-green bonnet.

"Father says that the tribes so enjoyed the socializing they did at the treaty signing that they won't let an excuse pass to do it again. Oh, do look at those Maori ladies on horseback! All in sateen."

"The colour doesn't match their tattoos," said Sarah irreverently. "And leghorn hats! Oh, do look at that fat woman with the pink velvet dress. It must have been made for somebody a yard smaller around the waist. Oh, I do wish that Sister Moya had been able to come. She would have loved to see this, all the local Maori ladies tricked out in their best English finery."

Rose said quietly, "I do so wish that you could leave Sister Moya out of at least some of the things we do together!"

"Where is she today?" asked Juliette.

"She is helping Sister Amy set up a school for the poor immigrants' children. Most of the church schools are exclusive, but this one will be open to everybody."

"Everybody?"

"Well, everybody of our faith, that is. I know that."

She tried to continue but the rest of her speech was smothered by a great roar from the crowd. People waved, hundreds of flags of all colours were brandished (some looking suspiciously like ships' signal flags, Stephen noticed), and the haka rolled off to a magnificent start.

It was a sight to congeal the blood. Over fifteen hundred warriors, naked but for white-tipped head feathers and clattering flax piu-piu skirts, leaped in unison, flourishing short carved spears, shouting and chanting. They pranced towards the now silent crowd and just when it seemed heads would be struck open they retreated with fearsome cries, struts, and leaps. Instinctively Sarah and Rose both clung to Juliette. Not only was she standing between them but she was the only one of the three who was not afraid. In her eyes the scene was breath-takingly beautiful.

"It's thrilling all right," agreed Stephen. And then he told Thomas what he had heard that morning on the beach.

By the time there was a lull in the chanting Thomas had fully digested the news.

"I'd not worry too much, lad," he said. "Hone Heke might cause all sorts of minor trouble, but he's no villain. The thing that will determine the outcome will be the Governor's handling of it, unfortunately."

"Why unfortunately?"

"He didn't make a very good impression with the Maoris to start with, did he? That massacre down in the South Island, I mean, where that evil fellow Te Rauparaha's men caused mayhem and got away with it. The Governor investigated and blamed the New Zealand Land Company. Well, maybe the Land Company does have their quarrels with the Government, but we've all got to live here alongside the Maoris and I say that how they are treated now will affect all of us in the end."

"You amaze me! I thought that you of all people would take Te Rauparaha's side."

"Because I'm a Maori fraterniser? Is that it? Sure, I take their side against injustice every time, but that problem down in the South Island was not handled with justice or injustice, only with weakness: and weakness with the Maoris is fatal. Respect counts for everything with them; for weakness they have only contempt."

"You make it sound very gloomy, Thomas. If Governor FitzRoy is no better than our past officials, then the outlook hardly seems promising."

"Outlooks seldom are," said Thomas cheerfully. He beckoned to Samuel to come and strike another lucifer match for his pipe.

Sixteen

In March 1845, less than a year after the Great Feast, the young colony was at war with itself. Over the past months stories about goings on in Kororareka had caused the mood in Auckland to swing wildly between amusement and alarm. Many people thought it hilarious that Hone Heke believed the flagpole was an evil talisman that prevented the lucrative trade of whalers from entering the harbour and that he should try to bring the ships back by chopping the thing down. But Royalists considered his actions an insult to the Queen. Hone Heke himself was flattered when the Governor, weary of having the flagpole replaced, set a reward on Heke's head. He laughed until one of his enemies remarked that having a price on one's head was rather like being a side of pork in a butcher's shop, there to be bought by anybody who wished. This joke delighted people all around the bay; soft grunting noises greeted him wherever he went. Enraged, Heke acted in desperation to save his mana.

"Is Te Rauparaha to have the sole honour of killing pakehas?" he asked loudly. The sniggering stopped at once. Confident that he had gauged the mood of his people correctly, he announced grandiose plans to march his two thousand warriors towards Auckland, gathering up more fighting men on the way. Preparations were begun at once.

Thomas heard this news when he was in the bush camp, up in the hills behind Auckland. They had just finished trimming a giant kauri log and were rounding up the browsing oxen to fasten them in twos to the drag chain for the long, slow journey down to the sawmill, when young Habbit rushed up.

"Already folks is swarming at the shipping office," the youth reported. "I just done what you sent me for an' got out as fast as I could. That town is a rum place right now. Makes you scared just to listen to the talk. Do you think the Waikato tribes will join in an' come after us as well?"

"Of course not!" said Thomas. "They want to live in peace with us just as much as we want to live in peace with them. Besides, what chance would they have against the soldiers' rifles and cannons?"

"But they're stealthy an' devious! Folks say they'll pick a moonless night an' all come creepin' to murder us in our beds, an' . . ."

"And that's enough," said Thomas. "We don't want a panic up here, especially not in front of all our Maori lads. I'll get the others aside one at a time and see if they want to carry on working or go into town. The men with families in Auckland may want to make sure they are safe."

"What about you, sir? You ain't afraid, are yer?"

Thomas was grim. "I'm going to see our Governor and see if I can't set a flea in his ear. I don't know what he's thinking of, but one thing's obvious: he knows as much about Maoris as I do about Eskimos. And that's bloody nothing!"

Governor FitzRoy was unimpressed by Thomas' concern and by his offer of practical help.

"We have our own trained negotiator," he said coolly. "Besides, we already know what this Heke fellow wants."

"Oh?"

"He wants a short, sharp lesson, which we are determined to give him. Troops have been despatched from New South Wales and will be there within the fortnight."

"But with all respect, sir, you are wrong! Hone Heke wants cajoling, flattering, an honourable peace, some way to fully restore his mana."

"We should bow to his impudence?"

"He's not being impudent. Not in his eyes. That flagpole was his originally . . . he donated it as a gift to Governor Hobson, so in chopping it down he feels within his rights. And this nonsense about marching on Auckland. It's only a bluff. He was saying this a year ago and nobody took much notice. Normally I would never dream of coming here and advising you how to run the country, but in this case we can avoid bloodshed and anguish if you simply go there, accord him full ceremonial rites, and discuss the matter."

"Thank you, Thomas Peridot. If you have quite finished raving, might I be excused? I have rather a lot of paperwork to attend to."

"No, I have not finished," said Thomas, his face tightening ominously.

"You called the Governor a braying donkey?" whispered Maire.

"He may be able to write a sentence without a dozen errors but for all that he's not one whit better than the fool he replaced. He's so bound up with smug, stuffy pride that he'd not listen to a single word I said. . . ."

"You called the *Governor* a braying donkey?"

"This country will be at war soon. At war! Do you know what that means? Our young men will have to fight against the young Maori men when all their energies should be directed towards understanding each other with sympathy and friendship. Instead of peaceful harmony we are going to have a shameful and totally avoidable war!"

"You insulted our Governor? Oh, Thomas, how could you, when I have tried so hard to maintain our high position? How could you do this to me?"

"Never mind our position," said Thomas. "It's our country we should be considering now."

When he returned to Auckland some five weeks later he dreaded the reception he might get from his wife, but to his surprise she seemed to hold no malice towards him. As he and Samuel rode up to the main store she glimpsed them through the barred windows and came hurrying out, discarding her serving apron as she dashed from the doorway. Below the black bonnet rim was the face of a tired, elderly woman and he guiltily wondered whether their social ostracisation had cut her that deeply.

"I hoped you would return," she said. "This town is in a turmoil."

"What about? And why are you working in the store? Where are the assistants?" asked Thomas.

"Haven't you heard?" she asked, searching their faces. "No, I can see not. The Government brig came beating into harbour last week from Kororareka. Oh, but there has been trouble up there! People killed, and the town sacked, and houses burned right to the ground. It's been terrible!"

"But what about the soldiers from the 96th? Wasn't a detachment up there? And we heard not three weeks ago that the H.M.S. *Hazard* was staying right off the beach at Kororareka itself in case there was trouble. Surely the military and the navy together could have stopped Heke? It *was* Heke, was it not?"

She nodded. "There is such a scandal about the military and the navy, for all the use they were!" She lowered her voice, then stopped altogether as three soldiers walked past, nodded politely, and continued on into the store. "From what we heard, all the armed soldiers did was to get in each other's way. To hear it from some of the women who have been in here, the only ones who helped to save the civilians were Bishop Selwyn and some of his people and the crews from some American whaling ships. When the trouble broke out they left off what they were doing ashore and helped to rescue those who were trapped by the fighting. The men from the *Hazard* beat it back to their ship at the first scenting of gunpowder and abandoned the women and children ashore!"

"I can't believe that!"

"I doubt they'd be inventing a tale to tell against those who had gallantly saved them from the jaws of battle," said Maire dryly. "You may take it that the *Hazard* has come out of this business smelling quite malodorous! Not only did the officers retreat at a brisk pace but they consoled themselves later and attempted to justify themselves by blaming the whole incident on the missionaries and the Bishop." She took a deep breath and tried to smile. "There has been such a tumult here since the refugees arrived. They are being crammed in where they can be fitted . . . the Bellwoods and Meyneys are staying with us. Needless to say, this town has taken a turn for the worse since the less pleasant of the Kororareka citizens arrived. I have already refused to serve more than a dozen faces which I have strong cause to recall vividly! I would sooner go out of business than accept *their* Government chits for free groceries."

Thomas had to laugh. Maire was so cool and controlled yet she had the Irish knack of reducing everything to the simple terms of how it affected her.

"We had enough riffraff here already. Still, they will give us an added interest in life."

"If drunkenness, idleness, and festering in the streets are of interest," she said tartly. "And there are so many of them. Many have nowhere to live . . . the streets are like army camps. We have had an American man-o'-war come in loaded with refugees and the whaler *Matilda* crowded with unsavoury-looking types. They all have been given chits for food, so we do continue to do well with trade, but oh, at what cost! And the worst of it is the servants have fled. Gone, vanished in the night."

"Mary and Tawa?"

"Not them, though it would be a blessing if they did go." The soldiers emerged from the store again, so Maire bade Thomas and Samuel follow her in and urged them to help themselves from a heaping basket of pears on the table behind the counter.

"What's this? Doing the Maoris out of a job?"

"Not from choice," said Maire. "We have had no Maori traders either—not for days now. Oh, we miss them!"

"As I was saying," said Maire, bolting the locks on the shop door, "we are reduced to serving in the stores ourselves and to fending for ourselves at home. Mary and Tawa have been rendered totally useless by the uproar and spend each and every day weeping and lamenting, and if it wasn't for dear Mrs. Meyney and Mrs. Bellwood we should be starving in our own home!"

"Why should the Maoris leave?" asked Samuel, wiping juice from his chin.

"It's the newcomers. They are filled with spite and prejudice against the Maoris, and seem driven to express that ill feeling in the worst of taste. They fling rotten matter and stones at them . . ."

"And dog droppings," supplied Sarah.

Maire gave her a swift glance. "They shout insults, accuse them of ingratitude, call them terrible names . . ." Another quick cold look to stop Sarah from contributing further specifics. "Truly they cannot be blamed for feeling that they no longer wish to be here, but it is so inconvenient. I do wish that this ghastly squabble would be over soon."

"I'm afraid that it sounds as though things are just beginning," said Thomas.

Leigh sat on the table in the kitchen swinging dusty boots and munching on a large red and green streaked apple. Juliette sat near him peeling apples in long striped ribbons and cutting the crisp white flesh into neat quarters. The china bowl at her elbow was half full of pieces of fruit floating in lemony-scented water. It was midafternoon but cool here on the south side of the house.

"I'll only be doing my fair amount to help," Leigh said seriously. "Everybody has to pitch in to stop a bully. That's what Hone Heke is, you know, a bully."

Juliette looked at him admiringly. His soft features seemed to have gained a firmness from the bold decision he had made that morning and his eyes had a hint of steely resolution in their depths. Oh, he was so brave. Only nineteen and off to fight in a war!

"If you don't stop a bully, then the next thing he'll be over your fence and in your yard, and if you don't stop him then do you know what would be the next thing?"

"No, I can't imagine."

Leigh said triumphantly, "Why, if he's not stopped then you will find him right in your very home with a knife point at your throat while all you had ever done to prevent it was to utter empty threats. It would serve you right, then, don't you think?"

"I suppose so."

"Of course it would!" He fished out a floating wedge of apple and pushed it into his mouth.

Juliette said doubtfully, "Won't Aunt Maire mind if you go away with the soldiers?"

"Of course not! Why should she?"

"I think that soldiers are brave and clever, but I didn't think that Aunt Maire liked the military much."

Leigh laughed. "In wartime everybody admires soldiers because they protect us all. Why, if you don't join in to help fight a war, then you are a coward, and you don't think that Mama would want me to be a coward, do you?"

"No, but I'm glad that Samuel is only fourteen, because Father wouldn't want him to fight. He says the Maoris are our friends and all this is a mistake."

"What do you think?" Not that he cared what anyone thought but her opinion was certain to be more agreeable than her father's views.

"I think you are wonderfully brave," she said quickly. Her eyes shone with an inner light and there was a gentle, soft expression on her face. "I can't wait to see how you will look in your uniform, but I shall miss you so much when you go away."

"Will you? Will you really?"

"Of course I will."

"I'll miss you too," he said.

Leigh was understating the truth when he said that his mother did not mind that he had enlisted. In fact, the whole thing had been her idea. When she had recovered from the shock of Thomas' quarrel with the Governor, Maire's first thought had been to mend whatever fences she could. An immediate visit with the Governor's wife had been brief and unproductive but at least she had not been snubbed. Then she had called on the most influential of Auckland's hostesses, all to some advantage: she had learned that the fighting in the Bay of Islands was expected to be brief and "safe" for Imperial troops; and that a platoon of civilians would be raised, and it would be these volunteers who would bear the brunt of any fighting. But it was pure luck that the ensign's position in the 58th became available on the journey from Australia. In the time it took her to arrange payment of the four hundred and fifty pounds' purchase fee she had restored the family honour, ensured Leigh's safety (for he would almost certainly have been called up with the civilian contingent), and thus by publicly opposing his views had struck a satisfying revenge against Thomas. This was much better than quarreling. Besides, this military commission seemed to give Leigh a definite sense of purpose. When he knelt beside her that night to say his Hail Marys in the privacy of her bedroom she was impressed by the new sincerity in his voice. After the intimate ritual she prayed aloud for his continuing safety in the vision of the Blessed Virgin. Her appeal was passive but so beautifully spoken that Leigh found himself blinking tears from his eyes when she had finished.

Her dislike of unpleasantness made Maire carefully skirt the subject of Leigh's commission when her husband arrived home. He would find out in due course but would not hear the news from anybody at Fintona. However, gossip has a way of propelling itself to the most unexpected corners, so when Maire looked up from her cash drawer one busy afternoon to see Stephen regarding her coldly from across the counter, her first thought was that he had heard about his brother and had come to give her his unwelcome opinion on the subject.

"I was not expecting to see you so soon this month, Stephen," she said calmly as she gave change and handed a wrapped bundle of candles to a customer.

"The *Lorendee* has goods for Kororareka which I thought best to off-load here before going on to Sydney. We had room for a dozen passengers and filled the places easily, so it is as well that we did call in. But there are pressing matters we must discuss." He smiled wryly. "I'm most impressed by your prices here at Peridot's Emporiums. Only one and ninepence for those candles! They'd cost two shillings in Wellington, and in any other store here too, I fancy."

"I trust that you did not make the journey to see me just to discuss the price of candles."

"Oh, but I did, Mama. I met Captain Corringham in Wellington and we went over the freight accounts together. This policy you are implementing of robbing the Richmond Line blind so you can undersell all the other shops in Auckland—it's most interesting and most ingenious, but what makes you think that you can get away with it?"

"Really, Stephen!" She glanced about the crowded shop, aware of the interest his raised voice had generated. "I insist that you postpone this discussion until a more convenient time."

"I'll give you ten minutes to close the shop, then."

"It is closing time soon anyway, but I cannot talk to you now. I have to hurry home: we have three officers and their wives from the 58th coming to dinner this evening and I have to supervise the preparations."

"I see. The military are the new elite, I imagine. Very well, I shall come to dinner too. We can hold our discussion over the soup course. The officers will be intrigued to learn how you cheat your own family out of their dividends by making the Richmond Line carry your goods for nothing."

"Stephen!" His words whipped patches of colour into her cheeks.

"Ten minutes, Mama, then all the customers will hear every word I have to say. In the name of Jove, I swear I am in earnest."

Her eyes grew hard and opaque. "Very well, but whatever you say will do no good at all. I am the major shareholder as far as votes are concerned. If I want to run the Richmond Line at a loss, then I am perfectly entitled to do so."

He knew that she was right but he shrugged easily and said with a smile, "Not without a struggle, Mama. Not without a fight."

Seventeen

It was Stephen's habit when he came ashore after each voyage to make confession in his own home church. He found it both refreshing and spiritually uplifting, and today he sought the experience also as a preparation for another frustrating interview with his mother. If he could not persuade her to budge from her policy of exploitation, then he would be forced to dip into his own savings to make essential repairs to the *Lorendee*, and this he was loath to do. If only there was some way to make his mother play fair. Not only was this ploy harmful to the Richmond Line and to the other members of the family as shareholders, but by using this unfair advantage she could stifle all other competition in the town. But Stephen was pessimistic about his chances of talking her around. No doubt she'd give him a smug "None of the customers are complaining!" and refuse to go further than that. Well, he'd have to threaten litigation if the situation grew any tighter. They could not afford to have ill-fitted ships putting out of port with winter storms almost upon them.

Father Markswell was on duty in the small church today, busying himself at the altar. When he saw Stephen he hurried towards him on softly shod feet, his grey hair reflecting the colours of the stained-glass windows as he moved through the sunlight.

"It is a relief to see someone out and about to be sure," he said. "This town is so jumpy that whenever I hear an unusual noise I have to smother the notion that Heke's men have arrived to murder us all where we stand."

"You could not hope to die in a better place than this. But why is this church not barricaded? As we were being

piloted in I noticed frantic activity up at St. Paul's. The
harbourmaster said that the building was being made into
a stockade, with the windows boarded up and padded with
sandbags, with slits for musket barrels to poke out . . ."

Father Markswell was clearly shocked. "Can you imagine our Bishop agreeing to such sacrilege?"

"No, I can't," laughed Stephen. "There'd never have
been any saints if they'd been prepared for the worst."

When he emerged the sky was low with ragged grey
cloud which had mopped up all traces of sunshine. Stephen
wondered whether he should strike out for Fintona on foot
and risk being drenched, or appropriate the convent carriage, which was parked at the roadside with the horse between the shafts, a sacking nose bag keeping it contented.
Jamming his cap down over his curls, he strode out in the
direction of the town.

"Stephen!"

He glanced at the carriage in surprise. One of the side
curtains was pulled back and Sarah's face was a pale blur
in the shadow.

"Have you been kidnapped? I knew I couldn't trust those
sisters."

She ignored the teasing. "Please get in for a minute,"
she urged, moving over and tucking her gathered navy
poplin skirts under her. "I waited for you to disembark and
followed you. Sister Amy said I might wait in the carriage."

"Sister Amy? Where is your twin, Sister Moya?" he
asked jokingly, noticing that her dress was the closest ap-
proximation one could get to a nun's habit.

"She is away again. Thames, this time. I do fear for her
safety in these troubled times. Will there really be a war?"

"It's inevitable, I'm afraid, but we hope it will be over
swiftly. The Governor is past the stage where he can
choose what to do, and it seems that the consensus of opinion is that Heke must be taught a lesson."

"You don't agree with it, do you?"

"I agree with Thomas. Governor FitzRoy on one hand
condoned a massacre by Te Rauparaha, and now he's
screaming for troops because a capering rascal chops down
a flagpole. Oh, I know there was more to it than that, but

Heke was pushed into sacking the town. No, Thomas is right."

Sarah shivered. "We are all waiting to see what Uncle Thomas will say when he finds out that Leigh is an ensign in the 58th."

"*What?*"

"Mama bought him a commission when one of the 58th ensigns died on the ship coming from Sydney. She says that he will be called up anyway so by doing this she is protecting him."

Stephen snorted. "Ensigns carry the flag and are right in the line of fire. But don't enlighten Mama, will you? Leigh will come to no harm in this little tour of duty. One or two skirmishes and it will all be over. But protecting him? I wonder. To me it smacks more of Mama striking back at Thomas for telling the Governor that he was a goat."

Sarah giggled. "A donkey. A braying donkey." She placed a gloved hand on his arm, suddenly sober again. "I came after you because I have a very important favour to beg of you."

"You ask, and in the name of Jove I'll grant it."

"I do wish you'd not say that, Stephen. It's almost blasphemy."

"Is that the favour?"

"Of course not! What a tease you are!" She grinned at his comical expression. "Stephen, will you please buy my shares?"

"Your Richmond Line shares?"

"Those are the only shares I have, you goose. Please, Stephen, can you buy them from me? Do you have the money to do it?"

"Of course I do, and I'd be happier to do it than you could possibly imagine. This would solve a gigantic headache for me. But, and it's a big *but* . . . why do you want me to buy them, Sarah?"

"The Church needs the money," she said simply and, catching a sight of his unguarded face, she rushed on. "You know I'm going to become a nun. I'm set on it, Stephen. I've known all my life that Jesus is the only dream for me. Never has my heart been in the things of a secular life. Really, I'm a nun already in my thoughts, my prayers,

my soul. So it doesn't matter that Mama is steadfastly refusing me permission, for as soon as I'm legally able to I
shall take my vows without her consent. And when that
happens the Church will receive all my worldly goods in
any case!"

"Then why the hurry to rid yourself of them now?"

"Because Sister Moya and I want to start up a school.
There are so many poor children here in town, practically
homeless and with no chance in the world. We have the
hall which we can use but need equipment, books, slates,
furniture. It will be so exciting! Sister Moya knows all
about running a little school, so I will be her assistant at
first, until I can cope on my own. I've not said a word to her
about this because I didn't want to get her hopes up and
then find out you won't buy the shares."

Stephen gazed steadily into her face. "The scamps will
run you ragged, you realise?"

"And what makes you think I'm not capable of holding
my own with the worst little horrors the Lord thinks fit to
send me?"

He leaned over and kissed her cheek with tender regret.
"You'd be a pearl of a mother," he said sadly. "Are you
sure you won't change your mind?"

"Stephen, you know me."

"Aye, that I do. I love and respect you, but I have to say
that it's a waste, because it is."

"Do you think Mama will be fearfully angry?"

"Yes, she will. Do you want to reconsider?"

She shook her head. "If I do there will be no school for
the poor children. I can't reconsider."

"Good," he said firmly.

A pall of gloom had deepened the sober atmosphere at
Fintona since the Meyneys and Bellwoods had arrived.
They brought their possessions which now choked the hall-
ways and completely filled the carriage shed, and they
brought that unpleasant aura of bad luck that clings to refugees. The horror of what had happened at Kororareka
seemed to have paralyzed the menfolk, who sat mutely on
the verandah in the sun all day, while the ladies busied
themselves with light work in the kitchen to lessen the

burden. With the girls still working in the stores, every pair of hands could find a task to do. Every day they talked about what had happened, tracing the details of that terrible evening over and over as though they hoped to erase it—like rubbing out a stain with a cloth. Mrs. Meyney was distraught over the fate of Georgina's bull terrier Rowf, which had dashed off in the uproar and was not seen again. She was haunted by the vision of his butchered carcass in a Maori *umu* oven and tormented by what she had to tell Georgina when she returned from Wellington with her husband.

"If she mentions that wretched dog again I shall scream right in her face," fumed Jane one evening as they sat around the table polishing the knives and forks.

"It's preying on her mind," soothed Rose.

"I don't care. Her constant 'Rowf this' and 'Rowf that' is getting on my nerves. I can't bear it."

"You are jumpy lately," observed Sarah mildly. "Look at how you shrieked when that moth swooped around the piano last night."

Abby leaped to defend her beloved Jane. "So would you have. That moth was *enormous*."

Rose said, "At least Mr. Bellwood has recovered somewhat. His fingers have remembered how to pinch."

"Yes," said Sarah. "Don't turn your backs on him, girls."

"Must you be so vulgar?" said Jane loftily.

Juliette put down her polishing cloth with a sigh. "I do wish that Leigh would come home again instead of staying at the barracks, training. His uniform looks so gorgeous, don't you think? I specially like that scarlet hat with the peaks in front and behind. What did he say it was called?"

"A shako," said Rose. "And he'll be home for dinner tomorrow evening, then the next day we shall all go down to the town to watch the soldiers march from the barracks to the wharf. We'll have to stare at him hard then, because we shan't be seeing him for a while."

Leigh seemed to be keenly aware of this too, as he talked to them the next night in the music room after dinner. His sisters sensed his unease as they fluttered around him and a companion, Ensign Deverell.

Sarah was saying, "This rifle is nothing like a musket at all!"

"It's the brand-new model," explained Ensign Deverell in a throaty voice. "This is a new percussion type of mechanism. Four feet seven inches long, she is, and she can fire three rounds every minute in a range of up to two hundred yards."

"My word!" said Sarah. "You could kill thirty enemy in ten minutes and the whole of Hone Heke's forces in ten hours. They don't need an army, just you by yourself, Leigh."

"It's not quite as simple as that!"

"Can you shoot it, Leigh?" asked Juliette.

The ensign smiled at this dainty girl with the luminous dark blue eyes. A delicate, enchanting creature, yet somehow he had not noticed her until she spoke.

"The term is 'fire' it, miss, and yes, he can. His target score is one of the highest in the regiment for a beginner."

"Really?"

"They teach you well in the military," said Leigh.

"I hope they taught you how to keep out of the way," said Sarah. "Oh, I do wish you weren't going!"

"I had to do something," Leigh said, but his voice quavered with the fresh nervousness of someone who has only just realised the enormity of what he is getting into. "If I'd not taken the Queen's shilling, then within this week I'd have been drafted by the Militia Bill which has just gone into law."

"What is that?" asked Jane.

"The barracks are buzzing with it. All the single men of Auckland town are going to be drafted. They'll be the ones used for cannon fodder. They'll be put in the front ranks and they'll be the ones most likely to be killed. Not that we will be out of danger, of course, but . . ."

"Jane!" shrieked Abby.

"Hush, Leigh," said Rose. "Jane has fainted."

Sarah was pulling a curl of feather from Jane's apricot feather boa. She thrust it into the lamp flame and as it hissed and singed she pushed the agitated Abby aside and waved the burning feather back and forth under Jane's nostrils.

"There, that's better. You fan her, Abigail. Rose, do you think we should fetch Mama? She might think that Dr. Havow should be called."

"No!" Jane sat up groggily. She coughed. "I'm not ill. It was just the talk of fighting, and killing . . . that's all. Please don't disturb Mama. She is packing provisions for Leigh to take tomorrow."

"More for the lackeys to carry," said Ensign Deverell.

"Lackeys?"

"We have lackeys to carry our kit, miss."

"Our kit is our things," said Leigh. "Our wooden water bottle, haversack, knapsack, mess tin, food, blanket, and greatcoat. But we are well loaded ourselves with the rifles, bayonet, ammunition pouches, swords, and the colours of course. But look at this." He undid his black-laced jacket buttons and drew out a flat, ugly pistol. "Look at what Mama gave me for a going-away gift. There, I thought that would make your eyes huge, Juliette."

"And I didn't give you anything! I thought so hard but I could think of nothing suitable for a soldier in battle."

"Nothing you could send by messenger," joked Ensign Deverell, forgetting for the moment where he was. For many months the mess hall had been his only social arena. Recovering quickly, he said, "You could not do better than knit socks. Soldiers always need plenty of thick, warm socks. They soften our journeys, keep us comfortable, and generally maintain our good humour."

"I shall knit you a pair too," offered Juliette.

"We shall all knit socks," said Rose. "And we shall all cheer you loudly tomorrow. Will you both wave to us?"

"Not a chance," said Leigh. "We'll have our hands full with the weight of the colours."

"We might wink as we go by," said Ensign Deverell.

The ensigns had been so mysterious about the colours that the girls were a little disappointed to see that they were nothing more than very large, heavy-looking flags. Ensign Deverell's was the Great Union flag, and Leigh carried a black flag with the Cross of St. George in one corner.

"I do wish that Leigh was carrying the other one," Juliette said wistfully. "The Great Union flag looks so splendid with that gold seal and the Roman figures embroidered in gold thread. The black flag is so plain and drab."

"But the regiment is called the 'Old Black Cuffs,' so what other colour could they have for their own flag, Miss Olivine?"

"Stephen!" She turned to look up into a tanned, laughing face. "We didn't expect you for another week, at least."

"It's amazing what a fair breeze can do," he told them. "If there is too little the sails sag, too much wind and they have to be trimmed, but this time we were lucky. We had a fast turnaround in Sydney, too. The load was all provisions for the military, so the lumpers had to give us priority. So the Old Black Cuffs are off to do combat, are they?"

"Yes, isn't it exciting? There is Leigh. Oh, if only he would look this way so that he can see us."

"It's going to rain," said Rose, hugging her cape tighter around her shoulders.

"They will look comical if they all break into a gallop when the rain comes down!"

As Sarah spoke the first drops scattered over the crowd who had come to cheer the soldiers. Then it began seriously, sweeping across the roadway like sharp cold strokes with a straw broom.

"Into the carriage, quickly!" shouted Sarah.

The Maoris ignored the rain. Stephen was surprised to see so many of them turn out to witness what was a show of strength against their race, and even more surprised to see that they obviously enjoyed the impressive spectacle of hundreds of briskly marching red-coated men. They marvelled aloud, counting the rows as they thumped past. Some held the very young ones up to watch. Most laughed when the rain struck, for the soldiers did not miss a beat. Heads proud, eyes levelled straight ahead, they marched like a red clockwork caterpillar to the waiting longboats.

The girls scrambled into the carriage with Stephen hurrying them along. Rain hummed on the roof. The ground was puddled with brown slush. Tamati hunched on the coachman's seat, wrapped in a black tarpaulin.

"Where's Jane?" asked Abby.

"You should know if anybody does," said Rose. "I thought she had to stay at home to help Mama?"

"She was going to follow with Belinda Godwin."

"Belinda was there, across the road from where we were standing. She'd not miss seeing Leigh off. But there was no sign of Jane."

"I suppose he's soaked to the skin by now," mused Juliette, gazing out to where the harbour was a mist of grey shadow stripes.

"He'll come home safely," Stephen told her.

Juliette felt her face warm suddenly with embarrassment. From the sympathetic tone of his voice she guessed that he knew about her feelings for Leigh, but how? Those feelings were private. Not even Leigh knew about them, unless he felt something too as he had kissed her goodbye last night. Even though it had been ruined by Aunt Maire walking in and catching them all laughingly exchanging farewells, the tenderness of their own precious few seconds still lingered with her.

They waited for another ten minutes, then Stephen instructed Tamati to drive home slowly.

"Perhaps we should stop at Godwins' in case she is still there?" asked Abby.

"Not while I'm here," said Stephen, who frankly detested Belinda.

"Why, Stephen!" said Sarah. "Don't tell me that you are afraid of Belinda. You're not fair to encourage her the way you do. Why, she has to come and practice flirting with Leigh when you're not here."

"I rather fancy that she is secretly fond of Leigh," said Rose. "Not that he is any fonder of her than you are. She is too bold by half."

"I'm worried about Jane. I wonder if anything has happened to her?" asked Abby.

"She'll be helping Mama, you'll see."

But Maire was alone in the parlour when Stephen found her a few minutes after they arrived at Fintona. And by then he was so tensed up with anticipation that his sister had left his thoughts completely.

Maire regarded him with distaste. Yet another unpleasant interview. She could see the signs and realised resignedly that there would be no fobbing him off. Very well, he would have his discussion, but there would be no satisfaction in it for him. Maire Peridot was not a woman who would allow herself to be bullied by her own son. She poured herself a measure of whisky and arranged herself regally in her high-backed chair, watching him coolly.

"You are a picture of utter elegance," Stephen told her as he raised his glass in a perfunctory toast. "The perfect picture of the lady shipowner."

"Get to the point, please. I have no patience with empty compliments, as well you know."

"Very well. I have been having an interesting time of things lately. After I checked Captain Corringham's records to see why the *Sarendee* was making almost no freight profit on the run between here and home, I decided to look over the *Marjoree's* books too."

"Really, Stephen, you are overstepping your authority! The *Lorendee* is your province. I never interfere with the way you use her. It is clearly understood that you keep to your own territory and leave the other two ships to my management. It is none of your business . . ."

"Oh yes, it is, Mama. When the running of one ship cuts into the profits of another I consider that to be my affair, and now when the whole Richmond Line is in grave danger of prosecution that too is my business. I notice that you are aware of what I am referring to."

"On the contrary, I have no idea what you mean," Maire kept her gaze turned towards her son but her eyes were fixed on a point slightly above his head.

"I rather fancy you do." He stood with his back to the fire. "What can you have been thinking of to throw the future of the Richmond Line into jeopardy just for your own greed . . . yes, greed! What other motive could you have had—other than gain—when you agreed to sell guns and ammunition to Te Rauparaha?"

"It was not to him! An agent in Wellington arranged the sale but it was emphatically not to Te Rauparaha! It was on behalf of a tribe near Wanganui. . . ."

"Te Rauparaha." Stephen downed his drink with a grimace. "But even if it was to some harmless tribe, the sale of arms to any Maoris is against the law. We could be fined so heavily that the Richmond Line could be crippled permanently. Who would pay that fine? The Peridot Trading Emporiums? I rather doubt it, somehow."

Her lilting tone became faintly wheedling. "It was a most attractive arrangement, Stephen. Greenstone was being offered. Greenstone! Just think of it! You know how enormously valuable that is. And there were other artifacts."

"Shrunken heads, no doubt, since we're on the wrong side of the law."

"They fetch a tremendous price on the London market."

"And an enormous fine if you're caught dealing with them."

"Really, Stephen, you are impossible! Sometimes I severely question your business acumen. One has to take risks to make a good profit. But why should you worry? Captain Filbert . . ."

"Captain Filbert faced being dismissed by you if he refused to do what you ordered."

"Did he say that?"

"And I believe him. I know he's too good and decent to indulge in black market practices. In fact, he told me about the deal before it went through, so naturally I put a stop to it at once. I have all your muskets and ammunition safe on the *Lorendee*."

"How *dare* you interfere! It is one thing to have the impudence to come here and tell me what I should and should not do, but quite another to interrupt my business arrangements . . ."

"Not any longer." He opened his cigar case and withdrew a thin brown cigar. "I'm retiring you as of now."

"Oh, no." She watched him take a taper from the jar on the mantelshelf and light it at the fire. "You have tried that strategy before and it hasn't advanced you very far."

"This time it will. Read this," and he handed her an envelope. "In there you will find an outline of the details from the transfer of certain company shares. Jane's and Sarah's, to be precise. I now have control of sixty per cent of the Richmond Line, while you, Mama, have the frustrating forty per cent which entitles you to an option only. From now on I control the shipping line."

"I don't believe you."

"Open it. See for yourself."

"Sarah and Jane would never sell. Not willingly."

"Be assured that I did not so much as suggest the matter. They both sold legally, and both for an above-market price. There is no way that you can reverse this."

She brushed the envelope from her lap with a gesture of impatience. "I shall refuse to take your word on this, Stephen."

"Do as you wish. Please consult Mr. McLeay if you have any doubts," said Stephen. He walked to the window and stood with his hands clasped behind his back, looking out into the garden.

His mother glared at him. Her composure lasted until the door was flung open and Abby rushed into the room. Then her temper snapped.

"Get out of here at once, you undisciplined little savage!" she cried. Her arms trembled as she gripped the arms of her chair.

Stephen turned around. "What is it, Abigail?"

"It's Jane!"

"Jane? Tell her to come here immediately. I wish to speak to that ungrateful wretch."

Abby shook her head, distraught. "She's gone! Jane has run away to marry Mr. Bragg! She's gone! All her clothes, all her things, everything! She's gone, and she didn't even tell me she was going!" With that she dashed from the room and slammed the door with a jolt behind her.

Maire's cold gaze fixed on Stephen. "You see what you have done with your scheming? This would never have happened without your interference. Now Jane has thrown herself away on that worthless labourer who must have somehow persuaded her to turn those shares into money. She could have been Lady Whytnorth!"

"Perhaps she didn't want to be," he said.

"What has that to do with making a match?"

"Everything, Mama," he replied quietly.

Eighteen

It seemed that nobody in the colony approved of the moves against the Maoris of the north. To those evicted from Kororareka the punitive expedition seemed too little and far too late; the citizens of Auckland cheered the soldiers away, then immediately began grumbling because they had gone, leaving them almost totally unprotected: while the New Zealand Land Company settlements lost no time agitating for troops to protect *them*. Surely the recent massacre at Wairau and the reports of tribes arming themselves proved that they were in far more urgent need of protection?

In Auckland, swollen with the influx of frightened refugees, the mood was of alarm. The shipping offices were besieged by desperate families trying to beg passage home. Property values plummeted as people tried to sell for whatever they could get. Stephen was badgered into accepting deeds for three houses, a coal merchant's yard, and a carriage and pair in exchange for berths and hold space. He kept the houses and paid the Richmond Line from his own pocket. To those who were unable to be fitted aboard he sold the rifles from the aborted trade deal. The Richmond Line lost nothing, and to Stephen it was a profitable, if depressing, morning.

For Maire it was far more depressing. The clever solicitor who had once promised that he could extricate her from any situation now told her that there was nothing she could do to regain control of the Richmond Line, not until Leigh turned twenty-five at least. Then perhaps they could petition the court . . .

"For the next six years I am forced to watch Stephen wreak whatever havoc he wills with my company?"

"I'm afraid so, if you are planning to stay in town. There is quite a scramble to leave, I hear."

Maire tugged at her gloves. "Mr. McLeay, I am not afraid of a few shouting Maoris now and I never shall be. The threat of losing my property is far more terrifying to me than the prospect of physical harm."

"Then today is a splendid day to be out. My secretary purchased a comfortable two-bedroomed home for his family this morning for less than ten pounds. Nine pounds fifteen shillings, I understand the actual sum was."

"But a good table is worth more than that!" She paused in the middle of fixing her veil, staring brightly at him through the net.

"People are panicking, Mrs. Peridot. I understand that you have house guests? They might be interested in buying themselves houses for next to nothing. There are quite a few about, I believe."

"Not as interested as I am," she said to herself as she stepped onto the carriage block. "Drive around the streets, Tamati. I am looking for 'For Sale' signs or evidence of people packing to leave."

"What about Mr. Bennington, *matua*?" Tamati used the Maori term for "mother."

"Later. What I have to discuss with him can keep."

As she settled herself in the carriage she was conscious of a fresh wave of anger. Her eagerness to acquire more property had blotted up her fury at her ungrateful, treacherous children. But Tamati's innocent enquiry reminded her. Stephen she could understand; Sarah was so devoted to the Church that even her disloyalty had a reason; but Jane's perfidy was beyond comprehension, beyond logic, totally unforgivable. How could she have thrown herself away on a miserable apprentice! The Honourable Simon Whytnorth could have been snagged so easily, for he was deeply attracted by Jane's cool indifference. The whole family would have benefited by a match between them—a match that she, Maire, had worked very hard to bring about. There was more to this than a simple romance and elopement, of that she was sure. Somebody must have helped Jane. She could never have engineered such a plan by herself. Maire's first suspicions alighted on Abigail. But when she recalled how distressed the girl had been at the discovery of the letter from Jane, she turned her mind to Juliette. Yes, she would be the guilty one. Unnaturally quiet—sly, in fact—and too much like that showy mother of hers to allow anybody's mind to rest easy. Juliette would have helped Jane with her underhanded deception.

Maire had purchased a dozen houses and three commercial properties by three o'clock. Quite enough to add an extra sting to the changes in her will that she had made that morning, but not enough to soften her attitude to Jane or to Tim Bragg. But her private interview with Jack Bennington went better than she had expected, and she was actually smiling as she emerged from his Queen Street office. Now she was ready to deal with Miss Slyboots, Juliette.

"I want you to tell me what you did to help Jane run away," she demanded.

Juliette felt very small in the shadows of the looming curtained four-poster bed but she spoke up boldly. "I didn't help her at all, Aunt Maire."

"There is no need to take that defiant attitude. You knew about Jane and Mr. Bragg, didn't you? You knew that he came here to the house."

Abby must have said something. Juliette relaxed. "Yes, I did know that."

"I thought as much."

Belatedly, Juliette hastened to explain. "I only saw them once, on the day of the race meeting. It was only by accident that I was out in the garden too, and Abby was very angry with me. She said that I was sneaking about and spying . . ."

"No doubt you were." So Abigail did know about it.

"No, truly I wasn't. It was such a romantic evening."

Maire successfully fought the urge to slap her. "Go to your room," she said. "You may come out after dinner and do the dishes."

The Bellwoods and Meyneys were sunk into deep chairs in the parlour, knees and shoulders draped with wraps.

Mr. Bellwood cupped a hand around his ear and Mrs. Meyney nodded her false curls as Maire briefly informed them that Juliette and Abigail were being punished for "complicity and deceit" and would be confined to their bedrooms except when occupied with chores. They were also to be on a diet of bread, gruel, and water until further notice. With a warning glare at the twins and at the softhearted Mrs. Bellwood, Maire advised everybody that if they fed the girls extra food they might find their own meals drastically altered too.

"They will suffer but not starve," she assured them.

"Sinners must be punished for the good of their souls!" said Mrs. Meyney.

"Exactly. And it is your responsibility to see that this is carried out to the full."

Maire also relied on Jack Bennington to see that Tim Bragg was punished, but she would have been dismayed to learn what actually happened the morning after her visit.

"She wanted me to fire you, lad!" said Jack. "Can you credit that? Naturally I told her that you were the best foreman I have ever had and even though she and I were old friends I could do no such thing."

Tim Bragg's eyes had an uneasy look in them and his thin face was flushed. I'm doing this for Jane, he told himself. For Jane and our future.

"There's no need for that, Uncle Jack. You don't need to give me no marchin' orders."

Jack Bennington patted his marcelled hair, staring at the young man shrewdly. "What is it, lad? Has the military given you marching orders instead? Well, we might have expected it, and when you get back . . ."

"No, sir, it ain't that." The "sir" was forced but made him feel better at once. By dropping the "uncle" he had cut an intangible tie and freed himself from guilt.

"They will call you up in a day or so. I knew that, so I assured Mrs. Peridot that her wishes would be carried out. She'll never know the difference, hey?"

"They'll not call me up. Not now that I be married."

"Married?"

"Wed day before yesterday, by special license."

"Wed?"

"Surely you knew that from Mrs. Peridot, what with Jane bein' her daughter an' all."

Jack roared with laughter. "I thought you had insulted her in some way, startled her horse or something. Mrs. Peridot doesn't take a slight calmly, you know. But this? Hey!" He whistled. "Jane, you wed Jane, and her mother all poised on the brink of marrying her off to that chinless society fellow! What a shock! Well, allow me to congrat . . ."

"No, sir!" said Tim firmly. "I'm leavin' yer as of now. I'm going ter 'ave me own shop, an' Jane an' me are setting up house around the bay. We bought a real cosy, pretty cottage all furnished fer only twenty-five pound from the Simpkins family, an' . . ."

"And this is your idea of gratitude," said Jack.

"I'm not owin' yer a thing! I paid yer me fare money an' then stayed on though I could 'ave earned much more for me craft from Terence Parkins, an' not a week's gone by that he ain't told me so. Yer got yer money's worth from my hide an' more, so there's no need ter take on so about no gratitude!" He turned and walked away, stooping to pick up his tools and carry bag with clumsiness, as if expecting Jack to kick him.

Within the hour Jack reported to Maire that he had fired Tim "as she requested."

The girls took their punishment stoically though Juliette found it particularly hard. Abby had the fortunate disposition of a happy glutton. She did not mind what she ate as long as the helpings were generous. Gruel or bread or roast beef were all the same to her. Juliette loved food. Sometimes she imagined that her life so far consisted of two plateaus and a valley, the plateaus being now and when her mother was alive and the valley being the time she lived at the Mission and had to survive on Mrs. Clerkwell's poor cooking. When she did go into the kitchen Maire was a superb cook. Better than that, she enjoyed a bountiful table and all those lucky enough to be at the house enjoyed sharing it too. The best of every kind of foodstuff delivered to the stores was always diverted to Fintona's crammed pantry to join dried apples from America, raisins from Australia, bananas, mangoes, pineapple, and oranges from Tahiti, and once a chunk of stringy pulpy sugar cane that Stephen had brought back from somewhere north of Sydney. Evangeline's menu had featured pork, fish, and pork again, but Maire had the money and the inclination to spend on variety. Her table offered smoky sausages, beef, lamb, aromatic stews into which she often emptied a bottle of good claret, and chicken dishes that defied praise. She was particularly fond of poultry. "A chicken is to a cook what canvas is to an artist," she would say.

Her most avid pupil was Juliette, who hovered around ("like a blowfly," said Maire in irritation) whenever something new and interesting was being concocted. She loved watching, adored tasting, and suffered the bleak punishment diet cruelly. Her throat knotted with spasms of longing as she served dishes of lamb ragout or fish coated in crunchy light batter, and it was awful to have to scrape wasted food into the pig bucket afterward.

But the ordeal was mercifully brief. Jane had been married a fortnight when Thomas came back home to stay until the weather cleared. Winter had set in with lashing rain and mists that wreathed the volcano cones and lay like soft scarves over the harbour. His arrival was looked forward to with apprehension by Maire, who fully expected a bitter, angry quarrel.

Thomas had no appetite for it. This war in the north had sobered him and he was so sickened at the futility of it all that lesser problems did not really exist. Why could the Governor not have listened and seen that Hone Heke was showing the same kind of defiance a child does when he sticks his tongue out at the teacher? Surely if he had been open-minded this would have been clear to him and there would have been no fighting. For the outcome was inevitable now. There had been no skirmishes yet, but there would be. The soldiers were going in to teach Heke a lesson that he did not need, and perhaps dozens of brave young Maori men would die who need not have died. He hurled this opinion at Maire as though it were her fault, then changed his tack: yes, he could see Leigh really had little choice and being accepted in the 58th was an honour. Yes, it was a shame about Jane; but it was done now and Jane had chosen for her own life. It was to be hoped that she would be happy.

"I fail to see how she can be," Maire reproved him, but with a light tone. His ready acquiescence astonished her.

"I shall let my own daughters choose," he said.

"And the sooner the better," said Maire. "Abby was completely hysterical when Jane eloped. I have never seen anybody in the grip of such uncontrolled passion. This has been an intermittent state over the last two weeks. Dr. Havow prescribed Nervene, which both girls have been taking, for the tantrums have upset poor Juliette too and brought back the nightmares. Dr. Havow advised a very restricted diet and lots of rest, which we have been strictly observing. . . ."

Thomas snorted. "You're not still consulting that quack, are you?"

With dignity she continued. "The doctor says that Abigail should marry as soon as possible. He says that a young woman of sixteen should not be suffering from this kind of hysteria and it would be damaging to allow her state of mind to continue. He called it a tendency to try to avoid real life, but a kind and patient husband and the natural condition of motherhood would quickly heal her affliction." She gazed at him steadily, not betraying her feelings.

"But Abby is just a baby!"

"She is almost seventeen, Thomas."

"I suppose you have a 'kind, patient' husband in mind for her too," said Thomas bitterly. He resented this suggestion, although he could see the wisdom of it. Abby needed love and affection more than most girls. She had doted on Jane and lost her. Maire was right; Abby did need the warmth of a loving home atmosphere. But not yet, surely not so soon.

Maire took a deep breath and said casually, "Mr. Bennington has several times expressed an interest in marrying Abigail. He would be a splendid husband. I know that I would have been pleased if he had only taken an interest in one of my girls." She broke off to stare in pique at

Thomas, who was laughing helplessly, his fatigue forgotten.

"Jack Bennington!" he repeated when he could speak.

Maire smiled thinly. "I suggest that you ask Abigail yourself what she thinks of the idea. You did say that your daughters would be allowed to choose for themselves."

"But surely . . . Jack Bennington!"

"Then ask her."

"Oh, I will . . . I certainly will!"

A few days later it actually stopped raining and the sky whipped off its grey cover to show blue again. Thomas leaned over the verandah rails and squinted up at the sun. Drops of water from the jasmine fell onto his neck.

"Let's have a picnic," he said at breakfast.

Maire glanced up from her kedgeree. "It will be soaking underfoot."

"We can have our food in the carriage with the top down," he pointed out. "Nobody need get wet."

"Or we could row across the harbour," suggested Samuel in a voice that slid disconcertingly from bass to treble.

"Good idea, son. You could row one boat and I another."

"We could race!"

"Would there be room for me?" asked Mrs. Meyney, patting at her pleated lips with a napkin.

"And room for Sister Moya?" Sarah glanced sideways at her mother. The nuns had been less in evidence around the house in the past few weeks, not forbidden but not officially invited either, and Sarah noticed the lack of approval keenly.

Juliette smiled and began clearing plates away. The syrup that she and Abby took three times a day made her feel lightheaded, but it was a delightfully pleasant feeling that took away all the hard edges and made the whole world gentle and somehow insubstantial. It had even taken the sharpness off her appetite. A picnic, she thought dreamily as she carried plates out to the kitchen and began rinsing them in a bowl of cold water. A picnic would be lovely.

Mrs. Meyney wore a large red bonnet and a red cape. She sat in the stern of Samuel's boat and shouted orders to

him which he doggedly ignored. Sarah and Sister Moya
giggled together. Abby sat facing her father, so quiet that
it worried him. She must be missing Jane. Juliette was in
Samuel's boat too, trailing her fingers in the water and
singing quietly to herself. Rose sat beside her, subdued in
apple green. Mrs. Meyney's voice carried like a ship horn
over the water. Maire had stayed at home.

"Let's sing a song!" suggested Sister Moya. She
launched robustly into the surprising choice of "Come
Where the Moonbeams Linger." Everybody but Thomas
and Samuel was able to join in.

A Maori canoe glided across their wake. Though the pad-
dlers knew Thomas by sight their reply to his cheerful
greeting was cool.

Thomas frowned, staring after them. "What a shame.
What a waste. We could have achieved a special harmony
with the Maoris that would be unique in the world today,
but bungling Governors with stupid pride are going to
spoil it all."

Sister Moya broke off in mid-line to peer at him sternly.
"Please, Mr. Peridot. We are going to enjoy ourselves today."

"And rightly, too," he apologised. "In the bush the
world's problems gain an unrealistic proportion. Abby,
dear, you look drowsy. Are you quite well?"

"It must be the Nervene. Sister Amy says it is dangerously addictive, to be sure."

"How could it be?"

"That's only what Sister Amy says."

Thomas understood why Maire had taken such a dislike
to this diminutive nun. Though she had a jolly disposition,
her suggestions did seem more like orders and her pro-
nouncements brooked no argument. Nuns should be self-
effacing and humble, decided Thomas.

On arrival Sister Moya and Sarah wandered off along
the beach arm in arm, their laughter streaming back like
fluttering ribbons. Rose and Juliette left their stockings
rolled up on top of the picnic hamper and paddled in the
lacy edge of the water.

Juliette trod on the sharp rim of a shell. When she
picked it up it glowed like mother of pearl and sat round

and pink in the cup of her palm. The water was so cold that her feet tingled.

Rose gazed across at the town. Her skirts were bunched in mittened hands and her marred face wore a clownish wistfulness.

"I do wish we could visit Jane. She must have been so much in love with Mr. Bragg, and he so desperately in love with her, for them to elope like that."

Instinctively Juliette looked around to see if anybody was within eavesdropping distance of the forbidden name, but only Mrs. Meyney was there, out of place and uncomfortable on the jetty steps and well out of hearing range.

"Don't you think that it must be wonderful? Imagine being loved so strongly that the gentleman could not live without you. Imagine such passion! Oh, Juliette, don't you long for something like that too?"

"I have never considered the matter," lied Juliette. Rose's intensity frightened her. It seemed to burst out of her with a force that breathed violence.

"I cannot bear to think of it without a ferocious envy. Jane has her own home, and could even have a family soon. It won't happen to me. I know it won't." The words sounded so sad and so unlike Rose that Juliette wanted to thrust a hand over her mouth to halt the flow of words. "I'm twenty," she continued passionately. "Twenty years old! Nobody so far has asked for my hand and I doubt that anybody ever will. When we go to dances or balls I am only asked to dance by grandfathers or uncles who talk about Napoleon and the Duke of Wellington all the time—as if Waterloo happened last month! Nobody wants me, Juliette. Nobody is ever going to fall in love with me. Oh, I would dearly love a home and family of my own. I dread the loneliness ahead of me."

"It *will* happen to you one day."

"I used to look at my face in the mirror and assure myself that my nose is not really as misshapen as I had feared. From all angles I inspected it, trying to convince myself. But it is no use, for I am implacably ugly."

"No, Rose, you are not!"

But Rose did not seem to see or hear her. She was gazing

across the bay as though somehow she could feel the
warmth of Jane's happiness from there.

Samuel had stationed himself at the far end of the jetty
to fish. Beside him stretched Tippy, pretending not to
watch the sea gulls because he felt too lazy to chase them.
Samuel regarded fishing as a stylised game rather than a
means of catching food. Fish were like women, the Maoris
had counselled. If they appreciated the artistry they might
consider rising to the bait.

The sun was hot on his back. His senses were flooded
with the salty smells of drying sand and rotting seaweed.
This freedom felt marvellous after the past three days of
Fintona's restrictions and discomforts. Living in a house
was so horribly complicated with so many rules and manners and matters of hygiene. At the bush camp he could
tear at his chunks of food with his fingers. That was the
life—raw and free and full of flavour. He tipped his face to
the sun and hoped the fine weather would stretch another
two or three days. If it did, then Thomas would declare the
wet weather over and they would be able to leave.

Abby and Thomas strolled over the springy grass that
carpeted the border between sand and earth. Here a small
park had been fashioned with shrubs; a meandering peb-
bled path and some grey picnic tables stood forlornly under
two pohutukawa trees. Abby wore a powder-blue cashmere
cape and gown, far too expensive for picnic attire. Her bonnet was the gift from Mr. Bennington and she looked se-
renely mature.

"Are you happy, dear?" asked Thomas.

"Oh yes, Father. I do enjoy living in a fine house, but I
cannot say that housework appeals to me. I'd rather not do
that."

"But you are happy? Do you miss Jane?"

"I do not wish to discuss unpleasant matters, please, Father, if you don't mind."

"Of course." They walked in silence. Two sea gulls on
the beach nearby flew off as they approached.

Thomas asked suddenly, "Have you thought of your own
future? Do you know what you want for yourself?"

"I am quite decided!" she said happily. "But then, I al-

ways have been. I want a fine house, a carriage of my own,
and enough servants so I never again have to wash another fork or spoon or scrape another carrot."

"Does this mean that there is a young man on the scene?
Someone who has captured your fancy, as they say?"

"Not a young man, but someone very kind. But I
shouldn't speak to you, should I? This is all a little premature."

He knew who she meant, but on such a lovely day it
seemed too ridiculously unsuitable to possibly be true.
Fearfully, yet hoping to bring her to her senses by making
her spell it out, he said, "Can you feel able to confide in
your father just a little more?"

She was sweetly surprised. "I could have imagined you
would guess at once. I would very much like to marry Mr.
Bennington, and Aunt Maire has hinted already that he
wants to marry me. Isn't that absolutely perfect?"

Thomas was unable to reply.

Dear Mama [wrote Leigh]. I hope that this letter finds
you in excellent helth as I am tho' suffereing from a slite
cold but not to bad tho'. The fellows of the 58th are a rough
lot but the officers proper gentlemen so am glad I am with
them. It is all very strange tho' and sometimes I wake and
forget what has happened, but will be accustomed in time
no doubt. Everybody is much taken with the Maoris and
call them blackes and admire the way they squat and
kneel all the time. Sometimes a chiefe comes aboard to
talk and they recline the whole time. This amuses all the
fellowes who stand about laughing but the chefes laugh
too and no insults taken. The maoris up here are more
greedy than in Auckland town and we have to bargain
very strongly for everything we want. Some of the officers
are so surprised by all the friendly Maoris and the fellowes
have to be warned constantly not to treat anybody as enemy yet tho' that time will come when we go to attack
Pomare's Pa soon tho' we must wait for the weather to improve as it has rained without a breake for more than ten
days now. I am much in demand from knowing a little Maori and amuse myself by inventing tales about what the
different Maori things meane, why some Maoris wear

string in their ear and some bone, or flax or a nail hung there. Of course it is all made up tho' the officers beleve me and it is all most amusing. Ensign Deverell askes to be remembered to you all. From your devoted son,

Leigh

Dear Leigh [wrote Juliette]. I am so glad that you are in good health and I do hope that your cold is quite gone by now. We were all so amused and delighted by the funny things in your letter and hope that you are still managing to divert yourself. I also hope that these socks fit. One pair is for Ensign Deverell as I promised.

We have had tremendous gales and storms here. One bad storm knocked over all the walls and buildings at the new Albert Barracks and they will have to be started all over again. Today it is sunny but only weak sunshine and all over town people are hanging mats and curtains out to dry and having them soaked by the torrents of rain.

Father is home now. He helped make up a petition for the governor about the Militia Bill but the governor would not see any of the men and as a consequence Father is rather angry. He says that the Maoris will fight only as hard as they are challenged but perhaps I should not put that if you are about to fight Pomare. We pray for you every night and know that you will be returned home safely.

She pushed the end of the pencil against her chin and considered the ending. "Your faithful servant?" No, that seemed rather stiff. "Your devoted stepsister?" No, too formal still. She frowned and then hurriedly wrote, "Your devoted friend, Juliette." Yes, that had a warmth and even a hint of affection. She folded up the letter and went to look for the sealing wax.

Nineteen

"I approve!" said Stephen, moving from the small dining room into the tiny parlour.

"It is all the Simpkins' furniture, but we like it too, which is fortunate. Do come and look at the back porch and I shall describe Tim's plans for alterations."

"In the name of Jove, I declare that alterations are more of a national disease than a pastime. Mama has altered Fintona three times in as many years and when Abby leaves she plans to turn your old room into an office with the theme of a Turkish boudoir. Can you imagine that?"

Jane smiled tolerantly. "The fashion papers say that Eastern décor is all the rage. The Queen herself began the fashion and she even has Indian attendants to make the theme complete!"

"Then our town is doomed to become an illustration from *The Arabian Nights,* for if the Queen likes it, then it must be good! I gather she has taken to dressing Prince Edward in sailor suits, judging from the sudden blossoming of young tars."

"You men must find something to criticise," Jane said lightly, adding as if it was of no importance, "When is Abby to be married?"

"March or April, I think. Not for quite some months yet. I say there, are you all right, Jane? Here, sit down. You look pale."

"It's nothing." But she did ease herself into a chair. "The doctor says I shall be perfectly safe. The saying is that one should never trust a doctor whose wife has died, but there is only a choice between Dr. Havow and Dr. Forster."

"Adrian Forster is excellent. He came out to treat a sailor on the *Lorendee* and was most efficient. He knew what he was about." He paused, suddenly remembering gossip that Dr. Forster's wife had died in a protracted hideous childbirthing. "Are you afraid, Jane?"

"A little," she admitted. "No, not really. These matters are in God's hands, but sometimes I cannot help worrying. . . . But it worries me more that Abigail has cut me off so cruelly. I know she hates me."

"How could she when you were so close all those years?"

"Because I didn't confide in her, I suppose. I didn't dare to in case Mama found out, and you know how Abigail gabbles so. But she has certainly cut me now. I almost bumped into her one day. She was with Mr. Flash Jack himself, hanging onto his arm and looking positively made of money, with poor Mrs. Bellwood trying to keep up and be a proper chaperone. Abigail saw me, I know she did, but she swept past into Merrington's and settled herself grandly at a counter chair while Mr. Bennington scurried around her like a helpful gnome. That snub wounded me, Stephen. Abigail was my dearest friend."

"She'll come round in time."

"I doubt it," said Jane gloomily. "Not after Tim walked out on Mr. Bennington. He'll never be forgiven for that. Still, we'll manage, and married life is fun. You should try it yourself."

"Marriage?"

"Why not! You're not afraid of the prospect, are you?"

"Terrified."

"I have another theory about why you've never married," she said reflectively. "I think you're waiting for Juliette to grow up."

"How can you do it?" asked Juliette as she rubbed polish into a pair of Maire's black buttoned boots. "Flash Jack Bennington! Abby, he's older than Father and not a quarter as handsome!"

"He is the kindest person in the world." She leaned on the verandah rail, posing in a sophisticated manner.

"You mean generous, not kind. They're hardly the same thing."

"I see no difference."

"But surely you don't *love* him?" When there was no reply she looked up from her furious rubbing to find her sister smiling at her in a decidedly superior way.

"I might have guessed that you would say something silly and romantic like that."

"But love is terribly important," insisted Juliette.

Abby swung a languid foot. "So are a lot of other things. Things which I intend to have." With that she marched off down the long verandah, her new morocco slippers pattering and her new lace parasol swinging jauntily.

Juliette's head bent over her task as she resumed more thoughtfully. There was no reply she could confidently give Abby yet she was positive her sister was wrong. If *she* loved Mr. Bennington the way I love Leigh, then it would be perfect for them both, she decided. Then a long echo stirred in her mind. Clearly she could see a young Abby, eight or nine years old, saying with pert assurance, "I shall marry a rich man because then it won't matter if I cannot sew or cook."

Attracted by the sound of her quiet chuckling, Stephen came to sit beside her. "It is good to see people happy in their work," he said, taking the boot and rag from her.

She stared out across the harbour, her chin resting in her polish-smeared hands. "Do you think that people should always marry for love?"

"Abby, you mean?"

"Yes. I was wondering about her—and about Jane," she added in a whisper.

"Jane married for love and seems positively radiant. But don't you worry about your sister. People often marry for practical reasons and never have a moment's regret. Abigail is possibly one of those."

She sighed. Stephen resisted an impulse to put his arm around her; she looked so slight and vulnerable, looking up at him appealingly.

"I worry about the future. What if . . . nobody loves me?" She recalled Rose's pathetic words and a chill crept over her shoulders.

"I think that the right man will love you very much," he said in a miraculously steady voice.

"Do you think so?"

"I'd bet my life on it."

"I'm glad you feel that way, because I have such terrible doubts at times. I wonder if I'm lovable at all. No, please don't smile at me like that, Mr. Stephen! I'm *serious!* I know that Aunt Maire doesn't like me, and though I love Father I don't think he cares for me either. When he looks at me it is with such an odd expression on his face. As if I hurt him, or offended him in some way." Her mouth turned down at the corners in an unhappy little twist. "I cannot understand it at all."

"I can," he said soberly. "I think it's because every time he looks at you he thinks about somebody he loved very much but who was killed a long time ago. That's why it hurts him to see you growing up to be so much like her."

"Mother, you mean?"

"Yes, the beautiful Evangeline. Everybody who knew her says so. It's your eyes, Juliette. They are exactly like hers."

"Nobody has ever told me that before."

"People would be much too afraid of hurting your feelings by stirring up old memories; I'm only telling you to help you understand your father."

"I'm so grateful that you did." She sighed again, a tremulous little sound. "I wish that I could talk to Father the way I can to you."

"I wouldn't advise it; some things go too deeply to be talked about. Your father is a proud man. Never mind. You can talk to me whenever you wish and about any subject under the sun. You know that, don't you?"

She was staring out across the harbour again, chin in hands. "Mmmm," she replied absently, then, "I wonder when we will receive another letter from Leigh. Do you think it will be soon?" She glanced at him in surprise. "Why are you laughing at me again?"

"I'm not, Miss Olivine. I'm laughing at myself."

Leigh felt as if it had been raining forever and as if he had been wading through sticky mud for almost as long. His boots were sodden, his dirty trousers plastered to sweaty legs, and his back was racked with fatigue. The war seemed to have been going on for nine years instead of nine months. Great chunks of that time had been spent out under oozing skies with the relief being a two-month stint camping amid the squalid ruins of Kororareka. Only the rats, fleas, filthiest grogshops, and most sleazy whores still remained there. That rest and recreation break had been almost enough to make Leigh want to row across the bay and beg sanctuary at the Mission, though he had been careful to let none of his disgust show as he drank and laughed and did his best to join in the bawdy hundred-chorus songs with his friends. Leigh had grown up in the shelter of the Church, believing sex to be a gift from God. So to see it used as a cheap pastime, a palliative from boredom, a subject of coarse humour was a complete revelation. He did not approve. Though he pretended to join in the fun he found a dozen excuses to turn away at the last minute, fearful that his inexperience would be laughed at.

Only Deverell suspected his distaste but because it was no more than a suspicion Leigh was let off lightly with a wink and a friendly jest. Leigh was grateful. This campaign would have been doubly hellish without the security of a friend.

The 58th Regiment—with some of the 99th Regiment, several hundred sailors from the *Calliope* and *North Star,* and parties of friendly Maoris—were gathered around and below a heavily palisaded pa. According to scouts, it was sheltering five hundred warriors together with the chiefs Hone Heke and Kawiti. Many officers believed that those with any sense would have crept up the hillside through the night-blackened bush to escape days ago. For almost a fortnight the pa had been suffering the bruising of constant shellfire; though kept up continually, it was so desultory that the main effect was to wear down the soldiers' nerves and prevent anybody from getting any sleep. Morale was poor. This was the fifth pa to be attacked since the punitive war began. Another dreary, muddy skirmish. Nobody really wanted to go on.

Leigh bit into a chunk of doughy damper. It tasted of the ashes in which it had been cooked and it stuck unpleasantly to the roof of his mouth, but he chewed it and swallowed it mechanically, then sucked down a mouthful of lukewarm, heavily sweetened peppermint tea. It was seven o'clock on a Saturday morning and already steamy hot. He stared morosely at the low sky and wondered if it would rain again today.

Deverell sauntered towards him, looking freshly shaven.

"Having a late breakfast again, Yardley? Tut, tut! These soft-living lads who don't know how to wake up in the morning will be the downfall of the 58th." He squatted on his heels and tore off a lump of Leigh's damper. "Have you seen the new Governor yet?"

"Only from a distance. He has better things to do than talk to ensigns."

"He was down at the river. They found a body in the flax. One of the Auckland volunteers, poor wretch. His head had been sliced right through at the temple. Grey and that fool Despard were there looking at it because the Maoris said he had been struck with a mere and Grey was interested in what sort of a wound the native weapons make. Despard said it was obviously a musket wound. I say, it's a bad thing he had to come back from Auckland. After the way Despard sent so many men to be butchered at the last pa, you'd think the authorities would have kept him away simply to keep the morale of the troops up. After all, they've sacked Governor FitzRoy over this bloody war, so why not an incompetent Colonel?"

"You'll be flogged if anybody hears you!"

"Only if Despard does, and he never listens, even to his officers' good advice. He's still down at the river bleating away about muskets. I don't think Governor Grey is very impressed. He's standing with his head tipped back staring at Despard with one eye closed."

"Did he say anything?"

"Not much. I gather that he's one of those types who says damned little but means every word of it. They say his wife is a delectable piece. Positively beddable with huge gorgeous eyes. Sounds like your Juliette."

"There you go again."

"Why not? Juliette is a beautiful lass, and beauty was made to be praised. Besides, she can make the softest, snuggest socks I've ever worn."

"I've noticed you've not changed them in months."

"Gives you something to gripe about. I say! I think they are actually aiming those cannon at long last. Those last three balls hit the palisade."

"They must have trained new gunners. Or else they're aiming at something else," said Leigh.

"I think they're actually doing something positive at last, and about time, too. Hone Heke and Kawiti must be just as tired of looking at us as we are of staring at them. I say! Another hit! Listen to that cheering. Don't get your hopes up, lads!" he called. "Even if they do breach the walls there won't be any action before tomorrow."

"Just as well. We've pork on the hoof for dinner. I agreed to pay the asking price, but after the last unhappy dealings with those little Maori scamps I made them include a full day's minding."

"Did you give him any money?"

"And have him resell the pig again to someone else? Not likely. Some enterprising fellow sold the same pig over twenty times last week when our provisions were low."

Later that evening they sat near a fire watching the joint of pork drip juice and fat into the embers while Deverell complained how long pork took to cook.

"There'll be chicken tomorrow, if the friendlies don't dash in the minute the enemy leaves and grab all the best pickings. Look at how they hogged the lot last time and only left us a few scrawny chickens and a couple of baskets of potatoes. They're supposed to be helping the army but if you ask me they're doing better out of this war than anyone."

"They're only following their customs," Leigh told him. "The Maori people have traditionally had so few material things that food supplies and other plunder are extremely important to them. Far more so than to us."

"Ah! I'm getting really sour on these Maoris, but for the life of me I can't help it. I went right off them as a race after that gruesome business at the last pa . . . Ohewai . . ."

"Ohaeawai."

"Your tongue is used to flicking around those barbaric words. But that business polished me off properly. It was bad enough that they tortured that poor wretch to death, but to drag in that dead officer and carve bits off him to be roasted and eaten . . . bloody cannibals."

"That was a rum lot and no denying it."

"I know you've been brought up here, so it probably wasn't so much of a shock to you." He shuddered. "I used to think these tattooed faces were quaint and picturesque, but no longer. I wonder what I'm doing here . . . serving the Queen? Ha! I'll wager that she doesn't give a tinker's damn. Better than that, I'll wager that she neither knows nor cares what's going on in this part of her goddamned glorious dominions!"

"This doesn't sound like you."

"So it's getting to me, too, eh? Sooner or later we all get struck down by dysentery, fever, and rabid cynicism—but not necessarily in that order. No, Yardley, I shan't succumb. This roast pork will lift my spirits splendidly and when it's done and I'm pleasantly relaxed I'll tell you all about that escaped convict woman I met in Bombay."

"What, again?"

"There are a wealth of luscious details I haven't even found superlatives to describe yet."

"I can't wait to hear," groaned Leigh.

Ensign Deverell looked at him slyly from under lids half closed against drifting smoke.

"You are a lascivious prude, Yardley. Isn't that so? You can join in the rioting but your little papist conscience gives you such a rollicking afterwards that it's not worth it, is it?"

"And you can find your own damned meal!" Leigh flared. "I'm damned tired of your criticism, telling me what I should do and what I'm a fool not to do, and prying into what I did do. It's none of your damned business! You can take your long nose and go and use it to sniff out a meal somewhere else!"

Deverell recognised that the outburst came because he had carelessly stabbed and accidentally hit the truth. But he was quick and smooth enough to recover swiftly and begin repairing the damage.

"I say, mate, I'm sorry! You know I'm only jesting with you, I'd never say a thing like that except in fun . . . you know that! I'm your friend, and if we don't stick together there's not much hope for us in this miserable campaign, is there now?"

Leigh glared at him.

For a second Deverell was tempted to stand up and walk away, but the pork smelled irresistible. So he stayed, he smiled, and he talked. Around a hundred campfires behind the muddy breastworks other soldiers were squabbling and talking with animation and anticipation. Today was the breaching of the palisade. Tomorrow could very well be the last day of the long, long war.

"It was bad luck, pure bad luck," repeated Leigh. He was seated under the rose arbour with his bandaged right leg propped comfortably on a bench. He was retelling the story for the benefit of Belinda Godwin, who leaned with studied grace towards him. Sister Moya and Sarah were ignoring the often-heard tale to search for quotations that might be suitable for the discussion panel at Saturday's Friendship Evening. Sister Moya was writing, Sarah whispering and giggling, and every now and then Belinda would look at them to reproach them for spoiling the account of Leigh's adventures. Juliette and Rose sat together on a low bench, heads bent over their embroidery while they listened once again. To Juliette the accounts of war sounded strange and thrilling, alien and yet, in countless details, familiar; for Turi had told her many things a long time ago which surfaced now in the descriptions of the wild hakas, the Maori soldiers naked in battle and the nights filled with the eerie laments for the dead.

"The Maoris couldn't get used to our strange ways," he was saying. "The way we dressed in red and black to be seen so easily in the bush. The way we marched openly and advanced without stealth was such a contrast to their own tactics. They could not understand our disregard for the laws of tapu. Maoris never eat before a battle or go about in such a businesslike way as we do. And what horrified them above everything was the way we carried stretchers ready for the dead and wounded. To them that is inviting disaster!" He paused ruefully. "I was more than a little pleased that we had stretchers, though, for I had good cause to use one myself."

"You were lucky that the musket ball didn't shatter the bone," said Rose.

Juliette shivered, recalling how close Leigh had come to having the leg amputated.

"Dozens of fellows were hurt worse than I," said Leigh with the right touch of modesty.

"Do tell us again how it happened," begged Belinda.

Juliette looked up from the muslin collar she was trimming. She wished that Belinda was back home, or down at the town, or anywhere but perched over Leigh, practically climbing into his lap. It was not fair that she should be monopolising him when it was Stephen whom she avidly pursued, with such enthusiasm that he was now forced to approach Fintona by rowboat from town rather than risk having her see him ride by along the roadway. This morning Juliette had met her at the door and had told Belinda plainly that Stephen was not at home, only to be told that she had come to see the "poor dear brave patient hero" . . . with flowers and chocolate, no less. She's setting her bonnet at him, thought Juliette indignantly. Stephen has made his aversion so plain that she is turning her attention to Leigh instead. Surely he can see that behind that flat doll's face her mind is working at baiting a trap for him?

"Do tell us again," said Belinda. "I should adore to hear how bravely you fought, how gallant you were."

"It was sheer bad luck," repeated Leigh. Juliette noticed his inscrutable expression and hoped that he was tiring of her silly voice as rapidly as the rest of them were.

But he obliged her. "We were all pressed into the actual charge towards the pa, even Deverell and I, so we took off our greatcoats and primed our pistols. Somebody shouted that a white flag was being hoisted but I didn't see it and obviously Captain Denny didn't either, for off we went, scrambling over the earthworks and through the ditches. Some of us dashed in at the breaches and others pushed at the main palisade itself; it was so weakened by the pounding of cannon fire that it simply toppled over and would have given the warriors an enormous surprise if they had been hiding behind it. To our astonishment there seemed to be nobody in the pa except for two frightened old hags who cowered behind the well and squawked at us. Some of the men were all for scalping them as the Maoris had done to some of our dead earlier."

"They really do scalp people?"

"As I said earlier, Miss Godwin, if you will recall. Captain Denny gave orders that the women were not to be harmed. But they ducked away into an underground chamber and immediately began ringing a bell to give alarm to the others; so perhaps Captain Denny was being rather too chivalrous, for right away the Maori warriors began pouring back into the pa through gaps in the back wall. It was quite an irony—us in the pa defending it from the rebels who were quite determined to reclaim it."

"Is this when you did something very brave, Mr. Yardley?"

"Only what any member of the 58th would do in battle, Miss Godwin. I was dragging a fellow officer to safety when a musket ball hit me and knocked me to the ground. So, as you can see, my brave deed hardly came to fruition."

"But it did! It made you into a hero!"

"Hardly a hero," said Rose. "Though we are very proud of him and think him extremely brave."

"Mama thinks that he fought the northern campaign all by himself," said Sarah dryly. "It is a wonder that she even lets him feed himself, so intent is she on pampering him."

"We are all extremely proud of Leigh," said Juliette. Leigh turned his full attention to her, looking into her eyes with a very slight smile, like a whisper meant only for her to hear. "Thank you," he said quietly.

"Leigh, tell me, please, did you have any dealings with Te Pahi's pa in the bay beyond the whaling station where we used to live?"

The smile slipped off and he said, "Te Pahi's pa? Let me see now . . . that would be south of Kororareka . . . ah, yes, we did go there but it was deserted, I think. Yes, it was deserted."

"But in the newspapers it was reported that . . ."

"Juliette, you know that you must not believe what is printed at the newspaper office. Why, if the facts of the matter lack excitement, then the gentlemen of the press will sharpen wits and pens and seek to compensate for it!"

At dinner that evening he tried to lay that argument before an enraged Thomas.

"So the brave forces attacked Ruapekapeka on a Sunday, did they? So that was the 'courageous assault' of which Colonel Despard was so pompously proud?"

"Please, Thomas." Maire set down her soup spoon and nodded to Juliette. "That Brown Windsor was delicious. You may serve the fish now." And to everybody at the table she said, "I trust you all read this evening's newspaper. Our Leigh was mentioned by name in the despatches. Colonel Despard praised his daring and selfless courage."

"Hey? Praised in despatches?" said Mr. Bellwood.

"You must be very proud of him," said Mrs. Bellwood.

"Oh, we are."

"Meyney will want to hear about this, hey, my boy? What do you say we take a stroll over there after dinner to tell him all about it?"

"Leigh cannot stroll anywhere, Mr. Bellwood," said Maire. "What do you say, Thomas? Is it not wonderful that Leigh was mentioned by name? Her Majesty's bravest troops, the Colonel said."

"It is splendid that Leigh is mentioned by name, but so is almost everybody else in the entire regiment." He stood up and shook out the rolled-up newspaper, which had been tucked behind a vase of freesias on the sideboard. "Look at this column, and this, and this. Hundreds of names! You might consider it wonderful; I think it suspicious. Colonel Despard is seeking to hide the truth with lavish praise, and he trusts that all who are praised will keep from speaking out about this shameful campaign. Listen to this, all of you."

"Thomas, please! The poached fish is served and the egg sauce is most delicate. It will not wait . . ."

"Neither will this. Listen, all of you, and hear the truth." He read, " 'The manner in which possession was gained of Kawiti's pa did not, in our opinion, justify the lengthened, pompous, commendatory despatch of Colonel Despard, in which a mere casualty of the defenders—being at prayers without the pa and enabling our troops and allies to enter unperceived and unmolested—is termed "the capture of a fortress of extraordinary strength by assault, and nobly defended by a brave and determined enemy." ' Now tell me, Ensign Yardley, did the attack happen when Heke and company were outside the pa conducting Sunday services?"

"Sir, we did not know what they were doing . . . we thought a defence would be made . . . we expected . . ." He gave up. "Sir, you should treat those newspaper articles with caution. They twist the truth to compose a livelier story."

"Leigh, do not excite yourself," said Maire. Leigh obediently stopped speaking. Thomas sat down again and dug knife and fork into his fish. He chewed, drew a bone from his mouth, and laid it on the side of his plate.

"So it is true," he said quietly. "There was nobody there. The attack was made on Sunday. Maoris never fight on the Sabbath. Everybody knows that. Oh, God, what have the British military stooped to, to do a thing like this!"

Leigh began to speak but his mother silenced him with a gesture of her hand. They all ate in uncomfortable silence.

"I wonder if this was the Governor's idea?" said Thomas suddenly. "I wonder if our new Governor is the type of man who would resort to low tactics like these to secure a victory? I wonder if the outpouring of praise—most uncharacteristic for Despard, you would agree—is really our Governor Grey's idea?"

"No!" said Maire in real fright. "Thomas, I beg of you, please do not pick a quarrel with our new Governor. If you know how humiliating it is for us to be cast aside, crossed off guest lists . . ."

"This is our country, Maire. If we do not see that fair play is maintained, who will? I repeat, this is our country."

"And we, your family, have to live in it," she answered coldly.

More and more often lately Maire was troubled by feelings of dissatisfaction. In marrying Thomas and later moving to the new capital she had laid the groundwork of a secure future that would embrace financial success, social success, and the fulfillment of her own personal ambitions. Though she was now wealthy in her own right, this central

ambition seemed to have been achieved without the development of all the subsidiary aims. She had hoped to see
herself by the age of sixty firmly enthroned as a matriarch
of society, with three daughters wed to rich and perhaps
even titled gentlemen, and two sons who followed her guidance for the family's glory. However, at fifty-six, she was
no closer to that ambition now than she had been in Kororareka. One daughter was cast out, another proposed to
underline the family's Catholicism by becoming a nun,
and the third was so cripplingly self-conscious that she
drove prospective suitors away with her forbidding manner. Stephen's open defiance was a bitter disappointment
(and she shuddered to think that he might be as good as his
word and actually marry some Maori scum!). So Maire was
left with only Leigh to be proud of. She had always loved
him best and it was comforting to remind herself that her
faith and affection had not been misplaced.

And the Peridots? Thomas could be the social salvation
of the family if only he would keep his troublemaking, rad-
ical ideas to himself. In the whole of history nothing had
ever been gained by going against the government; but no
amount of persuasion on her part would convince Thomas
of that. He was one of the most respected men in Auckland
because of his knowledge of Maori ways, his business acumen, his easy conversation and, despite long sojourns in
the bush and amongst the Waikato tribes, his surprisingly
courtly manners. He was the epitome of the ideal colonial
gentleman, attuned to the native life yet at ease in a
parlour. Maire was shrewd enough to realise that his ac-
ceptability was the positive that ruled out the negative
of her religion. She hoped strongly that Governor Grey
would live up to his reputation for being interested in the
natives' welfare—for then he would certainly seek Thomas
out and listen to his views. If only she could be sure that
Thomas would not force his opinions of the war on the Governor!

Yes, if only he was as malleable as he was over domestic
issues. He agreed mildly to almost all of her dictates con-
cerning the girls. Abby's marriage plans had come as such
a shock that he belatedly realised how little he knew his
daughters. When Maire began to explain why Juliette had

been given extra household work to do, he murmured that she knew best.

"Abigail is so occupied with dress fittings, and the work is good for Juliette. If she is kept busy she will stop brooding, and if she retires to bed exhausted she may avoid the nightmares which have plagued her since the Nervene treatment stopped."

"My dear wife, you may dote on Dr. Havow all you please and consult him to your soul's pleasure, but he is not to give Juliette Nervene. I had heard it was addictive and disbelieved the opinion; now Dr. Forster confirms it."

"I know what Dr. Forster said." She cut him off irritably. "You have told me twice already." What did *he* know about the competence of medical practitioners? Inverted snobbery, that's what it was, to take the word of a doctor who kept to his rightful place among the poor, against that of the grandson of a Duke. Yes, inverted snobbery and so typical of Thomas. But she smothered her feelings of resentment. It was odd how strongly her feelings towards the two Peridot girls had changed. Now Abigail was the one she favoured. Possibly the change of heart was because she would soon be rid of her, but Abigail had been so charmingly biddable over this marriage that Maire warmed to her to a surprising degree. It was now Juliette who so grated on Maire's nerves that she wanted to order the girl out of her sight. Juliette's hesitant manner was maddening. But above all her growing resemblance to Evangeline infuriated her stepmother.

Juliette was so happy to have Leigh home that Maire's dislike of her went unnoticed. These days she thought of little but him. It was fortunate for her that Maire had not observed Leigh's heightened interest in her after his return; if she had, Leigh would not have been permitted to recuperate comfortably at Fintona.

"I liked the socks very much," said Leigh. "They were the best ones that anybody received in the whole campaign." He pulled out a kitchen chair and sat opposite Juliette at the oilcloth-covered table.

"Were they?" asked Juliette, flushing with pleasure. "I knitted four and sent the best two to you. The ones that En-

sign Deverell got had a few stitches dropped. Not that it
was really noticeable, but I knew the mistakes were
there." She sprinkled the india-rubber knife board with
dark powder and rubbed a knife back and forth five times
on each side of the blade before wiping it with a damp rag
and placing it to one side.

"They looked perfect to me." He gazed around the
kitchen. It was uncomfortably muggy in here. Though the
fires had been set above and below the oven ready for the
preparation of the evening meal, they would not be lit for
another hour yet. But even without that added heat the
room was stuffy and humid.

Above them rain thundered on the roof. The knife board
made a hissing noise as Juliette concentrated on rubbing
the cutlery across it. The frills of her blue house cap hid
her face, and her neck was very white where it arched and
slid under the blue and yellow cotton dress. Her thin chestnut hair was tied back loosely with a snippet of black braid
and fell in curls down her back. Soft tendrils of hair clung
to her damp neck. Leigh hungrily contemplated the shape
of her shoulders under the floral material.

His voice was husky. "You don't have to stay in here the
whole afternoon, do you?" He paused and struggled to
make his remarks sound light. How she had changed in
the months he had been away. Her girlish prettiness had
fined into a delicate maturity that stirred him disturb-
ingly every time he looked at her.

"What about it?" he asked. "Tawa and Mary are visiting the servants at Bellwoods' and Rose has a music pupil.
I'm bored, Juliette. Why don't we go into the morning
room and have a game of brag? It's much more pleasant in
there."

"Oh." Disappointment clouded her face as she looked up
at him. "I should adore to do that, Leigh, but I truly cannot. Aunt Maire expects all this silverware to be polished
today and the egg spoons alone are going to take me an
age. They have been neglected for so long that they are
going to need a whole packet of Spanish whiting and hours
of rubbing."

"You'd not neglect them . . . even for me?" The question

was casually uncaring but he spoke in a tenderly low voice and placed a hand over hers.

For a moment she gazed at the hand that had captured hers. It was scarred now and marked by scratches of manuka branches received when the troops had moved through the bush. The sight of it filled her with so much emotion that her heart had to beat hard to prevent her from fainting. Nervously she glanced up away from the hand, across his red-jacketed chest resplendent with black braid frogging, and up to his face. His eyes met hers.

"Juliette," he whispered. Without letting go of her hand he swiftly changed his chair for the one next to hers, and in doing so his leg pressed against her thigh. It was accidental but seemed shockingly intimate.

"Don't . . . please don't turn away from me," he said.

Her closed lids were shadowed with the same dark blue as her eyes, and fringes of dark lashes trembled above her cheeks. His arms slipped around her and his mouth pressed clumsily on hers. She seemed so slight and vulnerable that it elated him with a pleasurable feeling of power over her. Cautiously he moved a hand around to cup one of her breasts. Instantly her eyes flew open; but he kept his hand where it was.

"I love you, Juliette."

"Oh." It sounded like a sob. Her hands were still on the table in front of her; as though waiting for her to resume her task. Her face was pressed into the hot skin of his neck, and tiny bristles prickled her cheeks. Her whole being was awash with the most numbing, overwhelming sensation of perfect happiness.

He was not surprised that they were interrupted; the kitchen at Fintona was heavily trafficked, and the Maori girls were due back at any time.

Tawa burst in, springing them apart as suddenly as the release on a trap. Her brown face was shiny with rain and her bunched curls dripped water over her shoulders.

"No umbrella, Tawa?" asked Leigh, covering his confusion with a show of good humour, while Juliette hurriedly began rubbing the knife blade back and forth over the pad.

"Mary, she got it. It's Sarah, she fell on the track. Looks like she hurt herself. I'm off to fetch the doctor."

"Sarah?" cried Juliette.

"Where?" asked Leigh. "I'd better help."

But Tawa had flung an oilskin cape around her shoulders and was gone again.

Only moments later Rose and Juliette peered anxiously out into the driving weather. Rain bounced off the hard lawn, and the trees at the top of the cliff had merged into the white haze. Leigh appeared as a dark blur, limping badly, staggering with a shapeless bundle in his arms. Mary's umbrella waved ineffectually above him.

Sarah was sodden and unconscious. While Rose hurried to fetch towels and rugs, Mary prepared hot cocoa. Leigh flexed her wrists and ankles looking for breaks.

"I think she's wrenched some muscles in this leg and given herself a nasty bump on the head," he told Juliette. "It's a good thing the girls were coming home along that track. She's soaked through, so who could say how long she's been there?"

"Probably hours. She and Sister Moya always dismiss the children when the weather threatens, so that they don't have to walk home in heavy rain. None of them have coats or changes of clothing, you see, so . . . oh dear, she's so terribly pale. Her breathing sounds odd. It's like a rattle."

"But she looks dreadful," said Juliette.

"I've seen some really sick people in the past year," Leigh reassured her. "She'll be fine, believe me."

Twenty

It was agreed between Maire and Dr. Havow that Sarah could have her first full day up on the day of Abby's wedding, provided that she took a double measure of Nervene that morning to ensure that she could not overexcite herself. The fall from the slipped-away path had given her bruised ribs and a nasty bump on the back of her head. Stephen had examined the scene of the accident when he returned home for the wedding, and he shook his head as he marvelled that Sarah had not plunged a hundred feet to the rocks below. Sarah was unimpressed. Because she had never really known illness she took this bout extremely poorly, with low spirits and a quiet misery that was completely out of character for her. She had endured the fittings for her new navy-blue silk gown with a mute passivity, and now as Juliette helped her dress she began to cry quietly.

"I don't feel at all well," she protested when Juliette tried to comfort her. "I've felt ill since that fall."

"Dr. Havow assures me that you have completely recovered," said Maire when she was summoned. "All that remains is for you to become accustomed to normal activity again. Now take your Nervene and you will feel better almost at once." She glanced at the other two girls. "Stand up straight, Juliette, and, Rose, do be nice to young Mr. Mannering. There is a Prince on his mother's side of the family and they are all respectably well to do. He will be feeling rather alone and fatigued after the voyage, so I am relying on you to entertain him and make him feel welcome in our town."

"I do wish Mama would not do this," sighed Rose when

she had gone. "I'm sure that Mr. Mannering is perfectly charming but I'm afraid that I dislike him quite intensely already."

Sarah dabbed at her eyes. "Even Leigh has not escaped her match-making," she said listlessly. "She is trying to interest Leigh in that empty-headed Belinda Godwin."

Juliette's face felt cold. She brushed a curl of Sarah's hair carefully around her finger. "I really don't think that Leigh could possibly be interested in her! Have you ever seen his face when she is simpering over him? He looks every bit as bored as Stephen does."

"Ah, yes," said Rose. "But now that an uncle in Montreal has died and left her a fur-trapping fortune the young men of this colony have begun to look at her in a different way. Whereas before she was something of a joke, now she is suddenly attractive."

"Leigh is too young for her!" persisted Juliette.

"He's twenty and she must be twenty-one."

"Not too young," said Sarah. "Fortunes don't happen along every day in a place like this."

"I suppose not," said Juliette. Her hands shook as she fitted the tiny cap of artificial delphiniums over Sarah's curls.

Rose pinched her cheeks as she leaned towards the mirror. "When I look in the glass all I really see is my nose," she observed sadly, then, recovering at once, she said, "It could be worse. I could be as fat as Miss Hopkins or have a strawberry birthmark on my brow like poor Lady Webster."

As they walked out together into the sunshine Juliette told herself, Leigh doesn't have to marry for money. He has the Richmond Line shares and his ensign's pay and Aunt Maire will settle a generous amount on him besides. I've heard her say that he will never go short of a pound and she will see to that. I know he won't marry that soppy Miss Godwin, no matter what anybody says. He loves me and he says so.

And to reinforce her sagging confidence, Leigh materialised as they walked down the verandah steps, told her she looked pretty enough to eat, swung her about until she cried out giddily, then limped up the steps and disappeared into the drawing room.

"Well!" said Rose. "He is in fine spirits!"

"Who could help but be?" said Juliette gaily. "Look at what a beautiful day it is."

The fickle March weather had decided to be graceful for Abby's garden wedding and had put on its best blue skies with fluffy white trimmings for the occasion. The freshly scythed lawn rolled smoothly to the fence line on all sides where late-blooming roses boasted the garden's only colour.

Thomas was supervising the erection of an awning, a skysail from the *Lorendee.* Maire followed him out onto the path.

Stephen leaned over the verandah rail, immaculate and darkly handsome in dark frock coat and trousers and a white ruffled shirt. Juliette thought, He looks like a man and Leigh still looks like a child, but was immediately ashamed of that disloyal notion.

He was saying laughingly, "What a pity it is, Mama, that you could not have arranged the wedding a month earlier. Then *two* Governors might have attended."

Nothing Stephen said these days seemed funny to her, so she replied stiffly, "I doubt that Governor FitzRoy would have been invited, though he was conciliatory to me at the end. Very conciliatory, in fact."

"Hmph!" said Thomas. "We've yet to have a Governor worth a dab of salt. I'm reserving judgement on this Grey fellow, though I'd have to admit he seems to have a knack for dealing with the natives. He's firm and if he can keep it up he'll get their respect." He moved away to assist with the placing of a supporting spar and when he turned back he noticed Maire staring doubtfully at him.

"Don't fret," he said kindly. "I shall not make one mention of the war or of the land sales all day today no matter how tempted I may be by the drift of conversations. I also believe that weddings and funerals are not fit places for politics. Satisfied?"

She nodded.

"Good. Now I want you to do something for me. Talk to Abby, if you will. The priest should have left her by now."

"What do you want me to say?"

His face darkened. "I want to be sure that she is really happy about this wedding. I've tried to discuss the matter with her . . . but it is difficult. . . . I thought . . . I mean, it is not too late to cancel the ceremony if she doesn't . . ."

Maire cut crisply across his dithering. "Abigail *wants* to marry Mr. Bennington. He would never have asked her unless he was sure of a favourable reply. She is happy, Thomas. This is what she desires."

"I know," said Thomas slowly. "And for some reason that saddens and depresses me."

Abby stood alone in the dim parlour. A candle burned in the bracket below the crucifix. Juliette noticed that it was reflected in her eyes like two hard, bright drops of gold. For the first time ever she admired her sister's beauty without a trace of wistful envy. Today all Juliette could think of was the squat little groom who would very soon be waiting at the chapel.

"You look beautiful," said Rose.

"Almost divine," echoed Sarah.

"Thank you."

"We came to beg a favour of you," said Rose.

"Oh?"

"It's about Jane . . ."

"Really," said Abby. "I don't think . . ,"

"She is ill," pressed Rose hurriedly. "Sister Moya told Sarah last week that Jane is getting very near to her time and things are not going well for her. I know that she would be so cheered by a visit from you, and it would be such a kind deed, such a wonderful gesture, if you and Mr. Bennington could stop by after the ceremony and . . ."

"I'm afraid that is impossible," said Abby. She picked up her bouquet. "Mr. Bennington would never agree to go to the Braggs' house, and besides, I promised Aunt Maire that I would never . . ." She stopped.

"Never what?" asked Sarah. "And what did Mama promise you in return, angel?"

With a swift movement Abby slapped Sarah across her face and hurried from the room.

* * *

"I wish I had hot rice pudding in here!" said Sarah, shaking her little cloth bag of rice as they waited outside the vestibule for the wedding party to emerge.

"Why rice pudding?" asked Leigh. When his sister shook her head he turned to Juliette. "You'll tell me, won't you?"

"No, for it isn't my secret."

He gazed at her thoughtfully. Juliette looked entrancing today—prettier even than Abby, whose complexion looked rather doughy against the white satin. The shimmering violet of Juliette's watered silk gown flattered her warm skin and intensified the deep blue of her eyes. She looked like a child with her hair shining loose in corrugated waves down her back. Then his gaze slipped a degree and he remembered with a shudder how those soft breasts had felt under the pressure of his palms.

"Tell me what the joke is! Why rice pudding?" he insisted. He crossed the length of the lower stone step and put an arm threateningly about her waist. "Tell me the secret! Tell me or I shall smother you with a kiss!"

"Leigh!" chimed the twins.

"You are doomed if you don't tell!"

Laughing, she tried to push him away. She ducked her head, her eyes shut, and she felt his fast breathing warm on her neck. Neither of them noticed the sudden fall of silence at first; but when Juliette opened her eyes with a feeling of something being amiss, her laughter choked in her throat.

The wedding party was grouped in the doorway, and Maire stood a pace apart. Her head was high, her expression cold and severe as a black frost as she stared at her son.

Leigh moved away at once.

Thirty privileged people sat shaded by the awning at the high table where crystal and silver graced fine linen and where young Maori girls flapped fans to keep the flies away. Other guests clustered around smaller tables on the lawn, seated on chairs borrowed from obliging neighbors. Every detail had been planned by Maire. As guests arrived they were tempted with claret cup or fruit juice, then with

concoctions of spiced meats and pickles. The soup was
served exactly half an hour after the Governor and his
lady arrived, and the other courses followed at Maire's direction while she watched the Governor for some hint of
when he was ready. She wanted to keep as long a break as
possible after each course, for there were many and some
were filling, especially those Irish dishes she had prepared
in honour of the time Governor Grey had spent in Ireland.
To her intense delight he noticed and appreciated her efforts. The chicken and potato soup he declared "a poem,"
the fish masked with cream sauce "ambrosia," and the
baked ham "exquisite." On and on it went through the
fowls with chestnut stuffing, the ox tongue with raisin
sauce, the aspics, the boiled meats, and the braised wild
pigeon pies.

Juliette enjoyed not a mouthful. She and the twins were
wedged onto a bench beyond the arbour, and Juliette had a
clear view of Leigh sitting at the high table beside Belinda
Godwin.

"Look at the way she's feeding him little morsels,"
hissed Sarah.

Rose said, "He wanted to sit with us but Mama made
him stay by her. And of course we know why Miss Godwin
was invited to sit there."

At that Juliette took heart. She reasoned that it didn't
really matter as long as Leigh would rather sit with her.

Then the dancing began. The pianist, two fiddlers from
Mechanic's Bay, and a piano accordionist were all dressed
in gypsy costumes. Their music was jerky and bright and
soon drew a silent crowd of Maoris who clustered around
the fence to watch and to listen. Oil lamps swung on temporary brackets, casting whirling arcs of moths out into
the night. It was a magical evening of looming shadows,
whispers, the click of fans, and scents of dying roses and
crushed grass.

The bride and groom danced the first waltz while all the
guests clapped or raised their glasses in a toast. Then the
band struck up for a polka and Juliette found Leigh bowing at her elbow.

They enjoyed themselves immensely, dancing one turn
after another. He gravely complimented her on her agile

toes and she praised his skill; then both laughed, for they
had learned dancing together with Jane and the twins at
the music-room piano. Juliette wished that she could bottle this happiness to wear later, like perfume. There was
something very special about dancing with the person you
loved, she decided. The whole world could see your happiness and the world's approval made it complete.

When the lancers were called Juliette squeezed her
hands together in delight. This dance was great fun: each
set was danced faster and faster until at the end a mad ri-
otous scramble ensued with the participants panting and
laughing helplessly (and the chaperones looking on in disapproving alarm). She turned to Leigh expectantly.

"I'm sorry, Juliette. The lancers would be too much for
my leg, and . . ."

"Your leg!" Immediately she looked concerned. "I had
quite forgotten it and here I have been selfishly dancing on
and on."

"Not selfishly." He placed a proprietary arm about her
waist and murmured that he would see her later. He then
walked directly to where his mother sat under the awning.
Beside her, looking flushed after the last brisk Roger de
Coverley, was Belinda Godwin. Within a minute Belinda
and Leigh were out with the others. The chords struck; he
bowed to her, she curtseyed to him, and in a flourish of
notes the lancers began. Juliette shrugged. Leigh could
hardly be blamed for obeying what was obviously a directive from his mother. At the same time she couldn't help
hoping that his leg might tire a little—just enough to cause
him to stumble and tread hard on Miss Godwin's foot. She
looked around for the twins. She had been talking to them
earlier, while they waited for Abby's grand entrance to the
dance. Rose was resigned to being a wallflower—Mr. Mannering had proved dull, disinterested, and had left the festivities when the Governor did, after the dinner speeches.
And though Sarah looked ill she refused to retire, saying
with a flash of her old spirit that she so seldom had a
chance to see so many people making fools of themselves at
one time that she was not going to miss a moment of it.

There they were, between the awning and the verandah.
Juliette slipped into the shadows and walked around be-

hind the dancers. She was just passing the awning when the sound of Leigh's name uttered in Mrs. Meyney's unmistakable tones caused her to stop and move a step closer. Maire was speaking now.

"Yes, I am so pleased with his recovery, though of course the 58th is off to Wellington in nine more days, so I hope no further mischief befalls him." She paused. "In a way I shall be pleased for him. He is obviously chafing here from having too little to occupy him."

"I noticed him dancing with Juliette," announced the loud voice. "He's extremely fond of her, isn't he?"

"No fonder than he should be," retorted Maire. "Not that it would do him any good if he were. I'm already looking about for a responsible widower to betroth Juliette to. Someone who can do us a favour in return, of course."

"Of course."

"She's not as pretty as Abigail but that shouldn't matter. She's young and biddable, and you know what these middle-aged widowers are like. . . ."

"It seems a pity that she couldn't marry someone her own age, just the same."

"With her background? Dear Mrs. Meyney, that would be *impossible.* What if she turned out to be disreputable, like her mother?"

Juliette bit her lip and leaned closer to the awning. She was too startled to feel frightened. What are middle-aged widowers like? And what did they mean by saying her mother was disreputable?

"Evangeline Peridot was *notorious!*" Mrs. Meyney's voice was slightly muffled as if she was eating something. "They said in Kororareka that she got her just deserts!" Another pause. "I always thought it was a pity about the children. They have been fortunate to have you, Mrs. Peridot. You have been kindness itself to those motherless children. As you have been to Mr. Meyney and myself."

"Thank you. Thomas is a dear, he really is. But the children are quite tiresome. Samuel is an uncouth savage. It was such a relief that he chose to go on a trading visit to the Waikato today. He lowers the tone of any affair. Abigail is a dear child, though I have had my moments with her, of course. You would not believe how spoiled . . ."

"Juliette!" came Stephen's voice from just over her shoulder. "What are you doing here? The girls are looking for you."

She looked up at him, trembling still from the shock of what she had heard. He stared at her hard, thinking for a moment that she might be ill.

Then Maire's voice came clear and sweetly through the canvas, saying, ". . . Juliette *seems* direct but I cannot help suspecting her of being devious and sly. Perhaps it is because she looks so much like her mother that one can be forgiven for assuming that she . . ."

"Everybody remarks on the likeness," Mrs. Meyney was saying, but Stephen did not wait to hear what mischief she might add. Seizing Juliette's wrist, he moved swiftly towards the house, while she skipped and stumbled to keep up. There, in the row of lights on the verandah, he held her by the shoulders and stared into her face.

"What did you hear, Juliette?" When she bit her lip and said nothing, he shook her gently and repeated with urgency, "Tell me what you heard!"

Her eyes slid away and fixed on the rosebud in his lapel. "Nothing. It was nothing, really. Your mother did not like my mother. . . ." Her chin and her gaze came up defiantly. "But my mother did not care for Aunt Maire either!"

"That's the spirit!" he said, capturing both her hands. "But tell me, what else did she say?"

"There was something." She hesitated. It was silly. Leigh was going to marry her, so why repeat this? "Aunt Maire said that she was going to find a nice middle-aged widower for me to marry, too."

"I could do a murder! Listen, my dear, in the name of Jove she had better not think of such a thing, but even if she does she cannot do anything until you are eighteen. After that we shall have to see what I can do to protect you, won't we?" As he spoke he searched her face but she gazed back at him with childlike trust and innocence. She has no idea of how I feel, he realised. Not the slightest inkling.

"I apologise for my mother. She has had many frustrations and a few bitter disappointments recently, but she has no cause to attack you. Put it out of your mind, do you promise? Now, hurry along; the girls are waiting. We are about to have an adventure."

"Like long ago on your ship, when I was seasick?"

"In the name of Jove! Fancy your remembering that. Not quite like that, Miss Olivine, but an adventure just the same."

She hesitated, wondering whether she should leave when Leigh must be looking for her. Glancing around uncertainly, she saw him over by the table where Tawa was dispensing fruit punch. Belinda was leaning against the front of his dress uniform, drinking from his glass. While Juliette watched he reached out and drew Belinda's hand and glass up to his lips so that he might sip from it. They gazed into each other's eyes as they drank. The sight appalled Juliette—she was shocked by such boldness, sick with envy.

"What is it, Juliette? Have you promised the next dance?"

She shook her head. It meant nothing, she told herself as she followed Stephen along the verandah; but she remained unconvinced. As she climbed into the carriage she noticed with dull surprise that her chest hurt.

Tim Bragg met them at the door, dishevelled and haggard, his voice a hoarse whisper. Absently he accepted the wedding bouquet and showed them into a bare parlour lit by candles.

"Doc Forster's in with 'er now. She 'ad the babe safe enough but the poor mite couldn't breathe proper an' it only lasted but an hour or so."

"And Jane?"

"She's fine, fine. Takin' it real well."

"If she's fine, then why is the doctor here at this hour?" asked Stephen.

"Dr. Forster 'as a lot of patients at the moment. There been a bad outbreak of fever all over town. Yer don't look too good yerself, Miss Sarah. Sister Amy said yer been sick an' that's why yer ain't been round lately." He jumped up from the straight-backed chair on which he had perched himself. "That'll be the doctor now."

Dr. Adrian Forster came into the room apologetically

and straightened with surprise when he saw the evening-gowned young ladies. He was a distinguished-looking man with a narrow face and dark hair thinning at the temples.

"Ah, Captain Yardley!" he exclaimed with pleasure.

"Might I present my sisters, Doctor? But first, this is Juliette Peridot."

"Ah." He looked at her closely and she had the oddest feeling that he was gazing into her soul, but in the kindliest of ways. "Yes, Miss Peridot. I knew your mother slightly. She was beautiful too."

"Thank you, sir," said Juliette with a lift of her chin. "She was the warmest and tenderest of mothers and a good person too."

"Of course." He straightened, letting go of her hand. As he did so his eyes met Stephen's. Neither man's face showed a hint of expression.

"My sister Sarah," said Stephen.

The doctor took Sarah's hand. "My dear, you are not at all well! How long have you been like this?"

From where she sat Juliette could see that Sarah was shivering. She looked mutely at the doctor with her dark-circled eyes and seemed unable to reply. Rose moved closer and put an arm about her sister's shoulders.

"She had a bad fall in the rain. It was weeks ago. Dr. Havow says that she is almost fully recovered."

"I see." He drew Sarah across to the candle flame and flipped open his brown carpetbag. She opened her mouth obediently while he depressed her tongue, and made no murmur while he turned up her eyelids and felt the contours of her neck with his slim fingers. At last he said that she was to go directly home to bed and was to stay there until he called in the morning.

"Without seeing Jane at all?" protested Rose.

Sarah said nothing. The fact that she did not argue alarmed Juliette. Sarah always challenged orders that ran counter to her wishes.

The doctor spoke kindly but firmly to Rose. "I'm afraid that your sister has the fever. Captain Yardley, may I please talk to you alone?"

* * *

Stephen allowed himself to enjoy a certain perverse pleasure in calling his mother away from the still bouncing festivities. After all, she had ruined the party for Juliette.

"I have no interest in Dr. Forster's opinions," she informed him when he had finished repeating what the doctor had confided.

"Not opinions, Mama, but orders. Sarah is gravely ill, and the Nervene is suppressing her will to combat the disease."

"I will not listen! Dr. Forster—if he *is* a genuine doctor—is making capital out of a chance meeting with this family to undermine Dr. Havow's prestige. No doubt he would love to gather a clientele of patients who are able to pay generously. I understand that at the moment he is destitute, utterly destitute. What kind of a doctor is he then?"

"One who cares more about people than money . . . not that you could understand or be sympathetic to that view."

Maire's face tightened. She breathed through her nose while she stood glancing looks of distaste at her son. He lounged against the marble mantel, apparently indifferent.

"I shall call Dr. Havow and see what he says."

"Good. You and I seem fated to have our differences of opinion but it would be splendid if for once a third person's well-being was considered more important than the outcome of our quarrel."

"Did Dr. Forster write a prescription for the druggist?"

He drew a folded slip of paper from his inner pocket and handed it to her as he left. Maire stood thoughtfully staring at the closed door and then deliberately tore the paper into shreds, allowing the scraps to fall over the hearth. If Stephen returned to the room he would see them there. She hoped that he would.

Juliette sat on the verandah steps, white in the moonlight. The party was over; it was past three but she did not feel in the least tired. She was too frightened to feel anything but apprehension.

Rose was on the other side of the softly lit window, sitting beside Sarah's bed. The Nervene had worn off, leaving her with fiercely bright eyes and scalding breath. The rest of the house was in darkness.

Juliette hugged her knees miserably. Those fears that had evaporated when repeated to Stephen now loomed in her mind. Aunt Maire would succeed. Leigh would marry his heiress and she would be sold off to a middle-aged widower. Now, without Stephen's laughter of dismissal and warm reassurances, those fears seemed perfectly tangible.

Leigh, she thought desperately. Oh, Leigh, prove to your mother that you really do care about me. Stand by me so that I never have to feel afraid again.

A low whistling from the darkness beyond the garden cut into her muddled thoughts. The tune was one of Leigh's favourites, but it couldn't be Leigh. He had disappeared from the party long before they played "God Save the Queen," and must be asleep by now.

The whistling came closer.

Oh, pretty lass, oh, bonny lass
With hair as gold as corn,
Walk with me at eventide
And through the sparkling morn.

It *was* Leigh! He vaulted the fence not a dozen yards from the gate and strode towards her, the moonlight brushing his hair with silver. He was in such a good mood that she instinctively wanted to hide her own dismal spirits, now plunged even lower with the ugly suspicion that he had spent these last hours at Godwins' with Belinda.

"Juliette?" He paused at the foot of the steps.

A moment ago she would have given even Clarissa for five comforting minutes alone with him, but now she couldn't reply.

"Are you angry with me?" he whispered, settling himself on a step below hers so that their faces were level.

"Where have you been?" she heard herself say, and instantly wished that she could have snatched the words back.

"I've been in the town, of course," he said, carefully casual. "The dancing was dull and my leg ached, so I decided to go to the Rising Sun and see what my comrades were doing to amuse themselves. There, now! Tell me that you are not angry with me." And he placed an arm about her shoulders.

She wanted to say that she did not care what he had been doing. She wanted to tell him to take his arm away and to stop nuzzling her neck. More than anything else she wanted to stop loving him, to still these treacherous ripples that were lapping tenderly at her nerves. He had ignored her for the entire remainder of the evening and had devoted himself to Belinda. Not one word, not one look had he given her. Pride forbade her to remind him that he had promised to return to her later in the evening. It was such a light thing that he had instantly forgotten it, so why should she show her hurt?

As if he could read her thoughts he murmured, "I knew that we would be together again this evening. Were you waiting for me?"

"No. I couldn't sleep."

"I wish that you had been waiting for me."

"Do you?"

"Just as I hope that you will miss me when I'm away at the fighting. I often thought of you when there was death and danger all around. The image of you gave me comfort. Promise me that you will think of me too."

Visions she had suffered many times this past year rose in her mind, visions of Leigh hurt, wounded, lying helpless in the mud. . . . With an involuntary whimper she threaded her arms about his neck and clung to the warm reality of him.

His hands stroked her back. "I shall miss you," he continued. "So far away and so much danger. I love you, Juliette, I love you so much."

She eagerly accepted his kiss and allowed it to soothe away her doubts. Nothing could harm her while Leigh loved her. He would stand by her and look after her.

Leigh's spirits soared. This was an unexpected bonus to cap a highly successful evening. What a rare and rousing little thing she was. How he adored her!

His hands pressed her body into a curve against his. Hungrily he slipped one hand around to fasten fingers over her breast. She struggled a little but her hands stayed knotted at the back of his neck and he was encouraged. Pulling his mouth away from hers, he concentrated his attention and his kisses around the pale, cool base of her throat.

"Juliette, dear Juliette . . ." His hand pressed its way down to her waist, then moved down to her ankle in one swift stroke. He held his breath, praying that she would not resist. The pressure in his chest, head, and loins was so intense that his body seemed full of a throbbing red haze.

"Juliette, I love you . . . you do believe me, don't you? I love you. . . ." His hand was at her knee where her garter marked the top of her stockings. Above that his palm slid over soft, exquisite skin.

"Oh, my God!" She stirred and he kept talking, feverishly. "I love you, Juliette, I do . . . I adore you. . . ." His hand was there with breath-stopping suddenness, there in the satiny gap between her thighs where warm, sweet moisture welcomed his touch, and down so soft that he merely might have imagined it.

He had cradled her head on the cushion of one forearm, and now as he propped himself to lean over her, the hard edge of the steps dug into his ribs and thigh. He was suddenly aware of how ludicrously uncomfortable a place this was for love-making, especially when the privacy and comfort of his own room were only a few steps away. Urgently, for the momentum of his lust made him reluctant to pause, he smoothed her skirts and tugged at her waist.

"Come, dearest . . . come with me."

She stirred unwilling. "Stay a while longer."

"Come," he whispered, helping her to her feet and guiding her along the verandah. They turned the corner where darkness gave way to a long ladder pattern of balustrade shadows and grey moonlight. They were almost to his bedroom, where the french doors stood wide open, when Stephen stepped out in front of them. Both Leigh and Juliette were startled; but while Juliette clung to Leigh in fright, his reaction was to immediately push her away in a confusion of guilt.

"What in the devil are you doing here?"

"Thomas asked me to wait up for you," said Stephen

calmly. He was smoking a cigar; the firefly tip drew bright circles in the darkness.

"But what are you *doing* here? Who asked you to stay in my room?"

Juliette was astonished by the rudeness in his tone. She was so happy that she felt like laughing aloud in sheer giddy delight. "Leigh loves me!" she wanted to shout. But why was he so angry? Had he and Stephen quarrelled?

"I'm sharing your room. It was rather too late to row out to the ship, so I decided to doss in with you. I hope you have no objection."

"Too damned bad if I do," muttered Leigh, pushing past him through the billowing curtains.

"We were taking a walk, and you frightened us," said Juliette. "I suppose he's upset because he may have thought that you were spying on us. Not that *I* thought so, of course, but . . ."

"I'll accompany you back to your room."

She hesitated, glancing into the candlelit room. There was no sign of Leigh. It seemed that he had no intention of returning.

"He is an unpredictable fellow," said Stephen.

"Yes." She took his arm.

Stephen drew thoughtfully on his cigar. "Mama has rather definite plans for Leigh," he said.

"Perhaps he has plans of his own!"

"Perhaps he has, but Mama and Leigh have a special kind of a bond, and Leigh invariably concedes to her wishes. He finds life easier and more pleasant that way. My brother is rather . . ." He considered and discarded the word "weak." ". . . rather easygoing while my mother is extremely strong-willed. There is no contest between them. Forgive me for bringing the subject up, but you should understand the situation if you are fond of Leigh."

Fond of him! How belittling to have her adoration described like that. Juliette felt suddenly very young and foolish, keenly aware of the contrast between herself and the sophisticated Stephen. He had spent the evening dancing with a dozen lovely young ladies, some wealthy, but most not; while once Leigh had been summoned by his mother he had spent his undivided attention on Belinda.

Could Stephen's analysis be correct? She shook her head. This was nonsense! Leigh loved her and said so. If she could not invest her faith in his word, then her love was a poor thing indeed.

They paused at the edge of the verandah where a long shaft of light bleached the colour from their clothes and cast their faces in sharp etchings. Juliette looked at Stephen. Her eyes were lit by an unmistakable, banner-bright happiness.

In the name of Jove, thought Stephen. If he's trifling with her I'll break his pampered neck, I swear it. But in his previous conversational tone he said, "Take care, sweet Olivine."

"Take care?"

"Don't squander your affection. Protect yourself. Hold onto your feelings until you are sure you won't be hurt."

"I promise. But then, perhaps I am sure already." And with a quick kiss on his cheek she darted inside.

Twenty-one

"And why did you not bring your dear wife with you?" asked Maire. "I do hope that Abigail is well."

"She is at the milliner's. *Some* wifely pursuits come very naturally to her, or so it seems."

"You have some objection to milliners?" She led him into the parlour and poured him a whisky. "We have had nothing but disruptions here lately. The wedding, then the Bellwoods having to be settled—and what a drama that was! And now Sarah refuses to get better. It is such an upset. Dr. Havow has a new treatment to try on her, some kind of electrical battery to vitalise her nervous system."

"And when is Leigh going?" He had glimpsed him in the garden reading poetry to Juliette.

"In two more days. Time hangs very heavily on his hands, I'm afraid."

"So I've noticed. Up to mischief, is he, hey?"

"What do you mean?" she asked sharply.

"Nothing, nothing. Harmless flirtation. Boys will be boys, hey? Nothing to fret about." He sipped at the drink hastily, aware that Maire's gaze was not friendly.

"Leigh is a dutiful son."

"Of course."

She tapped her fingernails on the silver reticule she wore at her waist. Relax, she told herself. It was foolish and pointless to be so touchy about Leigh. He *was* a dutiful son and she *did* accept his bland-faced assurances that there was nothing between him and that minx Juliette. It was idiotic to be so jumpy just because someone at the wedding had asked whether the two of them could legally marry. It was such a silly moment but it had spooked her, made her feel that she was seeing a situation between them that didn't exist.

"You're skittish as an unbroken pony today," said Jack frankly.

"Are you here on business, Mr. Bennington?" It came out a good deal less graciously than she had intended but that could not be helped. Surely he could see that her patience was stretched. And what did he want? Some petty complaint about Abigail? No doubt he'd have plenty of those, but she was a goodhearted girl and already showing her appreciation. Not many girls would think to send their stepmother a crate of whisky for a thank-you gift. She refilled Jack's glass.

"Thank you. I suppose I'd better get to the point, hey?" Jack tugged at his starched collar. It was damnably hot in the room, humid, too. "It's about Abigail."

"Not a complaint, I trust? She must be pleasing you if you're spoiling her already. A dozen new hats she had in her trousseau, you know. Her father insisted on it."

"I must know whether you instructed Abigail before she came to me. What did you tell her, Maire, about her duty? Did you prepare her?"

"She should have been satisfactory. Why?"

"The girl fought me, that's why. Shrieked, kicked, and resisted my most reasonable attempts. Furthermore she confided to Mrs. Hodges, the housekeeper, next morning and she, with great glee, I regret, has spread the news around. I fear that there is not a house with English servants in the whole town that does not know the state of my marriage. While Abigail, of course, remains unrepentant and completely stubborn. She informs me that I cannot expect her to submit to indignities."

"Oh dear." Maire knew from the tickle deep in her chest that later she would laugh and be hugely entertained by this, but Jack was too upset for her to so much as smile at him now.

"What can I do?"

"Fortunately I can advise you about that. Abigail loves pretty clothes and opportunities to show them off. I suggest that you remove all of the clothes from her wardrobe and lock her in her room until she decides to be . . . agreeable. You might even make a little bonfire outside her window and consign some of her favourite gowns and bonnets to the flames so that she understands that you are absolutely serious. And dismiss Mrs. Hodges. No, on second thought, do not dismiss her. If she acts as gaoler for you and reports this all around the town, then your prestige will be restored and the laugh will be on Miss Abigail."

Jack frowned and patted his marcelled hair. "This does sound harsh. Abigail is a sweet little thing and I really don't want to upset her."

"Poppycock! A woman has to respect her husband. And, after all, you cannot take her by force," she said, adding with unnecessary cruelty, "She is bigger and stronger than you, after all."

When Sister Moya returned to Auckland a fortnight after Abby's wedding she was shocked to see how ill Sarah was, and immediately begged leave from the Bishop to spend every day nursing her. Rose, too, had stationed herself beside her sister's bed, and Juliette kept busy in the kitchen preparing nourishing tea made by infusing a whole pound of the best minced beef in hot water. Very occasionally Sarah was able to manage a little. All day she lay on her heaped pillows, hair damply clinging to her head, her hot body racked by feeble coughs.

Dr. Havow called twice daily. In his delicate way he had implied that the illicit night excursion was entirely to blame for the fresh attack, and hinted that Dr. Forster himself might have transmitted the disease when he examined her throat that night. After all, he did spend most of his time visiting the most appallingly filthy hovels, so who could deny the possibility that he had spread an infection? The fever would run its course, he assured Maire, but meantime Sarah should begin at once on the course of one-guinea sessions with the electrical battery system to revitalise her energies. So a sedated Sarah was transported with sisters, nun, and with Maire every afternoon to the doctor's rooms.

Today Juliette did not accompany the caravan. She was busy baking cakes for the special dinner tomorrow to celebrate Leigh's last evening home. Mary and Tawa had gone

to await the fishing canoes to buy fresh seafood; and by
three o'clock Juliette was alone in the kitchen, separating
eggs, whipping butter and yolks into cream, and checking
the temperature of the oven by dropping a teaspoonful of
water onto the tray. Into the hot oven went a half dozen
pans of golden batter. Juliette wiped her brow on the corner of her apron, poured herself a glass of barley water
from the jug in the cool larder, and washed the mixing
bowls while she waited out the hour of cooking time.

She did not hear Leigh come in. Her singing covered the
tread of his soft-soled boots on the tiles. When he shot his
hands swiftly around her waist she gasped. She would
have dropped the heavy china bowl she was wiping if he
had not deftly taken it from her and set it down on the
table. She twisted in his arms and broke free, trembling
from the sudden fright.

"You gave me such a scare!"

He looked pleased with himself. "I hoped to find you
alone and here you are, all by yourself."

She frowned. "Leigh, you aren't breaking any rules, are
you? Aren't you supposed to be at the Albert Barracks
with the regiment?"

"They gave us leave. Generous, wasn't it? Back one day
and given two days' leave. We have forty-eight hours left
before we embark for Wellington. Look!" He produced a
small flat box covered in red paper. "I have a little surprise
for you."

A locket! She knew that's what it was. It had to be a
locket. Abby had been given one as an engagement gift,
and all the girls had made such a fuss of it, exclaiming over
the beautiful engraving and the cunning little frames inside for a miniature and a lock of the beloved's hair. Leigh
must have noticed how much she liked it. Now she would
have something to remember him by, a lock of his hair
sealed away close to her heart so that he would never seem
really far away.

"Aren't you going to open it?"

"Of course." Her fingers shook as she tugged the string
loose and unfolded the paper. Inside the box lay a small
pink artificial flower, a dog rose. Juliette had seen them at
Merrington's priced at two for threepence. Her disappoint-

ment was so fierce that it stung her eyes but she reproached herself and was smiling when she looked up at him.

"Thank you, Leigh. It's very pretty. Whenever I wear it I shall think of you."

"I want you to think of me all the time, and do you want to know why? Because I shall be thinking of you. You will be in my thoughts all the time."

"What will you be doing when you think of me?" She kept her voice light.

"I'll be at a campfire arguing with Deverell. We argue a lot. Or in the mornings I'll be trying to shave with cold water and a little tin mirror. . . . How do you think I would look with a beard?"

"Splendidly handsome."

"Then a beard it is. If my Juliette wants me with a beard, then a bristly, scratchy beard it is!" He held her at arm's length and allowed his eyes to drift in a leisurely manner over her face, feature by feature.

Within a minute she was feeling self-conscious and uncomfortable. "Why are you staring at me so?"

"So that I may better remember you," he said with a throb in his voice. "Oh, Juliette, I do adore you. I want . . ." He drew her closer to him, careless of her soiled apron against his smartly pressed uniform, and covered her mouth with his. She remained quite still for a moment, unresponsive to his insistent passion. Then she slid her arms up around his neck, and her body sagged against his.

He felt like cheering. Keeping her mouth prisoner, he swooped her up in his arms and carried her through the kitchen door and along the verandah. Then they were in his room with the scent of pomade and damp worsted and wax floor polish and she was lying on the bed, her head framed by his two arms as he leaned over her.

There was fright in her eyes, a little touch of apprehension which he smoothed away by murmuring her name and endearments over and over. This time she wore no stockings and the satiny feel of her legs made him draw in his breath as sharply as if he had plunged into a cold pool. She moaned and moved slightly as he found the secret place again and he panicked, thinking that she might push

him away or stop him—and she could not stop him now.
His blood was rushing so fast that he felt he would explode
if he did not have her at once. It was a clumsy, frantic business, fumbling with buttons with his right hand and
pulling up her skirts with his left, while all the time
kissing her as the breath choked in his chest and the
mounting, bursting excitement goaded him on.

He flung himself onto her and shoved himself into the
place his stabbing fingers guessed at. She cried out, a
strangled gargling in her throat, but it seemed to echo inside her head like the pounding of surf against a sand bar.

"Hush, hush, dearest," he murmured as he sucked and
nibbled at her lower lip. By now he was pounding at her
with frantic blindness, scrambling to his knees for more
leverage and then slipping and thrusting blindly at her
again. He was in a revolving drum of giddy sensation that
was whirling him with a fierce power of its own. At one
point his eyes flung open and he saw her anguished face,
the forehead laced with wrinkles of pain. He was drenched
in sweaty, glorious darkness. In those final, soaring moments of exhilaration it did not matter who she was—Juliette or a Princess or the lowliest slattern from the pa,
willing or unwilling—it made no difference to him.

But the minute it was over, when he had floundered for
his lost breath, an awful realisation crept over him.

"Oh, my God!" he said aloud.

Juliette was still. Their only movements had been to
straighten their clothing, she out of modesty and he in the
futile, ironic gesture of trying to undo what had just been
done.

"I'm sorry," he said. If only there was some way to re-
trace his steps to the kitchen and wipe all this out.

"Don't be sorry," she whispered.

He shuddered and closed his eyes when she turned to
gaze into his face. Depression weighted his chest; he felt
ill.

"Leigh, don't be sorry, please," she said. "I know that
you feel dreadful because you hurt me but I love you and
you love me, so don't you see that it makes everything
right between us? Nothing can separate us now. We really
do belong to each other, don't we?"

"Juliette, I am sorry . . ." he said thickly. "I didn't mean to . . . I really didn't . . . oh, my God!"

"What is it?"

He looked at her helplessly. If only he could get rid of this sticky, sleazy feeling that was suffocating him. Her expression was so damnably happy and trusting. A few minutes ago he had not given a single thought to either the act or its consequences. But now . . . How could he tell her that he never really wanted to do this? How could he find the words to explain that this, this act, was not really what he meant at all?

"We shall be together for always, now," she said happily, the words soft as a scarf tightening about his throat.

He was spared the effort of framing a reply. From beyond the doorway a cool voice said in measured tones, "I doubt that you will be together ever again. This room is and always has been strictly forbidden to you, Juliette. Now go to your own room at once. I wish to speak to my foolish son alone."

Juliette sobbed in the jolting carriage while Maire stared at her grim-faced. The older woman's arm ached with the satisfaction of the whipping she had administered, but even the network of stripes she had laid across the girl's back was not enough to hammer away the hatred. Whatever vengeance she wreaked for this would never be enough. And to think that Leigh actually encouraged the little trollop!

Rose and Sarah sat together at the doctor's waiting rooms. Both stared in surprise as Maire dragged Juliette past them and shut the door in their faces. Juliette wanted to die. Mary and Tawa, both big-eyed with fright, had held her arms as she was pressed flat on her face on her bed for the beating. Now the twins were witness to her humiliation. But worst of all was what lay immediately ahead. She had no notion why she had been forced to come to Dr. Havow and could hardly believe it when he lifted her onto an examining table and fastened her ankles into stirrups so she could not move; then flipped up her skirts. The exposure and examination were degrading and made even more mortifying by the fact that Maire insisted on remaining there to witness the whole sordid, uncomfortable business.

"Very recent," the doctor told Maire. "Within the hour, I should think. And a brutal attack, too, I would say."

Maire's back stiffened. An attack? For the first time she began to wonder if the good doctor did know what he was talking about. If there was any "attacking" it was in the promiscuous way this slut had thrown herself at Leigh.

"She was of course not a virgin."

"She most definitely was. Until an hour ago, that is."

"I am astonished to hear that. Utterly astonished." He inferred from her tone that she thought he was lying to protect the girl.

"It is the truth. The man used considerable force . . ." He paused and added casually, "Was it someone known to the family?"

Maire gazed at him with cold steady eyes. A handsome woman, he thought. She reminded him of a picture of a lion he had once seen. Something about her bearing and the impersonal way her look was fixed on him.

"She *said* that she was attacked by a fisherman. A Maori fisherman. I did not believe her, but now it appears that I must. You understand the shame which would descend on us, your clients, if word of this should seep into society . . ."

"Mrs. Peridot!"

"Quite. Be assured that the price of your silence will be added to the accounts."

They arrived home to find Mary and Tawa frantically battling a blaze in the kitchen. Apparently some cakes in the oven had ignited.

Juliette might have laughed about that as she sat locked in her dark room, but the humiliations and the whipping still hurt so deeply that she could not even manage a grim smile.

Next morning, after an embarrassed Mary had brought in her breakfast tray, Rose tapped on the window.

"Leigh crept into our room early this morning," she said. "He said to be sure to tell you that he is terribly, terribly sorry and hopes you understand. He wouldn't explain further, just said that you would know. Was it Leigh who broke the tantalus? If so you shouldn't take the blame like this. Mama would forgive Leigh. Somehow I cannot picture you breaking open Mama's whisky supplies. Tell the truth, Juliette. Mama is so angry with you and I know she is mistaken."

The tantalus? The whisky bottles? Oh, of course. An excuse to explain the punishment and disgrace.

"She is not mistaken," said Juliette wearily.

"Truly? Oh, Juliette, whatever were you thinking of? And I heard you screaming in the night. Did you have a nightmare?"

She pulled a wry face at Rose's expression of tender concern. Yes, a nightmare of epic proportions. Peaches rotting in her hands and footsteps drumming and the sun dazzling her so that she was blinded. Then someone hissing names at her, forcing her to drink, pinching her nose while a spoon grated against her teeth.

"Yes, I had a nightmare, but Aunt Maire gave me some medicine to make me sleepy. How is Sarah today?"

"No better; worse, if anything. She . . ."

"Rose!" came her mother's imperious voice. "Come away from that window at once!"

Her solitary confinement lasted only until midafternoon when she was ordered to make herself presentable to wait on table at dinner. Mary kept an obedient distance away as Juliette peeled potatoes in the scullery; but Tawa, who was less respectful of Maire's orders, popped in long enough to slip the package containing the dog rose into Juliette's pocket. She wiped her hands on her apron and took the flower out, staring at it as if searching for some clue about the giver.

Her feelings crystallised at dinner into a hurt, bewildered bitterness. When everybody filed in from their sherry in the parlour Juliette saw with a jolt that Belinda Godwin was on Leigh's arm. Maire seated them together at one end of the table with a proprietary concern that warned Juliette why she had been given this task. Leigh, she noticed, gave her one sick, apologetic look and then kept his eyes averted from her. He seemed so ill at ease

that despite her own misery Juliette felt genuinely sorry
for him. But if she had any question about why she was
given the task of serving, the reason soon became absolutely clear, for at the first opportunity Maire elucidated.
While Juliette was leaning politely at Mrs. Bellwood's
right hand to remove Maire's roe plate—and while her face
was only inches away—Maire confided in a loud whisper to
Mrs. Bellwood that Leigh and Miss Godwin would announce their betrothal after the toast to the Queen.

Surprisingly, Juliette found it easy to maintain an outward calm. Right now she was too doped with laudanum
and too unutterably weary to react with anything but
fresh depression, and the dinner party might have been
quietly uneventful but for Belinda herself.

From the beginning she had been jealous of Juliette, and
that jealousy had stirred into quite a nasty turmoil of feelings at the wedding. Now, with Leigh's affections assured
and her rival in the inferior position of acting the servant,
Belinda could not resist a little petty revenge. She watched
Juliette, waiting for her moment.

Juliette dished the soup with care; it was hot tomato
broth and tricky to serve. Belinda was the fifth lady served
and the only one who deigned not to thank her.

"How very careless of you," she said loudly. "You have
splashed soup onto the cloth." And indeed there was a tiny
pink spot where a droplet had run from the ladle.

Juliette said nothing. An apology might have been in order or it might not. It was a small matter and her mind was
too sluggish to form a reply, so she merely nodded and
backed away to attend to Rose.

"What are you doing?" asked Belinda snappishly. "Fix
it up at once! I cannot eat on a filthy cloth!"

Maire's brows raised at this comment. She took up her
soup spoon and began to eat, quite a breach of etiquette
since the gentlemen had not been served yet. But in unison
the other ladies also dipped into their bowls. Juliette set
the tureen on the sideboard and sponged up the drop with
a damp napkin before hastily finishing the serving. There
was an embarrassed silence at the table.

The next course, fish, was Mary's speciality. Hot
poached fillets of plump snapper had been smothered with

a fragrant sauce made of finely chopped mussels, pipis, mushrooms, ham, onion, and thyme. When Belinda had been served her portion from the deep oval porcelain dish, she turned to Maire with a conciliatory smile.

"What delicious food you serve your guests, Mrs. Peridot. I must congratulate you. What a pity it is spoiled by such deplorable service! I have been dished such a tiny piece that I fear I shall scarcely be able to taste it. Could such a clever lady as yourself not train your servants a little better?"

If Juliette had been feeling well her natural sense of humour would have allowed her to make a sharp and witty reply, but now she was weary and heartsore, capable of only a basic, primitive reaction. Without a word or a grimace she turned back towards the young lady and tipped up the dish. A torrent of scalding fish and boiling-hot sauce gushed into Belinda's red velvet lap.

"Is this portion more to your liking?" she asked, a split second before the room echoed with Belinda's shrieks of pain and rage.

She was out the gate and striding along the cliff path in the darkness when Leigh panted up behind her. She turned to face him.

"What do you want?"

"You can't run away like this. It's not safe."

"I might be molested, you mean?"

"Juliette, please don't." He grabbed her arms and forced her to look at him. Very faintly she could read his expression of humble remorse. "I really am sorry. Don't hate me. Please don't hate me."

She paused before answering. Tiredness had fallen away from her like a heavy coat on a hot day. "I don't hate you, Leigh. In a way I wish I did, but I don't. You just made it all up when you said you loved me, didn't you?"

"No, Juliette! It wasn't like that at all."

"Wasn't it?" She moved away, freeing herself.

"I did mean it. At least I thought I did, and . . ."

Her voice was heavy with sadness. "You thought you did but your mother convinced you otherwise and now you are engaged to Miss Godwin."

"She'll never marry me now. Not after tonight."

"I suppose not." The breeze was cold on her face, cleansing her with the scent of seaweed and sand grasses. "I suppose she won't marry you, but I'm not sorry, not at all."

"Neither am I really. Juliette, I . . ."

She interrupted. "I'm going away, Leigh. Going far away and as speedily as possible."

"But where?"

"I shall answer one of the advertisements for governesses that they put up in the newspaper office."

"Your father will never agree to that."

"I rather think he will." She began walking back toward the house. "In fact, I know that he will, for after the way you've followed me this evening I can guarantee Aunt Maire will do everything possible to assist me with my plans."

Maire blotted the letter carefully and handed it to Thomas, saying, "Here is the recommendation I shall send with Juliette. I have put a pound in her purse to give her a start. Her wages may not be very high to begin with."

"That's very generous of you. I cannot for the life of me understand it, but I'm so sorry that the child has been a problem."

"She has been unsettled ever since Abigail left."

"I know. But I worry about her going so far away. New Plymouth! That's a long journey from here."

"It was her choice." As she stood up the items at her waist—keys, chatelaine, and ivory lorgnette case—jingled together. "Juliette wants to go to New Plymouth. I did not agree at first. I offered to do what I could to see her speedily settled with a steady husband like Abigail's, but she screamed most ungratefully in my face at such a suggestion. Over and over she insisted that she wanted to go as far away as soon as she could."

"It sounds as though some particular incident might have upset her."

"You have questioned her. I think it was merely that the idea suddenly appealed. She is impulsive, you know, and may well decide to return home just as quickly. If she does, then our door stands open to welcome her."

"You have been more than kind," said Thomas warmly.

"I'm only trying to act as a mother should. Now you must not worry about her on the journey. Stephen will be home in a little more than a fortnight and will be going on to Wellington after a short break. I know that he . . . What is it, Rose? Can you not see that I am busy?"

"It's Sarah," she said, wide-eyed with fright. "Her breathing has gone all raspy and squeaky. Sister Moya is holding her upright to try to assist her. Should I give her some more Nervene, do you think?"

"I'll fetch the doctor," said Thomas.

"He'd not come out now. It's well past dark."

"I'll fetch him myself," said Thomas. "Mary! My hat and cape, please." He asked his wife, "Where are the doctor's rooms?"

"He'll be at his house now. . . ."

"I could show him!" said Rose. "Let me go and even if the doctor is out I could give Tamati instructions, for I know where practically everybody in Auckland lives.

"I am so dreadfully worried," Rose confided as the carriage trundled along. "Dr. Havow is a kind man but I wonder whether he really knows what is wrong with Sarah. After each treatment she seems improved for such a short time before she lapses back worse than before. Even the double doses of Nervene don't seem to help."

"That vile stuff?"

"Sedation is the key to recovery, or so Dr. Havow says. He takes Nervene several times a day himself to prevent his energies from being dissipated by the busy life he leads. Oh, do forgive me for prattling on, but I am so desperately worried about Sarah. I couldn't have endured staying in the house and watching her struggle for breath. Uncle Thomas"—her voice dropped to a whisper in the dark corner of the carriage—"I know that she's going to die and I feel terrified." She began to cry quietly. "I have this premonition. Twins often do have a special feeling about each other and I know that Sarah is going to leave me. I'm terrified, Uncle Thomas. She's not even twenty-two years old and she's so vital, so full of life . . ."

"You must put your faith in the Lord. If He wants Sarah, then He will take her no matter what age she is or how much she loves life. When Evangeline died I railed uselessly against fate, and my soul was in desperate torment until I determined to trust in God."

"You are right, and I feel ashamed of myself for having so little faith. But it is such a dreadful waste, and I shall miss her so . . ."

"There now, don't cry." But he spoke absently. A dreadful waste, aye, he thought. Evangeline and the little ones. Serious-faced Madeline, little Thomas, poor Regina, who was always wanting to fight with the world, and the sweet babe Melina. As always when he thought of them a rage of frustration rose in his chest, choking him. It was all very well to talk about God and faith to comfort a frightened lass; he'd never feel better until he'd had the satisfaction of seeing those bloody murderers swinging on a gibbet.

Maire brought a candle out to light their way inside, though the moonlight shone a ribbon along the path.

She realised at once that the man who accompanied them was Dr. Adrian Forster. But before she could protest Thomas was explaining with suppressed anger how they had been obliged to force their way into the house past an Amazonian housekeeper, only to find Dr. Havow and two companions in their cups and virtually insensible.

"I asked the fellow for advice and he was not even in any fit state to offer me any. So there was nothing to do but to find Dr. Forster, who was out on his rounds. He agreed to come at once. A decent fellow. Why you waste your time with that other poseur I cannot imagine."

"Mrs. Peridot," called the doctor from the sickbed. "Would you be so good as to show me the medication your doctor has prescribed?"

"Here it is," said Maire, agitated and annoyed. "Here, on the bedside commode."

"I mean the medication, Mrs. Peridot. All we have here are laudanum and opium sedatives."

"That is the medication. There is no other."

"My God!"

Maire's lips shrank primly to a thin line. "I trust Dr. Havow completely. We have a saying that there are four people one should trust: one's doctor, one's lawyer, one's spouse, and the commander of one's troops, and all in that

order. And not only do I trust Dr. Havow, but I must point
out that I do not allow blasphemy in this house."

"I apologise, Mrs. Peridot. I assure you that I will do
what I can to help your daughter." He leaned over Sarah,
who had lost consciousness. Her breathing sounded like
gravel being swirled in a bucket. In a low tone he said,
"You should know right now that I may be too late. Recently I have attended cases of scarlatina where the family
has not sent for me because they feared they could not pay
my fees. But in those cases, as now, where the skin has acquired this rough red texture, the fever is usually beyond
anything I can cure. All I can suggest to you, Mrs. Peridot,
is to add yet another name to that list of those in whom you
trust."

He turned away to look for something in his bag so she
was forced to ask, "Who?"

"God, Mrs. Peridot, God," he said over his shoulder.

Juliette knew that she would never see another nun
without remembering the harrowing echoes of Sister
Moya's crying. It had begun when it was clear that the desperate attempts to clear Sarah's breathing had failed; and
it continued through the lying in, and trailed out into the
fern-edged cemetery where she was buried next to a family
of eight who had died in a boating accident three weeks before. Juliette had been instructed to believe that nuns and
priests were accepting, but there was no acceptance in Sister Moya's abandoned grief. She was moved by the mourning and felt sorry for the little nun who had spent so many,
many afternoons with Sarah.

She was sorry for Rose, too, more than sorry, and she did
not know how to reply adequately when Rose sat on the
end of her bed watching forlornly as she packed her things
into her mother's old workbasket and begging her not to
go.

"Surely this will change Mama's attitude. Surely now
she won't insist on driving you away."

"She's not driving me away. This is something I must
do, for myself."

"I don't believe you. You can't be running from Leigh

because he has gone away himself and won't be home for ages, and anyway, he can't hurt you."

Not any more, vowed Juliette as she smoothed Clarissa's skirts and laid her on top of the neatly pressed undergarments. Leigh will never hurt me again, for I shall not give him the power.

"Then why, Juliette? Aren't we friends? Surely you cannot go away like this after this dreadful . . ." Her voice faltered. "I'm going to be so lonely now. Jane, Abigail, Sarah, and you . . . I don't think I could bear it."

"Please try to understand. I cannot change my mind now."

"You mean you won't, and it doesn't matter how hurt I am by your desertion."

"I wouldn't hurt you for the world, you know that!" She reached out to put her arms about Rose's shoulders. Rose angrily pushed her away.

"Yet you have, and you refuse to reconsider." She moved away, close to tears. "It seems to me that you can say one thing and mean another, and be as false to me as Abigail was to Jane."

"Rose! That's unfair!" But she was gone, and the click of the door seemed another accusation. It was a tiny, lonely noise and it pushed at the log jam of feelings in her throat, clearing a path through which the scalding, unreleased tears could flow mercifully, at last.

PART FOUR

THE
SEFTONS

1847-1852

Twenty-two

The *Lorendee* dropped anchor in a slow, even swell just beyond the breakers off New Plymouth town. From Stephen's cabin where she sat alone at breakfast Juliette could see a long sandy shoreline backed by rolling sand dunes and a brace of odd, tall rocks shaped like sugar cones. Standing tall above this scene was a perfectly symmetrical mountain, serene and pale as a blue and white watercolour on a grey canvas. The white must be snow, the snow of Mother's Christmas recollections. But from here it looked disappointing—no colder than a piece of white rag.

Stephen put his head in at the door. He was wearing his braided captain's hat. "Sorry about the commotion just now."

"I heard some frightful shouting and thumping. What was it?"

"A deserter from the 58th. Your soldier's regiment," he added, noticing that the gentle teasing did not provoke one of her usual shy blushes. Odd, that. "He ran away from the ship when it put in here on the way to Wanganui a few weeks back. They had him chained to a log earlier, when he was first captured, but he carved his way free, and he's not at all appreciative of the efforts made to recapture him."

"What will happen to him?"

"Flogged or shot, I suppose. Would you like more tea? I'll have the cabin boy prepare some if you wish."

"Flogged or shot? For running away?"

He smiled at her shocked face. "The Maoris may not think it cowardly to run away from the battle but Her Majesty's officers take a decidedly different view. In the name of Jove, Juliette, don't look so distressed. We cannot have people rushing about breaking the laws. What kind of a society would we have then? People who do wrong must be punished. It has to be that way."

He was still angry with her for refusing to discuss her reasons for leaving Auckland. "That seems a very hard attitude to me," she observed.

"I disagree. The laws are set by society and if we choose to break them we must be prepared for the consequences. I'm not hard, nor authoritarian either. If I stole something or—heaven forbid—killed someone, I would have no choice but to face up to society's judgement on me."

"I can't imagine you doing anything wrong."

"Neither can I, but who knows what waits around the next corner?" He came in and sat opposite her on a leather cabin chair. "What do you think of our mountain?"

"It's beautiful," she said, glad to change the subject. "Why didn't you tell me about it?"

"Partly so that it would be a surprise, and partly in case it was hidden by cloud. It often is, and I didn't want to describe it to you, then have you disappointed." He lit a thin cigar. "It must like you, to look so pretty for your arrival."

"Is that snow?"

"Yes. Not much at this time of year. In winter it reaches right down to the plain."

"Then I *am* disappointed. Mother told us all about snow and she made it seem somehow magical."

"It is. I'll tell you what. In winter, when the snow is right down, I'll come and visit you. Then see what you think. We can make a man out of snow . . ."

"No! Please, Stephen, please don't be angry, but we have been into all this. I beg of you, when you set me on dry land, please forget about me."

"In the name of Jove, how can I do that?" he exploded; then, sensing that she was perilously close to crying again, he made an effort to control his exasperation. "I thought of myself as a real friend, someone you could confide in, someone who would help you. I can tell that you are unhappy, and perhaps frightened, and I do wish you would let me help." He paused without much hope; she remained stubbornly silent. "Has that charming brother of mine hurt you in some way? If he has I'll . . ."

"Of course not!" She was prepared for this. "Why should I run away from Leigh when he has already gone off with the regiment? That would hardly make sense now, would it?"

He sighed. "My growing-up time was so brief that I tend to forget what it was like to be your age and have all the nerve ends so close to the surface. Every contact with life hurts so sharply, doesn't it?"

She turned her head away, fighting the desire to rest against his strong shoulder and pour out all her fear and misery. Perhaps she would never see this tender, considerate man again. And—if the ghastly probability that sat like a hunchback's lump on her shoulders should prove to be true—then she would never want to see him again; for if she did, she would see only disgust in his eyes.

He patted her hand. "There now, sweet Olivine. I do understand, truly I do." And to his astonishment that innocuous remark fell on her like a whip, provoking such a startled, guilty look that he wondered what sinister meaning could have been contained in those few harmless words.

He pretended to go along with her wishes, watching from the longboat as she followed the Maori sailor who carried her wicker basket and bundle past the high-tide mark. Beyond the dunes only tents and rooftops were visible. But when they were out of sight, he followed.

In this raw town Juliette could see a striking contrast to how Auckland had grown in the past four years. Here the shops were so tiny, the permanent-looking buildings so few, and makeshift dwellings so numerous. It was easy to find the town hall: a bare tin building right in the middle of town, opposite the London Missionary Society church. On the deep-rutted road outside waited a farm cart with a black horse and a thin sunburnt woman of indeterminate age. She wore an ugly yellow print dress and an incongruously elegant red sateen bonnet with little black bows set like butterflies all around the brim. When Juliette approached her she looked up sharply from the sewing heaped in her lap.

Stephen watched from behind the publican's dray as the woman jumped down to greet her, and when the Maori lad returned to where he was standing he fell in beside him for the walk back to the shore. He had seen all he needed to know.

Grace Sefton examined the lass shrewdly as she climbed awkwardly up onto the wagon seat, holding her cloak closed in front of her although the day was milky mild. The first sight of her was disappointing, and the way she moved was not promising either. She had been assured of a strong, healthy girl and this one looked thin and weak. But it could be merely that the sea voyage had knocked the colour out of her.

"Well, Miss Peridot, was it a fine and eventful journey then?" she asked in a shrill voice.

"Very well, thank you, ma'am." The woman's small brown eyes were studying her in a most disconcerting way. Her feelings of aloneness and inadequacy increased, as did her fears. What could she do if Mrs. Sefton turned her out? Where could she go? On the surface New Plymouth seemed a quiet place, not a town where employment might be easily obtained for a stray young lady.

Grace Sefton slapped the reins and the horse began to amble along the deserted street. Juliette clung to the wooden seat as the wagon jolted over the bumps and tried to give her polite attention to what Mrs. Sefton was saying. I shall have to tell her quickly, she thought. I must tell her, and the sooner it is done the better.

"Well now, you'd be a well-spoken lass, better than I expected for a home helper."

"My family are traders."

"I see. Then let's be having the reason you're so far from home. Come now, let's be hearing it."

"I beg your pardon?"

"A good family would nae send one of their daughters so far from home without a fine reason. I thought to get a poor lass, someone in dire need of employment; but you'd nae fit that description, not by a donkey's mile, my girl. There's money where you came from. I've nae seen quality cloth or fine sewing like that since I was in Edinburgh, and that's a pretty few years ago."

"The sewing is my own," said Juliette proudly. "And my stepmother imported the material for resale."

"Then perhaps you'd be telling me what it is with this stepmother of yours that she'd be shipping you off somewhere like a piece of goods when you're just the age to be starting up a life of your own. That doesn't seem right to me. I'm just a plain Free Kirk woman but that don't seem at all natural to me, I must say."

"I wanted a different life," said Juliette nervously. Then, because that reason did not seem to satisfy Mrs. Sefton, she began in a rush, bringing out her well-rehearsed story in such a tumble of words that it seemed to lose all the credibility she had hoped for it.

She doesn't believe me, thought Juliette in despair as the other woman repeated, "In the military?" and "Killed in action?" And her spirits sank when at the end of her speech Mrs. Sefton said bluntly, "And that will be a bairn you're carrying under that cloak, I suppose?"

"My stepmother knows nothing of that. Nothing at all," Juliette assured her.

"Then she most certainly should. And so should your husband's family. A widow with a bairn coming doesn't need employment. What she needs is care and plenty of it, especially a gently brought up young lass like yourself. I'm a mite too busy to be caring for you, Mrs. Peridot."

"Mrs. Yardley," said Juliette tonelessly.

"What's that you said?"

"My name is Mrs. Yardley. My husband was called Leigh Yardley. An ensign with the 58th he was, God rest his poor soul," she added grimly, hoping that it was not a dire sin to pretend that a living person was dead. She had quite enough sins to pray forgiveness for at the moment.

The wagon stopped at a pull on the reins, a gesture of finality. She was expecting it, but it stunned her just the same.

"I hope that you will be so good as to see this matter from my point of view," said Mrs. Sefton. "I have six sons to raise and nae time to care for the home." She held out her hands. "Look at these calluses! Our land is nae yet cleared and burned off, so all of us work all day and in all weathers. I've nae time to cook and mend and keep a cosy home, Mrs. Yardley, and that's why I sent for you. But you're nae what I wanted, so I can't take you. I need help, not a hindrance."

"Please, Mrs. Sefton, you must hear me out!" She clung to the other woman's lean arm and the reins quivered. At that the black horse began to plod again. Juliette interpreted this as a good omen and dashed on. "Please at least give me a chance. I *am* a good worker. I know how to scrub floors, to bake bread . . . how to launder and work around the house. I'm quick and clever and willing, and I'm begging for my life. Oh, I don't think I shall need special treatment or care when the baby comes. My own mother raised seven children and carried on without any ill-health or ill effects from childbearing. . . ." She trailed off, her face flushed with shame. This was a subject she knew of only from whispers or oblique remarks, yet she surprised herself with the amount she knew.

Mrs. Sefton jogged the reins. The girl's pleas had no effect on her practical and unsentimental mind, but the reasoning behind her arguments made sense. Also, she had not considered what it might be like to share her home with a younger, much prettier woman, or its effect on her lusty husband, Campbell. But an expectant mother would be a different proposition altogether. Campbell was like many big, blustery fellows; he was overawed and scared skittish of expectant women. And then there was the question of wages. . . .

She slid a look at the dejected Juliette, who yet had a look of proud defiance about her. She was clinging to the seat in a way that seemed to dare anybody to try to make her let go. Yes, she might well be as good a worker as she said, and her sewing was superlative.

Cannily she said, "If you're awaiting a bairn you'll nae be able to work as hard as I was wanting . . . and the matter of payment . . . well, I was nae wanting to pay much anyhow, and there's your food and keep . . . Why, what's to amuse you, Mrs. Yardley?"

"Nothing, truly." She could hardly repeat what Stephen had said: "Scots, eh? Then they'll have some excuse to

keep you and your wage at a distance from each other."
Aloud she said, "I do not expect much payment, Mrs. Sefton."

"Good!" said Mrs. Sefton. "Then it's done. I'll slip you a
shillin' a week so as you'll have something put by for the
bairn."

"That will suit, thank you."

"Well, lass, I fancy that we might do right well together.
You'll find it right peaceful here after the busy life of the
town, but we like it right enough. Nae neighbors to speak
of, but old Atholl Rykins on beyond the ridge. He 'purchased a Maori dictionary' some years back."

"I beg your pardon?"

"Took himself a Maori wife. Never seen her myself.
We dinna approve of mixing with them Maoris. Dirty,
thievin' lot they are."

"Not in Auckland," said Juliette, rather startled by this
view.

"An' the Maoris what belong here are good enough folks
too. It's the outsiders, stirrin' up trouble, they're the ones
we keep well away from. Let me tell you what I mean."
She launched into her story, obviously delighted to have
an audience; and Juliette, so relieved at the outcome of her
confession, would have listened to the dullest sermon.

The Seftons had arrived in New Plymouth five years before. There was a limited amount of Land Company property available, but they were fortunate in being able to
buy a farm that had already been partly broken in. The
wife had been burned to death when her skirts caught over
the cooking fire, and after that tragedy the husband lost
heart in the place. The Seftons sowed wheat, potatoes,
fruit trees, and vegetables and were just reaping their first
reward of crops when trouble struck.

"Them Waikato Maoris arrived and said, 'You canna
farm here! This is our land. We won all this land hereabouts in the war years back and this land is ours.' And a
right fuss they made, too—stole the hens, trampled the
crops, killed our horse, and poked a hole in the cabin wall
to fish out what they could from inside. Winkled out two
blankets and half the boys' clothes, they did.

"And then Governor FitzRoy came to sort out the fuss—a

right pompous fellow. He didna care whose land it was but he hated the New Zealand Shipping Company and saw a fine way to spite them. We couldna believe it, but he gave all our tilled, planted land back to the Maoris and told us to shift for ourselves. Not one penny piece did we get by way of compensation."

"That's *terrible!*"

"Aye, it was." The horse ambled along through the light, open bush, seeming to know its way home. "But Campbell—that's Mr. Sefton—an' me, we have plenty of Highland toughness in our souls. If the lairds couldna kill our crofter folks by chasin' them off the land an' burning their homes, then nae black devils are going to put us down. We may be plain Free Kirk folks but there's spirit there aplenty. We found this new land, an' we tithe our crops to the New Zealand Land Company. But maybe soon it will all be ours."

"It's a miracle that you're not bitter, Mrs. Sefton."

"Bitter? Aye, lass, I'm that, I admit, but only over one thing. Mr. Sefton an' me, we went back to visit our old land one day last summer. Ah, but it made me weep to see it. Fern, weeds, vines all choking the trees we planted. Our wee home with the shutters and the door hanging, dogs an' dirt lyin' about. No crops. All our work, all our toil gone for nowt. Those black bullies from the Waikato want their ears boxed till their brains scramble, aye, that they do." She shook her head, making the black bows jiggle. "Well, here we are, lass. This is home now."

When she heard that the Seftons lived on the mountain slopes overlooking the ocean, Juliette had pictured a pretty setting and a cottage with climbing roses; but what confronted her was a tiny, mud-plastered hut squatting on a bare earth yard. A flurry of drab red hens scattered as Mrs. Sefton yelled, "Halloo!

"Perhaps they're still up at the fields," she said, heaving bundles from the cart.

With a shout the unpainted door was flung open and three boys barrelled out like corks from a popgun. They were all of about a nine-year size with round, tanned faces and ears jutting out of a tangle of orange hair. All wore loose overshirts of the same ugly yellow print as Mrs. Sefton's dress, and all shouted at once—a jumble of words incomprehensible to Juliette. But their mother obviously understood, for she thrust her bundles at them and strode purposefully to the door, unpinning her ridiculous bonnet as she went, the boys hounding at her heels.

"Please let one of us shoot them, Ma!"

"I should! I'm all but ten!"

"Pa said we might use the gun when you say!"

"We got the gun down ready, Ma!"

"You what?" She turned on them and they hopped back a step in unison. She knew that they were baiting her but she snapped just the same. "I told you and I told you good! You'll nae touch that gun if you want to eat supper sittin' up at table." She glanced at Juliette. "That gun's so fraught and dangerous that if they did touch it they'd like as not lose a hand or a head. And it's always loaded, too."

Juliette followed them in, to find that the hut was much bigger than it seemed from the outside, but every bit as dreary as first glance had promised. Stacks of unmade bunk beds stood along one wall; a curtained alcove contained a lumpy double mattress, and near the fireplace was a narrow cot covered in a grey and red striped blanket. Assuming it was meant for her, she put her basket down beside it.

Mrs. Sefton was up on a chair reaching for something on a set of crammed shelves. As she dragged it out, Juliette gasped.

"A tupara!" she cried. "Where did you get that?"

"Nae, lass. It's nae a Maori thing and we've had it for longer than a donkey can remember," she said, squinting into the workings. Shooing the boys away, she commanded, "Hush now. Nae a sound when we go outside, do ye hear me?"

"Yes, Ma." All were obviously in awe of the old double-barrelled musket.

"What are you going to shoot?"

"Hogs, lass. Poachers. Wild hogs. They raid our garden and we bag them in return. Makes it fair."

Juliette looked out the one window but wouldn't have seen them if the boys hadn't pointed them out to her. They moved in slow circles in the patchy sunlight under the trees just beyond the privy. Mrs. Sefton stepped outside the cabin's other door and raised the stock to her shoulder.

The thin anguished squeal seemed to come before the smacking blast and was followed immediately by another shriek and another jolting report. The boys waited in the doorway until the second shot and then streaked away towards the pigs, shouting with excitement.

"It's a sow, Ma! There's piglets here, too."

"Then catch them and put them in the rabbit hutch, quickly. Don't stand flapping about."

Juliette hesitated. "Shall I start the fire, perhaps?"

"If you would." Grace's brown face warmed with approval. "I'll need hot water to singe the hogs, and I'll be busy till they're gutted and hung, and nae mistake. Pity they'll be too fresh to have a morsel of. I've nae tasted fresh meat in a right long time."

No meat! "What shall I prepare for dinner then?"

"It's supper, lass. Nae fancy dinners here. We'll have potato and cabbage, same as we always do. Potatoes in the bin there, cabbage in the garden. We'll need plenty, because old Atholl Rykins will be here, too. He's always here within an hour of that gun going off. He canna keep that nose of his in his own back yard, but nae matter. When he shows up he can help bristle the hogs. Can you manage the supper then, lass?"

"Certainly, Mrs. Sefton."

"Very well." She looked at the girl uncertainly. This was a new experience for Grace, having someone to give orders to.

"I shall be quite all right," Juliette assured her with a confidence she didn't feel. When Mrs. Sefton strode away, she had to fight the urge to sit down and luxuriate in a good weep, so depressingly dismal did her situation seem. Cabbage and potato—the same as always! Great heavens, what did they have for breakfast if that was their idea of a good main meal?

It was not until suppertime that she met the family properly, and then it was hardly a sociable moment, for they were tired, stained with blood spots, and smelling most unpleasantly of warm pork. But Juliette smiled and looked frankly into each face as she shook hands. Mr. Sefton was a hulking square fellow, red of hair and beard with freckles crowded over every path of exposed skin. He crushed her hand and boomed a few words at her, then laughed. She smiled weakly, not knowing what the joke was, for she had comprehended not one phrase of the heavy brogue. Grace rescued her quickly by explaining that Mrs. Yardley was a widow woman and they'd soon be having a bairn about the house again. This with a warning look at Campbell, to whom the news was clearly a surprise. She hurried on to introduce Craig, Cuthbert, Conway, Chester, Cameron (called Corrie), and Crispian, the junior member of the family at eight years old. Because Juliette looked rather dazed she explained they were all given names beginning with C like their father's so that the family name would quickly become strong in the district.

"If one does us right proud, they'll all take a share in the credit and if one should fall into trouble"—another sharp warning glare—"then they can all take a wee portion of the blame."

Mr. Sefton added something totally incomprehensible, to which Juliette nodded blankly.

"Cuthbert, go and see who's at the door!" said Grace, adding, "It'll only be Atholl Rykins but I don't know what can have kept him this late. Must be two hours since those hogs were shot."

"Is you all safe?" asked Mr. Rykins, who had a sad, toothless face and patched, baggy clothes. "I just came to see that nothin' were amiss."

"Aye, and hoping that it might be," whispered one of the boys to Juliette.

"Come in and welcome," said Grace. "We've a braw supper tonight and a young lass to cook it for us. Come in and set yourself down. What kept you so long?"

When the house was finally quiet Juliette lay on her hard little bed beside the fireplace and stared into the coals. Her mind was churning with doubts about her immediate future; yet at the same time she was set in the knowledge that she had had no other course of action open to her. Leigh had been long gone when the first terrible suspicions rose, and by then she had cut herself off from the rest

of the household by her insistence on going and her refusal
to discuss her reasons. Thomas had grown shoutingly angry with her and had decamped in a rage of frustration for
the bush, dragging Samuel, who had pleaded in vain for
her to change her mind. Rose was so hurt and bereaved
that she was scarcely speaking to her. And as for Aunt
Maire, Juliette could hardly wish to confide in *her*. Which
left Stephen, the one person she wanted to lean on for
comfort—and the last person she wanted to find out. It was
strange, but she could think of Leigh quite clearly and
without remorse. Shame, definitely, for the way he had seduced her; but no hatred and even some sorrowful understanding. But Stephen? Her mind shrank at the chilling
thought that he might learn about the baby.

"If he thinks ill of me I couldn't bear it," she said to herself. "Anything but that. Anything."

Twenty-three

"What have you called him?" asked Stephen. He hesitated and then decided not to call her "Miss Olivine"; it would probably only increase the strain between them. He had surprised her half an hour before kneading gritty brown dough at the kitchen table. The baby slept in a muslin-lined crate on a divan near the fire. She had glanced up, expecting one of the boys, but when she saw him the shock bleached her face and rendered her speechless. Stephen felt terrible. Forgotten were all the careful little phrases he had been rehearsing on the journey up. Awkwardness bristled between them.

He had not touched the baby either. A handsome little fellow, bonny, with dark green eyes and black hair, quite unmistakably a Yardley. It gave him an unsettled feeling to look into those steady, four-month-old eyes and realise that someday his own children would look exactly like this.

"His name is Leigh Yardley," she informed him in a tight voice. She did not add that it was Mrs. Sefton who had alerted the priest and insisted that the boy be baptised for his "poor, dead, brave father." Even in the face of such irony Juliette had been too ill with childbirth depression to argue. So "Leigh" it was.

"Leigh, of course," said Stephen.

She did not look up from the work, sprinkling coarse flour around the basin and punching the mass of dough as she flopped it over and over. Watching her, Stephen's patience began to stretch thin.

"You look well, Juliette," he said politely.

"So do you." Though apart from the first aghast stare of disbelief she had scrupulously avoided looking at him.

"It's very isolated here. A stupendous view, but isn't it lonely for you after Auckland?"

She thawed a fraction. "It is different. We have callers sometimes, and occasionally Maoris come to sell fresh fish or mussels. The priest called only once, and of course we get swaggies here. Wandering old men cadging a meal, mostly. They always want to talk. But I don't mind the isolation." Her voice warned him not to pity her. "In fact, when the Seftons go to New Plymouth once a month for church on Sunday and shopping on Monday, I generally choose to stay here."

"What, alone?"

"I'm not alone," she pointed out. "Besides, what harm could come to me? Mrs. Sefton showed me how to use the musket and there's nothing more frightening than wild pigs around here."

"If you say so." His eyes roamed with interest around the cabin. "This is a tiny place, but I must say you keep it tidy. In the name of Jove, what hideous curtains!"

"Around the bed?" She almost smiled. "That must be the ugliest cloth I've ever seen. Mr. Sefton bought a whole bolt of it when he was on one of his first shopping expeditions alone, and the family has had to wear yellow print ever since. Mrs. Sefton told me that she broke down and cried when he brought it home. There." She spread a threadbare dish towel over the basin and set it near the hearth, and pushed the sway so that the water pot was directly over the fire. "I'll make a pot of tea now. It's only green, I'm afraid, because green tea costs one shilling and sixpence a pound against black at two and eight. And there's no sugar. Mrs. Sefton doesn't believe in wasting good brass on things like food."

Stephen knew how much she appreciated fine cooking; yet he was uneasily aware of that "don't pity me" attitude in her stance. He was not quite sure how to proceed. "What do you people eat up here?"

She laughed without humour. "We have mashed potatoes or Indian corn porridge for breakfast, and potato and cabbage for supper. And bread, of course. Lots and lots of

bread. On Sundays there is no cooking so we fare better.
Cold boiled potatoes, cold boiled bacon, and cold hard-
boiled eggs."

"In the . . . Juliette, you shouldn't be here."

She pretended not to hear him. "It is a good healthy diet,
and it is teaching me a lot about gardening. I've been
forced into that out of desperation, and now we have tomatoes, sea kale, beans, even a few peas growing. I've tried to
introduce salads for Sundays but nobody but me likes the
taste of lettuce. I don't mind not having to share it. Between them they can consume an impressive amount of
food."

"How can you stand such a spartan existence?"

She ladled boiling water into the squat teapot and set it
on the table with two mugs and a plate of sliced bread.
Unwrapping a block of granite-hard cheese, she said
frankly, "I don't stand it, Stephen. I've taken to stealing.
Oh, you might as well know the rest of my sins and become
totally disillusioned. The Seftons go out all day with only
two loaves of bread and a crock of stream water; and I'm
supposed to have plain bread for my midday meal too.
Only I can't face that. It reminds me of . . . When I have
time I go down to the stream and catch a few kura, and if
there are vegetables ready I steam a handful of beans to
eat with my crayfish. But usually I steal an egg and coddle
it for my lunch. Mrs. Sefton would be furious if she
knew—I think she suspects because she's said that they
haven't had so many eggs to sell since I arrived."

"They sell the eggs when there are ten people here to be
fed?"

"Most of them. And all the rabbits, and whatever hens
go off the lay, and occasionally pigeons when the boys
shoot them. The only meat we have is pork because there's
a glut of that on the market, and half-wild bacon isn't
worth selling."

While she poured the tea he stared at her thoughtfully.
It was not going to be easy to break through that defiance
and say the things he wanted to. It was almost a year since
he had last seen the frightened young girl outside the town
hall, and in that year she had rounded and matured into a
truly lovely young woman. There was a new maternal

gracefulness in the slope of her shoulders and the curve of her neck. Her body was thicker, her face subtly altered. Marvelling at the change, Stephen was conscious of the hardest and most pressing desire that he had ever experienced. Shaken, he walked away and stared into the bleak yard until he felt a little calmer.

"This is no life for you, Juliette."

"Then what life do you suggest?"

He sat down opposite her and was about to speak when he saw that her face had hardened even more.

"What do you suggest?" she repeated with a flare of anger. "You can see my predicament—you knew it already, didn't you? You found out where I was and asked questions about me. Who told you? The priest? The storekeeper? Oh, it doesn't matter," she said in disgust. "I cannot alter what has happened, and I'm hardly delighted with this life. But it is made no easier by you coming here and telling me how poorly off I am. I know that already, thank you!"

Marry me, he wanted to say. Marry me and let me take you away. But her manner stopped him and he said, "What about Leigh? Do you keep in touch with him? Does he know anything about his son?"

"I do not wish to discuss that."

"In the name of Jove, Juliette, we have to discuss it!"

"Why?" Inside she was shrivelling, dying. He had not called her "Olivine" once. He was repelled by her shame; if she looked at him she would see it in his eyes. He had come to be businesslike and formal, to clear up the mess his brother had made. She wanted to shriek, Go away! Take your disappointed face and your disapproving eyes and *go*, so that I can break down and cry!

Her stubborn resistance maddened him, but yet he treated her with courtesy. If she had been one of his sisters he would have shaken her until she bawled. But this was Juliette and he kept his voice gentle and his hands tight around the blue pottery mug.

"We must discuss the matter because, in my quaint, conservative way, I think that this concerns other people besides yourself. Leigh, for example. Mama, Thomas, Rose, Jane, and Abigail too. This is the first living grandchild, do you realise that? A baby is not something you can run away with as though it is exclusively yours. It belongs just as much to its father."

She misunderstood him completely. Victorian law stated explicitly that all children are the property of their fathers, and Juliette knew—everybody knew—of pathetic cases where women had been driven from their homes and denied all further contact with their babies.

"How can you say that? Why would Leigh want the child?"

"And how do you know what Leigh wants?" he countered.

She pushed aside her tea, untasted. "I don't want him to know! I would rather leave here with my baby and try to find another shelter for us both than risk having to give him up—why, if Leigh took him he'd give him to Aunt Maire to raise! Do you really think I could endure the thought of that? How can you possibly suggest . . ."

He grabbed her wrist. She flinched, and he let go at once. "Of course I'm not suggesting that. I think that if Leigh knew about the baby he would offer to marry you." At that she ducked her head and made an odd, strangling noise that he interpreted as laughter. "I mean it seriously. Don't you want to marry Leigh?"

She did look at him then. He saw that she was crying and realised at once that she was not as toughened and defiant as he had supposed. In fact, her face had blotches of the same terror that he remembered from the last day he had seen her.

"No," she said forcefully. "No, no, no, no!"

"Why not?"

"Leigh doesn't love me." It sounded as though she was reporting the death of someone she had scarcely known. "Leigh said he did, then after . . . afterwards he said he didn't."

"My God! When I lay my hands on him, I'll . . ."

"No—don't be angry. He did mean it at the time."

"Why should you defend him? He's treated you appallingly, Juliette. How could he have done this to you?"

She stood up and went to lean in the doorway with her back to him. Apron ties crisscrossed her back and hung in a sloppy knot over her dark green skirt. "You probably imagine that I hate Leigh, but I don't." She gazed out across her vegetable garden, speaking so matter-of-factly that he knew she had spent a long time thinking about this. "I hate what he did to me and the way he treated me afterwards, but I do understand. You see, I thought that I loved him too, and not until later did I realise that I had been mistaken. I know that you'll think even worse of me than you do already but the fact is that I never want to see Leigh again. Never. I do realise that there is young Leigh's future to consider and the best thing for his sake would be to marry Leigh and give him a father, but I dread the very idea. I couldn't be Leigh's wife after what happened. I couldn't even face him again. There is a terrible loathing in me at the memory of that day. A terrible, terrible loathing."

His voice was very close behind her. "Poor Juliette. You have suffered dreadfully."

She stiffened. "Don't you pity me, Stephen Yardley! Your condemnation is quite enough for me to endure."

"I don't condemn you." He put his hands on her shoulders. She shuddered and he knew she was crying again.

"You must! You must condemn me. I'm immoral, and I'm quite unrepentant . . . and I steal, and . . ."

He laughed. "I don't condemn you, sweet Olivine." And with a sob she twisted in his arms and pressed against his jacket, crying helplessly. He stroked her shoulders and rested his cheek on the top of her cap, murmuring softly. "The stealing doesn't count, you've earned those eggs and more. And as for the rest, you're not immoral, nor are you unrepentant. What happened on the day you mentioned— well, for reasons of my own I never want to hear another word about that." As he spoke he was aware of a keen, hard edge of pain. The bastard, he thought. The spoiled, charming, utterly selfish young bastard.

"I thought you would detest me if you ever found out," she sobbed. "I thought you would be horrified and disgusted, and . . ."

He held her away from him and waited until she met his eyes. "Why do you imagine I would condemn you?" he asked as lightly as he could. "It's not as though you've killed someone now, is it?"

At the mock-serious look on his face she could not help but laugh.

In the autumn, as the melons were ripening, the garden was again raided by the wild pigs. When Juliette heard the sounds she found that she had no squeamishness about dragging out the old tupara and marching out to protect the vegetables she had laboured long, hot hours to tend. Grace had taught her to approach as close as she dared and to scan the bush beyond the raiders to make sure that none of the Sefton boys was approaching the orchard from that side. Quaking with apprehension, she put the gun to her shoulder and held her breath as she aimed. The tupara knocked her staggering backwards, and the blast was so loud that her head hummed and she was unable to hear the shrill indignant whistling of the pigs as they lurched away. Laying the musket carefully on the ground, she walked over to the partially walled garden. Half a row of carrots had been uprooted, and the remains of two pulpy melons were scattered among the dull leaves. But lying between two rows of potatoes like a sack rubbed over with coal dust was a large sow with a gaping red hole in her neck and pink froth rimming her jaws. Blood soaked blackly into the soil. Flies sang. The air was warm and wet with the sickly scent of blood.

Juliette bolted for the privy. Her stomach heaved and emptied itself. Bile stung her nose and raced down her throat in a long burn. From far away in the house she could hear the baby crying. When Atholl Rykins arrived an hour later, she let him begin the butchering alone.

Thomas wrote a letter for Stephen to deliver. It was brief and impersonal, a clumsily written and ill-spelled letter—and she wept over it when Stephen had gone. Nobody else wrote to her, nor did she write to them. She realised that she could not mend her friendship with Rose without confiding in her, and that was out of the question. But she hungrily questioned Stephen for news, any news, of home. Abby had a daughter called Dora and was expecting another any day. Jane had five dogs and a houseful of cats. Rose had a secret admirer, or or Stephen suspected. Maire had bought an expensive new carriage and the family was often invited to Government House. Governor Grey seemed especially taken with Thomas and respected his opinions about the Maoris so much that he had been asked to escort him on expeditions to the Bay of Plenty and down the Waikato River. There were now horse-drawn omnibuses in Auckland and a horse-drawn fire engine to pump water on any houses that might catch alight—if they got there in time to do more than douse the ashes. Leigh? Leigh was never mentioned by either of them.

The winter was miserable. When the mountain did show itself it was grey and forbidding. The two youngest boys developed colds and had to be nursed by Juliette, whose every chore was now hampered by a toddler with a rollicking sailor's walk. When the boys had recovered enough to go back to chopping down trees for the spring burn, Leigh stood at the door wailing for an hour every morning after they had gone. Even two days of sparkling, magical snow failed to console him. Juliette despaired. He was a healthy child, but from the beginning he displayed a determination to get his own way in everything.

One day she looked out through a fine curtain of rain. Two Maoris were walking through the garden. She opened the door and picked her way across the muddy yard, holding a square of oilcloth above her head to keep off the rain. One Maori man was fossicking in the vegetable patch, while the other was tampering with the door of the rabbit hutches. Both were heavily tattooed, with shoulders and backs bare despite the freezing drizzle. Juliette's indignation elbowed any fears out of her mind. Boldly ignoring the gun one carried, she marched over to them and loudly ordered them off in Maori. They gaped at her. At the sound of their own tongue spoken with such authority they dropped what they were doing and walked away, neither lingering nor hurrying, but glancing frequently over their shoulders at the unusual young woman who glared after them.

"You probably frightened the liver and lights out of them," said Stephen, dandling young Leigh on his knee.

"Probably . . . oh, Stephen, what's that? Not another

toy? Oh, it's a carved wooden horse! It's beautiful, and thank you, but you really shouldn't. You spoil him."

"What are uncles for, if not to spoil their nephews? Besides, if he has his own toys he won't want to play with that doll of yours. Boys shouldn't play with dolls, should they, young man?"

"Poor Clarissa! She was literally cracked on the chin the other day when this rascal dragged her down off the shelf. I've had to keep her locked away in the workbasket. I hate to say it, but a certain person will not do what he is told no matter how I try to coax him. The Sefton boys indulge him recklessly and I'm afraid that he is catching the very worst aspects of their manners. Do you know what I found him doing out in the yard the other day? Spitting! Spitting at the hens! He copies the bigger boys and they simply encourage him."

Young Leigh wriggled and looked so pleased with himself that Stephen was unable to look stern.

"A little mischief doesn't matter. Besides, I like to indulge you, too." He reached into his greatcoat pockets and tumbled out an assortment of brown-wrapped lumps tied with string. "Our galley cook has done you proud this time. There's China tea, and Darjeeling, two kinds of coffee, some black pudding and . . ."

"You shouldn't do it, Stephen!" But she looked pleased.

"I know, but how else can I wangle an invitation to stay to supper?"

"You mean you hate green tea!"

"I confess I could never really develop a fondness for it."

She laughed. It was so much fun when he visited now. "To tell the truth, I loathe it too. Find the Darjeeling and I'll brew us a pot this minute."

One hot summer evening the boys went eeling down at the creek bends where the water quietly ran through dark, deep hollows. They took nets and a machete, lit their way with a candle in a half bottle cradled in a sling, and crept out as soon as Leigh had fallen asleep. They came back screaming. Grace and Campbell tumbled from the lamplit house and Juliette waited fearfully beside Leigh's bunk, anxious that he might wake. Campbell hurried in holding

Crispian while their mother tried to subdue the others, all
trying to explain how he had tripped and fallen on the
lamp. When Juliette saw the open, pulsing wound in the
leg, she almost cried out; but Grace's reaction was practical and businesslike. She cuffed Craig, who was still crying, sent Cuthbert for her little inlaid sewing box, Conway
to fetch a clean cloth, Chester to bring a bowl of water, and
young Corrie (who looked distinctly green) to talk to Leigh.
Campbell held his son's shoulders while Grace pinched the
oozing lips of the long wound together and stitched it up
with her ordinary needle and thread.

Juliette was horribly fascinated and said later that she
could never have done a thing like that.

"Nonsense," said Grace. "You'd do what needed doing
right quick. You didna flinch from shootin' that hog, and
you didna run when those thievin' Maoris were into our
rabbit hutches. If it were your boy lying' there a-bleedin'
you'd nae hesitate before openin' up that sewing basket of
yours. When you came here you were nowt but a slip of a
lass but you're nae a child now, Juliette."

That following winter the privy almost overflowed after
a prolonged spell of wet weather. Grace complained about
the stench and then the boys laughed about it, making
crude jokes that stopped only when Campbell barked at
them. Though Juliette did not understand what he had
said, she understood when the boys began working with
buckets, picks, and shovels: they were digging a new hole.
In the early stage of excavation there was minor excitement when Conway unearthed a meat dish that Grace had
long ago given up for lost. It was encrusted with dirt, but
she received it with cries of joy. Apparently soon after they
came to the mountain there had been a scare that Maoris
were invading. There was no time to pack; Sefton would
not wait. So Grace and the oldest boys quickly smeared
their most precious breakables with pork fat and buried
them where the potatoes had just been dug.

"There was nae room on the cart so we did what we
could," she explained. "Aye, but I've missed this dish, that
I have!"

When it was finished, the new privy was over twenty

feet deep and would last for at least another five or six years—provided, Grace said, young Leigh didn't fill it all in again in as many months. He had been causing trouble in the household recently with his naughty habits. And he decided that the privy was a good place to play in, and especially to throw things down into. First it was only rocks and chunks of firewood, but then objects began to go missing. And one day Juliette caught him in the act of throwing a spade down the hole. That evening the privy hut was removed and amid hilarity Craig was lowered on a rope into the pit. With an improvised grappling hook he retrieved the spade, then a poker, a ladle, and two rat-traps. Juliette had already given Leigh a token whipping for the spade but now, when Campbell caught sight of the lad capering about and chuckling as if he had done something very clever, his temper burst. He unbuckled his belt and whaled into the child until the shrieks seemed to bounce off the mountain. Leigh sulked for days and never forgave the burly Scot for the thrashing (neither did Juliette). But no further objects went missing after that.

Juliette reluctantly admitted to herself that the whipping may have done her son some good, for she too had been finding him impossible to manage at times. Just the same, she felt indignant when she recounted the incident to Stephen; she had expected a sympathetic hearing, and he all but applauded.

"I thought you doted on your nephew!" she said.

"I do. And I consider him to be far too splendid a young lad to be spoiled by ruinous indulgence."

"But he's only three years old!"

"Aye, and learning every trick in the book about getting his own way. He's charming enough and I do dote on him, but don't let him strain your life."

"I know. I do my best, but . . ."

"He needs a father. You realise that, don't you?"

She was prevented from answering when Leigh came running in and flung himself, with puppy exuberance, into Stephen's arms.

"Come and play with me, Uncle Stephen."

"I'd love to."

Twenty-four

"It's nae right to leave you like this, not with the poor wee bairn so ill, and the weather bein' so mortal hot. Would you like for one of the lads to stay and keep you company, fetch for you and such?"

The boys sat wedged into the cart like sheaves around the cases of fruit. They were all carefully looking away and hoping not to be chosen.

"It's only a summer cold and he's over the worst of it. I'd rather be alone, truly. And I've a letter from Captain Yardley's sister which I must answer. He'll be back here any day now and expect the reply to be ready." She hefted the stone water crock up for Chester to take. "Don't forget this. You'll be needing a drink before you've trundled a mile under this hot sun. Doesn't the mountain look beautiful this morning? Even without the snow it seems to sparkle."

Grace was not interested in the scenery. She squinted out over the leathery bright sea. "I hope that Captain Yardley does come. It's nae right to leave you with a sick bairn." She looked hard into Juliette's face, ridiculous black bows jiggling as she turned her head. "There's somethin' else, lass. Last time we was in town we heard that there's been mischief done at farms like this, things taken when the folks was away at services and visitin' and such."

"I'm not nervous. Haven't I chased Maoris away several times?"

"It's said that these are nae Maoris. It's money, knick-knacks, trinkets, and the like been stolen. That's nae Maoris."

"Then it's a good thing that I'm here, isn't it? If they are pakehas, then they'll not come near when they see me. Now you'd best be going or you'll be late for the first service."

She watched them drive away and then settled herself on a bench beside the door in the shade, with Rose's letter and a cloth cap she was making out of an old pair of trousers for Leigh.

Rose's letter had been a joyful surprise and Juliette reread it slowly. She savoured the descriptions of entertainments and outings now so alien that it seemed beyond belief that she had ever participated in games of dumb crambo, danced the quadrille, or thrilled to the resonance of Byron's epic poems. And Stephen had been right in his earlier assumption: for not only did Rose really have a secret admirer, but she had eloped with him just as Jane had done.

Poor Mama is Furious and has Cut both Jane and me out of her Will, no doubt to make us Repent, and Regret what we have done; for in my Case I have no Doubt that she planned to have me for a Companion for her Old Age. But my only Regret is that I delayed for so Many Years, not having the Courage to Take the Final Step: How I wish that you were Here to share my Happiness! Stephen tells me that I am Cruel to allow this Silence to go on so long between us, and he said that you were Deeply Unhappy and had Good Reason to go away as you did. But can you not come Back again now? You have a Welcome Home here with Doctor Forster and me, and Jane says the Same for Herself. Do think about it, Dear Juliette. We miss you more than we can say,

                    Your devoted friend,
                    Rose Forster

Postscript. I cannot Resist penning my New name in Full. Doctor Forster sends his Warmest Regards.

Folding the letter, Juliette sighed to relieve the tightness in her throat. It was as though Rose's voice had been transported over the distance. The murmur in her ear awakened nostalgic longings for events half forgotten,

whispered confidences, laughter. Dr. Adrian Forster with
the kind, intelligent eyes. How perfect for Rose, Rose who
was so miserably certain that nobody would want her. And
in the bloom of her happiness Rose had tried to include
her. Auckland. A week away by ship and coach, five years
away in time, and a lifetime away in experience. Lost in
her thoughts, Juliette gazed out over the folds and ridges
of bush which stretched dark green and ferny soft as far as
she could see. New Plymouth was a smoky patch torn out
of one edge of the fabric, too far away to be anything as real
as a proper busy town. As it had done a thousand times before, the enormous, solemn silence of the bush reached out
to enfold her and to ease her soul. Presently her mind
drifted away from the treacherous eddies of memory. She
picked up the cap and threaded her needle again.

In the afternoon the heat seemed to expand over the
countryside. Leigh took a little broth with pieces of bread
softened in it and was again asleep before she had rinsed
the bowl. She ate a peach and went back outside. A gentle
current of air seemed to flow under the trees, so she moved
the bench and settled back to work.

She first saw the men when they were still some distance away, and she laid her sewing aside at once, glad of
the excuse to stop even this undemanding task. Looking at
them idly, she decided they were swaggies, or so it seemed
through the shuddering heat haze that lay across the path.
Father and son, she guessed; one bulky and thickset, the
other slight. They walked at a brisk enough pace for her to
assume that they had not come far, just from Zeffs's place,
no doubt. Old Mr. Zeffs lived alone and stopped all pas-
sers-by to exchange his hospitality for company and gossip. These two would probably not even want a meal and
would be happy to be on their way after a mug of tea, with
a pocketful of dried fruit to munch as they walked.

They were closer now but had not noticed her. They were
talking in the loud, extravagant way of people who are
confident they have the whole district to themselves.
Bursts of a whinnying laughter punctuated their chatter,
an odd kind of laughter which for some inexplicable reason
made Juliette suddenly pay sharp attention to them. She

had been mistaken in her first assumption: they were both
middle-aged men, though one was so rail-thin and springy
of step that it was easy to see why she had been wrong. He
was a dusty-looking rag of a man, and the other a lumbering ox by comparison, with a broad face and a thick ruff of
frizzy ginger hair that stuck out all around the rim of his
old felt hat. As she took in all the details of their appearance the strangest feeling gradually tightened around her.
Normally she would have stood up and moved forward to
greet the travellers; but there was something striking
about these two that prickled at her memory and held her
fast where she sat.

Then, when they were within reach of a tossed pebble,
the thin one turned to his friend.

"We're in luck, Blue! Just like the man said, there ain't
nobody here!"

"Douse it," ordered the other curtly. He turned his head
and Juliette glimpsed his profile, a broken nose so humped
that the bridge protruded further than the tip. "Douse it,"
he repeated. "We make sure first."

Juliette swallowed dry air down her dry throat. Fourteen years separated her from that sultry afternoon when
she had crouched in the tinder grass and seen these same
two men as they fled from the carnage they had wreaked
in the little cottage on the clifftop. Fourteen years—but it
might as well have been yesterday. She quailed as the men
came jauntily closer. She could feel her hands trembling
against each other, like helpless animals trapped in her
lap. If she could remain perfectly still they might go
around the house and not see her. If only she could . . .

"Well, hello there!" The thin man looked down at her,
and she gazed timidly back at him. There was an odd slant
to his head, something queer about the way he looked at
her. She was aware of an eerie sensation—remembering
that peculiarity and what caused it, seeing again at exactly the moment of recall the large wart on his eyelid that
pushed his eye half shut in a parody of a wink.

"Lookit this, Blue!"

There was no way she was going to be able to run. Her
only choice was to smother her panic and to stare them
down.

"Good afternoon, gentlemen," she managed to say in a miraculously level voice. "Are you passing through?"

"We ain't in no hurry, ma'am. No hurry, are we, Blue?" He laughed a high, skittering laugh and Juliette wondered if she had the strength to stand up.

Blue did not reply. He was staring at her bemusedly and when her eyes flickered nervously across to him she was startled by the recognition in his face. He can't possibly know who I am, she told herself.

She swallowed convulsively, then recovered her voice. "I'm sorry, but there is no work for you here."

"All alone, are yer?"

Leigh! In her paralysis she had completely forgotten him. She had hunched like a cornered rabbit, her mind racing around blindly, wondering how she could escape, quite forgetting that she had a child to consider.

"I think she is all alone, Blue. Ain't that fine, now?"

A moment ago those words might have made her literally faint with fear, but now indignation surged to the front of her mind. These two murderous bullies had scared her, but she was not going to stand by and let them hurt her son.

She stood up and was astonished to find that she was taller than either of them. An insignificant detail but it further dulled her fright.

"I am alone, for the moment," she said with a dignity meant to reproach them for their insolent attitude. Before they could say anything further in that overfamiliar way she added, "It is the Sabbath today, and I am expecting company later this afternoon. However"—she thought swiftly—"I could prepare you a light meal if you like. There are a few slices of ham which I could cook with tomatoes and onions. Would that please you?" Careful, she warned herself. Speak slowly. Your voice is dinning as fast as the clatter of gravel down a rocky slope. Be calm. Taking a deep breath, she continued. "Would you please be so kind as to pick me some tomatoes from the vines over there in the garden? I shall go and tend the fire. Oh, and please remove your boots before you come inside the house."

It worked. After doubtful glances, Blue shrugged and grinned, and they both unslung their swaggie packs and dropped them beside the tree. They were going to be tricked into going far enough away from the house for her to rush in, scoop Leigh up, and bolt for the shelter of the bush.

Straight-backed, she moved towards the door, then paused. As they ambled away their voices tossed clearly back to where she stood.

"I tell yer, Johnny, she's *got* ter be. She's the spit of Evangeline. Didn't yer see it? Evangeline? Bay of Islands?"

"Evangeline Peridot? Oh, my Gawd, but she is! But what . . ."

"Douse it! She ain't deaf, is she?"

Feeling ill and weak, Juliette slipped inside, shut the door, and put the bolt across. It was no use trying to run now, for if she did they would immediately know why and seek her out in no time. Her bright skirts would stand out like a beacon in the undergrowth and she could not rely on speed to put any distance between them, not when she had a sick child to carry.

Leigh slept as though drugged, his damp body sprawled over the tumbled bedding. Juliette moved past him with held breath. Through the open window she could see the men sauntering towards the privy. Johnny poked at the door and his high laughter carried right into the room. She shivered. Numb and barely aware of what she was doing, she dragged a chair over to the shelves and climbed up. Her hands shook when she pulled the weighty tupara down and cradled it in her arms. Beyond the propped-open door, beyond the yard and hutches, the men bent in the garden. She was aware of the passing of time; each second seemed clear and separate. She breathed deeply to quiet her jerking nerves; her breath made loud scraping noises in her throat. Now the men were turning and coming back, their cupped hands holding pyramids of fruit against their shirts.

The barrel grated rough and heavy on her arms; they were sweating under the long red sleeves. Everything around her faded until she was aware of only the weight in her hands, and the two men stepping over the low stone wall. She slid her fingers around the musket, groping for the triggers. When the men were less than ten yards from the house she forced herself out the door and into the patch of dense shade under the jut of the roof.

Her courage faltered badly when Johnny saw her and dropped the tomatoes. It occurred to her that they might both run, and if they did, she and Leigh were lost. She could not afford to waste a shot, for reloading this thing was a mystery to her, and if they ran now and returned later she knew that she would not be able to keep them out.

Neither ran. Both stood perfectly still, watching her, their thoughts unreadable.

Juliette's own voice startled her. She was convinced that any movement would weaken her defence, but still she said, "You know who I am. I am Evangeline Peridot's daughter. I know that you killed her, and my brother and my sisters. I was there that day."

Without pausing to think, Johnny blurted out, "Yer lyin'. Nobody was there."

"Douse it!" hissed Blue. But it was too late.

If there had been any doubts, that admission banished them. Contempt flowed through her like blood. These were brutal, cowardly men and now they were afraid of her. She raised the gun barrel slightly. She could be sure of hitting Blue if she fired. He was the biggest, she should shoot him first. No, perhaps not, she decided, considering them both again. Johnny was the faster and might try to overpower her after the first blast.

"Put that gun down," said Blue flatly.

"Yer heard him. Do like he says!" urged Johnny. "I bet she don't even know how ter work the thing! I bet she's only bluffing! She ain't much more than a nipper 'er-self . . ."

"Douse it!"

Juliette was not listening. She was a long way away— fourteen long years away—and contemplating a task to be done. The utu must be exacted; these men had to die and there was no other way the confrontation could end unless they outwitted her.

"I have to do this," she said coldly. "You would have killed me here, today, if I did not kill you. It is what you have been planning since you first saw me, isn't it? You came to ransack the house and would have killed me in order to do it."

Johnny's face slumped as though his facial bones had suddenly collapsed. "We wouldn't 'ave 'urt yer none, honest. We ain't lookin' fer any trouble."

"What about my mother?"

"Yer don't understand. That were different. Yer ma, she were a whore, a one-guinea whore, an' all we was wantin' were the money she had hid somewheres. She 'ad all the guineas off us, an' all we wanted was some of our money back. But the stupid doxy, she wouldn't tell us where she hid it, and we . . ."

"Douse it," ordered Blue urgently, noticing how Juliette's face had whitened and her expression grown tight and hard.

It was too late. She was hardly aware of having squeezed the trigger. An invisible force roughly pushed her back at the same time that it swatted the side of Johnny's face, dashing it into a star blaze of bright red, gayer than her dress. He made no sound, simply sagged backwards and fell with his arms at his sides.

Blue gaped at him disbelievingly, then swung his gaze towards the barrels. "It weren't *my* fault yer ma got killed," he pleaded desperately. "It were an accident. It weren't me . . ."

Juliette's stomach revolted. Knowing that she could bear this no longer—and knowing that she had no other choice—she jerked at the trigger, shutting her mind against what she was doing. Flinging the tupara away from her, she fled inside, feverishly bolting the door behind her.

She was leaning against it shaking, her ears ringing with the echoes of the blast and with the high noise of crying. Crying! Oh, dear Virgin, I failed to kill them! she thought in terror. They're alive! What can I do now? Then Leigh stumbled towards her, face crumpled with howling. She suddenly sobbed with relief.

"You woke me and my throat hurts!"

"I'm sorry, dear. The gun went off."

"Was it hogs?" He brightened.

"Yes," she said quickly. "Yes, there were hogs in our garden. I had to shoot and frighten them away."

"Where?" He moved towards the window where the shutter stood wide open.

Her nerves snapped. Even if he peered out for a split second he would see.

"No!" she said. Then, more mildly, "I chased them away. There's nothing to see. Now, I want you to go right back to bed and I'll bring you a drink. I crushed some apples this morning to make fresh juice to ease that throat of yours."

He tried to push past her. Though he was slight for four and a half, his determination gave him strength.

She held him by the shoulders. "Go back to bed, please."

"No! And I *hate* apple juice!"

"Sick people have to stay in bed until they are properly better. Now be a good boy, please."

"No!" His whole attitude was a caricature of defiance, with lowered head, jutting lip, and squared shoulders. Normally this posturing elicited a chuckle and a hug from her but not today.

"Do as you are told!"

"No, I won't!"

Exasperated, she shook him, igniting his temper. He yelled and hit her—only an open-palmed smack, but it stung her into retaliating with a swipe on the legs, the hardest blow she had ever given him.

He crumpled at her touch with an exaggerated shriek of pain, agitating her still further. Later she could make it up to him. Later she could be the loving mother. But the only priority now was to use any means at all to keep him from seeing those bodies.

Sweeping him up authoritatively, she carried him back to the far end of the house and dumped him on his bed.

He glared at her, tears standing out in his eyes.

"Do you know what a switch is?" When he nodded she went on brutally, "If you put one foot off this bunk, then I shall cut myself a springy switch and give you a real whipping. Now stay there!"

As she was bolting the shutters his voice rang out to her, "I shall stay here just until Mr. Rykins arrives!"

Mr. Rykins! Her hands froze on the shutter catches. Atholl Rykins—of course! He would have heard the shots and right now would be scurrying along the bush path to investigate. How long ago had the shots been fired? It seemed like hours. How much time did she have left? She had to cover all trace of what she had done, and she would have to do it quickly. But just in case Leigh had ideas about getting up she took the door bar outside with her and wedged it under the door handle.

Blue was gazing straight into the sun like someone staked out in the desert with a wet, red cravat slung casually about his neck. She turned her eyes away as she took hold of his ankles and dragged him towards the privy. The touch of him seemed to crawl along her skin, up past her wrists like ants swarming over sweetness. That same cloying smell that had revolted her when she shot the pigs now choked at the back of her throat, but she smothered her nausea and fought the horror. Quickly, quickly! There was only one place where the bodies could be hidden. It was a simple matter to remove the privy seat and to drag the inert lolling mass into the tiny outhouse; but it was a far more awkward proposition to manoeuvre Blue into the pit. Trying not to watch what she was doing, trying to ignore the gritty stickiness under her fingers, she tugged, pushed, and lifted until he dropped away into the darkness.

When Johnny had been disposed of she realised that her task was only beginning. The privy walls and platform floor were splattered with blood, and her apron was so soaked that the colour merged into the redness of her skirt. Worst of all, a lightly ploughed streak across the yard was a swathe of blood, hair, cloth scraps, and bits of nameless horror—all already singing with flies. She guessed that an hour had passed between now and the killings. Atholl Rykins would be well on his way here.

She moved in a blur, a panic of activity. Grabbing the spade from beside the door, she scraped up the worst from the yard, then dashed to the garden for a scatter of earth to spread over the marks of the blade. The flies lingered. Blood pounded in her ears. It were an accident, an accident, an accident, the rhythm seemed to say. Rushing on,

she tore off her apron and hastily donned a fresh one,
thrusting the bloody one into her workbasket. Leigh
stirred but did not look at her. Frantically she splashed
water into a pail, snatched up a scrub brush and soap, and
dashed out to the privy. It were an accident, an accident,
drummed her ears. The soap and water dissolved the blots
but a sharp eye could still detect a pink hue. She would
have to do it again later—there was no time now, no time
to change, no time to wash the crawling stickiness from
her body, no time to do anything more than sluice out the
scrub bucket as Atholl Rykins' whistling tune moved
closer across the ridge.

Accepting the mug of green tea, he hunched his shoulders and pointed his long, sad face towards the tomato
patch. "I bin over there an' I seen no hoofprints nor no
damage neither."

"I chased them away before they managed to break
through the wall," she said, trying to sound pleased with
herself. Her clothes stank so violently of blood that she
couldn't comprehend why neither he nor Leigh had commented on it.

"Reckon yer hit summat here in the yard, though. Them
flies seem mighty innarested in summat there."

"The boys killed a hen there yesterday," she lied.

"I didn't know that!" Leigh was sitting at the table in
his nightshirt, eating a peach.

"You were too sick to go outside, dear."

"I wish I could have watched."

Hastily she said, "I'll pick you some tomatoes to take
home, Mr. Rykins, if you will be so good as to load the
musket for me again while I do that? The pigs might come
back again, and then how could I frighten them?"

"I figgered yer 'ad better aim than that," he said darkly.
But he did as she asked, keeping busy and out of the way
while she filled a flax kit for him.

An hour after he had gone she sat on the stoop, bathed
and scrubbed, with fresh clothes on. There was still a lot to
be done before the Seftons returned, but Leigh was now determined to be out and playing. The work could wait. She
was exhausted, but at least that crawling stickiness had
gone.

Leigh came galloping round the corner, shouting in his still very hoarse voice and dragging a small trolley Stephen had given him. She looked up, flicked wet rope of hair over her shoulder, and began to say, "Don't play so energetically, dear." Then she saw the two swaggie packs in the jolting trolley, and her heart lurched. "Look what I found!"

"Oh, dear God!" she whispered.

"I found them, so they belong to me! That's what Craig says when he finds anything." The packs sat up in the trolley as jauntily as their owners had sauntered up the road. Leigh settled himself beside her and reached for them.

"What are you doing?"

"I'm going to see what's in there. There might be good things to play with."

"Oh, no, you're not!" She grabbed and swung them out of his reach. "They will belong to somebody."

"Who?"

"Never mind who. I don't know. They must be . . . they must have been left there and the owners will return for them. Perhaps the swaggies have gone looking for kura. Yes, that's where they must have gone."

"I'll go and find them."

She said sharply, "No, you'll not. You'll come inside right now. It's getting cool. Leigh, do as you're told, at once!"

He glared at her with resentment. "You're crabby as hell!"

"Who taught you to talk like that?"

"I taught myself!" When she relaxed enough to smile he said, "Will you make me a swaggie pack to play with?"

"If you pop off to bed right away," she promised.

Twenty-five

When Juliette woke next morning she lay staring at the ashes in the hearth for a long, cold minute. I am a murderess, she thought. A murderess.

It didn't seem real, so she whispered it. "I am a murderess." The sounds had no more sinister implication than the wind rustling the fronds of the tree fern against the walls. It was ironic; she would have smiled if she had not been too tired—smiled at the irony of her situation. When she had borne Leigh out of wedlock she believed that she had sunk as low as a person could. But killers went to gaol and were hanged, their bodies buried secretly in unconsecrated ground—disposed of like rats. What if someone came looking for those two? What if Atholl Rykins became suspicious? What if he had returned last night and seen her toiling in the lamplight, dragging rocks to dump into the privy, shovelling in loads of earth, sweeping the yard—scrubbing the privy, scrubbing her dress which ran red into the rinsing water. What if he had been in the orchard, watching? If he should fetch the police, what would happen to Leigh?

"Stop it!" she said aloud, swinging aching legs out of the bed and straightening her clothes with stiff, sore fingers. Outside, the yard looked so quiet and innocent that she could hardly picture yesterday's carnage. The sky was clear as water, the bush alive with the early morning crackle of birdsong; the rabbits in their hutches were waiting for their morning puha, the hens scratching in the yard. . . . She hurried to get a scoop of grain from the barrel, fighting the encroachment of gruesome thoughts.

Then, soon after, she found that she could not bring herself to use the privy; she had to go instead behind the house.

Leigh slept on. She smeared her cracked hands with mutton fat and began making the swaggie pack she had promised him. Ugly images waved in front of her until indignation took over and forced her to face up to her doubts. What choice had she? None. What would have happened if she had not killed the men? They would probably have raped and likely killed her instead . . . and Leigh, too. What would have happened if she could have summoned help and had the men arrested for her mother's murder? They would have been set free, no doubt, for who would accept the word of an immoral woman who had been a mere child at the time? And what if there was a trial? They could have—would have—said those same unspeakably vile things about Mother, in front of a courthouse full of avid listeners.

It had to be this way. Realising that, another thought occurred to her. Fate, or Providence, or God, or even some mysterious force in this, the Maoris' land, had brought those two men to her at a time when she was alone—and then had given her the courage and strength to do what had to be done. Perhaps she was nothing more than a figure in a grand design of utu, part of a pattern that ensured that the two men were punished for their crimes.

There remained only one last tiny doubt, a scampering mouse that had pattered around in her mind as she toiled through the exhausting cleanup, the mouse that squeaked repeatedly, "It were an accident, an accident, an accident." Was it accidental? Had they killed Mother and the children by accident?

Of course not, she thought as she turned the new swaggie bag the right way and checked the seams. How could five killings be an accident? she thought as she measured the lengths of rope for the handles. One perhaps, but not five.

Leigh shouted with a whoop of joy when he saw the bag. But though he reached up for it at once, she held it high out of his way.

"There's one very important thing," she said sternly.

"You must promise me most seriously that you will not say one word about the swaggies to anybody."

"Why?" he pouted.

"Because Mr. and Mrs. Sefton would be worried if they thought that swaggies were hanging about here when they were gone. We don't want to worry the Seftons, do we?"

"I don't care."

"Leigh!"

"I promise not to say anything about the swaggies," he said, chanting an incantation that would give him his new toy.

She sighed, watching him caper about with his arms thrust through the rope handles. Within an hour of the Seftons' return this evening the subject would be mentioned, but no matter. Her arms and back ached intolerably and she could hardly keep her eyes open. Yet she was gripped by such a clean, sharp hunger that she realised wearily that she had not eaten a proper meal since the day before yesterday. Last night Leigh had supped on cold leftovers from Saturday's dinner, but her stomach had contracted rebelliously at the thought of food. Now she was ravenous. She scratched up the ashes and hooked a pot of water onto the sway, reflecting as ragged ribbons of fire slicked over the roughly split wood that what happened yesterday was already far, far behind her.

While the water began to boil she heated a pan and extravagantly carved thick slices of pink ham. Recklessly she cracked three eggs for herself and two for Leigh. Her hunger made her eat rapidly; she craved more when she had finished mopping up the juices with a heel of dark brown bread. She was nudging the pan over the heat again when Stephen ducked his head in at the door. "Is this a late breakfast or an early lunch?"

"Uncle Stephen!" screamed Leigh, wriggling down from his place at table. "Look at what Mother made me! Look! A real swaggie pack!"

Juliette tried to smile. Stephen couldn't help it if his timing was unfortunate; she was pleased to see him no matter how tired she was. Reluctantly she put aside her plans to sleep all morning and unwrapped the ham again.

"I have timed my arrival perfectly," said Stephen when he had admired the pack.

"What? Oh yes, the ham. We had good luck a few weeks ago when the most enormous sow came fossicking in the garden. Craig shot it, and it's cured beautifully."

"Mother shot at some hogs yesterday," Leigh informed Stephen. "She fired the musket both times but she missed, and Mr. Rykins came all the way down for nothing."

Juliette's laughter sounded high and false. "He scored so well on the previous occasion, and this time all he received was a kit full of tomatoes." Glancing at Stephen, she noticed uncomfortably that he was staring at her as if he had never seen her before. Turning her back on him, she began cooking his food.

As he ate he watched her thoughtfully. She looked terrible; old, red-eyed, her hair tangled, her gracefulness eroded into stiff awkwardness. When she straightened from the fire she seemed in actual pain, holding one hand to the small of her back as an old crone might. His concern mounted until, when she set a mug of tea before him, he captured her hand in a gesture of compassion. But when he touched her the soothing words died on his tongue. Though she immediately tried to pull her hand free he held it fast and turned her wrist, prising the fingers away from the yellow-stained palm. In disbelief he stared at the ragged skin and raw, weeping blisters.

"In the name of Jove, Juliette, what have you been doing?"

"Nothing!" she said too quickly in that false, high voice.

"Nothing? Come, now . . ."

"A little gardening," she replied. "I worked late last evening, weeding, digging. . . . I moved rocks onto the wall to try to keep those wretched pigs out. It was the rocks . . . it must have been the rocks that caused these blisters. I was so busy that I didn't notice."

"That looks like the result of more than one evening's work."

"I told you, Stephen."

"And I find it difficult to believe you. You look as guilty as . . . Never mind. Juliette, you look utterly exhausted! There's more to this than a pleasant evening's gardening.

You've been slaving in the fields, haven't you? The Seftons have had you outside doing labourer's work."

She pushed the hot denial away, thinking wearily that it didn't matter what he thought. Instead she said that nobody made her do anything and that, believe it or not, her hands were raw from rebuilding the rock wall.

"I admire your loyalty," he said after a pause. "But it really is of no further consequence what the Seftons have been doing or not doing. I've come to take you away from here."

"I beg your pardon?"

"Sit down, Juliette. That's better. You make me nervous with your prowling around. Now listen. I have to go away for quite some time—two years or more. I'm developing a shipping company of my own, quite separate from the Richmond Line, though I'll still run that too. This is the time for expansion, Juliette! There is a magnificent future in this country and all it needs are people to develop it, people whom I and the shipping lines can bring in." He held both her hands gently. "But for proper development I need to be based in London where the customers are. I know the kind of people who would do well here, I can promote the country and at the same time learn the skills I so badly need for management."

"But I thought that you already knew everything necessary to run the Richmond Line."

He smiled. "I know almost nothing. Up until now the Richmond Line has been taking up the slack, as it were, getting the leftover custom which the bigger lines don't want. I plan to change all that."

Despite her weariness she found herself responding to his enthusiasm. "I'm sure you will be very successful, Stephen."

"With you beside me I shall be."

"Oh?"

"You don't think that I'm going to go away indefinitely and leave you here, do you? Sweet Olivine, this is the perfect opportunity for you and young Leigh to escape all this. We'll be in London for at least a year, then in San Francisco. I need a base there, and another in Hong Kong. We can try living in a dozen different cities if you like before deciding which one to make our permanent home. There's no need to look so puzzled. Surely you've realised that in a very roundabout and clumsy way I'm asking you to marry me."

"I didn't realise that . . ." she began, then the full import of what he said struck her and she pushed away from the table.

Stephen watched her as she stood at the window. His chair was tipped back in the manner forbidden to the Sefton boys. They always nudged each other and pointed surreptitiously when Captain Yardley relaxed like this, waiting half hopefully for a blast from their father.

"I am astonished by your reaction," he said at length. "Surely you must have guessed that when the time was right I would ask you to marry me."

"I had no idea," she whispered. "No idea at all. I thought you came to see me because you wanted to make up for what your brother had done, and because Father was worried about my safety, and because you were fond of young Leigh, and . . ."

"In the name of Jove, Olivine!" He wanted to go to her, embrace her now, but sensed strongly that it was best to leave her alone for the moment. "I've been coming here for almost five years. I didn't court you with romance and serenades because after what you had been through I didn't think you would really appreciate that. Instead I've tried to show you how I felt in other, more practical ways."

"And you have," she said listlessly. She turned to face him and he was shocked to see tears in her eyes. "You have been the most considerate, wonderful, generous friend to both of us. A hundred times I have realised that I didn't deserve such kindness as you have given me."

"No, don't talk like that. It's nonsense." He stood up.

She put up both hands as if to fend him off. "Please, Stephen, please let me finish. I didn't deserve your friendship and I certainly don't deserve your proposal. Stephen . . ." She was really crying in earnest now. "I'm sorry . . . I'm so terribly, terribly sorry but I cannot marry you."

He stopped a yard away from her. "You're serious, aren't you?"

She nodded, choking on a sob.

"But why?"

She shook her head dumbly and in a second his arms were around her. It was like being folded in a blanket and she pillowed her head gratefully against him. The scent of his jacket was a blend of tar, tobacco, and salt, a peculiar and distinctive aroma that reminded her instantly of her father in the early days and stimulated another wave of hungry nostalgia. She wept silently, without energy, simply sagging wearily against Stephen. No noise, no movement, just a flow of tears.

His voice was careful, braced up from within. "You don't love me. Is that it?"

She shook her head against his jacket, then belatedly realised that she had to be fair and that she had to try to make Stephen understand her predicament without elaborating enough to have him learn what had happened. Pulling herself away, she leaned on the window frame. How tempting was the impulse to accept him, tempting and totally impossible. Equally tempting was the desire to say, Yes, I do love you, Stephen. I love you far too much to bind you up with my future now. Not after what happened here. Then place it all on him, tell him everything. Impossible, all impossible.

"My feelings have nothing to do with it," she said when she could speak. "The simple truth of it is that I am not worthy of you. You deserve the very best in a wife and I am not even second or third best."

"Let me be the judge of that," he said softly.

"One needs to know all of the facts in question before one can judge," she rejoined bitterly. Exhaustion was beginning to claim her. "You must take my word for it, you must believe me."

Despite the anguish in her voice he was only partially convinced that she was sincere. He had known her for over thirteen years and had watched her grow and develop into a beautiful (and, he considered, eminently sensible) young woman. The business with Leigh was unfortunate but understandable. He had been knocked badly by it but had reasoned that most of the blame for that lay with Leigh's spoiled selfishness, which in turn should be placed at Maire's feet since he was a complete product of her indulgence. No, Stephen knew Juliette well enough to suspect that there was something else here that she did not want to tell him.

"Your speech is very pretty but I do suspect that it is only in order to ease my feelings," he told her.

He must believe her. "It's the truth, I do swear it to you. Do you not understand at all? Stephen, I do care about you. I look forward to each visit as soon as I have farewelled you on the last one. I care about you as much . . . as much as little Leigh. More, probably, in a different way. I do love you, Stephen, so please don't go away angry with me. I could not bear that. . . ." She looked him full in the face now, speaking almost defiantly and realising with a small patch of warm security that she had never meant anything more than the words she was uttering now.

He tried to stare her down but could not. His own feelings were swamping him, choking him. Reaching out with both hands, he dragged her abruptly against his chest, snapping her head back as he kissed her with a hard, angry passion. For a moment she was stunned and did not respond. He noticed this and thought angrily that she was seeking to play with him by uttering empty little declarations that he was not supposed to take seriously. In the name of Jove, he would show her that she could not dally with him like that and he did show her, with bruising mouth and hands gripping her brutally, one like a clamp on her jaw and the other swept tightly around her waist. It was not until her hands crept hesitantly around his neck that he realised she had made no attempt to struggle or to push him away. At once he relaxed his grip and became the tender lover. The hands that had gripped to imprison her stroked and fondled, and the lips were now adoring.

Paradoxically this gentleness unleashed a force of emotion that staggered him. He was no stranger to desire or passion. Women of all kinds had been admiring him since he was fourteen and freshly at sea, and he had never been one to let opportunities for diversion pass him by. This, however, was a new, completely different feeling. Always before he had been the one in control. Passions stayed within him and he only showed as much feeling as he wanted to. But when he took Juliette in his arms it was as though something in turn seized him and shook him until he was helpless. It goaded him and spurned him; he was kissing her as if she were going to be torn away from him and he must get enough of her to last him a lifetime. She was tenderness, the warmth of motherhood from his long-ago childhood, the endless flowing caress of a hot spring, the most precious, most fragile . . .

"Uncle Stephen!"

A little hand tugged impatiently at his coattail.

"Uncle Stephen!" The child did not seem to notice what was happening. "Uncle Stephen! I picked some beautiful melons for you to take back for your sailors to eat for their supper."

A rippling shudder of relief passed through Juliette's body as Stephen pulled away from her and tried to speak normally and naturally to the boy. The last few moments had been an agony for her, an agony all the more acute because she had precipitated the passion. She had sought to soothe Stephen's wounded feelings by telling him frankly that she cared for him, and instead of calming his anger she had stirred up a fervent emotion that could not be denied—but that somehow must be. If only she could think clearly! If only she was not so nerve-scraped and bone weary. She groped for a chair and shakily seated herself on it, tucking it in under the table.

"That is very kind of you," Stephen was repeating.

"Out you go." Juliette waved a hand at him.

Leigh clutched at Stephen hopefully.

"Put him outside again, please. We have to talk." It was the last thing she felt like doing, but it did have to be done.

"I don't want to go outside." Leigh burst away and came running to plead his case to Juliette. "Mother, you look all funny. Your face is red and your eyes are all fat."

She had to laugh. "I suppose they are. I feel very tired, that's all. And you, my boy, can help me by running along outside and staying there until we call you." She rested her hot face in trembling hands until the door had closed, then said without looking up, "That didn't make any difference, Stephen. I cannot marry you."

Evasions again. And now she was fenced in behind the table so that the closest he could get to her was to sit down opposite. A slow rage which had been sparked by the frustrating and somehow symbolic interruption began to smoulder below his breastbone.

"It's Leigh, isn't it?"

"Leigh?" Her head felt thick, stupid.

"Aye, my brother. That was all nonsense about never wanting to see him again, wasn't it? You still care for him, don't you?"

"No, I don't! I told you the truth about him and I'm telling you the truth now. I can't marry you because you deserve better. I can't do it to you, Stephen."

"Yet you say you love me?"

"*Because* I love you!" Again she began to cry. "Oh, please try to understand!"

"I'm trying, Juliette. In the name of Jove, I'm trying. Look, I don't care what you've done, what happened to you. That's all in the past." Desperately he added, "Remember once I told you that none of that mattered to me? You're not bad or immoral, or criminal! Really, Juliette, it's not as though you've *killed* anyone!"

Her response to that last time had been to smile. This time she buried her face in her hands and wept. He stared at her with a blank, angry hopelessness.

"That's it, then," he said after a long awkward silence. "I'll be on my way."

She raised her head. "Please don't be angry. I can't bear it."

"I should cut a caper and be delighted? Not likely, Juliette. I'll say goodbye now, and I shan't be back."

"Not ever?"

"I doubt it. I'm far enough over thirty now to decide that it's time I wed, and if you'll not have me, then I shall look elsewhere."

"Stephen!"

He gazed at her steadily. "Very well. I'll ask you once more. For the last time, will you marry me?"

"I can't," she whispered.

He nodded curtly. Perhaps he would be able to carry a picture of her in his mind looking just like this, hair straggling, brow grimed, swollen-eyed, hands callused.

She could live like this in his memory forever. Perhaps it was something worth hoping for.

"I'll miss you," she offered as he picked up his cap.

For a moment he looked as though he might say something else, but he nodded again and left. She heard Leigh calling to him and heard the livery stable's horse nickering softly. Then there was an awful, empty silence and she was too weary to cry.

He must have met the Seftons on the road, for Grace came bustling in, unpinning her garish bonnet and talking rapidly in the high-pitched agitated way she affected whenever she was upset.

"Mrs. Yardley, how *could* you turn that lovely Captain away? How could you do it, him so fond of you and the lad both? I tell ye, lass, I could nae believe my ears when he told us he'd nae be back again and then the reason why. Oh, lass! I wish with all my heart that you didna do that! Why . . ." Grace broke off. There was something very odd about Juliette. "Lass, are you feelin' quite well?" She stepped forward hastily, just in time to catch Juliette's shoulders and prevent her from slumping over into the fire.

PART FIVE

LEIGH

1853-1856

Twenty-six

Grace Sefton continued to be snippy with Juliette, scolding her for refusing Stephen's proposal, and within a week the reason for her dismay became clear. They no longer needed her and it would have suited their purpose very well if she had departed with the Captain for a new life of her own. On this last visit to town they had even found a room for her in a respectable lodging house and had made enquiries as to suitable employment.

Grace was relieved to see how placidly she took the news. What a strange lass she was at times! When she played with that son of hers she romped and laughed with real abandon and love fairly radiated from her. Yet one might have expected some emotion when she spoke of the lad's father, but there was none at all. She evaded questions about him with a complete lack of expression. It jarred Grace more than a little. Not natural, not to feel *anything*. If anything ever happened to Campbell—God forbid—she would welcome opportunities to speak of him but would never be able to mention his name without a decent watering of tears.

Nor did Juliette show any emotion when she stood outside the one-storey unpainted rooming house to say good-bye. Campbell wrapped her hand in his freckled fist and muttered something unintelligible and the boys lined up solemnly in order of age, all towering over her like orange sunflowers. Only Leigh cried, and he shrieked with an abandon that blocked out all the reassurances that he would see the Seftons "every month" and would be able to ride in their cart right along the edge of the sand dunes and back again.

"He needs a father," Grace pointed out briskly.

Juliette nodded. Mrs. Sefton meant it kindly and she was right, of course. Every day that separated her from the horror lessened its impact and reinforced her conviction that she had followed the only course of action possible. But no matter how hard she pondered the matter, Juliette could not decide whether Stephen would agree with that. She could not have accepted him without confessing everything—would he have helped her or insisted that she go to the authorities?

Meanwhile the sniping comments were chafing at her nerves. Mrs. Sefton's intentions were good but to harp on about the matter was pointless now. Juliette tried holding her tongue; it was so much of a struggle that one day she slipped and retorted that even if she *did* change her mind now she could hardly swim after the ship. Grace's hurt expression gave Juliette yet another guilt to add to the pile of guilts stuffed like dirty laundry into a corner of her mind.

As the apron was still stuffed into her wicker basket. In the heat of the panic that day she had thrust it in under the sewing things and had not rediscovered it until last night when she packed her belongings away. There it was, stiff and almost black, sticking to the lining at the bottom of the basket. There was nothing for it now but to leave it there and dispose of it later. Another privy would inherit more of her grisly secret.

The Seftons' privy she had scrupulously avoided. She hadn't been able to use it since the killings; and soon, to her horror, she found herself watching and waiting when others went into it. Unable to stop herself, she would pause at the window, gripped by a tension that only relaxed when the occupant emerged. And though it had been almost two years since he had done it, she became ridiculously afraid that Leigh might revive his old trick of dropping objects down there. Unable to caution him directly, she began to pick at him instead, to find fault constantly and to reprimand him angrily. Her edginess affected him in such a predictable way that within days the boys began complaining about his aggressive behaviour. Grace confided to Campbell that, though she loved Juliette, that boy of hers was too much to tolerate. She repeated this sentiment as they rode away on the cart, leaving Juliette trying to calm the screaming Leigh outside the door.

Mrs. Jollife came out. She wore gloves and a tiny cap and was the tallest woman Juliette had ever seen, more like a very thin man in a frilly dress. Her arms and wrists were like broomsticks, and the hair pulled tightly over her skull looked like a slick of grey paint on wood.

"I do not approve of children who throw tantrums," she said in a tone that silenced Leigh, though it could have been her appearance that stopped him. "Mrs. Yardley, is it?"

"Yes, Mrs. Jollife. I'm glad to meet you."

"Mrs. *Jolly-fee*," she pronounced. "Come inside, Mrs. Yardley. I do not approve of talking out in the street."

Nor did Mrs. Jollife approve of Roman Catholics, women who had to work, men, tobacco, eating in the rooms, or noise. Hers was a stiflingly respectable house and she prided herself on the fact. She gave Juliette and Leigh a room only just bigger than a cupboard with a tiny cracked window that looked over towards Marsland Hill stockade and the flax swamp beyond. At dinner in the cramped dining room, Juliette met the other half dozen lodgers, none of whom seemed under sixty, and she discovered that Mrs. Jollife did not approve of imaginative meals either.

Juliette found employment with a tailor who paid her two shillings and sixpence a day for hemming, lining, and finishing off garments. Leigh was installed in Miss Beech's nursery school at sixpence a day, and Juliette calculated that she could just manage without encroaching further on her savings. She had already spent sixpence on a piece of calico to reline the sewing basket, a task she would get to as soon as she could; and for the special price of five shillings and ninepence the tailor sold her blue serge and machine-stitched the main seams on a new suit for Leigh to wear to school. He was growing so fast that it alarmed her.

Her life was cramped and awkward. The rooming house was no place for a boy; she had so many complaints about the noise that instead of doing her own laundry and sewing in the evening she had to take Leigh for long walks to tire him out for bed, which meant that she had to rise before daybreak. He hated school and threw tantrums every morning outside Miss Beech's white gate until Juliette blushed with shame. She felt that this was surely the lowest point of her life. The only compensation was that her nightmares seemed to have stopped completely, and every night she dropped into a deep, refreshing sleep. That must be due to the long walks and the change of life style, she decided.

After a month at Miss Beech's school Leigh was expelled for disruptive behaviour. Juliette could have wept with despair as she listened to the list of his misdeeds. He could not stay with her at work—kindly as he was, the tailor would not allow that—and the other school at the old mill charged boys a full shilling a day. With Leigh sulkily lagging behind her, she returned to the tailor and asked if there was anything extra she could do to earn another sixpence.

"He has to go to school, and I'm hoping that the gentleman has more control over his pupils than poor Miss Beech has," said Juliette, pride forbidding her to reveal the true reason for the change.

Leigh tugged at her arm. "I don't want to go there! Mr. Beaconsfield has a cane and he whips the boys with it."

"Only if they misbehave, sonny," said the tailor. "You do as the teacher says and you'll have no cause to be afraid of him." To Juliette he said bluntly, "I think you've made a wise decision. He needs a man's guidance. Yes, Mrs. Yardley, I'll give you a little extra work to take home with you but not today. Go home and have a rest. It's Sunday tomorrow. Come back fresh on Monday and I'll see what I can find."

On Sunday it rained all day. Juliette took paper and a pencil from the high shelf over the door and set Leigh to drawing a picture while she emptied the workbasket and prepared to sew in the new material. Leigh knelt at the chair and sketched out a picture of a sailing ship while she tore the old lining away in dusty ribbons and planned how she might, when she could afford it, buy a small pot of yellow enamel to paint the exterior to match the new lining.

Leigh said, "Crispian said that Uncle Stephen isn't coming to see us any more."

"He might, dear." The lining tore easily where she had cut way the bloodied bits for disposal.

"But Crispian said that you sent him away and he won't come back again."

"Crispian was only teasing you. Is that a picture of Uncle Stephen's ship?" Along the bottom of the basket a short section of seam had been stitched in different colours.

"Yes. I wish we could see Uncle Stephen again."

"So do I, dear." When she looked closely she noticed that the section had been sewn and resewn many different times and with different-coloured silks and cottons. There must have been snippets of fifteen or more varied colours there, embedded in the seam.

"Now, why would that be?" She tugged at the base cover, freeing it with a rip and a shower of lint fragments. Underneath was a square of tacked woollen padding, but when she lifted that out she saw a layer of unidentifiable objects lying on the wickerwork base. They were small, round things like dozens of tiny cloth-covered buttons. But as soon as she picked one up she realised that they were coins which had been tightly sewn into scraps of fabric.

Coins? she mused, wondering. Coins wrapped up so they won't rattle? Why in the world would coins be. . .

And then she knew. She did not believe it until she had sliced through one wrapper with the scissors blade and seen the warm gold with her own eyes; but the truth had already moved in and was sitting indigestibly in the centre of her brain, while her ears rang with remembered innuendo. "We only wanted ter get some of our money back. . . . The stupid doxy wouldn't tell us where she hid it. . . . A one-guinea whore . . . a whore . . ."

All the warmth and strength flowed out of Juliette's limbs. Mother *had* been a whore and these were her earnings, hidden from Father. Her earnings, carefully hoarded and of such value to her that she had allowed herself to be killed rather than give them up. It was unbelievable. The filthy things those two men had said—Juliette had never paused to question, let alone believe them, and they were all true.

She shuddered and dropped the coin, pulling the lining over it. How could she have done such a degrading thing as sell herself to men like those two wretches? They were loathsome! And there must have been others. There were a great many coins there. Perhaps some of the other men were people she knew—people from the Mission, perhaps even Mr. Jacobson or Jacky Norris . . .

"Mother! Where did Uncle Stephen go? Why won't you answer me?" shouted Leigh indignantly.

"Hush!" warned Juliette, as rapping sounded on the wall. "Mrs. Jollife can hear you."

"Where did Uncle Stephen go?" he asked in an exaggerated whisper.

She answered absently, dazed. There was no need to ask herself why her mother had done it. Too clearly she recalled Evangeline's glowing face as she eagerly described the wonderful life she planned for them all in the beautiful house on the San Francisco hillside. It was that sudden, clear vision that turned all the disgust into pity and understanding. Poor Mother. Living in that isolated hovel had been too much for her. She loved beautiful things and was so restless that she had to feel she was contributing something to her future escape. That house in San Francisco meant so much to her that she had literally died for it. Poor, poor Mother.

She turned back the lining again and stared at the money. In her disgust her impulse was to dispose of that as something shameful too, but with understanding she knew that it must be used in a positive way. Just one of those guineas would pay the extra sixpences she needed for almost a whole year—now she would not have to sit up until late every evening doing piecework by lamplight. Her glance fell on the bundled gown that she had set aside to be mended, and she wondered, ridiculously, what Evangeline would say if she could see her scarecrow daughter with her faded patched dresses. On Monday she would purchase a length of that pretty emerald-green print from the tailor and spend her spare time making herself some long-overdue new things. Evangeline would approve; of that Juliette was positive. She removed the unwrapped guinea and slipped it into her waist fob before fussing with the

new lining. What did it matter where the coins had come
from? It was only money after all.

From that day onwards Juliette changed. Her guilt
melted away. In forgiving her mother she forgave herself—
even took a small pride in what she had done, acknowledg-
ing for the first time that to face up to such danger had
taken real courage. She no longer felt cowed by Leigh and
told him with firm kindness that she would have to punish
him if there were any bad reports from his new teacher. He
was still impossible to manage at times but now she did try
and he was making progress towards controlling his temper. To her enormous satisfaction she found that no longer
could Mrs. Jollife bully her. One morning when she
stopped Juliette and informed her that she did not approve
of lights burning in the rooms past midnight, Juliette replied blandly that she would do as she pleased in her room
and, if Mrs. Jollife would like the room vacated, then she
would be happy to oblige because it really was too cramped
for the two of them.

At that Mrs. Jollife retreated with a scuttle and a neat
snap of the door that would have done credit to a hermit
crab, while Juliette marvelled, thinking that six months
ago she would have been intimidated by such a woman as
her landlady.

There is a certain delicious freedom to be found in not
caring what people think, she told herself as she strode out
for work in her new green gown.

Even so, she was lonely. The only woman of her own age
she had met was Miss Beech, and Leigh's behaviour while
at her school was an insurmountable barrier to their ever
becoming friends. When a letter from Rose arrived at the
post office she read it a dozen times within the first hour of
collecting it, so hungry was she for news from what she
still thought of as home. The letter was as crammed with
goodies as an old-fashioned plum pudding, full of descriptions of cunning lace house caps with flaps over the
ears, red hats made of feathers, cashmere jackets, merino
cloaks, and a gorgeous barège evening gown, entertainments, parties, engagements . . .

* * *

Our Governor Grey is soon to Leave us in the midst of Such Bitterness it seems that Nobody likes him Except perhaps Uncle Thomas and then Only for his views on the Natives. There is to be a sumptuous Farewell Banquet for him soon, but already it is rumoured that Anybody of Consequence is Declining to attend, and even Mama has doubts about Going. Doctor Forster was offered tickets for Half Price and says we may go if he can obtain some Gratis for it should be an Amusing Occasion. If you were here we could go Together. I do wish that you would come Back here, dear Juliette. Leigh was asking after you and read your letter. He is not in the Military now—they had a Slight Disagreement, as did he & his Fiancee. Mama was furious. It seems that she is angry with All of her Children now, Especially Stephen, but we are so Happy for him. . . .

Later when Juliette sat beside the lamp and took up her pen to answer she was at a loss to know what to say. In truth she was so lonely and directionless now that the thought of Auckland town with the lights twinkling invitingly around the harbour was painful. She lay awake for a long time, miserable, and deriving no comfort at all from the knowledge that somewhere in the world Stephen was happily going about his business without her.

But then there was more to worry about in New Plymouth at the moment than personal happiness. Living right in the centre of town and sharing accommodations with two elderly women whose one entertainment was to attend sessions of the magistrate's court, Juliette could not help but become aware that trouble, unpleasant trouble, was brewing between the settlers and the Maori tribes from the Waikato, who still pressed their claims to the land.

"It's a scandal!" declared Mrs. Reburn. "Today a settler tried to prosecute some natives for letting their animals graze on his crops and the magistrate wouldn't listen to evidence that the fence had been deliberately torn down. He said the settler should take better care of his boundaries and threw the case out!"

Mrs. Wyatt nodded righteously. "And yesterday when a settler was charged with killing a pig that strayed into his vegetables the magistrate ordered him to pay ten shillings to the Maoris—even though the settler's family claimed it was a wild pig!"

"Where is this going to get us? Whose side is the magistrate on?" cried Mrs. Reburn.

Leigh stared at the ladies wide-eyed, but Juliette silently ate her potato hot pot and appeared to take no notice.

She asked the tailor next day what he thought.

"We're headed for trouble right enough. We've got three thousand settlers crammed onto a strip of land twenty miles long and six miles wide, with more settlers arriving on every ship that puts in here. And outside our little strip of land are better than two million acres which aren't being used for anything. The trouble is, some of the Maoris want to sell us more land, and some don't. The ones who don't are the troublemakers, and not only are they trying to make things unpleasant for the farmers but they are also putting strong pressure on the Maoris who would like to be friendly with us. They've even formed a League to halt all land sales."

"Will it work?" asked Juliette. She had read about the League in the local newspaper.

"Wait and see," said the tailor. "Some of those Waikato chiefs are mean and determined enough to make anything work if they have a mind to."

His prediction was proved correct several weeks later when fighting erupted between the League and the local friendly Maoris. One of the first targets was a well-respected Maori magistrate named Rawiri who owned land in the district where the Seftons had first settled. This land, though once farmed, was now choked with thistles and weeds, and Rawiri thought that it was a much better idea to sell it back to the settlers, who would use it properly, rather than see it degenerate further for the want of someone to tend it. But when Rawiri and his friends were pegging out the borders of the land to make it ready for a sale, an armed mob of the League crept up through the manuka and without warning opened fire, killing Rawiri and six others.

Rawiri's tribesfolk were outraged and at once began preparing to seek utu, but were talked out of it by the local constabulary, who assured them that this trouble had gone far enough. It was now a matter for the Governor. He would intervene and see that justice was done properly. Weeks later Colonel Wynyard, the Government Administrator, came to investigate. To the dismay of the settlers, instead of punishing the murderers he visited the League's local leader, Katatore, and actually shook his hand as though to congratulate him. They chatted amiably and the Administrator then departed without even trying to clear up the matter. Once again the town had been ill served by the Government, but this time with more serious consequences. War was now a fact.

Grace Sefton was brimming with it when the family next ventured into town. Some of the local Maoris had bailed up a League scouting party on the ridge below Atholl Rykins' house and fighting had carried on across the farms for two days and nights.

"We was sitting at breakfast one morning and all of a sudden the front door burst open and in came six brawny tattooed fellows, all armed with muskets and strung about with cartouche boxes."

"Weren't you terrified?"

"At first, but when they made us to understand what they was about, then we knew there was nae cause to fret. We knew some of them. One often came with mussels and fish for sale, a fine fellow with a twist of red silk in one ear. You remember him, lass?"

Juliette nodded. "I don't know how you can be so calm about being in the midst of the fighting."

"Aye, but that's easy, lass. When you've suffered as we have already at the hands of those Waikato rascals you'll cheer and help anybody who's trying to chase them away. Campbell helped. He took our musket and did his share, peppering the enemy out of the bush. They'll nae come back, I grant you."

"You're going back there?"

"Of course, lass," and she climbed back onto the driver's seat of the cart. "I'm nae scared, and neither are the boys. Well, I'll be off to fetch them now. They're buying us two goats at the stock sales. The prices are canny at the moment."

No wonder, thought Juliette as she watched Mrs. Sefton go. No wonder the prices were good. With families trailing into the town behind wagonloads of possessions and war talk being aired everywhere, no wonder goods were cheap.

Because Juliette had lived through a similar scare in Auckland ten years earlier she felt no unease at all. This situation was less threatening than Hone Heke's had been because the Maoris were only fighting each other, as they had done for as far back as anybody could recall. She saw no reason for alarm; and when a letter from Thomas arrived instructing her to come home at once, she dismissed the order lightly.

Dear Father [she replied immediately], I do thank you most warmly for your paternal concern but there is no reason why you should worry about my well-being. I am perfectly safe and among friends. At the moment I am lodged in a respectable boarding establishment and am occupied with genteel employment working for a tailor, which I enjoy very much. I have sufficient money put by so if any genuine danger threatens the town I shall be able to secure passage on a ship out at once. The authorities assure us that every precaution is being taken for our safety. . . .

She paused, pen hovering while she tried to select a few items of personal news to include. Through the window she could see Leigh on the wind-swept street flicking stones into puddles. He looked lonely and cold out there by himself, as lonely as she felt.

When Leigh came in to enquire how long it would be until suppertime, she was composed and sensible once more. He watched her melt the sealing wax over a taper and then pressed his forefinger into the soft red dab on the back of the letter. When he lifted his finger there was a fine pattern of whorls and spirals.

"It's not to Uncle Stephen," he said in disappointment. "No, dear."

"Who are these other people you write letters to?"

The question was not new, nor was the answer. "One

day you will meet these people. One day you will know who they are."

She could not keep from smiling wryly to herself. What a shock that would be for everyone!

Twenty-seven

Craig Sefton was married in the winter of 1855 when Juliette had been in town just two years. Mildred, Craig's bride, was the daughter of one of New Plymouth's five innkeepers (or licenced victuallers, as he always referred to his colleagues). Grace and Campbell had never approved of the fact that there were almost as many taverns as general goods stores in town, and they were shocked to their teetotal hearts at the prospect of their son driving a brewery wagon. But a whole year of opposition failed to change his mind, so they gave in and added their blessings to those of Mildred's family.

Juliette attended the ceremony in the Congregational Church, musing as she did so that this was the first time she had been into a Protestant church since heaven knew when, and the first time in any church since Sarah's funeral. A solitary priest made extended visits to the district every other year but there was no proper church for Catholics in New Plymouth. Juliette gave Leigh religious instruction in their room.

At the wedding she found to her surprise that she knew almost everybody. She was beginning to feel at home in this raw little town which still reminded her of a handful of wooden blocks flung higgledy-piggledy down amongst the sand dunes and marram grass. She had a few friends, too—nothing like Rose and Sarah, more "warm acquaintances," really. And Leigh was making reluctant progress at Mr. Beaconsfield's school. Whenever she was caught unawares by treacherous memories or Leigh asked about "Uncle Stephen," she was still swept by hopeless anguish; but apart from the pangs suffered in those rare unguarded moments, this was a happy time for her. She no longer had nightmares or feelings of guilt, and after all this time there was no chance that she would ever be found out. It was a secure time.

In these long months the situation around New Plymouth had not altered. Hostilities continued without loss of settlers' lives. Some timid folk packed their families aboard ships, but most of those who had trundled into town behind their wagonloads of worldly goods soon gave up waiting for the fighting to cease and wandered back to their farms again. Few new settlers came. In New Plymouth there were no refugees, few unemployed, and last year the most exciting "crime" had occurred when the local newspaper editor was called out by one Paul Jenner, a surveyor, who felt bound to protect some young lady's honour from real or imagined insults. The resulting duel had been bloodless and pointless but the interest generated in it proved what a quiet place New Plymouth was. Just as well, too, thought Juliette as she set off through the dark streets to the Brunswick Hotel for the wedding dance. She would never have entertained the notion of walking unaccompanied about Auckland town at night.

The social room at the hotel was used for parties, lantern-slide evenings, and musical glees when the town hall was already booked. Tonight it had been strung across with ruffled paper chains and lined with enough feathery fern fronds to decorate a gigantic bird's nest. Mildred, a freckled blonde, had helped her mother ice a large square currant cake and trim it with garish flowers of poisonous-looking pink sugar. The cake had pride of place among the cups set out on the tea table. Men from the North End timber mill were taking turns to keep the music going: flutes, a fiddle, two accordions, and a violincello all chimed up in little groups to liven the party and tempt people onto the scuffed dance floor. When she was crossing the blacksmith's yard, Juliette heard the piano strike up a tune and saw the laughing people at the lamplit windows, their faces shining and slicked with gold.

She danced with all the Sefton boys in turn, tapping her buttoned boots and keeping her toes moving out of the way of their clumsy feet. The danger added spice to the fun of it, and she was proud to deny to Mrs. Sefton that her toes had been mashed like potatoes.

"Doesn't Mr. Sefton dance?" she asked, thinking what a pity it was that Grace had to rely on her own sons to partner her. It spoiled the romance of the occasion somehow.

"Ah, he'll nae dance. He's a strong Free Kirk man, he is. And he'll nae go near the ale, neither," she could not resist adding.

Juliette smiled sympathetically. She wanted to say something flattering, but Grace had added ten years to her age with her choice of black worsted, and the greyish crocheted shawl nullified whatever elegance the gown might have had.

"Let me fetch you some refreshments," she said instead, and heaped a saucer with little cakes and crustless sandwiches, careless of reproving glances. What did she care if the serving maid of the Brunswick Hotel thought her greedy?

The evening was a treat. She laughed behind her gloves when Campbell stood up to speak and she understood not one word of his flustered speech. She clapped and cried out in delight as the newlyweds cut the cake with the enormous borrowed butcher's knife; and her eyelids prickled with hot tears of genuine admiration and pride when Cuthbert, Conway, Chester, Cameron, and Crispian rushed at Craig and exuberantly chaired him around the hall. "What fine boys they are," she whispered to Mrs. Sefton as the guests cheered.

"Aye, lass. If only . . . if only . . ."

Juliette knew what she meant. "Nothing ever quite turns out the way we hope it will."

"Life is life and dreams are dreams. Aye, that's true. Dreams are nae but wishing."

"Yes," whispered Juliette, who had pushed away a dozen futile wishes herself this evening. If only Stephen were here! If only he would return now, now that she had come to terms with what had happened. Oh, if only he would come back and tell her that he still wanted her! He couldn't be married—Rose would have mentioned it in her letters and there had only been that one, vague "we are so happy for him," which referred to his business ventures. Surely, surely it was time for him to return?

She left the party before it began to wind down because it was not fair to leave her babysitter Mrs. Reburn waiting up too late. Outside the streets were busy. Patrons fanned out from the doorways of the other hotels, which were beginning to close for the night. As she crossed Devon Street to turn down Ridge Road she glanced up at the lighted windows of the Albion Hotel. Spread along the upper part of each pane of glass was a bright decalcomania featuring red brewery buildings with tall chimneys frothing out white smoke as thick as the froth on the top of an ale mug. Huge buildings they were, a hundred times the size of the New Plymouth brewery, large enough to fuel a thousand taverns. As Juliette glanced up she saw a group of gentlemen and shopgirls standing up from their table, laughing with warm intimacy that gave her the sensation of being an outsider. Though her attention was drawn to the bright-faced girls—was that paint?—one of the gentlemen suddenly inclined his head in a questioning manner that reminded her sharply of Stephen. It was not Stephen, of course. More like Leigh if anything, only much older, thicker about the face and neck, and of course Leigh had no moustache. It was a ridiculous notion, but she scurried much faster to the lodging house on the back road. Mrs. Jollife was framed by her curtains, stitching a patchwork quilt. She looked like a wooden doll. Juliette paused to calm her galloping breath, and then silently trod along the path to the back door where Mrs. Reburn quietly let her in.

On Sundays she and Leigh always went for much longer walks than usual, to the sugar-loaf rocks, or around the stockade, or to the stream where the wide gully was thick with beautiful bush and they could see fantails, bell birds and tuis or parson birds, as they were called here.

"Why can't we go there today?" Leigh demanded. "I like going there best because it reminds me of living on the mountain."

"We have a better reminder today." She smiled as she knotted his barrel tie and adjusted the stiff wings of his collar. "After the services are over we shall picnic with the Seftons down near the beach. Won't that be fun?"

"It's too cold for a picnic."

"It might be warmer by then. I know! Let's go for a fine long walk right to the other end of town and read all the notices on the board. You can show me how well you can pronounce all the names."

He brightened at that suggestion. "Let's go past the flour mill and the sawing pits on the way."

"There will be nobody working today."

"Sundays are boring. They seem to last much longer than other days. Why can't we do anything but walk and pray on Sundays? I wish I could draw pictures or play draughts, or play with my hoop or my kite."

"None of the other children play on the Lord's day. You really wouldn't want to be any different, would you? Besides," she added as they strode out along the windy street, "today we do have something special to do."

Eddies of powdery dust swirled around their boots. The roadside weeds were grey as the overcast sky. They had the roadway entirely to themselves. Wind fluttered the leaves of the cabbage trees at the edge of the raupo swamp and the sound of the sea thundered softly beyond the sand dunes. Juliette looked at her son and warmed inwardly with pride. He was a ruddy, strong boy with Thomas' determined chin and none of her feminine delicacy. Though he was still difficult and strong-willed and his temper caused problems at school, Juliette reminded herself that one could hardly expect a seven-year-old boy to be perfect, and surely spirit was preferable to meekness?

"There might be something on the notice board about the *Lorendee*," he said. "Or will Uncle Stephen have a different ship by now?"

"I really don't know, dear."

They were back in Devon Street again, walking under the overhang of shop verandahs. Dogs sniffed at the verandah posts. In a cart parked outside the baker's some Maori children quarrelled in a mixture of Maori and English. Towards them rumbled an open carriage driven by a young Maori lad from the livery stables. It contained three people she had seen in the Albion window, two shop-girls and the gentleman who had reminded her of Leigh. The girls were laughing extravagantly, flattering the gentleman on his wit, and he looked pleased with himself, in his striped suit and white silk cravat, with a dove-grey belltopper pushed casually back off his brow, his white-gloved hands looped easily about the girls' shoulders.

Juliette faltered. The carriage drew closer and the gentleman spoke loudly, giving the driver instructions. Juliette heard the familiar voice above the flap of the reins and the brisk clipping of hooves and now knew that the man *was* Leigh. Older, stouter, puffy around the eyes, and with moustache and long, curving side whiskers—but definitely Leigh.

There was a sick buzzing in her ears. She had seized young Leigh's hand and must have squeezed it too hard, because he tugged it away with an angry exclamation. The carriage rolled closer still.

Run! thought Juliette in panic. But already it was too late. Leigh was leaning over to whisper to the girl on the far side of him. She giggled and shoved his shoulder in a carelessly tipsy way. For a long moment he stared right into Juliette's shocked face. When the carriage had gone past, Leigh shouted and tried to drag himself to his feet. Playful hands held him down and fresh gushes of laughter bubbled in the wake of the vehicle.

"Who were those people, Mother?"

"I don't know . . . people from the hotel . . . I don't really know . . ." She looked all around.

"They knew you. That man shouted at you."

"He was mistaken. . . . I think that I may have looked like someone else. . . . Come, let's hurry, shall we?"

"I think we should wait. The carriage has turned around."

Juliette grabbed her son's wrist and darted up the narrow alley between the baker's ovens and the blacksmith's yard, then out over the swampy ground around the churchyard. Urging Leigh to hurry, she matched her step to his, dragging him as fast as hampering petticoats would permit. The organ was wheezing the introductory notes to a hymn and they could hear people shuffling and coughing, preparing to sing. By the time the first bars had sighed

away Juliette and the boy had skimmed past and were
climbing the path between the sand dunes, panting with
excitement as their feet crunched on the gritty track.

"Who *was* that? You were running away, weren't you?"

"Nobody, nobody! I felt like running, that's all. Look!
It's going to be fine after all."

The sky was clearing; far above their heads thin ribs of
cloud stretched across the blue. Her heart was jumping
queerly. He might not have recognised her, that shout
might not have been at her, the carriage might have been
going to turn anyway—she must not worry! But it would be
best to be careful, just in case. What was he doing here?

They reached the top of the rise and when she saw the
four ships riding at anchor she understood at once. He
must have arrived yesterday—passengers were usually
put ashore to spend the Sabbath on land and wait for reloading to resume on Monday. He would be gone tomorrow. The encounter had been merest chance, that was all.
Sheer bad luck.

Leigh raced ahead as they took the downward path. She
walked sedately, though the road, the boardwalk and fishing jetty were deserted. Even the sea gulls looked disconso-
late, she thought. Waves dashed along the beach. At the
far end of the beach the sugar-loaf rocks were misted by
wind-whipped spray. Just as Juliette reached the last
stretch of path an open carriage swung around the corner.
It was the same carriage but now with only one occupant.
Leigh climbed out.

"Well, well, well!" he said.

Juliette said nothing. There was nothing to say.

"When I heard the *Southern Eagle* was putting in here I
wondered if I might see you. Rose told me that you were
living in town now."

She nodded, not looking at him. The wind was cold on
her cheeks.

"Rose said that you were employed by a tailor. She said
nothing about the governess' position."

"I beg your pardon?" Then she realised that he was
watching Leigh, who was racing along the jetty making all
the sea gulls wheel up from their sentry points along the

railing. "Oh yes, didn't you know that?" Stay there, she urged her son silently. Don't come back whatever you do.

He cleared his throat. "Actually, I'm on my way home from the gold fields in New South Wales. Bathurst, actually. Didn't do too badly at all for myself," he confided. "But I chose the *Southern Eagle* because I knew she'd be putting in here and there's talk that there might be fighting here before too much longer."

"I thought you were out of the military," she remarked, her eyes on the boy, willing him to keep his distance.

"Slight misunderstanding. But never mind that. I'm glad I saw you. You're looking well, and as bonny as ever."

She swallowed nervously. "Won't your friends be missing you?"

"They'll not be very friendly after the way I bundled them out of the carriage. I was astounded to see you take fright, Juliette. Why did you run away from me?"

"I imagine that with a little thought you could discover a reason for that."

"That was a long time ago. Can't we be friends?"

She wanted to say, "That's impossible," but realised that all she really wanted to do was be rid of him. Besides, she could not entirely blame him for the past. She had loved him desperately, though, looking at him now, it was hard to imagine why.

"Everything is long forgotten. I assure you of that."

"Good!" he said in a "that's settled, then" tone. Young Leigh was now running back along the jetty, waving something he had found. To Juliette's alarm Leigh began walking to meet him, obviously planning on making the boy's acquaintance.

She pushed past him quickly. "What have you found? Oh, that is a pretty shell. Would you like to go down to the beach and see if you can find any others like it?" And with a determined grip she steered him around towards the boardwalk steps.

Leigh's gaze was fixed on his father. "Were you in the carriage with those two ladies?"

"That was me."

He frowned, shrugging at Juliette's hand. "Do you know us?"

"You are a sharp lad, aren't you? No, I do not know you but I am well acquainted with your governess."

"I haven't got a . . ."

Juliette cut in desperately. "Go on! See how quickly you can find me ten pretty shells. Quickly, now! I'll count to a hundred."

Off he dashed, unable to resist a challenge.

"He's rather a handful at times," she said.

"A good-looking lad." But when she glanced up she could see that he was watching her keenly, and her heart began to jump again.

"Do give my regards to everybody in Auckland town," she said, striving to appear normal. "Please give my love to Rose, and to Father, and Samuel . . . why, if I'd known that you and I would be bumping into each other like this I would have had letters written for everyone." She paused. He was still watching her thoughtfully. "You must excuse me now, Leigh. I am meeting friends for a picnic lunch, and I'm probably late already. So I'll not take up any more of your time."

"Yes," he said. "I didn't want to embarrass or upset you, please understand that. But I have never forgotten you."

"Please don't . . ." She turned away. Young Leigh was scrambling to his feet and beginning to pick his way back through the heaped driftwood.

"I remember you with tenderness and affection. You haven't changed at all, Juliette. It's astounding, but you are still as beautiful and sweet-looking as when . . ."

Rapidly she said, "Please, I implore you. That was all a long time ago. I don't wish to be reminded."

"I understand that. Forgive me."

"Mother!" yelled the boy. "Mother! Come and look at this!"

"Mother," murmured Leigh thoughtfully.

"It's a game we have. He's an imaginative boy. He likes to invent situations." She tried to look directly into his eyes. "I'll say goodbye now. Don't forget to give my best wishes to everybody." With that she hurried down the steps and onto the hard-packed sand, hoping against hope that he would go and knowing full well that if she looked back he would be there standing against the sky, watching.

As soon as he realised that they were moving away he scrambled down from the jetty and hurried in pursuit.

Juliette saw him coming after them and stopped. The wind buffeted her bonnet, pulling one side away from her face and snapping the long chin ribbons.

"Please go," she begged. "We have nothing more to discuss."

His eyes were on the boy. "I think that we have." A little smile nudged under the soft fringes of his moustache. "What's your name, sonny?"

Juliette had often imagined what she might do—how she might feel if the constabulary had arrived suddenly to question her in connection with the discovery of two bodies. Now she knew exactly how she would feel. Numbly she stood by while her son innocently said, "Leigh Yardley, sir!" And because he knew from experience what the next question would be, he added obligingly, "And I'm seven years old. I'll be eight years old in October."

"Well, well, well. What a coincidence! My name is Yardley too."

"Really? Are you related to Mother, then?"

"You might say that." Again the soft smile.

"And do you know our Uncle Stephen? His name is Captain Yardley and he's a sea captain. I miss him. He used to visit us all the time."

The smile dropped.

Juliette said quickly, "Run on ahead, please, Leigh. I want to talk to Mr. Yardley."

"So do I!" he pouted, immediately defiant.

"There now, you'll be a good fellow and do what your mother wants, won't you, lad?"

"Go and see if the Seftons have arrived," urged Juliette. When he had gone she said, "We shall be picnicking there, by those pine trees. Please go. My friends will be there already."

"Uncle Stephen, eh?" said Leigh nastily.

"Stephen has been very good to us."

"Good at keeping secrets, too. He wouldn't tell me where

you were. Wouldn't give me any news of you. Damn his eyes! He had no right to keep this from me."

"I told him not to tell you. I never wanted you to find out."

"Why not? He is my son, isn't he? He can't possibly be Stephen's because then he'd have married you instead of that Danielle creature, and the boy's a Yardley all right. No mistaking that face."

"Married?" she whispered.

He did not hear her against the rumble of surf. He grabbed her wrists, his eyes glowing. "Why didn't you tell me? Juliette, you should have told me! Why, I'm overwhelmed! I had no idea, no inkling! My son! Named for me and everything. This is astounding!" He let go of her wrists and his eyes raced to where the boy was climbing through the soft sand towards the dunes. A thought occurred to him. "What have you told him? What have you said about me?"

"He asked me once and I told him that you died in the war," she said, feeling that she, too, had died. Married! The clean sea smell that usually braced her and reminded her of Stephen now choked in the back of her throat.

"Oh dear. Well, you had to tell him something, I suppose, and we'll soon think of a way around it."

"I beg your pardon?"

"Juliette, I can't leave on the *Southern Eagle*. I can't possibly go away now. Surely you realise that. What a fine, healthy boy he is! The image of me, don't you think? You have done a splendid job of bringing him up. I must congratulate you."

He sounds as though he is thanking me for looking after a pet dog for him while he has been away, she thought. Indignation rose, mercifully blotting out the pain of his news.

"Yes, he is your son," she said tightly. "A son you wanted nothing to do with. If you think that you can waltz into our lives now and . . ."

"Just a minute, Juliette!" He was holding his belltopper rim with one hand and the other he tipped under her chin, forcing her to look at him. "You cannot accuse me of not wanting anything to do with the boy when I had no idea . . ."

Interrupting firmly, she declared, "You wanted nothing to do with me and that is the same thing. I had to risk terrible disgrace alone, I had to make a future for the boy, and I have lived all this time virtually in exile. And why? Because years ago you decided that you loved me and then once you had had your way with me you decided that perhaps you did not care for me after all! You treated me despicably and I tell you that you have no right to come into our lives after all this time, disrupting and upsetting young Leigh, causing us harm."

"Juliette!"

"Please understand this," she said evenly. "I want only one thing from you, and that is that you go away and leave us alone."

He looked regretful. "I can't do that. I have no intention of hurting you or upsetting the lad, but surely you can see this from my angle. He's part of me. I couldn't go away now, not without even having a proper talk with him. Look, I'll tell you what, I'll take lodgings at the hotel and call on you both regularly. I'll not say who I am, I promise you. All I want is to get to know him. Surely you can understand that."

She hesitated. She wanted to refuse but knew that she frankly had no choice.

The boy was balanced on a large egg-shaped rock, waving his arms and shouting. They turned towards him to catch what he was saying.

"Mrs. Sefton says there's plenty of food for Mr. Yardley too. Come on! They're waiting for you."

"Shall we go, Mrs. Yardley?"

Juliette felt like crying.

Leigh's delight in his son was unbounded. He waited for him each afternoon outside the old mill and each afternoon he had a different adventure planned: horseback riding, canoeing on the river, climbing the sugar-loaf rocks, riding a longboat out to the ships that were being unloaded, watching the soldiers drill at the fort, or sitting up at the bar in the Albion to sup lemonade while Leigh drank whisky and yarned to the men there. Each afternoon Juliette returned from work to an empty room and did not see her son until dinnertime. Leigh usually wangled an invitation to dinner. He told Mrs. Jollife that he was young Leigh's second cousin and charmed her into making him welcome at any time, and coaxed her and the elderly lodgers into fits of laughter with his stories of the war and his exploits on the gold fields.

"Oh, you are a card, Mr. Yardley," exclaimed Mrs. Wyatt. "Do tell us again about how you officers in the military invited Hone Heke to dine with you."

"Ah, that was when we were laying siege to his pa," Leigh would begin, setting down his fork so that he could use both hands for dramatic illustration.

Listening, Juliette watched her son's face glow and his eyes shine with delight as he followed the tale.

She was hardly surprised when one evening as they were preparing for bed the boy said, "I've decided that Mr. Yardley is much more fun than Uncle Stephen. I like him far better, don't you, Mother?"

Juliette did not trust herself to reply.

"Mr. Yardley said that he would have been to see me years ago except for Uncle Stephen not telling him about me."

"That's hardly fair, dear."

"Yes, it is! Mr. Yardley said that what isn't fair is that he would have liked to have known all about me when I was little. He said that I should forget Uncle Stephen because he's living in London and he's never coming back."

Good advice, thought Juliette, but easier given than taken. Aloud she said, "Have you cleaned your teeth?"

He took the rag and pot of tooth powder, dabbling the tiniest bit onto the rag. "What should I call Mr. Yardley?"

"Mr. Yardley, of course. Come on, polish those teeth."

He rubbed briskly, then stopped. "He says I mustn't call him 'Uncle' because he's not my uncle. What is he, then?"

"Clean the back teeth too, dear," said Juliette over her shoulder. She had her long nightgown on and was plaiting her hair into braids.

Leigh put the pot back on the shelf and the rag into its jar to soak. Climbing onto his low corner cot, he said, "Mr.

Yardley is ever so charming and gentlemanly, don't you think?"

"Everybody says so," agreed Juliette.

Leigh nodded. "Even Mrs. Reburn, and she told me that she hardly likes anybody. Do you think that he's a natty dresser?"

Juliette said lightly, "Gracious! Who taught you to talk like that?"

"He did. I do wish that you would come out with us when Mr. Yardley invites you. He says that we would have twice as much fun if you came along."

"That's nice of him. But I'm usually busy."

"Will you be busy on Saturday? If you're not, will you come with us to the Hospital Fair? There's going to be a slippery pole, and a woodchopping contest, and Punch and Judy show from Wellington, and Mr. Yardley says that he will buy me all the toffee apples I can eat. Do say that you'll come too."

"Wriggle down now, and I'll tuck you in."

He tugged at the rag on the end of her braid as she bent over him. "Do say that you'll come. Mr. Yardley wants you to."

"If you promise not to be ill from eating too many toffee apples." Her lips brushed his cheek, and with an effort she said, "Aren't you lucky to have a friend like Mr. Yardley?"

"Do you think so, really? I'll tell him that, and he'll be ever so pleased. He has the notion that you don't care for him, so I'll tell him that he's very much mistaken!"

Juliette lay staring into the darkness. Outside an owl cried sadly, and inside the room Leigh's even breathing was punctuated by the clicking of the brass clock. She felt trapped. Oh, she had been jealous and left out of this friendship between Leigh and his son but so far not actually threatened. Until tonight she'd assumed that Leigh would soon tire of his son and would go away, but now she wondered if she had been stupid to think that the situation would resolve itself so easily. Was he getting at her through young Leigh? "Forget Uncle Stephen because he's never coming back." "It would be twice the fun if you came too." Had Leigh said those things hoping that they would be repeated to her? Perhaps the time has come for a show-down, she decided.

"I must thank you for your kindness to young Leigh," she said. They were standing with an assorted cluster of farm wives, brightly dressed soldiers, Maoris in head scarves with pipes between tattooed lips, and eager-faced children awaiting turns. The children on the roundabout screamed, "Look at me! Watch me!" as the mechanical horses cranked up and down, flinging out their hooves.

"It's truly a pleasure. You have no cause to thank me."

She twirled her black parasol and said casually, "He will miss you when you go."

"Oh, I doubt it."

"But he will. You have been very good to him and I'm grateful. When are you going home, Leigh?"

"I do have to go soon, now that you mention it." As he moved his head the hoop of shade moved up and down his face. "I have Richmond Line business to attend to, and my Bathurst monies will be waiting at the Auckland bank. Not that I should worry a lady about such things." He smiled that soft, nudging smile under his moustache. "It will not be for some weeks yet, but I shall give you ample warning of when we shall be going."

"We?"

"You don't think that I'll go back to Auckland alone, do you?"

"All off" shouted the roundabout man, wiping the sweat from his brow. "All off! Roll up, roll up! Roll up for the ride of a lifetime!"

"What do you mean?" asked Juliette in an urgent undertone. She had gone very pale.

"That was great fun!" Young Leigh was panting as though he had been cranking the handle instead of sitting on one of the horses. "Can I have another turn?"

"One will do for now," said Leigh.

"Oh, all right. Then let's go and find the greasy pole. There it is!" He dragged his father along, and Juliette followed slowly. "Oh, heck! They're not falling into a water bath after all."

He stood staring while Leigh moved a few paces away to

where some Maori youths were shovelling earth away from the hangi oven. Steam frittered from the layered leaves uncovered by the spades and the savoury aroma of cooked pork drew more people to watch.

Young Leigh studied the two boys who struggled and wrestled on the greased pole. "It would be better with water!"

Juliette said, "I suppose it's too cold just now, so they're using a bed of fern instead."

With a yell of triumph one boy flung the other down to the ground. He slipped, legs flailed, and he too lay laughing on the springy fern heap.

"I want to try that. It looks like fun."

"No, dear. You will ruin those good clothes."

"Of course not!" he declared in disgust. "They give you old ones to put on. See—the boys are going into the tent to change. Give me a ha'penny and I'll try my skill."

"No!" she repeated. "It's not clean to put on other people's clothes. You could catch something horrid."

Leigh pulled a sour face. "Mr. Yardley said it would be twice the fun if you came, but it isn't!"

"Please don't fuss, dear. Shall we go over to the concert platform? I think that the Sefton boys and Mr. Sefton are going to give us a bagpipe tune. Mrs. Sefton said they've been practising for months. Do you remember the time Mr. Sefton started up his bagpipes and we all ran outside because the noise was so earsplitting?"

"No," he said shortly.

"I say, I say there," said his father, returning and seeing his glum expression. "What's tweaking your tail, then?"

"I want to go on the slippery pole!"

"Of course you shall." He flipped a halfpenny to the boy and winked as he ruffled his hair.

Juliette was furious. When young Leigh had disappeared into the tent she said, "I wish that you hadn't agreed to let him go on that dirty thing. I had told him he couldn't."

An apology would have soothed her, but he said, "Why not? It's only a bit of fun, so where's the harm?"

"It's dirty."

"Ah . . . boys are immune to dirt, Juliette."

Without thinking she burst out, "Whose son is he?"

"Mine. He's my son." He stared at her, not smiling.

The day went suddenly cold. She bit her lip, regretting her outburst.

He put a hand on her arm. "There, now. He's yours and he's mine too. Let's not fight over him. There's no need to, you know."

In a voice that trembled she asked, "What did you mean when you said that 'we' would be going to Auckland? Are you planning to take him away from me?"

He laughed at that. Beyond him she glimpsed a shopgirl giving him the glad eye. I should be flattered that others think him handsome and charming, she thought. But I don't, I don't feel flattered at all.

"What did you mean, Leigh?"

"I'm sorry. I wasn't laughing at you. Do you think I'd hurt you after all you've been through? I know that legally I could take the boy away, and I think that he would come with me, but I'd not do such a cruel thing to you. What I meant was we shall *all* go back to Auckland town. The three of us."

"You can't be serious."

"Of course I am. I have a smart little cottage in Auckland town right next door to Benningtons'. We can all live there very comfortably. Of course we'll have to get married first, there's no point in scandalising the populace too drastically, but as I see it there won't be much talk."

"You mean, you'd not be affected by it."

He ignored her. "Father Murray will be back here in three or four weeks' time, or so they say at the Albion. We might as well wait for him and have a proper religious ceremony, don't you think?"

She gaped at him, unable to reply, and he smiled back at her with the steady confidence of one who knows that he is so completely in control that there is no question of the outcome.

"Come now, Juliette," he coaxed.

"Oh!" she cried in exasperated rage. Turning, blinded by tears, she began walking swiftly in the direction of the lodging house.

Twenty-eight

Everybody thought the match a splendid idea. Young Leigh dashed home from the fair bursting with excitement. At dinner the lodging-house ladies perched around the table twittering with delight, and Mrs. Jollife was so pleased that she opened a bottle of Spanish sherry so that they could drink a toast to the happy couple. How fortunate that young Leigh would have a father at last, they all said. A doting uncle turned into a loving father. How delightful.

Leigh accompanied her to work and told the tailor she would not be returning. He chose the fabric for two new gowns for her while she stood by miserably. What a fine thing it was that the boy would have a father, said the tailor. "It will be the making of him," he declared.

Juliette saved her tears for Mrs. Sefton's shoulder and, to her dismay, Grace was happier than anybody. More than that, she alone had shrewdly guessed the truth.

"I thought all along there was somethin' odd in the way you sent Captain Yardley away, and the second I clapped eyes on Mr. Yardley I knew the reason. Aye, lass, I guessed you were nae widow woman. I guessed it all along."

"How did you know?"

They paused outside the saddlery shop. "Nae black clothes, nae ring, nae pictures. I guessed it easily enough."

"But you said nothing?"

"It suited me to say nowt. Campbell has an eye for a pretty lass, and I knew he'd show ye nae but respect if I told him you was a widow." She grinned, showing her gums. "I don't see nae reason to tell him owt different now, do you, lass? He thinks that 'Leigh' is a common name in the Yardley family, and let them all believe it, I say."

"Thank you . . . thank you so much."

"You mark my words, it's a fine thing you done, raisin' that boy alone. These things happen an' nae mistake, but better to do what you done than to give the bairn to the Maoris. Aye, there's some right snowy-haired bairns in these Maori tribes and I could tell you of a few so-called respectable folk who put them there."

"It's the same in Auckland," said Juliette. She paused, frowning. "I want your advice, please, if you will. Your help and advice. Mr. Yardley is forcing me to marry him. He'll take Leigh away if I don't, and he can do it, too. I've seen a lawyer and, according to him, Mr. Yardley has every right to claim him. There's nothing I can do. But I don't want to marry him. I dread the thought, I dread it. . . ."

Grace's small, hard eyes screwed up thoughtfully. "You know what it is? You've become too independent. That's what's ailing you. It's nae natural for a woman to live alone like you. Once you're wed, the feelin' will go, right enough."

"You don't understand," pleaded Juliette. "I don't like him. I hate the thought of marrying him."

"Don't like him? A fine agreeable fellow like Mr. Yardley? That's nae possible, lass. You're too independent, that's what's ailing you. Everybody likes Mr. Yardley."

Pausing helplessly, she realised that she could hardly confess that it was Stephen she loved. Not after having turned him down, not after having driven him to marry someone else. What a mess! What a ghastly mess she had made for herself to wallow in.

"You're right," she said listlessly. "I'm lucky, he is a fine man, and young Leigh dotes on him. I should be pleased."

"You should be on your knees thankin' the Lord for the marvellous good fortune He's sent you. Aye, that you should."

She knew in advance what Father Murray would say. First he would scourge her for pretending that Leigh was dead. She had the sin of not confessing truthfully. Doubtless he would expect her to answer to that. Then she had the business of having Leigh baptised as a legitimate child when he was illegitimate. And she could imagine the scolding he would give her if she proposed to reject the marriage and perpetuate her immoralities. It was better to say nothing at all.

Of course, she could have run away. There was ample money in the basket lining to take her and young Leigh completely around the world, and she might have done so—kidnapped her own son—except that Leigh had the foresight to anticipate such a move. Since the day of the fair he had accommodated the boy in his room at the Albion.

She gave up.

Graciously Leigh acquiesced to Mrs. Jollife's pronouncement that she did not approve of ladies staying in public hotels, and he brought his bride back to the lodging house after the wedding. Mrs. Jollife stage-managed the little dinner that evening (with champagne provided by the groom), and stage-managed their wedding night, too, thought Juliette when they were ushered self-consciously into Mrs. Jollife's own low-ceilinged bedroom which was lined with a papering of pages from English periodicals featuring the coronation and the royal wedding.

"Properly bridal and most suitable for the occasion," simpered the landlady. Juliette felt that she would never be able to look at another picture of Queen Victoria without experiencing this heavy, champagne-dulled dread.

Turning away from Leigh, who was thanking Mrs. Jollife at the door, she sat on the far side of the bed which had been draped with the best harvest-pattern quilt. He locked the door with a flourish and stood with his back to it.

"You're my wife now," he told her harshly. "There'll be no more nonsense, do you understand?"

She looked at him over her shoulder without replying. A tiny flicker of understanding illuminated her mind. Now he wanted more. He was not satisfied with marrying her—he wanted her to adore him, to revere him as she did long ago. She would never do that, never!

He stood in front of her and she kept her eyes on him, but

now without fear. That beaten feeling was gone. He was waiting for her to speak but she would not give him the satisfaction of showing any kind of reaction. Suddenly he jerked the lace cap off her hair and began plucking the hairpins from the chestnut coils. Her eyes were fixed on his face but he would not meet them. When her hair slipped loose and fell around her neck, he paused. She could tell that he longed to press his face into the waves but her passive eyes stopped him. Roughly pushing her around, he began tugging at the rows of covered buttons that studded the length of her spine. She made no move, did nothing to assist him. He spoke but she showed no sign of having heard him. Only when he reached the buttons on her lower back did she stand up without being asked so that he could peel the cream silk gown away from her body.

Her silence aggravated him even more than she had calculated. By the time he had mastered the intricacies of her corset laces, bodice fastenings, and the drawstrings of three petticoats and camiknickers, he was boiling with a frustration brewed of passion and disappointment. If he'd picked up a whore in the main street she'd have had the decency to undress herself—preferably while he watched. This haughty calm had him properly unnerved. It had taken him half an hour to disentangle her from most of her clothes and all he'd achieved was a glacial disinterest that was dampening his ardour properly. Damn her eyes! She'd agreed to marry him, so what was she playing now? There she stood in her short shift and garters staring him right in the eye as if she dared him to go any further.

His control snapped. Drawing back, he suddenly slapped her hard across the face. She saw the blow coming—he knew that she did—yet she neither flinched nor ducked to avoid it. And although the momentum of the blow sent her staggering back a pace she recovered her balance instantly and stood as she had been a second before, staring at him coolly.

That was too much. If she'd collapsed on the bed he could have comforted her, apologised. He could hardly hit her again. It was bad enough that he'd exploded once; striking women was something only a cad would do. Snatching up his coat and topper, he planned to make a dignified exit but even that was denied him. He forgot that he had locked the door and an embarrassing, frozen moment of comedy followed as he fumbled with the key.

He returned two hours later to find her lying quietly in bed, the lamp turned down, apparently asleep. Fortunately the ale he'd consumed had bolstered his courage and numbed all sensitivity. Swiftly, without tenderness, he consummated the marriage. She did not make a sound.

When he began to snore she crept from the bed and knelt on the floor by the window, gazing out across the silver toy town and the silver toy fort. A cloud floated across the very peak of the mountain like a flat silver hat. Juliette wept quietly, the tears soaking her crossed wrists.

"Stephen," she whispered, "oh, Stephen, what have I done?"

In the days that followed she found herself almost reluctantly admiring Leigh for the bluff cheerfulness he affected to mask their dismal marriage. Occasionally she would catch him looking at her with naked wistfulness and she reminded herself that she had given him a fair and just warning. He had married her against her will and therefore he could not really expect an affectionate wife. But despite her resentment she could not help feeling sorry for him, and after the first few days of adjustment a certain sympathetic kindness crept into her attitude.

Leigh's response to that encouraged her to hope that he might change his mind about returning to Auckland. True, New Plymouth had lost its charm for her once there was no prospect of Stephen's return, but anywhere seemed more attractive than Auckland and the malicious gossip that would undoubtedly greet them there. Whenever she felt that he was in a receptive mood Juliette tried suggestions that they settle in some other town, Wellington perhaps, or even Sydney. People said that Sydney town was a lively place with a picture of a harbour and all manner of interesting things to do.

"No," said Leigh, lighting a cigar. 'It's no use going on about it. We're going home."

"Then perhaps we could stay here?" she suggested in desperation.

"You stay if you like. But there'll be a flare-up of the war here soon. I should know, I've seen all these signs before. This town is no place for my son."

She could not resist asking, "Have you considered what your mother will say when she finds out that you and I are married?"

His laughter sounded relaxed but she detected a shifty unease in his eyes. "Mama will be enchanted."

"I rather doubt that."

"I honestly don't think that I should concern myself with what she thinks. We have had a few rather severe differences of opinion lately."

"I see. And I'm to pay her out, as it were?"

He said flatly, "You, my dear Juliette, are my son's mother. No less and certainly no more." With that he ground the cigar out in Mrs. Jollife's best Wedgwood dish and stood up abruptly. "I shall be very late this evening. Please be so good as to see that everything is packed and ready for the ship tomorrow."

She caught at his sleeve. "Leigh . . ."

"Yes?"

She paused. When it came to the point of confiding her news she did not know how to word it. "I suspect a happy event"? "A brother or a sister for Leigh"? No. Perhaps it was too soon to tell for certain. She would wait.

"Yes?" he prompted impatiently.

"Have you told Leigh yet?"

"All in good time," he said, meaning that he had not. She knew why. He was racking his imagination trying to think of some explanation that would not portray him in a poor light.

The procrastination almost cost him dearly. In his haste to have the whole unpleasant business of breaking the news to his mother over and done he dragged Juliette and the boy to Fintona without preparing either Maire or young Leigh for the interview. Juliette's protests were pushed aside. She braced herself for what she was convinced would be a scene and with head high followed Tawa through the gleaming, elegantly furnished rooms. The house smelled exactly as she remembered. Beeswax, rose-scented potpourri, and the tang of jasmine blossom combined so nostalgically that she would not have been surprised to hear the rickety tinkle of Jane's piano playing, or Sarah and Sister Moya giggling together on the settee.

Overawed, young Leigh groped for his mother's hand. "I'm scared," he confessed.

"Of course you're not!" his father told him at once in a voice that forbade contradiction.

Maire sat in her high-backed chair on the verandah in the sun, her feet on a hassock. Tawa had explained in a whisper that she was recovering from a bad attack of gout. At the first glimpse of her—regal, black-gowned, and forbidding—Leigh grasped Juliette's hand again. Even she quailed slightly, but she shook off the fright, reminding herself that, whatever quarrels Leigh may have had with Aunt Maire, he was her favourite child. This interview would therefore be worse for her than for any of them. In a matter of minutes she would hear that he had married the girl she despised. Juliette could even feel a trace of pity for her.

"Good morning, Aunt Maire," she said pleasantly, as though she had been away for the weekend instead of nine years.

Maire's eyes flicked from Juliette to the boy and back again. While Leigh approached and kissed her cheek she sat immobile, her glance flicking back and forth.

He laughed to cover his disappointment. "Is this any way to welcome your son home? I've returned from the gold fields positively laden with bounty, wealth, and good will."

She did not look at him. "Who is this?"

Juliette said, "Say 'good day' to your grandmother, dear." She tugged her hand free and pushed him forward a pace.

The boy stood unhappily clutching his ribbon-banded straw hat in one hand. He looked very handsome in his striped jacket, knickerbockers, and long ribbed stockings. Handsome and very like Leigh had been at his age.

"Good day, Grandmother," he said.

Maire's breath seemed constricted. She grasped the

ivory head of her walking cane and whacked her son on the ankle. "I insist that you tell me at once. Who, or what, is this?"

Belatedly Leigh realised that he should have first told his son everything. This was no way to break the news to him. Without answering his mother, he strode to the french doors and bellowed for Tawa. In the silence that followed the boy spoke.

"I'm your grandson, ma'am," he said politely. "My name is Leigh Yardley and I'm eight years old."

Tawa appeared, silent on broad bare feet. "What is it, matua?"

Leigh said, "Take the boy out to the kitchen and give him a glass of lemonade and some cake. Would you like that?"

The relief was enormous. White-faced, Leigh disappeared into the house behind Tawa. Maire's voice followed them through the morning room, as she railed at Juliette.

"How dare you! How dare you come back here with some gutter-snipe you plan to pass off as my grandson! Leigh Yardley indeed! What nonsense! And you . . . how gullible can you be? I cannot in the world imagine what you were thinking of when you allowed her to persuade you to bring her and her . . . brat to Auckland, but you had best turn around at once and deposit them both back exactly where you found them. Really, Leigh! To bring them here, to Fintona! Who saw you come in? Who has seen you with these two since you arrived in Auckland?"

Juliette noticed without surprise that Leigh did not have the courage to admit that it was his idea. Instead he tackled the least important issue she raised.

"We arrived this morning, Mama, and came directly by carriage from the wharf."

"Thank heavens for that, then. At least the situation is not as bad as it might have been."

Juliette said, "I'm afraid that it is a good deal worse than you imagine. I did not persuade Leigh to bring us here. For myself, I would much rather have stayed in New Plymouth. But, as a wife must follow her husband, I therefore accompanied him home."

"You've *married* her? I don't believe that you could be so stupid."

"She's the mother of my son, Mama!"

"What nonsense! She has a child, that's incontrovertible. No unmarried woman would burden herself with someone else's infant unless she was mentally deficient and she is certainly not that. But your child? Yours? How gullible you are!"

Juliette said, "It won't do to distress yourself, Aunt Maire. We do understand that the truth is abhorrent to you, but . . ."

"Silence her, please, Leigh. It's bad enough that she is here without having to listen to her as well."

"I'll not be silent while you attack me," she returned in calm tones. "Would the boy be named 'Leigh Yardley' if he was anybody else's child? And you have had the opportunity to study his face closely. You, if anybody, should be able to see at once that he is a Yardley."

"Pour me a glass of water please, Leigh," she said, and while he busied himself at the trolley she tapped her fingers restlessly on the arm of her chair. It was a full two minutes before she spoke again.

Dabbing her lips with a linen napkin, she said, "Yes, he is a Yardley—or he looks very like one. But is he yours, Leigh? Did it not occur to you while you were rushing headlong into this unfortunate and ill-advised union that there might be another reason for the child's likeness to our family?"

"I don't follow you, Mama."

Her tone was pleasant now, lilting with the musical hint of Irish accent. "Think, dear, think carefully. Who has been keeping in close contact with Juliette all these years? Who else is a Yardley, capable of producing that child?"

"This is monstrous!" said Juliette, provoked at last into anger. "Stephen has been nothing but kindness itself to me and to young Leigh. He found out why I had to go away quite by accident and he kept in touch because he was concerned about our well-being. It is despicable of you to imply anything else."

Maire smiled. "I think you protest too much."

"And I am not listening to another word," said Juliette

to Leigh. "When you have quite finished listening to these poisonous lies you will find us waiting in the carriage." She hesitated and added, "I think that I had best tell the boy the truth before someone else does."

"I'll come with you."

"That's right," said Maire. "Go running like a little lap dog."

The unpleasantness of the past half hour had jolted. Even after they were settled in the carriage and rattling along the fern-edged road, Leigh was still scowling and Juliette on edge. Only young Leigh seemed happy as he prattled on about the refreshments and the basket of kittens in the kitchen.

"Their fur was really hot from the warmth of the fire! Why do cats like to stay in warm places when they don't really need to because of their fur coats? Have you got any cats or kittens at your house, Mr. Yardley?"

"There's no need to call me 'Mr. Yardley' any more, son," he said gruffly. "You may call me 'Papa.' "

"Oh, good! I wanted to call you 'Father' when Mother and you were married, but 'Papa' is even better. That kind Maori lady said that I must not call that old woman 'Grandmother' either, but Grandmaire like my Aunt Abigail's children do. Grand-maree," he pronounced carefully. "Grandmaire, Papa, Grandmaire. Oh, Papa, I was frightened of her!"

Leigh frowned. "No son of mine is frightened of anything, do you understand?"

"But . . ."

"Do you understand? Yes, I saw you when we went in there trembling and holding your mother's hand like a namby-pamby. We'll have no more of it, is that clear?"

"Yes, Mr. Yardley."

"Papa. Yes, Papa."

"Yes, Papa."

Twenty-nine

Leigh's cottage was an unpainted wooden structure sitting in the centre of a lot covered with fern and long straggly grass. He pushed open the rickety gate and shrugged as he surveyed it.

"I know it's not much, but I almost always stayed at Fintona and only had this built as a renting proposition." He nodded to the trim white-painted house next door. "I suppose we could have that, if you prefer."

"Is it Abby's house?" It was a far more attractive place with frilled curtains at the windows and gardens vivid with flowers.

"No, that's Stephen's house. Abigail and Jack Bennington live in the next house along—though it looks empty too. But I know that Stephen won't be using his place."

"Perhaps it's rented too," said Juliette. "That garden looks cared for. This house will do for us, won't it, Leigh?"

The boy pulled a face. "It's ugly."

"And I'm longing for a cup of tea," said Juliette briskly. "Let's go in, and I'll see if I can light a fire and brew a pot of tea."

Inside, the cottage was as unprepossessing as the outside, and the only furniture was a broken chair and two packing crates. Juliette had purchased utensils and food at the store by the wharf so they were drinking tea and chewing wedges of buttered bread when Abby arrived to rescue them.

Juliette glanced up from the fire and saw someone at the door but at first glance failed to recognise her sister, so bloated had Abby become, with eyes sunk deep as sofa buttons and a muffler of chins. But the voice, the hair, and the elaborately beautiful gown could mean only Abby.

"Oh, my goodness! What a surprise!"

"I've just been to Fintona and heard the news, so naturally I had to come and see for myself." She trailed her crinolined, ruffled skirts into the room. Four children followed her in and stood behind her, gaping at young Leigh, who drank his tea and ignored them.

"How good to see you, Abigail!" said Leigh.

Juliette kissed her sister. Her cheek was smooth and tight as an overstuffed sateen cushion.

"Be careful of my bonnet. It took the milliner the best part of a week to make." She tipped her head to one side so that Juliette could admire the complicated pattern of finely pin-tucked silk. "And what a sly fox you are!" she accused Leigh. "No wonder you never married either of those heiresses! All the time you were nursing a guilty secret. Well, well! You've almost given Aunt Maire apoplexy, and that's the truth. She didn't even notice my new gown, she was so upset. What do you think of it, Juliette?" Without waiting for a reply she said in a disapproving tone, "You have not changed one speck! Still drab and scrawny as ever. It seems incredible that Leigh married you after all the times he's told me that he much prefers a woman to have some meat on her bones. Well, you can't stay here, can you? I mean, this place might be all very well to rent to somebody who hasn't ever known any better, but it's not for people like us." She smiled at young Leigh, who was staring blankly at her. This cottage seemed roomier than the cramped lodging or the cabin that had housed ten people at Seftons'. "We'll find something better for you, won't we, now?"

"Really, Abby, this will do very well. . . ."

"It so happens," continued Abby, "that we have just moved into our new Russian-design manor house and our old place is ready for renting. The agents were going to advertise it this week, actually. It is all furnished because naturally we didn't want to take one stick of old furniture into our new home. We were only going to ask fifteen shillings a week for it, which is a bargain, you'll agree."

"Oh, of course," said Juliette, thinking it sounded a great deal of money.

"Then it's settled."

"It does seem the obvious solution. Thank you, Abigail," said Leigh.

"Good. Well, I must say that, despite what Aunt Maire says, that boy's a Yardley, all right, and everybody in town will agree to that. Look at those eyes, that hair! He's you all over again, don't you think? Not like mine—they're a bit of everything, like pedigrees."

Mongrels, she means, thought Juliette. The children were the most artificial little miniature adults she had ever seen, though in all fairness they were rigged out to visit their grandmother. Even the toddler gurgling in the doorway was trussed up in over-ruffled clothing with a ridiculously elaborate bonnet.

Abby was summoning them forward. Hal was a burly, dark boy, Jon a chunky lad with fair colouring, Alice the baby, and Dora seemed about Leigh's age with a solid build and ringlets like her mother. Another baby, Edward, was apparently at home with his nurse.

"Go on, Dora. Give your cousin a kiss," said Abby.

Leigh looked alarmed. He was standing with his back to the wall like a knife thrower's assistant.

"Go on, Dora. Do as I say."

Leigh was starting to laugh when he suddenly looked at his son's apprehensive face and the smile faded instantly.

"Come on, son! You know what a kiss is, don't you?"

"I'm not sure, Papa." He looked at Juliette. "Is that what Uncle Stephen gave you once?"

"Oh, my!" pealed Abby. "Uncle Stephen kissed Juliette! Is that so?"

"That will do, thank you, Abigail," said Leigh coldly.

"I'm sorry, I'm sorry. Well, I'd best be going. One of the servants will bring the key around shortly. Have fun settling in, won't you?" Still laughing, she gathered up her brood and was gone.

Juliette sighed. "I was very upset about something once and Stephen comforted me. That's all there was to it."

"I don't want to hear about it." He plucked his belltopper from the mantelshelf and dusted the brim with long, sweeping strokes. "I'm going out and shan't be back until late."

"Very well. Leigh and I will manage the move on our own. I'll see if I can persuade Abby's servant to stay and help us move the trunks."

"I don't want to stay here!" cried Leigh. He did not know what had happened to ruin the comradely picnic atmosphere, but somehow he felt responsible.

"I need your help, dear," said Juliette.

"I want to go with you!" he pouted to his father.

"Another time," said Leigh. As he moved past Juliette he added, "I want to see if there are still as many agreeable people in Auckland town as there used to be."

While Juliette packed up the food items Leigh stared sulkily into the fire. "Why is Papa angry?" he asked after a long silence.

She hesitated, then thought, Why not? "Papa is your real father. He is angry with Uncle Stephen because Uncle Stephen didn't tell him about you. Your father went away to war and I didn't see him again, but Uncle Stephen looked after us. Papa really should not be angry about all that, but he cannot help it, and it will make things much better if we don't mention Uncle Stephen any more."

He poked at the flames with a stick. "That's confusing."

"It is, I agree. But we don't want Papa to be angry with us, do we now?"

"No. Papa is so much fun. But I'm afraid of him when he's angry."

"Don't make him angry then. Do you want another slice of bread before I wrap it up?"

Abby was back again next morning with the four children before Juliette and young Leigh had finished their bread-and-tea breakfast.

"Why are you whispering?" she asked after she had declined a cup of tea.

"Leigh is still asleep. He came in rather late last night."

"Marriage hasn't changed him one speck then," she said just as loudly. "Nor you. You look terrible today, too. Yesterday I thought it was the journey . . . fatigue and so on, but you're so pale. Are you . . ."

"Really, Abby!" She glanced at the children.

"They won't know what I mean. Anyway, I've just called in to leave them here. I'm going to the dressmaker's for a long fitting session and I thought that young Leigh might like to get acquainted with his cousins. I shall send our coachman in for them when I have finished shopping. Merrington's have a shipment of new French bonnets." She stood up, gripping the window sill for leverage.

On the way out she noticed the old wicker workbasket still sitting on the floor near the door, waiting to be unpacked.

"Gracious me! You still have that old thing? For goodness' sake, Juliette, get rid of it. Use it to light the fire or something. Look at how the wickerwork is coming unravelled on the lid and how scuffed the corners are! You should be ashamed to be seen with such a battered old thing."

Juliette smiled mysteriously. "I have good cause to be rather fond of that. It belonged to Mother. Do you recall how Father gave it to me when you wanted Clarice?"

"Clarice?"

"My old doll. Surely you've still got Clarice."

A plump rumple creased her brow. "That tatty old doll with the grubby yellow dress?"

"She had a yellow dress and bonnet. Like this." Reaching into the workbasket, she drew out Clarissa, who still looked fresh and pretty.

"Yes, I recall the one. Why, it must be years ago that it was tossed into the fire."

"You did that to Clarice? My Clarice?"

"She was dirty and smelled musty."

"How *could* you, Abby? How could you have done that?"

"What an odd creature you are, Juliette. Now I remember. You were ridiculously attached to that doll, weren't you? I never could understand why. Fancy being so sentimental and intense over something so unimportant. It was only a doll."

Juliette was compelled to bring the matter right out in the open now. "If you felt like that, why didn't you give her to me? She was mine, after all."

"Oh, I don't know." An airy shrug that made her violet silk cape rustle. "Father gave her to me, I suppose. Why rake it all over now? That was years and years ago and not even particularly important then."

"It was very important to me."

"What a queer creature you are!" repeated Abby, pulling on her cachou-coloured gloves. "So foolishly sentimental. Still, it hasn't helped you along in the world, has it? Look at where you are now. I chose to use my common sense and have six servants and a carriage of my own."

"I congratulate you," Juliette could not resist rejoining.

As soon as she had gone, baby Alice set up a long, monotonous wailing which provoked an angry bellow from the bedroom. Picking her up, Juliette discovered that her diapers were sodden and looked around in vain for a basket that might contain fresh linen. She rapped on the window. Leigh was bouncing in the branches of the apple tree, showing off, while the other three, not suitably clad for tree climbing, watched admiringly from the path.

"No, Aunt," said Dora earnestly. "Mama does not worry about having fresh diapers for Alice. She always cries when Mama goes away and leaves her."

"This happens often, does it? You are left with people while Mama goes shopping?"

"Not often, Aunt."

"Nearly every day." Hal scowled. "She can't leave us at home because baby Edward is sick and Nanny can't look after us all, and Mrs. Wilson said she would leave being housekeeper if Mama made her mind us."

"I see," said Juliette.

When Leigh wandered out, yawning, he laughed at her predicament. "It seems to me that your sister now has seven servants."

Ruefully, she agreed. "And those children seem half starved, too. You should have seen them eat the lunch I set out. This house is going to cost us a great deal more than fifteen shillings a week."

The move to Auckland town was neither as bad as Juliette had feared nor as good as she had dared to hope. Jane was cordial to her, Rose lukewarm, and they both managed to convey an air of disapproval. People she had been friendly with years ago now looked the other way. At church the congregation pretended that she was not there,

though Leigh was greeted as usual. Mrs. Meyney snubbed
her in a very obvious way when Juliette literally bumped
into her outside the bootmaker's in Fort Street.

"I'm grateful for your visits," she confided to Samuel
one afternoon in the late summer. "It's so good of you to
take the time to ride so far to see me."

They relaxed on chairs under the apple trees with
glasses of the ginger ale Dora had helped Juliette to make.
Below the garden the town spread out like a pretty pat-
terned quilt. It was so warm this afternoon that the trees
and bushes seemed to droop like flags on a still day.

Samuel coloured slightly, rolling the glass between his
leathery palms. He'd been a lad of almost seventeen when
she left and in the intervening years seemed to have
crossed directly into old age. His face was tanned and crinkled as a dry leaf and his hair bleached white like old rope.
Incidents and accidents had scarred him with a missing
fingertip, a puckered cheek, and the heritage from a rolling log—a pronounced limp. But for all his premature
aging nobody could have mistaken father for son. Thomas
was spry, walnutty, and bursting with a vigour that kept
him constantly moving, while Samuel moved with slow de-
liberation, dragging that leg, and speaking in a voice
brushed heavily with soft Maori intonation.

"It is good of you, Samuel. You have a long way to travel
each weekend and I appreciate it."

"It's not so far now that we're felling trees closer to
town. Those railway lines we put in make a big difference,
too. We can come into town every week, no problem."

"All the same, it's good to see you. I can't go out now, of
course . . . and nobody comes but Abby, and then only to
leave the children. She never stays more than a minute."

"You shouldn't be having to mind her children all the
time," said Samuel. "It's not right. Not when you're . . .
unwell."

"I considered asking Father to help me sort the problem
out, but since I hardly see him either . . ."

"It wouldn't be any use asking him. He dotes on Abby.
Spends far more time at her place than he does at Fintona,
and whenever he's there Abby and all the children are

there too. It's so peaceful here." Leaning forward to pour himself another drink, he asked, "Where's young Leigh?"

"He and his father are at Fintona too. I think Aunt Maire has overcome her aversion to him, and he's conquered his fear of her." She sighed. "I don't mind. When I see young Leigh and his father together I do feel envious because they dote on each other so much. But when there were just the two of us young Leigh was so dreadfully naughty at times that I seriously despaired of ever being able to manage. He's a different child now. I can understand why he was like that, because I missed Mother terribly when she died. Do you remember her very clearly?"

Samuel squinted through his glass at the bright patches of sunshine. "She was beautiful and she had a soft voice. I don't know whether I remember that or whether it's because I've heard those comments so many times over the years. Hey, Julie, do you mind if I tell you something really confidential?"

"No. Please tell me." She held her breath, waiting, wondering whether it was the secret about Mother. Did Samuel know about it too? Surely he wouldn't tell her!

"Remember the first day we came to visit you here? How Father hardly spoke to you?"

"I thought he was disappointed in me. Disgusted, or ashamed of what I'd done. Not that I can blame him . . ."

"No, nothing like that! I think that maybe he feels angry because you went away and didn't let anybody help you—maybe Rose feels that way too. But he wasn't disgusted or anything." He lowered his voice. "When we left here, Father cried."

"Cried?" she said, shocked.

Samuel nodded, his face solemn. "I can tell you, I was embarrassed. Didn't know where to look. Finally I thought he must be sick or something so I asked what was ailing him, and do you know what he said?"

"What?"

"He said that he was overwhelmed when he saw you because you look exactly like Mother used to. He said that it was agony to look at you. He said he didn't know where he would dredge up the determination to face you again."

"Poor Father."

"It rocked me, I can tell you. He said it's your eyes. When you look at him he sees Evangeline staring right back at him and he can't stand it."

"I'm glad you told me, Samuel. Now I'll not be hurt that he visits so infrequently."

"And I'm pleased that you understand. I thought that you might be upset—that's why I didn't tell you before. He's pleased about your marriage, did you know? Only—don't laugh, now, promise—he's really disappointed that you didn't marry Stephen."

Juliette didn't laugh. Staring into her glass, she said, "It must be the right weather for confidences."

Caught up with his own joke, he did not notice her reaction. "Father was almost annoyed when Stephen married that young lady from Sydney. Danielle somebody-or-other. He was sure that Stephen was going to marry you. Of course, he understood when he saw the boy."

"Of course." She glanced across at the white house with the crisp frilly curtains. "Who lives there, do you know?"

"In Stephen's house? Nobody—that is, he does when he's here, but I don't think he's been in Auckland town for ages. He and his wife were here about two years ago."

Two years! All that time she'd been hoping he would return and all that time he was married. With an effort she said, "I sometimes see people there. Gardening, clipping the hedge."

"He has some family look after it for him." He shrugged. "I never knew Stephen all that well. Nor Leigh, come to think of it." He laughed. "You're the expert on the Yardley gentlemen, I'd say."

She closed her eyes. "Please don't make jokes like that in front of Leigh."

"Jealous, is he?"

"Stephen's name is never mentioned here. When we first came to Auckland Leigh didn't seem to mind hearing chatter about what his brother was doing but his good humour has worn out. Or perhaps he's simply tiring of domestic life. He's very seldom here."

He thought how ill and drawn she looked but he said, "It could be just that he's found out."

"Found out what?"

"About Stephen asking Father for permission to marry you."

Her drink wobbled dangerously over her knees. "He did that?"

"Oh yes. He made a special expedition into the bush, all very serious, then the next thing we hear he's married someone else. Hey, maybe I shouldn't have told you that."

"It makes no difference," she said wearily. "My life seems to be in a proper mess, but when I look back on each of the crossroads I know that there was no real choice. So if by magic I could be spirited back a dozen years the pattern would only repeat itself and here I would be today, sitting in the shade with you while Leigh's at his mama's house."

At the bitter note he said gently, "Would you like Father to have a word with that husband of yours?"

"About being more attentive?" She laughed. "Thank you but no. I prefer it this way. Truly."

During the clammy wet weather of the Auckland winter Leigh's disenchantment with domesticity deepened until he was coming home only to change his clothes and leave the soiled ones for her to launder and press. Juliette did not mind for herself but it infuriated her to see young Leigh trying to smother his disappointment when evening after evening his beloved Papa failed to return for dinner. Occasionally she began to reprimand Leigh for his neglect of the boy, but always stopped before the words had formed, remembering how he had reacted on the only occasion she had gone so far as to complain. "Perhaps you'd both prefer the magnificent Uncle Stephen to me!" It was the swiftness of the retort, not the ugly tone, that stunned her. Thoughts of Stephen must be lying very close to the surface for him to have flung that at her so quickly. It's Aunt Maire, she realised as she swallowed her criticisms. She's probably feeding her son full of doubts and questions about those lost years in New Plymouth.

In the meantime Juliette was becoming increasingly hampered by her advanced pregnancy and so irritated by the constant noise of five children that she would have put a stop to their visits except for two things. Leigh thrived on the company of his two boy cousins and the older girl,

Dora, was a treasure of a help for Juliette. She could sweep, dust, peel vegetables, and look after baby Alice, all with the calm plodding manner of a pioneer mother. Only when quarrels flared or when baby Alice decided to spend all day screaming did Juliette's nerves fray.

One grey rainy afternoon as she and Dora put away the lunch plates she noticed that baby Alice had toddled out of sight. Mindful of possible dangers, Juliette sent Dora to see if she had wandered into the parlour. She checked Leigh's room where the boys were huddled on the floor playing with an army of miniature tin soldiers.

"No, Aunt," said Hal. "But Alice said she wanted to go home."

Home? Yes, it was possible that she'd gone outside. When she'd tossed the basinful of washing-up water out onto the lawn Juliette had noticed that the back door was ajar. But surely she wouldn't have gone out into that cold, drenching rain. Surely not.

But the baby was nowhere in the house. Directing Dora to stay inside, Juliette picked up her skirts and with a square of oilskin held over her head ventured out. The bare trees offered no shelter and Alice was not hiding under the soggy drooping branches of the evergreen hedge, so Juliette squelched up the path and out onto the road.

There she was, already at least a hundred yards away, a tiny white blur on the puddled road, moving with steady determination in the direction of her home. She shrieked angrily when Juliette splashed towards her, and yelled and kicked when she was picked up.

"No!" she bawled. "No! Wanna go home!"

"You'll go home soon," promised Juliette. "I'll dry you and then it will be time to go home, but please don't kick me, dear, you might hurt . . ."

"No!" she screamed, convulsing her limbs, slipping from Juliette's grasp and landing in a heap. Watery mud splattered Juliette's hem and all over Alice's delicately embroidered day dress.

Grasping her wrists, Juliette tried to persuade the child to her feet. Alice stayed doggedly in a soaking lump, bawling defiantly. It was clear that she was going to have to be dragged every inch of the long way back to the house.

Juliette felt like crying too. Her legs ached, her back ached, and the two-year-old Alice was screaming constantly. Gazing about helplessly, she wondered if she could tow the child to the nearest house, then summon the boys to help. Rain beat in her face and wadded Alice's coiffured hair. The child's skin was freezing to the touch. Feeling cruel and wretched, Juliette began to drag. She had succeeded in manoeuvring Alice only a dozen yards when a hansom cab sloshed towards them and the driver yelled, "Having trouble, missus?"

"Could you please help me?" cried Juliette, pausing to wipe the wet straggling hair off her brow.

With a "Hey-up," the driver leaned on the reins. At that moment the side canvas was pulled back and Stephen's voice said, "It can't be! Juliette, what in the world are you doing?"

"Oh, sweet Virgin!" prayed Juliette, hoping that she was mistaken. She wanted help from anybody, anybody but him! A hundred times she had imagined seeing him again. One day they would meet by chance, at an elegant party perhaps (though that part of her daydream was totally ridiculous since she had not been invited to a single social engagement so far), and she would look so beautiful, be gowned so elegantly, that he would regret forever that he had married someone else. And here she was, dripping from stem to stern with mud, hair plastered. How could she possibly compare with his wife now? His wife! If Danielle was with him she would die! She would run, she would throw herself under the iron cab wheels . . .

He was alone and apparently not repulsed by her appearance, though he was appalled when he had heard the full story. She and Dora had bathed Alice and pinned her in a petticoat and shawl.

"What can Abigail be thinking of? You're in no fit state to be her unpaid governess."

"Hush!" She nodded towards Leigh's door where the five children had been closeted. "Dora is a help, and Leigh is glad of the company. I've only been able to fit him into a morning school—the same as the Bennington boys, so they see a lot of each other. Oh, the noise tires me and baby Alice is impossible, but at least I'm not lonely."

"You need a servant. Someone chatty and pleasant like Gladys Benks, the lass who keeps my house aired. She needs a position and she'd be perfect."

"Me with a servant? Stephen, I've been a servant for so long that this seems like a vacation." She paused. "You've not asked what I'm doing in this part of New Zealand."

"I know already. I heard the news months ago. You'll forgive me for omitting to send a letter of congratulation."

She looked at him then, the first proper look since he'd rescued her. He was smiling, and it was still the same Stephen yet subtly different. His hair had thinned, the bones of his face seemed finer somehow, and his eyes, which used to have the warmth of melted butter, were distant, cool.

"You married before me," she told him.

"I told you I would, and I'm a man of my word."

"Do you . . . have you any family?"

"Not yet."

Idiotically, that hurt. If he'd said "no" or "yes" the words wouldn't have stung, but "not yet" had implications of tender togetherness that struck painfully.

"I'll make you some tea," she managed to say.

"Later." His hand was around her wrist. "I want an explanation first. Why did you marry Leigh? Was I right? Was it him you hankered after all that time?"

"It hardly matters now."

"Oh yes, it does," he said, his voice deceptively silky. "Your rejection of me has been a burr in my side ever since. I've been over and over it a thousand times and I'm no closer to knowing the truth. When I heard about Leigh I decided that must be it—you really wanted him, and I was actually pleased for you, but now that I see you I very much doubt it. I do realise that this is hardly finding you at your best but you're not happy, are you, Juliette?"

"What does it matter?"

"Because I care, and I want to know the truth," he said, not letting go of her wrist. "You're miserable, and from what I've heard from Tawa, that brother of mine spends most evenings up there if he's not on the town . . . that he takes young Leigh up there, and without you. That hardly seems an ideal situation to me. So why did you do it? Why did you marry him? Was I right in suspecting that it was him you loved all this time but you refused to admit it to me?"

"Of course not!" She tried unsuccessfully to free her hand. If only she could excuse herself long enough to wash and change this soaked gown for a fresh one. But he was staring at her so intently that she realised that her appearance was of no importance. He wanted answers, truthful answers.

Defiantly she said, "I've not told you everything, Stephen, but I do not consider that a crime. After all, I don't expect you to confess everything you have ever done . . ."

"Nor would I. A fair enough comment."

She made herself look him in the face. "But I've never lied to you either. Not once. Especially not when I told you that I never, never wanted to see Leigh again, let alone marry him."

"Then why in the name of Jove did you?"

She sighed. "He saw me quite by chance and, though I literally ran, hoping and praying that he'd not seen me, he followed. I tried to brush him off; I allowed him to assume that I had a position as a governess. But just when I thought that he'd go away and leave us young Leigh called me 'Mother' and that was the end of my hopes." Her eyes clouded and she looked much older than her twenty-seven years. "Of course Leigh asked the child what his name was and you can imagine the rest."

"I see. Leigh was overwhelmed with paternal instinct."

"Enough to make it firm and clear that he was prepared to take young Leigh away if I didn't marry him."

"He threatened to do that?"

Alarmed by the sudden dangerous tone in Stephen's voice and anxious that, whatever other impressions he gained, he was not to go away feeling sorry for her, Juliette changed tack, saying with all the warmth she could muster, "He and young Leigh took to each other from the beginning. They adored each other. In a way I felt envious but I could see it was for the best. Young Leigh had been difficult for me to manage on my own, naughty and disobedient—and he missed you, of course. Once his father showed up he was a different child altogether." She forced a smile. "Let me brew you some tea now, and you can tell me all about your life. How long are you here for?"

"A week this time, but from now on I'll be staying here fairly regularly . . . if you can call once every few months regularly. We're living in Sydney now. Danielle's mother is critically ill—something that's been building up for some time, but she's not expected to live much longer, so we moved back from London to be near her." He still had her hand captured and was rubbing the fingers gently between finger and thumb. "Are you going to tell me why things have come to this?"

"What do you mean?" Though she knew very well.

"This. Here we are, almost but not quite strangers. Why did it have to be that way? Why did you send me away, Juliette?"

His tone was as soft as the touch of his rope-scarred hands. He still loves me, she realised. Despite everything he still cares as deeply for me as I do for him.

"Why, Juliette?"

"I don't know whether I could ever tell you the reason," she said. "But this much I will say. Something terrible had happened. Something truly horrible. It had nothing to do with you or with Leigh, but I could not have married you without telling you everything. Honestly, Stephen, I don't know whether I ever will tell you." She paused and the rain drumming on the roof seemed to fill the room with whispers. "If you were not married and I was not married I might tell you now, but otherwise I cannot."

"Had someone . . . harmed you?"

She was going to say, "No, I was not raped," but then decided to let him think that if the idea had crossed his mind. "I will not discuss the matter further. I can't discuss it."

"Juliette, I hate to think that . . ." He broke off and stood up suddenly, letting her hand go.

Leigh stood in the doorway. A belligerent, scowling Leigh with the puffy, ale-flushed expression that had become too familiar since their return to Auckland town.

"Brother! Welcome and congratulations!" said Stephen.

Leigh shook the drops of rain from his overcoat and flung it over a chair back. He ignored Stephen's outstretched hand.

"I was not expecting you home," began Juliette.

He ignored her too and stood surveying them both with an odd little smile of triumph and contempt, his hands braced on his hips.

"Let me take your hat. The water's running off it." Juliette got up awkwardly.

He put up a hand to stop her. "This is a fine thing, don't you think? A man comes back to his own home and what does he find? He finds his brother holding hands with his wife. What do you say to that, hey?"

"In the name of Jove, don't be so ridiculous."

A burst of laughter came from behind the children's door, making Leigh swell with increased indignation. "So you've locked the young ones away so that they can't hear or see what's going on. Oh yes! Don't deny it. I suppose you've been oozing that charm of yours all over and no doubt she's been telling you what a neglectful, uncaring husband I am. Oh, I can hear it all now."

He's ill with jealousy, thought Juliette. Sick to his stomach with it. It's not just me—he's jealous of Stephen's manner with ladies and the fact that they all appreciate him. He's probably been nursing this spiteful envy all his life and I never realised it until this moment. No wonder his name rankles in Leigh's mind.

"Don't be ridiculous!" said Stephen in disgust. "How can you be serious with such notions? And as for Juliette complaining about you, she's uttered not one word against you and that's the simple truth of it. One might say that she is considerably more loyal to you than you are to her. If you were a halfway decent fellow you'd apologise to her at once."

"No! Leave it be!" She had sufficient experience of Leigh's tempers to have discovered that the best way to treat them was to remain calm and not argue.

"Apologise! I come in and find you sniffing round her like a dog and now you want me to apologise! Why, I'd sooner . . ."

Stephen's fist struck him on the side of his jaw, spinning him around and toppling him to the floor, bringing the chair with his wet coat crashing over with him. Then there was one of those hollow silences that follows bad news.

The children! thought Juliette. A silence stretched from there, too, and she could picture them crouched around the ranks of tin soldiers or bolt upright on the bed, listening with a frightened awe. As Leigh unfolded to his full height she hurried to the door and opened it a slice, saying, "There's nothing to fuss about. Just a little quarrel. All of you stay in here, won't you, and, Dora, take care of baby Alice."

"Who is there?" Leigh wanted to know.

"Just Papa and another man," she answered evasively.

Hal shrugged as he regrouped his cavalry. "Mama and Papa are always fighting at our house."

Not like this, I hope, thought Juliette, standing with her back to the door.

Warily the brothers circled one another, waiting for an opportunity to land a punch or lash out with a crippling kick. She watched with unhappy resignation. It was nonsense, utter nonsense. Stephen's face was devoid of humour; it was clear that he was determined to give his brother a thrashing, to punish him for what he considered neglect—and for all the misery he'd inflicted on Juliette long ago. She wanted to cry out, "There's no need to do this!" but when her gaze switched to Leigh's gloating face she realised that no part of this quarrel was Stephen's. Leigh had provoked it, Leigh desired it, and Leigh was determined to thresh his grievances out with violence.

Springing forward suddenly, Leigh struck Stephen on the shoulder and he replied by slamming a fist hotly into the centre of Leigh's face. Juliette felt ill. "Please, Leigh! Please stop this brawling. No good can possibly come from it," she urged as he picked himself up.

His moustache was scarlet and blood dripped from chin to cravat but he glared at her with a righteous exhilaration. "It's a little too late now," he said, rubbing his wrist across his bloodied mouth in a gesture of disdain.

She understood. Leigh was totally bored with her and with marriage and this scene was a perfect way to end his commitment. Who took the worst of the beating was immaterial: the fight was the thing. In the eyes of friends and family—and especially in his own eyes—he had caught her out with Stephen and was avenging his honour. He would soon depart with the satisfaction of knowing that he had done his best to be a good husband and the collapse of the marriage would be entirely her fault. She had seen the approach of this crisis in a score of hints and inferences and had been too weary and ill with pregnancy to recognise them as signs of chafing discontent. His prolonged absences, his criticism of everything from her appearance to the food she placed on the table, his sudden rages, the neglect of his son, his unconcealed irritation whenever young Leigh tried to bid for his attention. Leigh was sick to death of them and she had not had the wit to realise it.

He would go no matter what she or Stephen said, but he could go without suffering more damage. With determination she strode across and grabbed Leigh's arm.

"That will do," she said quietly. "If you want to leave, then go, please go now. Imagine what the children would think if they should come out and see this ugly scene? Wouldn't it be best to just go quietly now that you've made your point?"

He tried to shake her off. "Ordering me out of my own home now! A fine wife you've turned out to be. A fine wife from the first night! Too fine for me to touch . . . cold, infuriating, damn your eyes, you bitch!"

She tried not to flinch as he all but spat the last words in her face. Out of the corner of her eye she could see Stephen step closer with his chin aggressively forward. "Please just do as you wish, stay or go," she told Leigh.

Frustrated by her calm, he glared at her and without another word slammed into the bedroom. There came the scraping noise of a tin trunk being dragged from under the bed, and later the splashing of water into the basin. Juliette and Stephen stood silently, several paces apart and not looking at each other. Eventually Leigh emerged, freshly washed, his face blotchy. Picking up his coat and jamming the saturated topper on his head, he flung the door open and paused on the stoop for a moment, a looming figure with the tin trunk at his feet and a backdrop of grey, streaming rain.

"I hope you both rot in hell," he said bitterly.

Juliette sagged into a chair.

"It's all right," soothed Stephen. His face was stricken.

"He'll not hurt you. But, Juliette, I am so dreadfully sorry."

"It's hardly your fault. If you had not happened along to-day I should probably still be trying to coax baby Alice indoors, and Leigh would still be trying to concoct a positive reason for leaving. He's been wanting to go off to the Coromandel ever since the gold strike was made but I've been too obtuse to read the signs. It's not your fault, truly."

"He cannot just desert you like this. Not when you . . . ." He walked away in embarrassment and then turned abruptly. "I feel responsible. I am responsible. I'm as jealous of him as he is of me, and for the same reason, it would seem."

"Jealousy is ugly and corrosive."

"True. And what you need right now is practical help. Even if Leigh hasn't deserted you, then I'll make over half his Richmond Line income to you. There's enough of that to support you comfortably, to pay young Leigh's school fees and enable you to hire a servant. No arguments, please, Juliette. I shall send Gladys Benks over this evening."

Foolishly, she began to cry. The tension that had been building up in her for months had now, in one swift stroke, dissipated, and the relief was enormous. A sweet delightful feeling as comforting as sliding into fresh sheets. She sobbed with joyful release, pressing her face into cupped hands and then into the curve of Stephen's shoulder as he stooped to embrace her.

"There, there, sweet Olivine," he murmured. "Nobody will harm you. You'll be taken care of, I promise."

"Oh, Stephen! I didn't want you to feel sorry for me. You should be happy in your life and not waste any time feeling pity for me."

"How can I pity you when I admire you so deeply?" he asked, soft-toned. "I'm not sorry for you. I know that you will make a splendid success of your life. Look at how you've triumphed over the setbacks so far. How could I pity someone as brave as you are?"

"Are you sure?" she whispered against his warm neck. He smelled of bay rum and tobacco, and she longed to drift off to sleep like this—with his arms protecting her and the beautiful manly scent of him against her face.

"I'm sure." He was smiling. Her eyes were closed but she could tell by the lilt in his voice.

"I couldn't bear it if you felt sorry for me. I couldn't stand that."

After a long silence he said, "There have been things which I was sure I could not bear the pain of, yet when they had to be faced, somehow the strength was there to go on with life."

His voice was sober now; she dared not risk asking what he meant.

PART SIX

JULIETTE

1857-1861

Thirty

Gladys Benks was a lumpy Cumbrian girl with a floury complexion, an avid interest in gossip, and the kind of unobtrusive capability that enabled her to give the impression of having stopped by for a chat while she stoked the fires, whisked the house tidy, and cooked up a full roast dinner. Her arrival provided a welcome distraction that postponed the nasty prospect of breaking the news to young Leigh of his father's departure. Stephen had offered to have a talk with the boy but Juliette adamantly forbade it.

"It's best if you don't see him at all—not this time, at least," she said. "If anybody is to be blamed for this, I don't want it to be you."

Leigh did not ask any questions for a few days. The rain continued montonously and she kept him home from school, afraid that his slight cold might develop into something more serious if he was caught in the rain. Rain did not stop the Benningtons from coming, however.

Gladys laughed when the coachman had collected them the first day. "Eeeh, but she's a one, that Mrs. Bennington! Always parks her children off on any that'll have them. She tried it with the Captain's sisters, you know, but they both give her a short shrift, that they did!"

"How do you know so much about them?" asked Juliette, hiding a smile.

"We just live down the hill, an' our family used to do for them . . . me pa still does the gardenin' like he used to here. Eeeh, but they're a funny lot, her with her fussin' over clothes an' gowns an' hats an' him with his fancy piece."

"What?" Juliette knew it was wrong to encourage her but she was so starved for gossip that it was more than she could resist to say, "What did you say? Mr. Bennington . . . Mr. Jack Bennington has a fancy piece?"

"Eeeh, yes, ma'am, that he has." She sat back on her heels, the clay rag in her hands. "She's a young Maori lass, by the name of Rosaleen Teipa. Has a baby by him an' all, name of Patrick. It's said that she's a princess but I've noticed that every one of them Maoris what keeps company with English fellows all claims to be princesses. She's most likely a sailor's brat; she's fair enough an' real pretty, too, for all that she's no more than a child." She bent over the hearth again, applying the white clay paste in sweeping strokes. "Mr. Bennington parades her everywhere, to the races every meeting, sitting up like a proper wife in his carriage. Eeeh, but he treats her grand!"

"No more than a child," whispered Juliette. "Just as Abby was a young girl once. Poor Abby."

"Beggin' your pardon, ma'am, if I trotted tales out of the classroom; but Mrs. Bennington, some say she don't mind. She has all she wants."

"I suppose she has," murmured Juliette. Everything she ever wanted. All her dreams come true, and a few that she hadn't bargained for.

She dreaded breaking the news to Leigh so much that she kept inventing excuses to put off the moment, and eventually of course the chore was done for her. He came back from morning school with his shirt torn, his tie and one tooth missing, and his face crimson with graze marks. Wordlessly he handed her a note from the principal. He had been suspended, it curtly informed her, for "obstreperous and intractable behaviour."

Sitting down carefully, for her time was so near that every movement caused discomfort, she took the boy's grubby hands in hers and gazed at the bruised knuckles. "What was it all about?"

He scuffed his boots on the floor, looking sullen.

"You do have to tell me, dear."

"It was Hal and Jon's fault!" he burst out. "They should be the ones to be caned!"

"Oh dear, it was as bad as that? Tell me, were you fight-ing with them?"

Shaking his head, he admitted, "I was fighting every-body else—but they started it! They told the other boys that Uncle Stephen came here and chased Papa away. Then they laughed and said that Papa hates Uncle Ste-phen because he wanted to m-m-marry you! So when the other boys all teased me I hit them."

"Fighting never solved anything, dear," she said gently, stroking his hair back from his flushed brow.

He pulled away. "Where is Papa? Did Uncle Stephen chase him away?"

"Now where did you get hold of a notion like that?"

"Dora said that Uncle Stephen was here that day—when you put us all in the bedroom and there was quarrelling. Was that Papa and Uncle Stephen?"

"Yes, but that's not the reason Papa went away. He has gone to the gold fields. Remember when he told you about looking for gold?"

With a cold face he said, "Papa told me that if he went to the gold fields again he would take me with him. He said a son would be a great help and that with my sharp eyes I would find more gold than him."

"That was a long time ago, dear. Sometimes grownups forget promises when circumstances change."

"I don't believe you!" he shrieked suddenly. "I don't be-lieve that at all! Papa wouldn't forget! He promised! He promised to take me with him!"

"What's all this, then?" asked Gladys, hurrying in with a basketful of potatoes.

"I hate Uncle Stephen!" Leigh stamped. "I hate him, I hate him!"

"Stop that this minute!" scolded Gladys, grabbing his upper arms and giving him a shake. He was so astonished that he was silenced at once. "Now what do you mean by this nonsense?" she demanded. "Don't you know that your ma's not to be troubled at a time like this? She needs lookin' after, and peace an' quiet. That's what she needs."

"What for?" asked Leigh, subdued but still sulky.

"Why, for the baby, of course." When he looked disbelieving she said, "Don't you know you'll soon have a little brother or sister?"

"Is that true?" He stared wildly at Juliette. "Hal and Jon said so but I didn't believe it."

"You should be pleased, and be helpful to your ma."

With a wild look back at her he dashed from the room. Juliette frowned and said, "I should have told him. I should have prepared him for all this."

"Don't you fret, ma'am. He'll come round to the idea. Now I'll make you a nice cup of tea. Would you like that?"

"That sounds lovely." Juliette smiled.

May Yardley was born as the first buds began to burst on the apple tres. A week later Abby's sixth child, Lena, was born—a surprise to Juliette, as Abby had been out and about all through her pregnancy, the secret concealed by her excessive stoutness. Leigh was disgusted that both his new cousin and his prospective brother were girls. He pulled a face at the mewling creature and informed Juliette that he wanted nothing to do with it.

"I hate girls, all girls! I'm never going to be married. And I don't want a stupid sister!"

Starched aprons rustled as Gladys appeared. "Your ma needs rest! Out you go now!" After shooing him out the door she returned to the bed to plump up the pillows and voice her opinion. "You're too soft with that lad, ma'am. He shouldn't be allowed to upset you. The Captain said most particularly that you were not to be upset."

"We have agreed not to discuss the Captain," Juliette reminded her. "And as I have said before, there is nothing wrong with Leigh except that he misses his father very deeply."

When she had gone Juliette closed her eyes and wondered wearily if she was abysmally bad as a mother, or did it just seem so to her?

Rose and Jane reassured her when they came to see the baby.

"Boys need a man's influence," said Jane knowledgeably, her bonnet plumes nodding. "Leigh was the same after Papa died."

"Yes, he was. You would remember that," agreed Rose.

"Perhaps if Stephen could spend some time with him when his ship comes in. The *Mondrich Princess,* is that it, Jane? It was so clever of him to name his own ships all the same, the *Mondrich Princess,* the *Mondrich Queen,* and the *Mondrich Duchess,* but I must confess that I never can remember which of them is under his command. They are all so very similar, don't you agree?"

Jane commented dryly, "Our Rose would be confused by anything. At the Queen's Birthday Ball she committed quite a faux pas by greeting the new Governor's wife as 'Mrs. Grey' instead of 'Mrs. Gore-Browne.' "

"And what did she say to that?" asked Juliette, sitting up in bed and relishing this very different kind of gossip.

"She did not mind, for she told me disarmingly that grey and brown are both drab colours and easily muddled. Direct and charming, that is our new First Lady," said Rose.

Jane looked up from feeding scraps of sultana cake to the two silky terriers that squirmed in her lap. "I'm sure that it will only tire poor Juliette if we talk about Governors and such. You will have had enough society chatter to last a lifetime when you lived at Fintona."

"Please tell me all the news! What exciting happenings have you been to? Have there been any Sheridan plays recently? And the Haydn concert that was on in the Town Hall. Have either of you been to that?"

Summer slid pleasantly by in a golden procession of picnics on the lawn with the Bennington children and hazy, drowsy days. During the long evenings Juliette sat on the tiny verandah watching gold and apricot sunsets over the harbour, remembering those days at New Plymouth when the silence of the bush reached out to enfold her. And if the day had been a happy day for young Leigh, with no tantrums or outbursts, then Juliette would be conscious of a feeling of perfect contentment. But summers never last; by April, when May was at the fretful teething stage, winter set in again with a recital of thundering storms and lashing concertos of rain.

"The Maoris all reckon on it bein' a jim-dandy of a winter, ma'am," said Gladys, shaking her umbrella at the doorway. "We'd best lay in a stock of dry firewood and have my pa fix up a clothesline across the fireplace for the wee babe's things."

As the weather continued Leigh grumbled about being housebound. He moped about with his soldiers and sulked over his collection of pictures, saying how unfair it was that his cousins never visited on the really stormy days, and every day was stormy now. School closed. Juliette and Gladys both stayed in and relied on peddlers and the grocery-cart men for their supplies. The only people who seemed impervious to rain were the Maori children who hawked vegetables and sleds of firewood door to door at highwaymen's prices. As she dug into her purse Juliette commented that Hone Heke himself could not have done better, at which they always giggled proudly.

The rain kept falling long after it seemed that there could surely be no more rain to fall. Floods closed all the roads out of town and washed out Thomas' logging railway. The camp closed and the men returned to their families, but instead of staying with friends this time, Samuel knocked on Juliette's door. She greeted him with delight. Did she have room for him? Of course she did.

"I have a companion," he said, whistling keenly out into the rain. Nails rattled on the steps and in dashed a black and white terrier with very muddy paws. Without so much as pausing to wag its tail it braced four legs on the floor and shook itself in a whirring of spray.

"It's Tippy!" cried Juliette. Then, "But it can't be. Tippy would be a terribly old dog by now."

"No. Tippy died of old age," said Samuel, hanging up his coat. "The tusk of a wild pig helped him on his way in the end. He was too slow and stiff with rheumatism to nip out of the way. I got this dog immediately after that. This is Mrs. Tippy."

Leigh knelt, laughing as Mrs. Tippy flailed her front paws on his shoulders and snuffled with flicking tongue around his neck. "She's adorable!" he cried. "Why didn't you bring her before?"

"She usually stays at the bush camp—helps to keep the rats down. But I brought her with me because she's going to whelp soon. I hope you don't mind, Juliette."

"Mind? Of course not." She was watching Leigh's joyful

face and thinking, Why didn't I think of this? Aloud she wondered, "Have you homes for all the pups?"

"I was planning to drown them," he said without thinking; but at a glance at her horrified face he said, "I suppose we could find homes round the town here. What do you say, young Leigh?"

"I'd love a dog like this! I'd really love one."

"Then it's settled. I'll have to teach you to look after a pup, won't I? Town dogs need care, you know, and you'll have to learn all about them if you're going to have one of Mrs. Tippy's children."

One morning shortly after that, before the rain had lightened from black to grey, the whole household was roused to the kitchen by tremulous cries from Mrs. Tippy. Leigh fetched the box of warm rags he had prepared for the nest and Samuel settled himself sleepily on the floor to reassure his dog with an even stream of conversational patter and comforting strokes as she gazed up at him with huge eyes filled with pain and trust. After she had fed May, Juliette mixed a brew of brandy and milk which she administered with sisterly sympathy. Leigh was not allowed to watch. By midmorning three yellowish pups squirmed sightlessly around pink nipples and Samuel tried to guess which of the camp dogs could have been the father. Mrs. Tippy, who alone knew the answer, lay back contentedly with what was undeniably a look of pride on her whiskery face. Leigh was allowed in now on condition that he was quiet, and he had just finished naming the three (a highly exciting process) when a frantic knocking was heard at the door and Rose's parlourmaid Marama, shivering and dripping, handed a sealed note to Juliette.

"You can be sure it won't be an invitation to one of those dinner parties of hers," said Samuel, watching as she broke the seal of blue wax and carefully unfolded the damp, smeared paper.

"Hush, she'll hear you." Juliette jerked her head towards the open door beyond which Marama now stood steaming herself off near the kitchen fire.

"I don't care if she does," said Samuel heatedly. "Those sisters are all alike—yours and Leigh's. They come around here as though they're making charity calls, but do they invite you into their homes as if you were their equal? No, they do not, and it makes me so angry . . ."

"Hush, Samuel, do. What you say is true, but there is no call to become agitated. I dare say that you care as little as I do for formal occasions. They are tedious affairs at best—you know that. It is kind of you to champion my cause, but I do prefer a quiet, informal life. . . . Oh dear. How terrible!"

"Bad news, plainly enough, but what?"

Her eyes were almost frantic as she scanned the rest of the letter. "There's a fever epidemic. It's struck suddenly and dozens of Maori children from the other side of the harbour have died. They will not learn to keep the children warm instead of cooling them off when the fever strikes. . . . Oh my! Poor Abby! Little Edward and Alice have become critically ill—Dr. Forster is not treating them but he has heard that they are not expected to live. Listen to this. 'Baby Lena has been spared so far, and the older ones are comparatively safe, but before you go flying around there like an angel of mercy, Juliette dear, please be warned. The fever is dangerously infectious, and you should not allow your dear little May to come into contact with it at all.' " Looking soberly at Samuel, she said, "It must be! Rose has underlined the words 'dangerously infectious' three times. And she goes on to tell me not to let Abby's children inside our door until Dr. Forster advises us that it is safe. There, Samuel! Would you not consider Rose to be a friend even if she does not invite us to her grand evenings? But poor Abby! Do you suppose she needs help?"

"With six servants and enough money to hire every doctor in Auckland town? I doubt it."

"You sound heartless."

"I'm not. But that sister of ours has been making use of you and I'd like to see that stopped if I can."

Before the afternoon was over he was not only grudgingly testifying to Rose's friendship but admitting that she must have psychic powers, too. Gladys came scurrying into the parlour where they were toasting cheese before the fire and whispered that the Benningtons' coachman had arrived with Abby's three oldest children.

"He says they're wrapped in blankets and lookin' miserable as death, ma'am," she blurted, thrusting a note at Juliette. "Shall I tell him to bring them in here to the warm?"

"You'll do no such thing," said Samuel.

"What can I do?" asked Juliette unhappily as she looked up from the pleading letter.

"You'll send them home quickly, before they catch their deaths of cold. What can Abby be thinking of? Fancy sending them out on an afternoon like this!"

Tears of pity blurred Juliette's eyes. "She asks if they can stay in this house to recuperate until the danger is over. She says they feel at home here. How can I turn them away?"

"Because the doctor told you to. Don't be a fool, Juliette! What are you doing?"

She was shucking off her slippers and buttoning her boots. "Fetch me my old bonnet and shawl, Gladys, will you, please?"

"You can't be serious," Samuel told her. "Abby is selfish and thoughtless, but there is no need for you to expose yourself and your family to any danger. Especially when you have been specifically warned."

"Rose said nothing about me, only the children. Of course I must go and see if I can help."

Gladys helped with her coat. "Eeeh, ma'am! It's a grand house, the Benningtons'. I ain't been there but I hear it's ever so handsome inside."

"I've not been there either, and I'd prefer the first time to be under happier circumstances." She nodded to the coachman. "Come. Let's take the children home."

Juliette was admitted only to the front hall, where Abby listened with tearful anger while she tried to explain that it was best for the children to be cared for in their own home near their own parents.

"We've puppies there, newborn puppies, and with Samuel staying the house is crowded and noisy, so I thought you might prefer it if I came here to nurse them. I'll stay as long as you need me . . ."

While she talked Abby glared at her. The moment Juliette paused her sister's bitterness spilled out.

"What colossal impudence! It's your fault the children are ill! Your fault entirely, yet you refuse to do one simple thing to help me!"

"Excuse me, please!" Juliette cut in. "How can this be my fault? It's an epidemic, Abby. The illness is widespread. I've not done anything to harm your children."

"Oh no? Let me tell you that baby Alice has been snuffling ever since that day you neglected to mind her and allowed her to become soaked to the skin. She has never properly recovered from the chill she received then, so whose fault is that, may I ask?"

Juliette drew breath to point out that baby Alice had visited half a dozen times since then and had exhibited not so much as a sniffle or a croak. But she stopped without a word of indignation, and instead said gently, "I'm sorry that Alice and Edward are ill, and I hope they'll be better soon."

"Do you? But not enough to offer practical help, I see. You are so ungrateful . . . false . . . the worst kind of jade . . . living in my house, accepting my hospitality . . . after all I have done for you, finding you somewhere to live . . ." Bosoms heaving, she moved on in lurching sobs. "I didn't care that you disgraced your family . . . behaved worse than a whore . . . brought your bastard here to flaunt . . . I stood by you . . . I was your friend and what a fool I was . . ."

Shocked, Juliette opened the door and let herself out into the rain. Everything her sister said was nonsense but that did not blunt the sharp edges of her accusations. Because there was nothing to say she had no choice but to let them be. It was not until the next evening when news came that baby Edward and little Alice had died that the last sting of Abby's words melted into compassion.

On the long trudge home from the Benningtons' Juliette contracted such a severe chill herself that Dr. Forster confined her to bed with peppermint vapour treatments and warm oil compresses. For more than a fortnight she was too ill to look after the children, too ill to climb out of bed, and far too ill to attend the pathetic double funeral. Unaware of her illness, Abby sent a stinging letter vowing never to forgive her. Worse, Thomas himself came with the singular purpose of reprimanding her.

"Father, you're not being fair to me," protested Juliette weakly. "I have been loyal to Abby, but don't you see that I simply couldn't risk my own children becoming infected, and . . ."

"That's not how she sees it," he told her, avoiding her eyes. "She has stood by you, visited almost every day when most people would have snubbed you. She is dreadfully hurt by your attitude and so am I. Sometimes I have been almost pleased that your mother is not here to see what has happened to you."

"It's so unfair," wept Juliette later. "He wouldn't listen to me at all. If only I still had Rose's letter to show him."

"It would make no difference," Samuel told her as he tried to offer awkward comfort. "Abby has his ear and the claim to his sympathy."

"I don't begrudge her that for a minute. Those poor children; it's so terrible when they are taken so young. But you understand, don't you, Samuel? Young Leigh and May are all I have in the world . . . I couldn't risk losing them."

"I understand. But you're wrong in saying that those two are all you've got. I'm here, and I'm your friend."

"I don't know what I'd do without you. Truly I don't."

"You don't have me all the time. In fact, I'm going to have to return to the bush camp next week and I don't want to leave you in this miserable state. There, now. You know that this unpleasantness will blow over just the minute our Abby decides she could do with your services again. You know it will."

But as winter slid towards spring there was not one word from the Russian manor house above the harbour. To underline her antagonism Abby visited the school and informed the principal that young Leigh Yardley was an undesirable influence on her sons and if he was not excluded from the school she would remove her boys and take her considerable patronage elsewhere. Now poor Leigh had a two-mile trudge to Sister Amy's classes where he was given tuition in the company of some of the roughest ragamuffins in Auckland town, boys who immediately dubbed him "Yardley-Bastard" and ragged him about his "foine voice" and clothes. Every afternoon he trudged home and sulked dejectedly in his room; even his enchantment with the pup Skippy faded as pleasure has a habit of doing when there is nobody to share it with.

Gladys was indignant. "If the Captain could see what was going on he'd have somethin' to say, that he would."

"The Captain sees that we have the means to live. That's all that interests him," said Juliette. Since that first unfortunate meeting there had been no sign of Stephen. Obviously he'd changed his mind about coming ashore regularly and just as obviously she could guess why.

"Eeeh, but ye're wrong, ma'am. Every time his ship comes in he goes directly up to visit me da to ask about what you're doin' and how you're copin' on your own, and me da always tells him that I'm doin' a right proud job of lookin' after you."

"He goes out of his way to ask about me?"

"That he does, ma'am. Says he's particularly concerned, what with you bein' his brother's wife, and him gone away an' all. Right decent of him, I'd say, but then I always did think the Captain was a real gentleman. Bighearted and kind, too. But don't you think it's odd that he don't come an' see you himself? He never comes near his own place no more. Me da were ever so disappointed when them rhododendrons was lookin' so splendid an' the Captain just said he'd take da's word for it. Said he were too pressed for time. Surely he can't be so busy that . . ."

"Please, Gladys," interrupted Juliette. "I have a frightful headache."

That spring was the loneliest Juliette had ever experienced. May was a placid baby, not interested in play and content to sit on a rug gurgling to herself. Leigh moped after his cousins and asked endless questions about when his father might come home. It seemed to Juliette that every attempt she made to jolly him along ended in bitter recrimination about both losses. Neither Jane nor Rose could call—Jane had suffered yet another miscarriage while Rose's first baby was due at any time. And a much-antici-

pated visit from Samuel was ruined when Mrs. Tippy
failed to recognise her son and almost killed him. Leigh
bawled, Skippy whimpered, and Samuel swore furiously
as he bandaged the pup's front legs. It was an occasion best
forgotten. Even the newspapers could offer no diversion, it
seemed; bad news crammed the pages. New Plymouth was
featuring prominently again with accounts of forts being
erected and churches barricaded to protect the populace
when the expected uprising swept over the town. Juliette
grew more worried. No reply came to the anxious letters
she wrote to the Seftons. If only she could talk to her father
about it, for he would know more than anyone else
whether there would be fighting. But Thomas had not
called after the scolding and pride forbade her to make the
first healing move. If he thought so ill of her it was best
that he stay away.

A fortnight before Christmas came wonderfully welcome news. Rose, after a week's exhausting labour, had
been safely delivered of a daughter. Dr. Forster called to
tell Juliette himself, his face glowing with pride and relief.
He had been so afraid, so terribly afraid, that history
would repeat itself, he said. Because no visitors would be
permitted until Rose had recovered her strength Juliette
wrote her a note of joyful congratulation and enclosed it
with a delicately embroidered nightgown she had made
from the finest lawn.

"Eeeh, but that will look a treat on the baby, ma'am,"
said Gladys. "Would you like me to take it around to the
doctor's house on my way home?"

"You may take it now if you like, and take young Leigh
with you. Skippy needs to be taken for a walk. No, wait. I'll
pick a bouquet of those red roses to go with them. Roses are
so appropriate for her and those have a heavenly fra-
grance."

Armed with secateurs and a basket in which to lay the
blooms, Juliette hurried down the path to where scarlet
roses rioted over the fence that separated her house from
Stephen's white cottage. As she selected and snipped she
suddenly heard a woman quite near, on the other side of
the fence.

"They are gorgeous roses, Mr. Benks," the voice said in

a peculiar hard accent. "Rose will appreciate an arrangement of those by her bedside."

Holding her breath, Juliette moved close to the fence
and angled herself so that she could see a thin slice of what
was happening in the next garden. For a few maddening
moments she could see nothing, then her patience was rewarded by the sweep of a navy-blue crinolined skirt on
which rested a black-mittened, very white hand. A young
woman's hand. Juliette moved but the next gap was more
obscured by the profusion of blooms and leaves on the
other side and it was not until she had tried several positions that she finally was able to see the young woman's
face.

It was nobody she could recall ever seeing before, a
honey-blonde young lady—sweet-looking rather than
pretty, with too heavy a jawline and too low a hairline, but
appealing for all that with friendly brown eyes.

"Will this do, do you think, Mrs. Yardley?" asked Mr.
Benks and at the same instant the girl turned. She was obviously pregnant.

"Why, that's really lovely!" she said in the same harsh
voice and, taking the flowers, which were wrapped loosely
in a cloth, she walked out of Juliette's view.

Shaking like a thief, Juliette fled back inside. "Gladys,"
she said as she set the basket on the kitchen table, "have
you ever met the Captain's wife?"

"Why, yes, ma'am, but a long time ago it were. More
than a year before you came here, I'd say."

"What does she look like?"

"Mrs. Yardley?"

"Yes." Miraculously she could hear the name, know to
whom it was referring, and still respond normally.

Gladys considered carefully as she tied the strings of her
grey bonnet. "She's taller than you, ma'am, with lighter-
coloured hair—not as fair as mine, though. She's neither
plain nor pretty, but it's her voice I recall best. Fair put me
in mind of a duck, that it did."

So it was she. Juliette said faintly, "That is an Australian accent."

"Beg pardon, ma'am?"

"Never mind. Look, I've changed my mind about the flowers, so if you like you may take the baby gift now."

"Quite right," agreed Gladys, fastening her cape. "I always think roses are far too sweetly perfumed for a bedroom. Especially a sickroom."

"Yes."

"Are you feeling well, ma'am?"

Juliette was trembling on the brink of tears but she managed to shake her head, shoo Leigh out, and slip a bottle of cider into Gladys' basket, telling her to stop by and chat with her mother on the way home.

"Don't hurry back," she said, waving them up the path. "It won't matter if dinner is late tonight. I'm not feeling hungry."

Not feeling hungry! She almost laughed at that as she bolted the door and collapsed onto a chair. Not feeling hungry! She doubted that she would ever again be able to swallow a single mouthful of food. Why, she didn't care if she died . . . it would be better if she did.

Sharp rapping at the front door interrupted her abandoned fling into self-pity. Gladys, she thought as she plucked a handkerchief from her sleeve and hastily scrubbed at her eyes. Gladys forgotten something again. But with her hand on the knob she paused. Gladys would never come to the front door.

Juliette took a soft step backwards and slipped into the parlour where she craned her neck to peer around the edge of the lace curtains. There on the porch was a woman dressed in a navy-blue crinoline and a navy-blue bonnet with a white shawl draped over her shoulders for concealment of her condition.

"Mrs. Yardley, are you there?"

Juliette shrank back from the window. She subsided onto a low hassock where she remained huddled and silent long after Stephen's wife had crunched her way back up the shell path.

Thirty-one

Juliette's bedroom overlooked the town from a wide bay window, low enough and sufficiently close to her bed so that she could lie there on summer nights and enjoy the view of the sparkling town without even lifting her head from the pillow. On clear nights the scattered lights reminded her of tiny holes poked into a black kettle, or of glowworms in the cave Thomas had showed them when they were children. In moonlight the town was spread with silver frost that made her nostalgic for the mountain snow; and on rainy nights the picture blurred like one of young Leigh's earliest attempts at watercolour painting, when black and yellow were his favourite colours.

One night in late summer her windows stood wide open to the air, and she was wakened by an insistent clanging of bells. Sleepily she pressed her face into the pillow, mumbling to herself. Fires were a constant hazard in this dry hot weather and, like babies, they always seemed to arrive in the dead of night. Another fire bell chimed in, adding its strident tongue to the barrage of noise. From her alcove in the hall, May woke and set up a fearful cry.

Juliette reluctantly rolled over and opened her eyes. All her room was awash in a glare of orange light. Sitting up, she saw leaping flames and realised that the hot colour on her walls and ceiling was the reflection of a huge, spreading fire in the centre of town. Tall flames danced along the rooftops of a row of buildings near the waterfront. The ships moored close to the wharves looked like charred twigs on a flat sheet of copper.

On and on clanged the bells. Juliette groped for her slip-

pers and stumbled as she hurried from the brightness of
her room into the black hall. May clung to her.

"Mother?" called Leigh nervously. "Is that you,
Mother?"

She paused in his doorway. "Come into my room and
watch the fire. It seems as though half the town is burning."

"Can I bring Skippy in? He's been barking for such a
long time that I thought robbers must be creeping around
the house."

"He's probably barking at the bells. But bring him in
anyway."

"I'm scared." He snuggled up against her on the bed
next to May. "Will it spread up here?"

"I don't really think there is any danger of that happening."

"I've been lying awake for ages and ages. I thought for
sure that something horrid was happening."

"Fires are horrid. They destroy homes and sometimes
kill people."

"Sister Amy says they clear away the old to make way
for the new."

"That's a shrewd observation." She put her arm around
him and found him shaking. "This is almost like a picnic,
isn't it? Shall I fetch some cake and lemon barley water so
that we can make it into a real one? I doubt if any of us will
get back to sleep tonight. What do you say? Shall we have
a picnic?"

"Pi'nic!" said precocious May, cheering up and clapping
her chubby hands together. "May wants a pi'nic!"

"May wants everything," remarked Juliette fondly, ruffling the dark auburn curls.

"May is spoiled!" Leigh's fingers tightened on his
mother's arm. "There *is* a prowler here! There is!" And as
the door swung open he squealed in fright.

"Sorry to startle you, ma'am," said Gladys. "Only I
didn't know if you was awake or not, though me da says
the Devil himself couldn't sleep with all this racket goin'
on. Gracious! What's this? Oh, it's the dog and I all but
tripped over him."

"But what are you doing here, Gladys? You gave us all quite a nasty fright."

She turned from the window, a bulky silhouette, and said, "It were me da what sent me. He said the Captain would never forgive him if he let you stay here on your own while all this fuss were goin' on. My, but it looks hot down there! Me da says it put him in mind of 1847 when there was a huge fire in Rochester that almost gobbled up the whole town. Hundreds of folks died," she exaggerated, adding with regret, "there'll be nobody hurt with this one, unless it be a fire fighter. Me da were down in the town earlier and he said they got everybody out."

Leigh had recovered his courage completely. "Why don't we get dressed and go down there too?"

"Because we have an excellent and safe view from here. Oh, listen to those cracking noises. That must be windows exploding with the heat. We were going to have some cake and barley water, Gladys. A picnic."

"I'll fetch it, ma'am."

"I wish we could go down there! We are too far away to see everything properly from here. Oh! I do hope our school burns down!"

"That's possible, dear. But think of how upset Sister Amy would be if it did."

"None of them folks are venturing too close to the flames," said Gladys, placing the tray on Juliette's bureau. "Look at how they're keepin' well back. The 'eat must be terrible down there. Terrible."

"I'm astonished at how fast it's spreading," said Juliette, holding a glass so that May could sip from it. "Father said years ago that those houses should never have been built so close together, and those ones behind Shortland Crescent were a real fire trap."

"They'll not be there come mornin', ma'am. Eeeh, ain't that the Ospray 'otel catchin' alight now? Look at them curtains streamin' fire out of the windows. Fair makes your blood run cold, don't it?"

"Pretty!" sang May, clapping her hands. "Pretty fire, pretty fire."

"The Ospray Hotel? But that's just up the road from the old Peridot Emporium."

"You can see the sign all lit up by the flames," said Leigh.

"It *is* close. Oh dear, I hope it doesn't go up. Samuel said that Father has been working there for the best part of a month, supervising a complete refurbishing of the place. He said that when the renovations are completed it will be one of the most modern in Auckland."

"Could be that it will be the only store in Auckland town left standin'," said Gladys.

Leigh was disappointed. "The fire is not even going in the same direction as the school. Do you think it might spread that way?"

"If the wind changes. But I hope it stays right where it is. There's been quite enough damage done tonight. Gladys, have you seen any signs of fire fighting? There seem to be crowds down there watching but nobody actually doing anything to put the fire out."

"There's some folks wearin' their arms out ringin' those bells, and that's about all that's bein' done, I'd say."

"The Emporium is alight!" shouted Leigh.

Ripples of flame were tiptoeing across the roof in the advancing breath of the fire. Already the houses of Shortland Crescent were black-toothed shells glowing orange. A sticky odour of smoke had spread even to the cottage on the hill. May wrinkled her nose and coughed.

"How ghastly for Father," whispered Juliette. "Why is nobody stopping the spread? Surely they have a whole regiment from the Albert Barracks, so what in the world are they doing? Why haven't they pulled some of the older houses down to make a firebreak?"

Thomas was wondering the same thing at that same moment. His was not a querulous observation but a demand, loud and cursing. Working frantically with a group of hastily mustered helpers, he was racing against the flames to clear all the goods he could ferry from the shop to the relative safety of the old Kororareka house, which stood alone on a wide lot next door. Part of this building had been let as rooms and part retained as a storehouse for freshly imported shop goods. Right now the whole building was being doused by anxious tenants who flailed at the pump in the yard and sluiced buckets of water over the walls and roof.

Muttering darkly about army bungling and military inefficiency, Thomas raced into his Emporium and staggered back out under load after load of merchandise. Already he had conceded that he would probably lose the Emporium itself; it was now only a question of how much valuable stock could be salvaged before those greedy flames began licking at the woodwork.

"Never mind the food," he called to one of his Maori assistants who was carrying out a large wrapped ham. "Try to save the dress goods first. The trimmings, buttons, needles, scissors, thimbles, and so on. All the small, expensive items. Hurry! Bring out as many of them as you can."

Though three lamps blazed inside the store they were unnecessary, for the fire outside lit the night with dazzling brightness. Like a hot day in hell itself, thought Thomas; there was more than a touch of madness here. Twice he had been caught dangerously close to the bush fires that can wrap and consume whole hillocks and valleys in the space of a drawn breath. But this was a different kind of terror—wilder, garbled, more sinister under the clamorous festival excitement. Thronging the streets was a multitude of insane, babbling, shrieking lunatics, or so it seemed to Thomas. It was so hot that breathing hurt, searing scalded lungs. Sweat lubricated his body until his clothing seemed to be plastered on.

"Here it comes!" yelled one of the tenants perched on the old house roof. A bucket swung in a glittering arc as he jumped down. Thomas hurried out onto the verandah and down the steps for the next load, pushing past the spectators angrily.

"Get out of the way if you can't do something useful!" he shouted as he elbowed his way through.

"No, Paritau, no! Stay out! It's not safe now!"

Like yellow weeds, the flames sprang in full-flowered clumps right along the eaves of the Emporium, sprouting and multiplying as they watched. Thomas shook off restraining hands and plunged back into the narrow rear door. One more load. The cutlery boxes had not all been cleared. If he juggled them carefully he would be able to scoop up all that remained.

Inside, the room was filled with choking grey soup.

Smoke had curdled through cracks and swelled to fill the room from floor to raftered roof. How eerie it is! he thought. Like an underwater cave, unbreathable, with shafts of weak light angling through the sudden gloom. A crackling noise loud as gunshot fired nearby and glass rained around him. Where were those cutlery boxes? It was so difficult to see and the smoke made his head ache . . . muddled his thinking. Ah, here. This seemed like them.

Outside in the yard, Gerald Brook stood nervously tugging at his blond moustaches. Nothing could persuade him to go inside that building now—Thomas must be crazy to have returned in the face of those flames waving all around the walls. It was like marching right into an open coal range. His eyes hurt. Morbidly he wondered whether eyeballs could solidify like boiled eggs in blasting heat. What a bloody damned thing to happen right after all the work they'd put in to flossie up the shop. Weeks of work gone in a few moments' conflagration. What was Thomas doing? He'd been in there a damned long time. "Come on," he urged under his breath. "Come out of there, old fellow. It will start caving in soon."

Out of the smoke ran two Royal Artillery men. Recognising the uniforms, Gerald hurried to intercept them.

"Why in hell hasn't something been done to halt this fire? Surely there should have been a firebreak made long since! It should never have been allowed to get this far."

"All under control. This building's going to go up any second now. Should save your house here from destruction. Doing what we can, sir. Bad business, this. Apparently ignited on purpose." Both men looked around purposefully. "Have to sacrifice the store. Shame, really. Been here since the town was founded, they say. Still, arson's a bad business too. Can't be helped."

"Hey, wait one damned minute!" Gerald grabbed the soldier's sleeve as he fired a shot from a pistol directly up into the air. "What do you mean, sacrifice the store?"

"Bag of powder under the front door and dynamite all round. Risky business but it will powder the building to nothing. That will stop the fire creeping this way."

"Is the powder set?" Gerald looked frantic.

"And the fuse lit. Just gave the signal. One shot. Had to check first, make sure nobody was near."

"Thomas Peridot is inside there!"

"Surely not! Full of smoke in there."

"I tell you he is. Quickly! Stop that fuse somehow, quick, for heaven's sake!" Cupping hands to mouth, he yelled, "Mr. Peridot! Your life is in grave danger! Hurry! Come out at once!"

It is doubtful whether there was any hope of Thomas hearing, so loud were all the other noises. But at that moment he emerged from the smoking doorway, moving jerkily under the weight of the armload of boxes. As his eyes cleared he saw Gerald a dozen paces back across the now empty yard; he was shouting and gesticulating with such a desperate urgency that it was obvious something important was happening. Thomas turned to see what it could be, and in that instant the building exploded. For a fraction of a second the doorway was a glaring yellow eye and Thomas a black, burdened shape fixed in its iris. And then the violence slammed down in a crushing wave with a blast that shook the blood from Gerald's face and whacked him effortlessly over onto his back. He did not see Thomas crumple under the force, or the scarlet dragon's tongue that scraped over his fallen body.

From the cottage window the blast was beautiful—a red and white chrysanthemum with a bright fiery centre.

"Pretty!" cried May, applauding. A second later she screamed as the delayed shock of the blast drummed the house and rattled the window frames.

"Wow! That was louder than a hundred rolls of thunder!" said Leigh in awe.

"Hush, now, hush," soothed Juliette, calming the terrified little girl.

"Must have been exploded on purpose," said Gladys. "The military done that, I'd say."

"But that was Father's store. They blew up the Peridot Emporium!"

"Eeeh, ma'am! Look at all them little fires. That big explosion scattered lots of bits of burnin' wood and started fires all around. Half the town will be gone by mornin'."

Leigh pressed his face eagerly against the window glass

as he counted the tiny yellow flickerings beyond the perimeter of the main fire. "If it burns down the school, there will be no more lessons for months and months!" he said hopefully.

It was late next afternoon before Juliette heard the news about Thomas. The morning had been spent in the company of hundreds of other curious citizens, strolling in blank shock around the blackened streets that only yesterday throbbed with life. Now it was difficult to recognise most places, and only by deduction could one tell where the baker's had been and where the little shop that sold riding clothes had stood. Gladys was away collecting the laundry, Leigh reluctantly at lessons in the untouched convent hall, and Juliette was in the kitchen scrubbing young May in a tin bath, marvelling at how dirty she had managed to get on their walk.

"You are a clever girl, aren't you? Fancy getting soot right down under your stockings and up into your pretty curls. What a clever lass!"

"Me clever! Me clever!" May laughed, throwing her head back in extravagant enjoyment; then stopped suddenly. "There's a lady here!" she whispered.

Abby filled the doorway. "A touching domestic scene. But surely one of your servants should do that? I never have anything to do with such messy procedures."

"Then you are depriving yourself of a lot of fun," Juliette told her as she got up from her knees. "What a surprise to see you, Abby. May, this is your Aunt Abigail. Say 'Good day' to her, there's a clever girl."

"Good day." May hung her head.

"If you get out now, dear, I'll dry you in front of the fire."

"I want to stay in longer!"

"Very well. Do you mind talking to me in here, Abby? I don't like leaving children unattended, and . . ."

"From what I recall, you specialised in leaving them unattended," her sister remarked coldly, making it clear that this was definitely not to be construed as a cordial social visit. "I care not in the least which room we discuss our business in, for I have no intention of staying a minute longer than I absolutely must. No, thank you. I would not care for a cup of tea. I have come to tell you about Father."

"Oh!"

"You do not seem alarmed. Yet surely you must have heard. Everybody in the entire town would have heard."

"Heard what?" She dried her hands and put the towel over a chair within May's easy reach. "If it's about the emporium, we saw that go. It's a terrible shame. I can recall when that was the only building on that particular part of the waterfront. We were so upset to see it burn."

"I knew that you were unfeeling, but this is too much!"

"Whatever do you mean?"

"Just that Father was burned almost to death. Don't tell me you didn't know," she accused her. "You must have heard the news."

"Oh, God, no, I didn't know. When? How?"

"He was near the shop when the explosion knocked him over and he was horribly burned in the blast. All his clothes . . . his hair . . . he's not expected to live more than a few days at the most. I was with him most of the night. Samuel has been sent for and he should be there at Fintona by evening." Seeing that Juliette wanted to speak, she hurried on in the same tone. "Dr. Havow says that a fitter man might have been able to escape but poor Father has had so many worries lately that he is quite run down. Really, Juliette, you must accept that much of the blame for this rests with you. All the worry and shame you have brought on the family has taken its toll on him. He is quite worn out. When this terrible . . . terrible thing happened he had no chance of getting out of the way."

"I will not bother to argue with you," said Juliette evenly. "What you think of me or what anybody thinks is really of no concern to me . . ."

"Obviously!"

". . . but no matter what you say I doubt that Father is worn out with worrying over me. What does matter is Father himself. Where is he? Is he at the hospital?"

"He is at Fintona, and two nurses have been engaged to give constant care. He is in terrible pain."

"I'll come to see him as soon as Gladys comes back."

"That is why I came to see you." She tugged a handkerchief from her waist fob and held it under her nose. "You can hardly imagine I came here from choice. Oh, poor Father! I feel so distraught that I cannot think clearly."

"Then sit down and let me make you some tea."

"No!" She recoiled as if Juliette had proffered arsenic. "I must go back to Father."

"Please tell Aunt Maire that I will be there within the hour."

"There will be no need for messages. You are not to be permitted to see Father." Abby tucked her handkerchief away in a gesture of triumph. "Aunt Maire says that you have caused Father enough anguish already, and I must say that I cannot help but agree with her. She says that under no circumstances will you be allowed in to see him."

"Abby!"

"I merely came to inform you of her decision," said her sister righteously.

"But Aunt Maire cannot forbid me to see my own father!"

Abby smiled.

"If I wish to see Father—and I do—then she is not going to stop me."

"I rather imagine that she will," said Abby.

Tawa looked frightened, unhappy, and extremely embarrassed. But she gripped the door handle tightly and peered apprehensively out at Juliette.

"Please don't be angry with me. I don't want no trouble. Please go away, Miss Juliette."

"Tell me, Tawa, is Father any better today?"

"No better an' no worse." Glancing over her shoulder, she said, "Please don't come back. Mrs. Peridot, she growls at me when you come here."

"I've resigned myself to the probability that I'll not be able to say goodbye to Father," she told Samuel when he came to visit one evening. She would have expected him to help but he just shrugged uncomfortably, his face haggard. "It's probably best that you don't. He is very ill, Juliette, and . . ."

"And you also think that I should not be allowed in."

He stiffened at her tone but still did not meet her eyes. "I don't think that at all, but it's not up to me. If you try to force your way in, there'd be a terrible fuss and that would probably upset him. So all in all I do think it best. He is in such a bad way that he hardly knows anybody. I'm sitting up with him nights and sometimes he doesn't acknowledge my presence the whole night long."

"No wonder you look tired."

"I try to sleep during the day but it's pretty harrowing when he starts calling out."

"Well, come and rest here. It's quiet, and I can even take May out all day to let you have the place to yourself."

"No, I must be there. In case . . . you know, Julie, this is pretty ghastly for everybody. How long ago is it since Mother was killed?"

"Twenty years."

"To Father it might as well be yesterday. He calls out for Evangeline all the time and he keeps apologising to her, shouting out at the top of his lungs that he did his best to find the men, and would she please forgive him because he didn't avenge her. I tell you, it's chilling. He calls Aunt Maire 'Mrs. Yardley' as though he hardly knows her. When he starts in on his shouting, my skin crawls. It really spooks me. I thought he'd forgotten that business years ago. He's not mentioned it to me once since we left the Bay of Islands."

"And now it's worrying him?"

"Yes. He must have set himself the task of looking for whoever killed Mother and the children, and because he hasn't managed to find them he is afraid to die and face her. I've tried to tell him it won't matter, that Mother will understand; but he's inconsolable. And it's dreadful to think that he'll die raving instead of with dignity."

"Not only dreadful, but unnecessary."

"What's that?"

"Never mind." She was deep in silent thought for a long time, then said, "Is there any way, any way at all, I could get in there without Aunt Maire knowing?"

"Not unless the doctor brought you in."

She shuddered, recalling Dr. Havow's plump, freckled hands and his ogling eyes. "I couldn't ask him. That's quite out of the question. Is there any other way? Think, Samuel, think!"

"I don't think it's a good idea . . ."

"Please, Samuel."

"Yes, there is someone. Stephen. Aunt Maire said that his ship is due in port tomorrow morning. If anybody will be able to help you, Stephen can. Mary and Tawa take no notice of me, but they'd do anything to please him. Even defy Aunt Maire."

Juliette paused in the doorway of the Captain's cabin, suddenly unsure of herself. Stephen was busy writing at a narrow desk below the porthole, head bent, unaware of her presence. He was dressed smartly in braided jacket, breeches, and high polished boots that filled the cabin with the scent of leather. His face was set in earnest furrows as he concentrated on the document before him. Though it was less than two years since she had seen him, he had aged markedly.

The light outlined thinning curls—grey curls, she noticed with a wrench—and the softened jaw resting on the white silk cravat. But it was the haggard, weary look that jolted her most. Surely this was not Stephen, this middle-aged man who looked as though he had all the worries of the world on his mind. Stephen was a creature of the sun, tanned and golden with glossy dark hair that would never dull, and flesh that would remain eternally firm. Surely this tired-looking man could not be her Stephen!

Then he glanced up, saw her watching him, and in the first unguarded moment was flooded with a joy that was as plain to her as it was painful for him. The moment was brief. Control clamped swiftly over him, transforming him into the polite stranger; and she was left wondering whether what she had seen was a mirage: not an impulsive, radiant delight, but a trick of the light.

I won't accept that, she decided as she stepped into the cabin. That was his expression, mirroring my own thoughts. He still loves me and that brief glimpse proves he cares. Married or not, a father or not, he still thinks of me, dreams of me as I dream of him.

Her exaltation was crushed almost immediately.

"What brings you here, Juliette?" he asked with weary patience and no warmth. "I heard the news about your father from the pilot. Is he any better?"

"He's dying," she said brutally, and was immediately overcome by the accumulation of her miseries. When she collapsed, sobbing, Stephen kept his distance, playing the impeccably courteous gentleman; he seated her in his chair, fetched her a tot of brandy, and produced a pressed, folded handkerchief. He neither put his arms around her nor soothed her with loving words. Hungering for both, Juliette was desolate.

"He was terribly hurt . . . one eye is blinded and he is burned almost all over . . ." She wiped her eyes. "I came to see you to beg for your help. Aunt Maire will not let me in to see him, and I must see him. I must."

"Won't let you in? That's incredible."

"It's true. I have been to Fintona every day since the fire but the servants won't allow me past the front door."

"Perhaps he is too ill for visitors."

She made a choking sound and recovered. "Thirty-one chiefs have been to see him so far. *Thirty-one!* And more are coming, or so the newspapers say."

Stephen whistled. "They thought a lot of your father."

"So do I. We've had our differences, but surely I should be able to have one last meeting with him."

"You certainly should. Even dear Mama should have a more generous sense of fair play than this." He smiled bitterly. "It would seem that she has never forgiven you for stealing her sons away from her."

The silence that followed this observation was so unbearably poignant that Juliette quickly glanced away and said, "I must see Father and unless someone can help me it means pushing in and causing a scene. That would only distress him. Stephen, will you please help me? Samuel says that Tawa will keep out of the way if you ask her to, and if someone could let me know when Maire is going to be out of the house . . ."

"This is quite a conspiracy, then?"

She nodded. "You are the only person I could come to for help."

"So it is not my charm that brings you here after all," he

said in a curiously ironic tone that she could not fathom. "I shall, however, be pleased to assist in any way I can. Thomas has been a good friend to me."

So cold was the last stab that it brought tears to her eyes, tears she tried to blink away before he noticed them.

He did notice, and felt guilty; he made up for his casual cruelty by becoming totally pleasant, asking after young Leigh and May and Gladys, enquiring how she was managing on the portion of Leigh's income that he sent to her each month. And had she heard from Leigh? She in turn felt even guiltier, for she should have politely asked after his wife and the baby (if it was here yet). But Danielle would certainly have described her as a most peculiar and unfriendly person who refused to answer her door, and who instructed her servant to say that she was "indisposed and unable to receive guests"—five days in a row! After being so blatantly unsociable, it would smack of the worst hypocrisy now to make sympathetic enquiries after Danielle's health.

Fortunately he did not seem disposed to discuss his wife and the visit concluded cordially enough. As arranged, the hired coach came for her later the same afternoon. She arrived at Fintona white-faced with the anxiety of the interview ahead. An hour earlier, when word came and she had packed the children off to Gladys' house for the evening, she had almost panicked in revolt at what she had planned to do. Instead she had fortified herself with an inch of brandy and the stern reminder that everything she had done so far was for Evangeline—this would be for Evangeline as well. And what did it matter if Stephen heard her confession too? Perhaps it was as well that he did find out the truth behind her anguished decision not to marry him. What did it matter if that bitter cool in his eyes shaded to contempt? One was as bad as the other; she no longer had his good opinion to lose. Accordingly she poured another brandy and strengthened her resolve.

He was still in the pleasant mood that had been upon him when she left the ship. As he described his part in the conspiracy she thought she could even detect a faint twinkle of mischief, a hint of the old, teasing Stephen.

"The Governor's lady was delighted to assist—oh, I

didn't tell her the reason for wanting Mama out of the house, simply said that poor Mama was under such a strain, and if she did not have some relief I would be concerned for her own health. All true, as it happens. She is suffering very severely from the worry of what happened."

"And Aunt Maire went quite willingly?"

"The invitation was so charming she could not do otherwise. The Governor's wife requested the company of the wife of the town's first citizen. That impressed her."

"It would."

"We had best go directly in. I doubt if we have very much time." As he helped her out of the carriage she noticed that he-appraised her costume with a distinctly puzzled look. Traditionally she should have worn sober colours to visit a deathbed, but to bolster her courage she had donned her prettiest pink and black gown and a pink bonnet trimmed with ruffles of wide black lace: a garden party gown that she had made herself last winter out of boredom and the vague, vain hope that one day she might be invited to some special occasion.

"I thought that Father might be cheered up," she explained. "He always loved to see Mother in pretty clothes, and Aunt Maire never wears anything but black or grey, so . . ."

"Quite." She could tell he disapproved, but she shrugged to herself. With the brandy glowing warmly inside her, Juliette followed Stephen down the long, dim hall.

Thomas was bedded in the room she had once shared with Rose. The harsh light had been dimmed with both curtains and screens, though the windows stood open to the warm afternoon. Despite the ventilation a dreadful sickening smell of decay struck her forcibly as she stepped into the room. Unprepared, she gasped as the stench stung delicate membranes in her nose and throat.

Stephen heard her strangled breath and saw the look of horrified revulsion on her face. Warningly he squeezed her upper arm hard and shook his head firmly, pointing to the bed. She understood at once and almost vomited. The stench was her father's body actually rotting off his living bones.

She hesitated at the doorway, composing herself until she was calm. Stephen misunderstood and asked in a whisper if she had changed her mind.

"No," she said. "But could you please leave me here alone?"

"I'll see."

Together they approached the bed. Thomas was propped up on pillows and swathed with endless yards of bandages. Only his fingers and half of his face were exposed. There the flesh was scarlet, raw. They moved around the bed so that he could see them with his good eye.

His gaze wavered between them, then settled on her. Thomas' lips trembled. There was soft grey stubble on his chin, sprouting between the blistered patches; but he would never be able to shave himself again. Noticing that detail, Juliette's insides twisted with such acute pity that she almost broke down. Stephen's fingers dug into her arm.

"Evangeline," murmured Thomas.

"No, sir . . ." began Stephen, but Juliette looked at him and shook her head fiercely. Stephen couldn't know that Father had been asking so pathetically for his dead wife. Aunt Maire would hardly be likely to have told him such a thing.

"Evangeline . . . Evangeline . . . you came." His voice was hoarse with delight. "I have been asking to see you."

"He's raving," whispered Stephen in dismay. "Should I fetch the nurse, do you think?"

She shook her head again, more positively. Bending forward slightly, she placed a hand on her father's cheek. "They told me you wanted to see me, Thomas."

His arm jerked. She placed her fingers over his, and he grasped her hand at once.

"Evangeline," he insisted, tightening his grip on her hand. "Forgive me, Evangeline. I tried to find them, I tried my whole life long. Every time I went on a trading journey up north . . . to the Waikato . . . to the Bay of Plenty. On every trip I asked about it until everybody was sick of me. Someone must have known something, but they wouldn't tell."

"Please put it out of your mind. It doesn't matter now."

"But it does!" He struggled to sit further upright. "I did

everything I could. Never stopped trying . . . please believe me, Evangeline. Someday, someday I would have seen those filthy murderers swing from ropes. I had to avenge you. I had to do it, so why didn't it happen? Why couldn't I find them when I tried so hard?" He fell back onto the pillows, exhausted and tearful.

Juliette dabbed her handkerchief at the frothy spittle at the corners of his cracked lips. Stephen was looking at her with a question in his eyes. She could see what he was thinking—that she was tiring her father and should end the visit before his reminiscences became too morbid.

"I can never rest with that burden on my mind. I can never rest . . . it haunts me, Evangeline. How can I face you when I have failed so abysmally?"

Juliette swallowed the tangle in her throat. If only Stephen would leave the room so that she could confess everything in private. But it was clear he intended to stay. Staring at her father's wasted face, she began speaking quietly to him, the words coming naturally, with no need to consider or compose.

"I have come to see you for a special purpose, Thomas, to tell you that I *have* been avenged. Years ago both the men who murdered me and our poor babies met the fate that they deserved. You could not find them because they were already dead."

"What . . . how? How did it happen?" He was struggling again.

"Please rest, Thomas. Do not excite yourself. Just lie quietly and listen. Do you recall on one of our excursions seeing two men being drummed out of Kororareka? One was a short, slight man, very thin with a wart over one eye, and the other a thickset fellow with curly reddish hair."

"Vaguely," said Thomas. "One was called Blue. They were very short, both of them."

Stephen knew instantly who she was talking about. A moment ago he had been wondering how to stop this insane charade before real damage was done to Thomas' fragile and already unbalanced mind, but now he could see that the story Juliette was concocting might help soothe his last days. Concocting? She had just given a very accurate description of two men he remembered well—men he'd actually seen in New Plymouth town on one of his last visits there, come to think of it. Intently he watched Juliette as the story unfolded, and as she spoke a prickly feeling of unease and inevitability crept over him.

"Those were the men who killed us. They came to steal from you on the assumption that, since you were a trader, you would be certain to have valuable items and money hidden somewhere in the house."

"Oh," groaned Thomas. "And I never did, just to protect you from that very possibility. Oh, Evangeline, I am so sorry. It was all my fault."

"I insist that you must rest," urged Juliette. "They found nothing and killed me anyway. It was not your fault. Nobody could ever blame you, Thomas."

"But how . . ."

"As the men were running away from the cottage Juliette saw them. You might recall that she and Abigail were hiding in the grass beside the track. Juliette saw them clearly, but later when she went into the cottage and saw the blood . . ." She faltered and almost stopped, but was encouraged by Stephen, who squeezed her shoulder reassuringly. "When she saw that, she was so shocked that the image of the men went right out of her mind. It was not until she saw the men again, years and years later, that she remembered everything."

"Juliette saw them again? Where?"

"When she was in New Plymouth. One afternoon when she and her son were quite alone these men came to the cottage. She recognised them instantly."

"But how could you be sure?" asked Stephen, cutting in. "I mean, how could Juliette be certain? That was a long time afterwards."

"She was sure because of what the men said," replied Juliette steadily. "One commented on her resemblance to Evangeline Peridot and later, before she killed them, they admitted what they had done."

"You *killed* them?" Stephen said in a shocked whisper.

"Juliette was very frightened," she continued, ignoring Stephen. "The men knew she was alone and recalling what had happened to Mother—I mean to me and the children—she was terrified that a similar fate would befall her and her son. She would have run away if she could, but she bore in mind a piece of excellent advice you had once given her, Thomas."

"Me?"

"Yes, dear. You had instructed her to run from danger only if she could be sure that an escape was possible. Otherwise it was important to stay and stare the danger right in the face. Juliette had no way of escaping, not carrying an ill child, so she took the old tupara down from the shelf, made sure that these were the men who killed me, and then shot them both."

"What did she do with the bodies?" asked Stephen faintly.

"She put them in the privy and dumped rocks on top of them."

"She did that? Little Juliette did that? Why did she never tell me?" wondered Thomas.

"She never told anybody. Not even those she loved and trusted. You see, she doubted whether she had done the right thing and was afraid. In killing those men she became a murderess too."

"No!" said Thomas. "It was utu. She had to do it. I must see her and thank her. She has not been to visit me yet. . . . I don't understand that . . . never mind, I shall send for her."

"No!" said Juliette quickly. She glanced up at Stephen for help.

"Juliette is away . . . in New Plymouth at the moment," said Stephen. "I will tell her when she returns."

"I'll be gone then. It will be too late to thank her."

"She will understand," said Juliette. "She loves you."

His expression cleared. "I know. When she comes back, Stephen, you must give her my mere. I would like her to have it. Do you think it would be a fitting reward for avenging my Evangeline?"

"A mere! Oh, Thomas, your life's dream come true! Why, even Captain Cook himself was unable to get one. But who gave it to you? Where is it? May I see it?"

"It's on the dresser." Stephen brought it over and placed it near his hand.

Juliette picked it up. A magnificent mere, flat, emerald, and so translucently thin that the veins in the greenstone glowed as though alive. The handle and one curve had been carved with intricate scrollwork fine as any tattoo, and from the base of the handle dangled a tuft of precious black and white huia feathers.

"Oh, Thomas! I always knew that you were deeply loved and respected by the Maori people, but until this moment I never realised how important you have been to them. Those chiefs must truly love you. I feel so touched . . . so proud of you."

"There, now. Don't cry. Do you think that Juliette will like it? I admit that the mere is the only material thing in this whole life that I have ached to possess; but it is a meagre gift indeed when compared with what she has done for me."

"Juliette has been compensated already."

"How?"

"For years she was plagued by terrible nightmares, but they stopped as soon as the utu was completed. Never since that day has she been disturbed in the night."

A sound had drawn Stephen to the window. He turned suddenly and said, "We must go now."

"No," pleaded Thomas, groping for her hand. "Please stay a little longer."

"I cannot." He looked so stricken that she found herself adding, "Be patient, dear. We will be together again soon." Bending over him, she pressed her lips to his cheek. Turning his head awkwardly, he found her mouth. She fought the urge to pull away, reminding herself that for the moment she was Evangeline. It was the oddest sensation. "Soon, dear," she whispered, then she and Stephen were out of the room and swiftly walking along the corridor to where the carriage was waiting out of sight behind the stables.

Stephen was still watching her with the same flat gaze when later, back at the house, she poured them both glasses of honey-coloured sherry and set sugar biscuits onto a blue and white china plate. He said nothing when she thanked him for his help. He said nothing when she explained that the children were with Gladys and would not

be back until dark. Even when she said it was good of him
to invent the excuse that she was in New Plymouth he did
not reply.

She handed him his glass and sat opposite him on one of
the pretty parlour chairs. He refused a biscuit. They sipped
their sherry in silence.

Finally she could bear it no longer. "I knew that you
would be angry. Now can you understand why I had to
keep everything from you?"

"I'm angrier than you can possibly imagine." Glass in
hand, he strode to the window where he stood for a long
time with his back to her. Abruptly he turned, his face
cold. "Why didn't you tell me? I was there! I was there just
after it happened, wasn't I? You were worn out, distraught, your hands in tatters. That was not from gardening—I knew that at the time. That was from disposing of
the bodies, wasn't it?"

"Stephen, please . . ."

"In the name of Jove, what a thing to do with them!
Where did you come by an idea like that?"

"From young Leigh."

"You mean he *helped* you?"

"Of course not. But he gave me the idea. I remembered
how he kept throwing things down there. . . . It's just as
well. I would never have had the strength to bury them."

"But why didn't you tell me that day? Why, Juliette?
Our lives would have been so different if only you had seen
your way clear to confiding in me."

"Would they?" she said bitterly. "Would our lives have
been different if you knew I was a murderess?"

"What you did is hardly the same thing as . . ."

"It's all the same thing. I recollect your views on that.
You regard all taking of life as criminal, you told me so
years ago when you explained why you would never fight
in a war. And don't you remember what you said to me
when I was so ashamed of having young Leigh out of wedlock? 'It's not so bad,' you said. 'It's not as though you've
killed somebody.' Yes, your very words. You said that to
me again, after I *had* killed somebody—two somebodies!
Really, Stephen, can you blame me for keeping silent? I
dreaded the thought of a trial, gaol . . . perhaps being

hanged, and young Leigh growing up knowing terrible things about me. Who'd have looked after him? Aunt Maire, no doubt. Do you think I could endure the thought of that? Really, Stephen, you're not being fair when you insist I should have told you. I'm a *murderess*. How could I have confessed that to you?"

He said, "You keep repeating that as though it was the only thing that mattered in your life."

"At the time it was. Right now it is."

"And all the years between?"

"I never thought of it. I suppose that makes me even worse."

"Not at all. Don't you think that I have sufficient imagination to realise what your fate would have been if you had not killed those men? Of course I do. We both know that you had no alternative. Self-protection is hardly the same thing as an aggressive act of murder."

She refilled her glass. After a long, reflective pause she said, "That is the crux of it. How do I really know what would have happened? At the time I thought they would kill me, and I saw that as the only outcome, but afterwards I was not so sure. I killed them partly for a trivial reason—only it didn't seem so at the time."

"Oh?"

"They were saying vile things about Mother . . . they used it as an excuse for what they did. I couldn't stand to hear their accusations—and that's when I pulled the trigger." She looked at him and noticed that his face was carefully non-committal. "I found out later that what they said was true."

"Oh?"

"You knew about Mother all the time, didn't you? When I heard Aunt Maire gossiping at the wedding and you insisted that I tell you everything she had said, that was because you already knew about her."

"People talk, and we should take no notice."

"What people do reflects on their children, surely? What she was like reflects on me, and these terrible things I've done will reflect on Leigh and May."

"Rubbish!" he told her crisply. "You have no right to judge your mother in any way *except* as a mother. She treated you well, didn't she? Even those Mission ladies most spitefully jealous of her beauty and her pretty clothes had to grudgingly allow that she was an exemplary mother to you children. And consider how your father still loves her. He has been married to Mama for eighteen years, and now that he is dying all he can think of is that soon he will be with his beautiful Evangeline again. Don't you think that devotion counts for something? You cannot dismiss her as unworthy because she has been discovered to have had a few human weaknesses."

"You're right. I forgave and understood her a long time ago, and at the same time my own doubts seemed to vanish. It is odd how we can look back and see truths that should have been clear at the time we needed to see them. If only the truth would advertise itself a little more distinctly!"

"There is no such thing as the absolute truth. Even great religious truths are coloured by men's opinions and change with time."

"Some truths do not," she said as she refilled her glass. "The way I feel about you, for example." Gracious! This was a day for confessions. She could no longer meet his eyes but she pursued the thought frankly. "I must have loved you since that day long ago when Leigh bullied me and took my Christmas penny. I can still remember how you looked, pushing those girls on the swing, and how you told me not to cry. I was terribly impressed that a grown-up gentleman should bother to help a bratty little girl who had landed herself in a pickle. From that time you have had your own place in my heart, yet because of a foolish infatuation I did not realise the significance of my feelings for you."

"You *were* a bratty little girl, too, your face smeared and your mitten torn, yet proud as a boy of the way you had whacked Leigh over the ear!" He laughed and bent suddenly, placing his hands one on each arm of her chair and lowering his face to brush a kiss onto her brow. It was a light, almost absent-minded gesture meant as a tender recollection of the people they both once were, but as he lowered his face she turned hers up to meet it in a hopeful ture, and instead of forehead his lips found her warm, starving mouth.

"I love you," she whispered as her arms wound gently about his neck.

He groaned as though in pain, hesitated, then returned the kiss.

Her eyes closed and she stopped thinking. The day was blurred, befuddled. So much had happened. Too much, far too much for one day. The nerve-stretching interviews, tears, bitterness and recriminations, the raking up of past unalterable events, the torment of seeing Thomas so close to death. It was all a dream, and this was a dream too, Stephen with his arms about her, Stephen dragging her out of the chair with a desperate hunger and pressing her against him, Stephen kissing her with such fervour that she realised—it was miraculous but true—he had been as sick with longing for her as she was for him. Was it in a dream that she responded dizzily, clinging to him? It must be, it must be. Real life could not be so unbearably vivid, the sensations so acute that she felt she must cry out if he touched her. In real life Stephen would not kiss her like this, not pick her up, bunching her crinolines with practised expertise, nor would he prop her against the bedpost and swiftly unloop the dozens of covered buttons down the front of her dress while she gazed at him from a great dreamlike distance, wondering at it all.

"Sweet Olivine," he whispered, making it real.

His fingers found the ribbons that tied her petticoats and the laces that tightened the corset about her waist. This morning she had dressed with special care. She was now foolishly thankful that she had worn her best camisole and crinoline cover, both trimmed with broderie anglaise and threaded with narrow pink ribbons. While he stripped the dress and undergarments from her she shivered mutely—not from cold—and watched his strong brown hands, fearing to speak in case a word from her might turn this back into a dream again. His hands were rough against her skin as he dragged the coverlet back and bundled her into the bed. Her throat was too dry to swallow, her limbs had no strength of their own. She closed her eyes, waiting, and it occurred to her that she had waited all her life for this to happen—all her life, and now that the moment was so close the waiting seemed intolerable. When she felt his breath on her cheek she opened her eyes again. By now she was so lulled into a state of happiness that it was with a disquieting jolt that she looked into his face and saw there an expression of anguish.

"Stephen!" In concern she placed a hand on his cheek. "What is it? What's the matter?"

His voice sounded tortured too. "Forgive me, sweet Olivine. It shouldn't be like this."

"But, Stephen," she said, frightened, "I love you."

His face was bleak. "I cannot bear the pain. I cannot stand it. Sweet Olivine, please forgive me."

"But why . . ." she began but the question was smothered uncompleted as his mouth covered hers. Tenderly she stroked the side of his face and tried to recapture her evaporated happiness but now her mind was flooded instead with anxiety. Why was he so desperately unhappy? What was wrong? This was not how she had imagined it might be if Stephen ever made love to her. This was no drowsy ecstasy filled with loving, leisurely caresses. This was the grappling of an agonised being who clutched her with rough, fervent hands in such panic that he seemed driven by the fear that at any time she might be torn away. Goaded by some unknown torment, he urgently slipped off her last garments and lay pressed against her, gasping, his skin scorching her and hands trailing ripples over her skin. She was afraid to speak, afraid almost to breathe. His skin was silky as a child's yet knotted with muscles which surged under her fingers as she clasped her hands behind his back. The coarse, springy hair on his chest grated on her breasts. But despite his desperation and her fear she welcomed him. Willingly she clasped his thighs with hers and when he pierced her she was momentarily overwhelmed by such a strong sense of coming home that she cried out.

He misunderstood her and asked distractedly against her hair, "Did I hurt you?" She shook her head, dumb with happiness. It seemed to Juliette that the room closed in on them, wrapping them together in a haze of shadows. Gentleness welled up within her and her heart bled tenderness, but he was unreachable and separate, still raging with unabated violence. Oddly she felt no pain, not even when he thrust into her with such force that he seemed to be trying to break loose from unseen demons that tormented him. She soothed, silently caressed, but he did not seem to notice. When it was finally over and he clung to her, shuddering, she had the distinct feeling that she was actually comforting him, a child awoken from some terrible nightmare.

Her bliss lasted beyond the next afternoon when the *Mondrich Princess* sailed on the full tide. Stephen had left fairly hurriedly after the love-making but she understood and was calm. Of course he had a thousand matters of business to attend to. Of course he must go before Gladys brought the children back. Of course he wanted to see Thomas again. . . . Her happiness was untouched by this flurry of embarrassed excuses. She understood perfectly that someone like Stephen—a man of impeccable honour—could hardly seduce his brother's wife (or be seduced by her) without suffering an unpleasant attack of conscience afterwards. She understood, and did not mind. He had acknowledged the depths of his feelings for her and that was the only matter of importance. Even if such an interlude never occurred again she would always have today's experience to remember.

Juliette deliberately chose not to dwell on the many false notes—Stephen's dull tiredness all day, his expression of anguish, the uncharacteristic violence in his manner, and the speed with which he made his farewells afterwards. So elated was she that none but beautiful thoughts entered her mind.

Samuel came to see her the morning after Stephen's departure, bringing a thin package which he said was her revenue from Richmond Line profits.

"How is Father?" asked Juliette, tucking it into her fob. A letter, she guessed. A personal note from Stephen, sealed and importantly secretive-looking.

"Much better, surprisingly. You know, if he was well enough to argue he'd not let Dr. Havow within a mile of him, let alone submit to being his patient, but I have to admit that he's doing Father some good. Oh, he's no better in his health but he's content."

"Why, what is he saying?" she could not resist asking.

"He must have had a dream about Mother, I think. He says that she visited him and told him that soon they would be together again. Full of it, he was, his voice glowing almost. You can imagine how delighted Aunt Maire was to hear him talk like that. This has been a nasty blow to her. Fancy. being married to someone for all those years and then when he's dying all he raves about is his first wife."

"I feel almost sorry for her. She's always been good to him."

"Ah, but Mother was beautiful."

"She was."

As he left, Samuel said, "I'm sorry that you didn't get to see Stephen. I was sure he could help you sneak into Fintona somehow, but he said he was sorry, time was too short. Seemed awfully abrupt, actually. Not his usual self at all."

"Never mind," said Juliette. "I've accepted the fact that my presence in the sickroom would only be upsetting."

"That's the funny thing. Father kept saying what a wonderful daughter you were. He's changed his attitude completely."

She stiffened her face to hide the smile. "You mean Abby."

"No, you. Juliette. He repeated it several times. Makes it a real pity that you can't get in to see him."

"Indeed it is," she agreed.

When he had gone she leaned against the door and broke the seals on the package. She was right. It was a letter, but only a very brief one.

Dear Juliette,

I know it is presumptuous of me to beg your forgiveness but please try to pardon my inexcusable lapse of behaviour on the occasion of our meeting yesterday. I find it deplorable to realise that I should have been so blinded to all decency and honour that I could weaken as I did and give in to feelings of the moment. It is my abject hope that you will judge me less harshly than I must judge myself. Please try to forgive me.

Sincerely,
Stephen

"I don't believe it," she whispered, staring at the neatly penned rows of writing. "I simply do not believe this! 'Lapse of behaviour'! 'Feelings of the moment'! Of the moment! Oh, damn you, Stephen Yardley! Damn you, damn you to hell!"

May rushed into the room and hesitated. Leigh strolled past her quite unconcerned. "May wants to know if we can have a sugar biscuit. Are you crying because Grandfather is sick?"

She nodded.

"He is old, anyway," Leigh said callously. "Can we have a sugar biscuit?"

"No, you may not. Now out you go, quickly." She poked the crumpled note into her sleeve, ready to be dropped into the kitchen fire at the first opportunity. Feelings of the moment! How could he be so cruel?

She had to bite back caustic words when Samuel confided after the graveside ceremony that Father had liked Stephen better than any man he knew.

"Really?" was all she allowed herself to say, her face wooden behind the black veil.

"He thought the world of Stephen. Do you know that right at the end he asked that you would promise to take care of him?"

"Me take care of Stephen?" she asked coldly. "Why in the world should I do that?"

"Because of all that he has been through, I suppose. I know that Stephen gives everybody the impression of controlled self-sufficiency, but I think Father was right when he called him a lonely and unhappy man."

"Really, Samuel, I can't imagine why."

"Haven't you heard the news about him? I would have imagined that Jane or Rose would have kept you informed."

"They never discuss their brothers with me." She

stopped on the gravelled sidewalk, the wind plastering the veil over her face. "What is it that I should have heard?"

"That Stephen's wife died, of course."

"Danielle? Oh, Lord, no! When? What happened?"

He looked decidedly embarrassed. "I wish you would ask one of the girls . . ."

"No!" Her fingers dug into his wrist. "You tell me. When did she die?"

"It happened just a few weeks before he was here. . . . Do you recall that I told you he seemed unusually tense and quiet? It would appear that was why. Danielle had died some time before that, so no wonder the poor chap was distraught. He must have been knocked sideways by it because he told nobody, and it was not until the ship had gone that the news spread. His officers told their friends and so on." He handed her up into the crape-ribboned funeral carriage. "Poor Stephen. And now he has a baby son to look after too."

"Did she die in childbirth, then?"

"Some time later," he said with vague unease. "She caught some illness which mothers are susceptible to. Look, you'd best ask Rose or Jane. They know all about these matters."

Thirty-two

Three months after Thomas' death, when Auckland was well into the slushy winter season, Maire sent for Abigail. She asked that she come without the children as there were some extremely important and confidential matters to be resolved, and a quiet atmosphere was needed in which to discuss them.

As she scanned the violet-scented note Abby's first impulse was to refuse. Pregnant again, she was in her most peevish disposition, but even if she had been filled with a radiant kindness her impulse would have been the same. After Thomas' accident she had almost lived at Fintona, and after the funeral she had called on her stepmother daily. But as soon as Thomas' will was read her visits stopped abruptly. As she brooded over the monumental injustices contained in that document, Abby began to suspect that Maire might perhaps have manipulated Thomas into changing it at the last minute. This idea was at first utterly ridiculous but it gained positive credence as the weeks went by and no word came from Fintona. The fact that Maire made no friendly move towards her seemed to underline her guilt.

Reading the note again, Abby decided it was too bad. Today simply did not suit. Aunt Maire was showing no consideration to summon her there at such short notice. She would regretfully decline. If the matters to be resolved were so earth-shattering, then they could wait until it was convenient for her to discuss them. Aunt Maire could rage all she liked. It would do no good.

"You are late, Abigail."

"I'm sorry, Aunt Maire. Hal and Jon . . ."

A flicker of gout-swollen fingers dismissed the remainder of Abby's apology. Tawa set an enormous silver tea tray on the table and stood by, waiting for further orders. When Maire nodded, the Maori woman tucked both hands under the bib of her long starched apron and bustled from the room, turning to close the door behind her. Abby did not even notice; her mind was itching from the burr that the summons had implanted. Why did Aunt Maire want to see her so urgently, and alone?

Her stepmother was in no hurry to enlighten her. As Maire calmly poured tea into gold-rimmed cups, Abby fancied that there was a new tightness about her. She might have expected to see a wilting widow but Maire was more serene and self-possessed than she could recall. Her grooming was impeccable, with even the two white streaks in her hair arranged in perfect symmetry; her black silk gown was stylishly cut, and her voice only faintly wavered with age, as she enquired about each of the children.

"And your husband?" Maire passed the sugar bowl. "I trust that he is in good health?"

"I seldom see him."

"The situation is unchanged then? You must be patient, Abigail. As I told you before, these unfortunate incidents are not uncommon in today's irresponsible society, but they do pass. Mr. Bennington will tire of the girl eventually and when he does you will be thankful that you said nothing."

"I am ill with being patient! This has been going on for so long . . . how many years? Five? Six?"

"Patience, patience."

"It is difficult to exercise patience when he is spending money on her and that brat of hers—money which rightfully belongs to us. That is the bone which sticks in my throat." She gulped her tea in a long mouthful and passed the cup back to be refilled.

"Put it out of your mind," said Maire, passing her the plate of cakes. "Put them down there so that you can easily reach the plate should you want another. Mary baked them especially for you. No, Abigail, you can take comfort in the fact that you are well cared for and respectable. Not like some people we know."

"Juliette, you mean?" asked Abby, a cream cake inches from her mouth. Balancing it on her lap plate, she said with indignation, "It's her own fault if she is received by nobody. She insisted on brazenly returning to Auckland, dragging the boy after her. What else could she expect? It's no wonder Leigh finally abandoned her."

"Personally, I never could understand why Stephen had such sympathy for her," remarked Maire. "He seems to have come to his senses at last, though it took the death of his poor wife to bring that about. I was thankful that on his last visit here he made no attempt to visit her. No doubt she would have inveigled him into smuggling her into Thomas' sickroom. I dread to think what effect that might have had, because he was in such a wretched state of delirium already."

"So I believe." Abby swallowed a mouthful of cake and dabbed her lips with a napkin. "What happened to Stephen's wife? There seems to be such mystery surrounding her illness."

"I think that Stephen felt in some way responsible for it. Some men feel very guilty when their wives die in childbirth."

"Like Dr. Forster? They say he had terrible depression after his first wife died."

"His was with good reason," sniffed Maire. "The man is an incompetent fool. Look at what happened to poor Rose. She all but died too. However, I did warn her, and if people choose to ignore rational warnings . . . But Stephen's wife did not die in childbirth. She was safely delivered of a son while Stephen was on a voyage to San Francisco. Some weeks later she caught a milk fever and died the day before Stephen arrived back in Sydney. It was scarcely his fault. Such a thing could happen to anybody. Still, now he has a son to worry about, so doubtless that will stop him from wasting his sympathies on Juliette."

"Everybody worries about Juliette," said Abby sourly. "I thought it was so unfair the way Father left that valuable mere to Juliette and only a worthless piece of jewellery to me! I sent that brooch to be valued and do you know

what Mr. Jury had the impudence to offer? Four shillings!
Do you have any idea how much that mere must be
worth?"

"Thousands of pounds. Many thousands."

"Exactly. I asked Samuel if he would agree to contest
that part of the will. I mean to say, it's hardly fair that he
should favour her so much above the two of us even if his
financial bequests were more equitable. But Samuel refused to consider the matter. He had the gall to say that
Juliette should keep the mere, because she is the only one
in the family who would never be tempted to sell it! I mean
to say, what is the point of having something so valuable
unless one intends to sell it?"

Maire made a soft clucking noise with her tongue. "I
rather imagined that you might feel like this, and that is
why I sent for you today. I am going to give you an opportunity to redress the wrong which has been done to you."

"And how might that be accomplished?"

"To begin with, I have decided to make you and Leigh
my sole beneficiaries. Mr. McLeay is drawing up a new
will which will divide everything I have between the two
of you. Naturally Leigh will be granted the larger portion
but you will be provided for so handsomely that I think you
could do well to forget your father's will and any injustices
therein. As I said, he was not really himself at all in those
last days."

"But what about Jane and Rose?"

"You, my dear, have been far more dutiful and devoted
than any daughter could be, and more. As one grows more
mature one more clearly understands the value of loyalty
and devotion."

"You have always been very generous to me, and to the
children," said Abby, torn between excitement at the prospect of the enormous bequest that had been hinted at and a
nagging little suspicion that this promise might be used to
extract all manner of services and favours from her.

"I shall continue to be just as generous to you. The new
will shall do nothing to alter that. Now, Abigail," and her
voice smartened up a pace. "I would like you to tell me
something. How fond is Mr. Bennington of Dora?"

"Dora? Well, she is not like the boys, of course, Hal so forceful, Jon so clever . . ."

"Yes," said Maire. "I do not require a complete recital of their talents. Only Dora, please. How fond of her is her father? The truth, please."

"The truth?" Flustered, she reached for a piece of cake with chocolate icing. While she bit into it her eyes moved restlessly around the room. "Very well," she said after she had considered carefully. "The flat truth of it is that he has not paid her a moment's attention since she began to talk. He finds her exceedingly dull—which, I'm sorry to say, she is. Lena is a bright, chattering girl but Dora is always overlooked because she never has anything diverting to say."

Maire nodded, her lips pursed.

"But why do you want to know about her?"

"I need a companion, Abigail. Someone to fetch and carry for me, to see that my instructions are properly carried out. Someone who will grow used to my little ways. Dora will be perfect. I realise that she is only twelve years old but she is mature for her age, biddable, and reads very nicely in a clear voice. All that remained was to find out whether her father would miss her if she came to live here." Noticing that Abby looked a trifle stunned, she decided to be generous. "I assume that you would not object if I rewarded her with a small wage, perhaps a pound a week to begin with?"

"A pound?"

"To be given into your keeping, confidentially, of course."

Dabbing the napkin over her chins, Abby said, "I shall have Nurse pack her things tomorrow. She will be delighted when I tell her the good news." Dora would whine and cry but a slap would fix that attitude. Living with Maire would soon cure her of her sulky, complaining ways. Always asking to be allowed to visit Aunt Juliette again. She'd soon forget Aunt Juliette once she was settled at Fintona.

"Do have another cup of tea, Abigail. The pot is still half full and this Darjeeling is too precious to waste." As Abby passed her cup over Maire noticed that her upper arms were enormous, as thick as the hall umbrella stand.

"Thank you. It *is* refreshing tea."

"You are more than welcome. Your loyalty means a great deal to me, Abigail."

"You can rely on it, Aunt Maire."

"Good. There is one last thing I require of you. This is not a request but an order. Do you understand?"

She could hardly be surprised that Maire wanted more. Dora's company was hardly worth a pound a week and a generous bequest. She looked at Maire enquiringly as she forked up a portion of spongecake.

"You are to make up your difference of opinion with Juliette."

"What?" A crumb sucked down the wrong way and Abby coughed harshly, napkin to mouth, face turning red. When she had recovered sufficiently to speak she said, "You don't understand. I cannot ever reconcile with her. She was abominably heartless when poor darling Alice and dear little Edward died. And then there is the matter of Father's terribly unjust bequest. How can I possibly . . ."

Maire was smiling. "I think that you will do it, Abigail, and do it gladly when I explain. It will be easy for you to pretend. You don't have to be agreeable to her, simply say that Leigh's cousins miss him, tell her anything you please. You don't even have to visit her as long as she suspects nothing. All I want is for young Leigh to be brought regularly here to Fintona."

"Are you saying that you prefer him to my boys?"

"Of course not! But we have a great deal of preparation to do and all of us must help with it. The boy misses his father, doesn't he?"

"Dreadfully. Sister Amy says that he is disruptive and disobedient in class but she forgives him his appalling behaviour because it is so obvious that all he needs is for his father to return."

"And so he shall."

"Leigh is coming home again? To Juliette?"

"Not to Juliette. He is coming to Auckland—in September, he thinks, but it could be later. Nobody must know."

"Why not?"

"Really, Abigail. You can be positively obtuse at times. Because when he comes home he intends to take his son away with him. That is why. And we must prepare the boy for the event without anybody suspecting. Not even him." Seeing that Abby was about to ask another question, she continued, "He must not know because he could inadvertently warn Juliette. What we shall do is bring him here often and mention Leigh constantly to the boy. Show him photographs of his father, speak of him with praise, build up that desire in the lad's mind. When Leigh arrives the boy will leave without looking back."

Abby forked another heap of crumbling cake into her mouth. The expression of pleasure on her face had nothing to do with the food.

"You will help me, Abigail?"

"I should be delighted, Aunt Maire. Positively delighted."

Thirty-three

Summer began early in 1859 with a long dry spell that seemed to suck the moisture out of every living thing. The trees' spring green faded instead of deepening to emerald. Gardens withered and the newspapers were filled with complaints about the annual dust nuisance. Every time a cart or gig passed along the road, a yellow veil of gritty dust drifted over Juliette's house. When Mr. Benks came to trim Stephen's hedges, he was pressed into moving the clothesline to a far corner of the garden beyond the beehives so that the dainty items Juliette preferred to launder herself had at least some chance of drying cleanly.

On the Saturday before Christmas, as Juliette stirred a jelly of grated hard soap and boiling water, she watched May and young Leigh playing together down in that corner, amusing themselves as they competed to toss beanbags into a wicker basket Leigh had pegged on the line. She marvelled, thinking that a few months ago it would have been impossible for Leigh to play for so long without losing his temper. The renewed association with his cousins had sweetened him so much that now she and May actually looked forward to his arrival home from school each day. Children should be enjoyed and appreciated, thought Juliette, as she poured cold and boiling water into a basin and tested the temperature.

As she lathered her hair with the jelly she noticed that May was developing quite a formidable skill with the beanbags. Despite the gap in their ages she was showing a determination to keep up with Leigh in everything; and he, in his good humour of late, seemed happy to encourage her. He seemed proud of the way she always knew what she wanted and would accept no substitutes or excuses. Already she had decided that she would become a nurse—a real, proper nurse. When Juliette pointed out that only nuns could respectably become nurses, May had firmly stated that she would therefore be a nun first. She had been most put out when Sister Amy laughed patronisingly at her solemn announcement the following Sunday.

"Nobody is going to stop me from doing what I want," she declared, her baby face pouting. Juliette silently cheered. No, she thought now as she rinsed her hair with jug after jug of lukewarm water, nobody will disarrange May's life the way I weakly allowed mine to be. She has the courage of her ambitions, whereas I never knew what I wanted, not until it was too late.

So deeply engrossed was she with pondering this idea that when Samuel came whistling around to the porch she wrapped a towel around her hair and asked him without thinking, "Samuel, do you know what you want from life? Really know?"

Dropping his haversack, he answered with a smile, "I want a simple life. Hard work and good food, a little fun to break the monotony . . . and a better welcome than that from my sister when I haven't seen her for months!"

"Oh, Samuel, I am sorry!" and, laughing, she embraced him.

From the garden came the sound of snarling dogs. The quarrel rose sharply to a yelping and the children ran shouting towards the house.

"Oh, I forgot . . . and it appears that Mrs. Tippy likes her son no better this time." He strode down the steps and yelled fiercely at Mrs. Tippy. She immediately came cringing towards him. May rushed to be scooped into his arms.

"Why are you here so early, Uncle Samuel?" asked Leigh, grinning as Samuel ruffled his hair. "Christmas isn't until the end of the week."

"To tell you the truth, I was hard put to think of a good excuse to come to town, but then I decided that it must rain soon, so I'd leave the camp in case it did."

"If it rains this week the pre-Christmas race meetings will all be washed out," said Juliette slyly.

"Race meetings?" said Samuel, all innocence.

Leigh laughed aloud. "You knew about them all the time. That's why you're here, isn't it?"

"You sound as though you know all about it."

"I do! Mother is going to the meeting tomorrow."

"She has a lovely pink dress to wear," announced May. "I want to go too, but I'm not allowed. I have to stay with Mrs. Benks and she won't let me get myself dirty."

"I see. That is a shame. But what's this, Julie? You going to a race meeting?"

"I know. I've not been for so many years that I hate to think about it. But this time it's actually Abby's idea. She suggested it on Thursday when she came to bring the children. It was most out of character; usually the coachman either leaves her brood here or whisks Leigh away for the afternoon. But on Thursday she suggested that a day at the races might be a pleasant outing for me. She's sending the coachman at nine to collect Leigh so I shan't be able to change my mind."

"My! She must be feeling generous!"

"Possibly. I should give her the benefit of the doubt, but this sudden thoughtfulness puzzles me. Come on in and I'll make us some tea." As she sloshed the basin of soapy water under the lemon tree she cautioned, "Please don't leave the door open. I have an enormous bag of honeycomb dripping into a basin and every winged creature imaginable seems to be attracted to it."

"I noticed the lace stretched over the windows as I came along the path."

"Not beautiful, but it's effective at keeping them out. Flies and bees are a menace this year."

"I hope you've not been stung," he said as he carried May indoors.

"No, but Mother was when she opened the beehives!" reported Leigh gleefully.

"And I had to stay inside," said May.

"*You* opened the hives, Juliette? Why didn't you get Mr. Strater in?"

She prodded the fire. "Last year I did that, but he took almost half the honey for his trouble. So this year I made a wee smoke lamp from a cracked teapot and managed quite nicely by myself. You should have laughed had you seen me in my hat all shrouded with muslin, and my funny teapot."

"You *would* have laughed when a bee crawled up Mother's leg!"

"Uncle Samuel doesn't want to hear about that. Off you go outside, both of you, and I'll call you in when it's time to wash your hands."

"Is that the same boy who wouldn't do anything for you at all last winter?" asked Samuel when they had disappeared without one murmur of argument.

"The same boy. He's happy now, that's what it is."

That evening they sat companionably under the apple trees as darkness thickened and the lights woke up in the town below.

"You can still smell the smoke when the wind blows strongly from the north," said Juliette. "It's a frightening odour. After what happened to Father I feel quite differently about fires."

"All they need is to be treated with respect. No reason to be afraid of them. Still, fear is unreasonable. I'm terrified of the ocean, so terrified that I'll never go on another ship no matter what the purpose of the journey. If you can't get there by land, forget it! Others are afraid of heights . . ."

"Or Maoris. Remember how Jane was . . . is still, I suppose? Gladys is much the same. She coaxes Leigh into reading the alarmist stories in the newspapers."

"Not so alarmist."

"The Seftons seem to think it will come to nothing. The three oldest boys have joined the Volunteer Brigades and go into town every weekend for training, but they merely regard it as a great lark. And Mrs. Sefton says that the forts being constructed all around the countryside will never be used for anything other than grain stores. Why are you looking so parson-like? Don't you agree with her?"

"Do you recollect that game we used to play down by the sea wall at the Mission? The one where one person smacks another lightly, then that person responds a little more briskly and so on, until it escalates into a real fight? What was that game called?"

"Slapsticks. I hated it. Abby always used to pick on me and slap me so hard the first time that there was never any contest. I always gave up immediately. But what about it?"

"Father had a theory that the Maori tribes are playing that game with us. They can't make up their minds whether they like us being in New Zealand or not."

"Isn't it a bit late for that?"

"Of course it is, but that's not the point. You know how the Maoris love drama, and it's a long time since the Treaty and the Bay of Islands war. At the moment they are making a lot of fuss about whether they will try to scour us all out of New Zealand—the fact that they couldn't possibly do it is quite incidental to the argument. But the danger is that, with all this talk of Maori kings and unity against the pakeha, they are becoming so bound up with the idea of their own power that they are actually believing those doctrines of theirs. Father said that the tribes will never settle until there has been a full-scale trial of strength, which would be a tragedy, a terrible tragedy. I thought Father was being uncharacteristically pessimistic; now I think he was right. It's inevitable, Juliette, and it's very close. I see it in the faces and the manner of those Maoris I've been trading with recently and, quite frankly, I doubt whether there will be many more trade expeditions into the Waikato now."

"The Waikato? But that's right on our doorstep!"

"Relax! They are a lot farther away than you may imagine, and besides, their real concern is what is happening in New Plymouth right now. Their main leader, Wirema Kingi, is down there at the moment, I believe. No doubt stirring up whatever trouble he can. No, I can understand the Maoris' fears. Every time I come into town it seems to have gained another hundred houses and a few score more tents. No wonder the Maoris feel more insecure with all the white sails they see arriving every week."

"What will happen to the Seftons?"

"Don't worry about them. The ordinary citizens will be safe. It's the soldiers who will slog it out, and they're there willingly for the pay and for the adventure."

"I hope you're right." She brushed away a moth that

had settled on her sleeve. The darkness was almost complete. In the hedge the cicadas were finishing their long scratchy chorus and all around them was the scent of dry grass and Juliette's lavender cologne. "We had better go inside now. Tomorrow will be a long, full day."

He yawned. "No doubt I shall see a few faces I know."

"And several thousand unfamiliar ones, too. Sometimes as I stroll along Queen Street I cannot believe that this whole place was a wasteland of brown fern. Look at it now! Just look at all those lights."

If Abby's strange behaviour had puzzled Juliette, next morning she was even more perplexed to see her sister outside the main gates of Epsom Race Park in a hansom cab. Gladys pointed her out, and Juliette scoffed, knowing Abby thought hansoms very common. But it was definitely Abby, swathed in baby blue silk, her hair bunched up in a girlish froth of ringlets under a blue cap. It was plain that she had not wanted to be noticed there at her vantage place: when Juliette and Samuel crossed the road to greet her, she made no attempt to be pleasant.

"What a surprise!" said Juliette. "I didn't expect to see you."

Abby kept her eyes on the flow of traffic. "Is there some rule which excludes me from attending?"

"Of course not. Only, you did say that you had planned to do something special with the children today."

"What? Of course, I'll be joining them later. Miss Grymble is bringing them here, I mean."

"Here, to the race meeting?"

"Yes. They wanted to come for an hour or so, and there's no harm in that, so I agreed. Miss Grymble has taken them all in the coach to fetch Dora from Fintona."

"If they're coming here, then I might as well take care of Leigh myself, because . . ."

"Don't you trust Miss Grymble with your son, then?" Abby flicked her the briefest hard glance. "Don't you think a London-trained governess meets your high personal standards?"

"I say there, Abby . . ."

"It's all right, Samuel. I meant no criticism of the governess, Abby, and you know it. My only concern was that she might have more than enough children to worry about without any extra. And you do realise that the boys are inclined to indulge in mischief when they get together?"

"She can manage perfectly well, thank you." She opened her fan and closed it with a clip, still watching the road.

"One more thing, Abby. Leigh mentioned something about going to Fintona, but no sooner were the words out than he looked embarrassed and guilty. I really do think . . ."

Abby cut in angrily, saying, "I don't know what you mean, I'm sure! I have taken him there once or twice with the others when I have gone to visit Aunt Maire and Dora, but there is no secrecy and I do resent the implication. Now, if you will be so kind as to excuse me, I plan to enjoy myself today and you are making it far from easy for me. . . ."

"She certainly is hiding something," said Samuel as he steered Juliette across the thronged roadway.

"Something serious is obviously bothering her," said Juliette slowly. "Something extremely serious, I should think." She raised her head to look at Samuel as she spoke, and as she did so her attention was snagged by the sight of a very familiar figure. Up the road towards them swept Flash Jack Bennington's open landau. Jack himself was seated at the reins waving his shiny black topper to everybody who called out to greet him, and beside him sat Rosaleen Teipa.

Juliette paused, staring, and Samuel looked up too. "I say," he said. "There's Mr. Bennington. And look at that beautiful young lady he has with him! Who is she, do you know?"

Gladys, who had rejoined them at the roadside, answered facetiously, "Why, she's just a young lady he met along the way and kindly offered a lift to." Samuel knew nothing of the scandal and took this remark at face value, staring admiringly. She was part Maori yet obviously someone of class, for she was dressed in the height of style in a dark red sateen gown with a white rose at the breast. Her hair had been artfully coiled into a complicated chignon arrangement so that it appeared as though a shiny black snake was wound around and over itself on the back of her head, and on top of this perched a saucy little frilled white topper. With her dark eyes and perfect oval of a face she was the most beautiful creature Samuel had ever seen. It was incredible that she should be attending the race day alone, but there was no sign of any chaperone. And when Abby suddenly appeared in front of the landau and spoke to the girl, she climbed out alone and walked away into the crowd with impassive dignity.

Gladys giggled and poked Juliette on the arm. "Eeeh, but I'd like to be a fly on the horse's rump now, that I would. Mrs. Bennington's sent her off with a right proper flea in her ear, but I'm wonderin' what Mr. Bennington will have to say about that."

"He's not the first husband to be found out and I dare say he'll not be the last." She glanced around swiftly. "What has happened to Samuel? There's no sign of him."

"Look, there he is." Gladys pointed towards the ticket window under the grandstand. Samuel was standing there in the short queue. By the time they had strolled part of the way towards him he was hurrying back with a fistful of blue and white slips of paper.

He spoke rapidly and excitedly. "Here are some tickets for you both for the first two races. If you are in the main grandstand after that I shall find you there." He nodded to Gladys. "Will you ladies both excuse me?"

"Of course, Samuel. You don't have to stay with us."

With another nod he was away, walking very fast and weaving his way between the groups of people. Gladys looked after him, her face blank with disappointment. "Thanks for the tickets!" she called, but he did not hear her.

Her white parasol with the wreathed trimming was some distance ahead of him. He would have caught up within minutes, but twice was hailed by his campmates who insisted boozily on regaling him with their exploits of the previous evening. In the thick of the crowd it was a wonder he managed to keep her in sight, and hardly surprising when, at the small pavilion grandstand, he lost sight of her completely. He walked a few paces to the rear of the stands, then retraced his steps. Perhaps she had come this way to join her family, and in that case she would be lost to him forever, for the only chance he, a stranger, had of speaking to her was if she was alone. No chaperone would think of permitting such a thing.

It seemed that she had vanished. Samuel swore silently but viciously; then he had to laugh at himself. He, Samuel Peridot, chasing after a young woman he didn't even know and who probably would have wanted nothing to do with him. Smiling at his own foolishness, he strode into the pavilion and looked for a place to sit down.

The girl was there, huddled on one of the seats level with his head. She was crying silently, a handkerchief quickly dabbing away the tears.

"Excuse me, please," said Samuel. He positioned himself on the seat in front of her so that he could look up into her face. "Are you in some kind of trouble? May I be of assistance?"

She looked embarrassed but shook her head firmly and glanced away. Up close she was even more beautiful than he had thought.

"Please don't be angry. I know that it is not proper of me to talk to you, but when I saw you in my brother-in-law's carriage I was so impressed that I had to at least try to talk to you."

"Your brother-in-law?" Her voice was thick as clotted cream, with a soft Maori accent.

"Yes," said Samuel eagerly. "Mrs. Bennington is my sister. Do you know her too?"

The girl's face was suddenly hard and angry. "You got a cheek, coming to talk to me like this. I suppose *she* told you to come."

She began to rise out of her seat and Samuel stood up too, taking her hands and saying rapidly, "Nobody told me to do anything. I followed you because I think you are beautiful, and I cannot for the life of me understand why you should be angry. Why should my sister mind if Mr. Bennington gave you a ride in his carriage? Look here, Miss . . ."

She looked away again, knowing that he wanted her name, but not willing to give it.

He tried again. "My name is Samuel Peridot, if you will permit me to introduce myself, that is."

"Peridot? Not Mr. Paritau's son?"

"That's right."

She smiled and put things right between them at once. "I am Miss Teipa. Rosaleen Teipa. My family thought very highly of your father, Mr. Peridot."

"So did I, Miss Teipa."

She was looking at him with a shrewd expression. "Have you not heard my name before?"

"No. Should I have?"

Smiling evasively, she said, "I wouldn't say no to a cup of tea, Mr. Paritau." And as she descended the steps she tucked a hand into his elbow.

Jack Bennington was not happy. There was a hard white patch around his nose, stretching down to his mouth and across his cheeks. Abby noted it with satisfaction and told him that he looked as though he had been stung on the nose by a bee.

"Or several bees, I should say," she added.

"I am going to turn this carriage around and drive you home at once."

"Do as you like," she said implacably. "I would be here again within the hour. And pray don't go getting any fancy ideas like locking me into my room again. That may have worked when we were first married and I was a stranger in your home, and that poisonous Mrs. Hodges was the combined housekeeper and prison warder. The situation is slightly different now, Mr. Bennington. I give the orders to the servants; I have hired every one of them, and I have the power to arrange all the little things which make their lives comfortable. No, I think that it would be rather a waste of your time to take me home, or to tell them to keep me locked up. They will all be loyal to me this time."

"But what do you want? What are you doing here? You have never come here before, so why put in an appearance now?"

Abby fanned her cheeks languidly. "Enough is enough,

Mr. Bennington. I am tired of being left at home while you attend these social froufrous alone. Besides, this is one of the first occasions I have been able to attend. Do you realise that since our marriage you have arranged to have me with child almost the whole time?"

"Abigail! Do watch your tongue! We are out in a public place!"

"I see. It is all very well for you to do as you please in public but I must be careful with everything, even my speech. Is this to compensate for you, perhaps?" A swift look told her that he was growing very angry indeed so she thought it prudent not to pursue that subject. "Very well, dear. I shall speak of innocuous things today. Are the fashions not pretty this season? I think that the gowns all look like Canterbury bells with the ladies' shoes like little black stamens."

"Oh, bloody hell!" muttered Jack.

She took his arm as they went into the champagne tent. Sipping from a tulip-shaped glass, she gazed around her with enjoyment.

"Ah, Mrs. Bennington!" exclaimed Mr. Antony, a Governor's aide whom Jack loathed. He trotted towards them on dainty booted feet, flashing a yellowish smile. "How very splendid to see you here, Mrs. Bennington. We are not usually honoured with your company on these occasions."

"My husband insisted that I come this time. He promised me that the Governor would be here in person to start the celebrations."

"He will be here shortly, don't you fret!" And he laughed as though he had made a terrific joke.

Jack glared at him. "I thought that our Governor was busy in Taranaki stirring up the blacks."

"We rather think that the trouble has now been settled once and for all," said Mr. Antony with pride. He rocked back on his heels as he spoke. "The Governor publicly paid one hundred sovereigns for a piece of land under dispute, and it seems that everybody is happy about that. The Waikato chiefs and their men were there to see it all. They made no protest, but if they change their minds later that will be rather unfortunate for them, I should think. Colonel Gold and the 65th are there now, keeping an eye on things." He laughed again. "In a way it is a pity that it is all over. Those Maoris are damnably cunning, and some of the things they did to stop the land being surveyed were quite entertaining. Did you hear how they sent the oldest and ugliest women from the tribe to kiss and embrace the surveyors, so that they could not do their work? Wherever these poor fellows turned, there were these grotesque women, tattooed, wrinkled, and stinking of fish oil, pleading to make love to them. It must have been gloriously amusing!" His laughter faded when he noticed Jack's stony face. "Well, well. Perhaps you have heard that story before. Ah, there is the Governor now. A word of warning, Mrs. Bennington. Make certain that you have enough champagne in your glass for two toasts. At the Queen's special request there will be a toast to the Prince Consort as well."

Jack said deliberately, "I'll not raise my glass to that arrogant German swine."

"Mr. Bennington, please!" Abby began to apologise to Mr. Antony, but when she turned to speak to him he had slipped away. Before she could say anything further to her husband, two of the ranking society matrons stood before them. Abby greeted them with hastily smothered dismay. It was plain that Jack was determined to be as disagreeable as possible. Her victory was going to be turned into a hollow defeat by his atrocious behaviour. It was certain that his rudeness would reach the Governor's ears, and if he insulted these two as well she might as well tear up her visiting cards and put away her "at home" invitations. Socially she would be ruined.

"Mrs. Bennington!" they trilled in duet. "How delightful to see you. My, how kind you are to bring your wife with you this time, Mr. Bennington."

Abby let go of his arm and silently prayed that he would go away. He stayed.

It was nightmarish. They chattered idly about the dreadful uprisings in India, and the fears that the Maori tribes might be taking the Indian natives as their examples and be planning to similarly plunder and murder. They discussed the bizarre accident Mrs. Tiary suffered when a bridge had snapped under the weight of her wagon, throwing her out and breaking both her legs. All the while Abby tried to join in the gossip and all the while she was waiting and fearing the comment from Jack that would smash her social prestige into dust. Twice she allowed herself to glance nervously in his direction. What she saw was not reassuring; he was standing calmly by with a bland smile on his face and an unconcealed expression of contempt in his eyes. Abby shivered and jumped back into the stream of the conversation. Perhaps if she ignored him he might go away. If only he would grow bored and drift off to talk to somebody else. He stayed.

When there was a small pause in the talk she said to him quietly, "This must be boring you, Mr. Bennington. Please feel free to join the gentlemen if you wish."

"On the contrary, I am fascinated," he said with a sarcasm that made both matrons raise their eyebrows.

Abby included them both in a sickly, apologetic smile.

Jack said, "Here comes your Governor. Look pretty, dear. I think he is going to talk to you." He spoke very softly in a honeyed tone that made Abby ill with apprehension.

"Why, Mr. Governor, sir!" said one of the matrons with a bob that was almost, but not quite, a curtsey.

"Pray do not allow me to interrupt your conversation."

"You have arrived in time to give us your views on the Princess Royal's new child, sir," said Abby quickly. "Do you not think it splendid that the Queen has become a grandmother?"

"Quite splendid, indeed."

"I don't think it's splendid at all," said Jack loudly. "It was bad enough for the Queen to marry a German upstart, but now her daughter has gone the same rum way. Soon the royal families of all Europe will be crammed with German swine!"

The silence rang in Abby's scarlet ears. Her eyes blurred miserably. The Governor, shocked, had been about to nod curtly and leave them; but on noticing her distress he paused and asked kindly, "I believe that you yourself were blessed with a son recently, Mrs. Bennington. What have you named the child?"

Abby blinked and looked at her husband, her heart cold

with impotent rage. "I decided to name him Kendrick, sir, since the name Patrick was already taken. If it had been a girl Mr. Bennington planned to name her Rosaleen."

There were probably thirty people within earshot, and all thirty had been already struck silent by the brazen insolence of Jack Bennington's loud remarks. Now the unexpectedness of Abby's announcement made them gasp collectively. Jack's face bleached like bone. Those who could see his expression began to titter. The Governor smiled, pleased by the neatness of the put-down. Someone farther back in the tent called, "Bravo, Mrs. Bennington!" and there was a spattering of applause. Jack turned stiffly and walked away, and the whole tent erupted into laughter. It was a truly extravagant joke, the laugh of the season. Everybody thought it riotously amusing except Abby. She stood clutching her quivering glass, watching her husband's back through eyes filled with tears.

Juliette and Gladys found a shady position in the upper half of the main grandstand, high up near the rafters where the breeze was cooling and the view excellent. From here they could see the entire course, most of the crowd, and the notice board where the payouts were tabulated. Juliette studied the programme she had been given at the gate, deciding to make a serious business out of choosing which horses should take responsibility for her threepenny bets. Gladys had a more successful hit or miss system, so instead of pondering her choices she hopefully scanned the crowd for a glimpse of Samuel. One of the tickets he had bought them had won the handsome dividend of six shillings, and she wanted to share the good fortune with him.

"Samuel won't expect you to do that. Put it all on the next race or keep it to spend later."

"Do you think that Mr. Peridot has forgotten all about us?"

Noting her downcast face, Juliette understood. With gentle pity she said, "He has been away from town for months and there are probably a hundred people here who would like to talk to him. Maybe he's over at the far slope talking to some of his Maori friends. He feels more at ease in their company than he does in ours, I'm afraid. Look, why don't you go and place the next bets? I shall wait here for you."

"Will you be all right, ma'am?"

"Perfectly. Now off you go."

Below and to the right of the main pavilion were the gaily decorated champagne tents where a delicious buffet would be laid out for invited guests. Beyond that was the Royal Pavilion, where guests could watch the races from the comfort of padded chairs, and where waiters circulated with drink trays. Society throats were not permitted to become dry, nor society appetites unsated. From her high vantage point Juliette watched the lacy parasols and the dove-grey toppers, the frock coats and swaying crinolines. In the space of a few minutes she recognised more than a dozen people she had once known, people who today would pretend that they had never seen her before. Yet if her life had been only slightly different she would have been mingling with that elegant crush instead of finding her place here with the seamstresses, washerwomen, and farmers' wives. As she surveyed the groups of fashionable people she saw Rose and Dr. Forster chatting to the Governor and his lady while they strolled from one shady awning to another. The Governor plucked a flower from the garlands draped along the tent posts and handed it to Rose with a hint of a bow. Rose tipped her head back, laughing, and Juliette hastily turned away though there was no danger she might be noticed. All pleasure in the day had gone. Suddenly she badly wanted to be home, where she could sit in the garden and watch the children and never have to think about everything that had been closed to her.

When Gladys arrived back, Juliette had almost conquered her treacherous feelings of self-pity. The girl had such an odd look on her face that Juliette asked, "What is it? Have you seen that straying brother of mine?"

"No, ma'am. I ain't seen him. It's the Captain I seen. Captain Yardley."

"Oh." Her heart sank. "I hope that he didn't see you."

"Oh yes, he did, ma'am. But it were you he was looking for. Said that he called at the house an' then went to our house an' me da told him where we was. Real lucky he was, I reckon, to find us in this crowd."

"Very fortunate."

"He said he'd wait for you over in the gardens, at one of them little tables where they're servin' Devonshire teas. Eeeh, but he must be anxious to see you, ma'am. Walked all the way from the town, he did, because there weren't no coaches to be had."

Juliette made no move to rise and a moment passed. Gladys, who stood waiting to accompany her, said, "He looked real serious, ma'am. He said you might not wish to see him and, if so, would I please tell you it was important news about Mr. Yardley."

"Leigh?"

"That's all he said, ma'am."

He had chosen a quiet table hedged in on two sides by thickly flowering hydrangea bushes.

"I ordered coffee for a change." He spoke cheerfully as he helped her into her chair.

"Coffee would be delightful, thank you." She took her cue from him, acting as if they were friends who enjoyed each other's company every day. "Samuel will be pleased to see you. He's somewhere about."

"He may have been here earlier, but as I turned in at the gates I saw him riding towards town in an open gig with a young Maori lass. A stunning-looking girl, beautifully dressed too. She was hanging onto his arm and he looked as pleased as my cabin cat with one of the ship's rats."

"Oh, poor Gladys. I think she is rather sweet on him."

"Speaking of Gladys, why are you here with her?"

"What do you mean?" She glanced towards the long trestle table under the oak trees where Gladys was drinking tea with her friends.

"I mean exactly that. Why have you come to one of the most important events of the year with only your maid-servant for company? You should be over in the enclosure with Rose and Jane and their friends."

"Should I indeed?" she asked in a strange little voice.

"Yes, you should. It's not right that you . . ."

"Please leave the subject be."

"My sisters have not snubbed you, have they?"

"No, they have not, and there is no call for you to look so angry. I cannot help the way society is, and I cannot change it. While I admit that, yes, I would like very much to be over in the enclosure, there's no reason why you should feel sorry for me. My only concern is for the children. I dread the thought that they might be slighted or treated badly because of me, and that is the reason that I am considering moving. Naturally I have no way of knowing whether I would be socially acceptable anywhere else, or even if I am able to leave Auckland without Leigh's permission, so if you have news of him, please let me have it. Have you seen him somewhere? Is he coming home, perhaps?"

"He is there now—at least, I think he is. I called at Fintona this morning to see Mama and as I walked up the path a bearded figure rose from a chair on the verandah and hurried around the corner of the house. I gave pursuit and called out to him but there was no sign of anybody in the rooms along that wing. Later I asked Mama if Leigh was there. She told me the very idea was nonsense—why should he be skulking about like a criminal? Why indeed? I wondered, but it puzzled me. So on the way out I calmly asked Tawa if she would please give my brother the message that I expected him on board the *Mondrich Princess* for drinks at seven. She said, 'Very good, Master Stephen,' and I said casually, 'What do you think of Leigh's beard? Did it tickle when he gave you a kiss for hello?' She laughed and then suddenly looked frightened and said, 'No, Master Stephen, Leigh's not here.' It's obvious he is, and it's obvious he wants to have his presence kept a secret." Looking directly at her, he said, "But I want you to go there and see him. I'll take you if you like, now."

"What for?"

"I want you to ask Leigh for a divorce. Now. Today."

Flustered, she spread her hands appealingly and said, "I've thought of doing that, but do you have any idea of the horrible things I would have to prove against him in order to obtain a divorce? And then there is the matter of our Catholic wedding service. Oh, Stephen, I have thought of all this before but I am caught in a hopeless situation."

"I realise the hurdles look formidable, but you have no

marriage at all now and Leigh shows no intentions of wanting to return. Therefore I think it eminently possible that he may agree to a separation, at least."

She said slowly, "Why are you so insistent on this, Stephen? Why, after all this time, are you wanting to help me?"

"Why, after the way I treated you, you mean. I'm sorry, Juliette. I hated myself for months after that day. I was boorish, rough, I bullied you into it, never pausing to consult your feelings. Afterwards I felt so dreadful that I couldn't get away from you fast enough."

"So there were no urgent matters to attend to?"

"Just my wretched conscience. Sweet Olivine, to me you are something precious and beautiful, yet that day I treated you like a . . ."

"No."

"You don't sound in the least angry."

She stared into her cup and spoke so softly that he had to bend his head forward to catch the words. "I would not have missed that afternoon no matter what the price." Her head stayed bowed; all he could see of her were the ruffles on the top of her bonnet.

"Nor would I," he admitted. "But if you knew what miseries I have suffered over that afternoon . . ."

"As I did when your letter arrived. I hated you then."

"Hated me?" he asked, genuinely surprised.

"It seemed terribly cruel to describe what happened as a regrettable 'lapse of behaviour,' but when I heard the news about Danielle I understood at once. Realising what a terrible time that was for you helped me to perceive the reason for your distress. I was so very sorry to hear about her death."

"It was not very pleasant." For a long time he said nothing, staring moodily up into the branches of the trees as he tapped his fingers on the table top. "I blamed myself," he said. "We had quarrelled before I went away on that last voyage. She had nursed her mother for years, giving her all her time, constantly keeping her company, feeding and bathing her, getting up in the night to her . . ."

"What a wonderful sacrifice."

"A needless sacrifice. We argued often because I saw no

reason for her to tire herself out with the heavy tasks when I could have hired a dozen nurses. Every time I did employ somebody Danielle concocted a pressing reason to get rid of them. She enjoyed the feeling of martyrdom, or so I would say when I came home yet again and found another nurse gone and Danielle exhausted. It reminded me of the time I found you at the Seftons', haggard and almost dead on your feet. No matter how I coaxed, pleaded or insisted, the situation never improved. Then, when her mother died, Danielle slid into a depression and only came out of it when she found that she was expecting young Stephen. For several months she was happy and lively. She even agreed to have a holiday over here. When her time was close I decided to stay ashore. She insisted I go on that last voyage because I would be back in plenty of time, and then we quarrelled very bitterly. All the other unhappy disagreements were raked up and slung at each other. In the end I left feeling furious. The baby arrived weeks earlier than expected, she became ill, and when I disembarked again in Sydney it was to find that I was a father and a widower all in one blow. It was dreadful to have parted from her in anger and never have the chance to make amends." He looked at her and said, "This conversation is becoming far too morbid."

"Regrets are senseless pain," she said.

"True. One learns to stop blaming oneself eventually, I suppose, but I've not reached that fortunate state yet." He stood up and helped her with her chair. "Let's go and see if I have better luck finding a carriage for the journey back to town than I did on the way out."

Seated companionably in a hansom, he told her, "This is ridiculous, Olivine. We should have been married years ago, you and I. Do you know that there are only two things in my entire life which I regret not doing? Both of them are immoral."

"What are they?" She smiled.

"One is that I did not kidnap you from the Seftons, forcibly carry you away. I should never have allowed you to send me away that day."

"And the second?"

"The second is that I am not in the process of eloping with you now."

"It would be a little difficult to kidnap me at this very moment. I would not be able to leave without the children and, though May would be easy enough to collect, Leigh is . . ."

"What is it?"

She stared at him, not seeing him, her face drained and white. "Oh, God, Stephen . . . I think I know why Leigh is being so furtive about being here. Oh, please, I hope I'm mistaken!"

"Mistaken about what?"

"Suppose Leigh is hiding out at Fintona because he intends to take his son away? Suppose my dear sister Abby has helped to make the plan possible, and that Aunt Maire thought up the idea in the first place? Oh, Stephen, let's hurry there as fast as we can and, please, God, let me be wrong!"

"I cannot imagine what you are talking about," said Maire. Stephen had marched into the house without going through the formality of knocking on the door. With Juliette in tow he strode through one room after another until he found Maire in her bedroom. She was seated at the bureau in front of a large mirror. Her gown was protected by a swathed muslin cape, and her magnificent black and silver hair flowed over it. A nervous European girl was plaiting sections of hair for the evening's elaborate style. Maire watched every move critically in the glass.

"I am referring to my brother. You remember him, Mama. That irresponsible, hopelessly spoiled mother's boy who has made a career out of throwing away money and ruining people's lives. Leigh Yardley, his name is."

The servant looked up at the name. Maire saw her in the mirror and whacked her sharply on the ankle with a long cane. The girl gasped and bent her head over her task.

"There is no point in badgering me. I told you that he has not been here."

He moved around so that he could look right into her face. "The *Mondrich Princess* berthed this morning with a full cargo of store goods for the Peridot Emporiums. Bolts of Italian velvets, Chinese silk, porcelain from Holland, the best of British pots and pans, bonnets from France . . . No, I'm not exaggerating. This is the order you have been waiting for. With these goods you will be able to carry out your policy of offering higher-quality articles than any of your competitors can hope to find. I put myself out for you, Mama. I felt sorry for you, losing Thomas. He was the best friend you have ever had. He could see those venomous glands of yours and he liked you in spite of them. He admired your good qualities and ignored the rest of you. You were fortunate to have him, Mama, and I felt so sorry when he died that I made a real effort to buy you a truly dazzling array of goods."

"The French parasols . . . did they arrive?"

He nodded. "All there. What a pity you will be seeing none of them."

"What do you mean?"

"I mean that one good deed deserves another, and one filthy deed also deserves another. Merrington's head office in Sydney heard about this shipment and sent a representative along to negotiate a price for the whole cargo. Most impressive. The Mondrich Line will make an awesome profit from what they offered." He nodded to his mother. "Good day to you, Mama. I'll be on my way back to Sydney now."

"But you can't do that!" She put a hand up to stop him.

"Can't break a business contract or be as deceitful as you? Come now, Mama. I'm your son, remember? My, but you seem to be having difficulty recalling your sons today."

Maire glared at his reflection with sudden defeat. "Leigh was here. He was here for three days but he has gone now."

"Where did he go?"

She shrugged. "How should I know? I don't know which port he chose to leave from nor what his destination was."

Juliette's voice croaked under the strain. "Where's my son?"

Maire's lips pressed together.

"Mama! Juliette asked you a question!" snapped Stephen as the silence stretched out.

Grudgingly Maire said, "The boy wanted to be with his father. His father had every right to take him."

Though Juliette had guessed what the outcome of this interview would be, the news still struck her a numbing blow. Unable to speak, she was conscious of two things: Stephen's arm supportively about her shoulders, and the mirrored gleam of triumph in Maire's eyes.

Stephen bent his head and muttered, "Don't let her see she's upset you. Hold on tightly." Aloud he said, "We shall find them easily. You can be certain of that."

"Oh? And then what will you do? I tell you truthfully, the boy wanted to go with his father. In front of Judge Benham he said so."

"You had the judge here to witness this cruel business? I can scarcely believe it. What an abysmal, rotten . . ."

"She's probably right," whispered Juliette despairingly. "Leigh would have gone willingly, and there is nothing at all that we can do."

"There you are," said Maire. "Even she knows when she is beaten." Her glance seemed to dismiss Juliette once and for all.

"Very well, it is done and cannot be undone. But what you did was a terrible thing. Not just to Juliette, but to the boy. Has it not occurred to you that he needs a proper father? Even a blindly indulgent mother like you must see how ill suited he is to bring up a son alone."

"You always were unjust in your attitude to your brother."

"Mama, I shall argue no further, but neither will I return. You and I have completed our dealings. Our association is over. Merrington's will have the cargo and any other cargoes of ours that they fancy. I feel confident that the White Star Line or some other will import your goods for you—at a price, no doubt, but their service is reputedly excellent. Good day, Mama."

"Come back, Stephen! I'm not finished talking to you."

"Goodbye, Mama."

"Stephen!" She banged the cane loudly on the floor. "Stephen! I want to talk to you!"

In the hansom he tried to console her. "Say what you

want me to do to help and I'll see to it at once. Shall we begin a search?"

"I don't think it would be much use, do you? Aunt Maire
seemed very confident. I inferred from her attitude that
they were long since gone. Leigh would have planned his
departure well." She said hopelessly, "In any case, do you
think it would do any good if they've had a judge there and
everything? Young Leigh won't want to come willingly.
He idolises his father, absolutely adores him."

"I hate to give up, and if there's any chance at all . . ."
She shook her head miserably, so he suggested, "Shall we
pack your things and have them delivered to the ship?
Would you like to come away with me now?"

"I'd love to. I'd love to go away from this place and never
return. But I hate to give up, too, and I know that Leigh
will be bored with his son in a short time. Do you think
then that I might have a chance of getting him back?"

"Without consulting a lawyer—which I shall do first
thing in the morning—I can't be sure. But if we find them
and the lad does want to come home, and if we can prove
that he is not being properly cared for . . ." Noting her sudden anguish, he said, "I don't imagine that Leigh will have
a home as such. He'll probably take the boy to hotels,
rooming houses, and so on. Actually, the more I think
about it the more positive I feel. Young Leigh is certain to
become homesick after a spell and that will cause difficul-
ties."

"I can't imagine that his father will have sympathy with
homesickness. But he will miss us, and Skippy. That dog
even goes to school with him . . . I mean *went* . . . Oh, but
I'm going to miss him so terribly. . . ." She shook her head
against feelings of weakness. "Right now I am in the grip
of a hideous anger. Perhaps it would be as well if you let
me off at the corner of Parnell Rise. The angrier I am the
easier it will be to say what I must."

"You are going to visit your sister?"

Juliette nodded. "I blame neither Leigh nor Maire too
harshly. Abby is the really treacherous one here. She pretended a concern for young Leigh and made a truce with
me for the sole purpose of helping them steal my son. I'd
best see her now, and if she's not home I shall wait in her

parlour for her. Do you know what hurts most of all?" she
asked, her face still. "Abby has always had everything she
wanted—beauty, money, servants, a position in society,
Father's affection. And yet with all that she can display
such small-minded meanness. For the life of me I cannot
understand why she hates me so viciously."

"Then ask her," said Stephen, rapping with his cane on
the roof of the cab.

Juliette planned to say that she had come personally to
collect Leigh, and then see what her sister said. But when
she was actually there in the parlour confronted by the
sight of Abby chewing on a thick slice of pink cream cake,
she was too angry for anything but a direct approach.

"Why did you do it?" she demanded.

"Do what?" Abby relaxed against the cushions of the
purple velvet sofa.

"You know exactly what. How helpful you were, how
pleased to think of me going out for the day to enjoy myself, how dismayed to actually see me there after you had
carried out your filthy little part of the plan . . ."

"Really, Juliette!" She rang a little brass bell on the
tray. "I shall have to have you escorted to the door, I'm
afraid. You cannot come here and make scenes in my
house."

Juliette ignored her. "To think that I felt sorry for you
when your husband arrived with his paramour! No wonder
he finds another woman more congenial if you are really
as vicious and spiteful as you have demonstrated today."

"How dare you? You, with all you have done! What do
you think the people of Auckland say about you? I feel
ashamed to be your sister! At least I've helped young
Leigh by sending him away from you. I'm not in the least
sorry about it, either. Do you imagine that he wants to
have a slut for a mother? Don't you suppose . . ."

It took only a short pace and a wide swing of her arm.
Abby screamed, more in fear than in pain, so Juliette
swung her arm generously and hit her again. Then once
more even harder.

In scurried the maid, her puzzled gaze switching from

where Abby sobbed on the couch to where Juliette stood coolly pulling on her gloves.

"There was something stuck on her face and I removed it for her," explained Juliette.

"What were that, ma'am?"

"An insufferably self-satisfied expression," said Juliette. "But I think it has gone now. I'll see myself out, thank you."

In the hall she paused to straighten her bonnet at the coat-stand mirror, and as she retied the ribbons the front door burst open and Jack Bennington barrelled through with only the briefest nod to acknowledge her presence. He looks furious too, she thought, looping the bow. The parlour door slammed but did little to muffle the angry roar that boomed out from the room beyond.

"You'll tell me what you've done with her or you'll feel the back of my hand, I swear that you will! I might have known there was more to your scheme than to give me the pleasure of your company today. It was one thing to disgrace yourself in front of the Governor, but to set that young scoundrel of a brother of yours after Rosaleen—that was going one gigantic step too far. You'll regret the day you planned this mischief, I tell you! Now, out with it! Where has he taken her?"

Abby whimpered something.

"Don't waste your breath denying it! I know you've been plotting and scheming something for weeks. As soon as I saw your sister in the hall I knew it was all your doing. He's been staying there, and you've been round there hatching your little plots. Go on, admit it before you try me too far."

There was a heavy silence, then a thump and a shriek from Abby.

Juliette bit her lip delicately and shrugged at her reflection. Samuel and Rosaleen Teipa, the mystery Maori beauty. Of course. But Jack Bennington was on the wrong track completely. She was certain that until this morning Samuel had never seen the girl. She could have returned to the parlour and straightened the matter out. Indeed she could. On the other hand, if she did that she would interrupt Abby's extremely interesting afternoon. Another shriek made her shrug as she picked up her parasol. Abby deserved this so thoroughly, it would be a pity to spoil it for her.

Quietly she let herself out of the front door.

Thirty-four

The war had already stuttered its first in a series of minor skirmishes when Leigh and his son arrived in New Plymouth. Their clipper approached land in the late afternoon. All they could see of the shore was a string of cottony breakers and a low muffler of cloud.

"I don't think this is the right place, Papa. There must be a mistake," said the boy.

"Why is that?"

"Where is the beautiful mountain?"

Leigh patted his shoulders, proud he should remember "But the mountain only shows itself to ships which have virtuous women on board, son."

"What does that mean?"

Leigh's friends laughed. "Let's hope you never find out!"

"We'll find good fortune here, eh, son? More adventures than you ever dreamed of."

"Yes, Papa," he said doubtfully. "Do you mean ale and tossing dice in the evenings?"

"That's everyday stuff here. We'll have some real adventures, so cheer up. Why the long face?"

"I get tired and sleepy waiting for you outside hotels. It's so cold and uncomfortable, and I miss being at home."

His father's voice was playful but a hard note lay just below the surface. "What's this talk? I think you'd better reconsider your attitude there, young man. I didn't go to all the trouble it took me to claim my son just to have him moan for a wet nurse." He clapped him forcefully on the back. "Cheer up, there, son. New Plymouth town will be different from Sydney. You'll be a volunteer in the army;

that's not like anything else in the world. There's nothing to give you quite the same thrill as having a musket in your hands and the quarry in your sights."

"What's quarry?"

"The thing you are aiming to shoot, of course."

"You mean kill?"

"Of course, kill!" he said heartily. "What else do you think an army is for?"

"Mother says that armies are to keep the peace."

When he laughed the brisk sea breeze tugged his beard into floating shreds. "What else would you expect? Women always try to make things look pretty. Listen, son. Armies are full of soldiers, right?"

"Yes, Papa."

"And soldiers have guns to shoot and kill the enemy, is that not so?"

"Yes, Papa." They were closer to shore now. Row after row of tents poked up white and ghostly behind the sand hills. Hopefully young Leigh said, "Perhaps the men in the army office will guess how old I am."

Now there was no warmth at all in Leigh's voice. "You'll tell them what I said and you'll come out with it straight and clear. I'll be right behind you. If you say you're fifteen and I say you're fifteen, then you are fifteen, my boy! Is that clear? And call me 'sir' now, not Papa. We're soldiers now, aren't we?"

"Are you sure the military will want us?"

"What? Two fine brave soldiers with their own muskets, bayonets, pistols, and some ammunition? Son, they will snap us up. We'll be at-easing and attentioning before we have even had a chance to look around the barracks."

"Proclamation!" announced a poster on the notice board beside the bridge railing. Young Leigh read:

"The inhabitants will in future be required to have a candle or lamp at their front windows at night ready to light in case of alarm, and are desired to secure their doors and lower windows. The police to see to this.

C. E. Gold,
Colonel Commanding the Forces,
New Zealand

New Plymouth, 20th April, 1860."

"Colonel Gold, eh?" said his father, reading over his shoulder. "I wonder if the military has changed as much as this town? Hardly know the place, would you?"

New Plymouth's quiet air of dignity had gone, trampled underfoot by the jostle of people who crammed into the muddy streets. Two carts were bogged down to the axles in Devon Street, and great queues of laden vehicles waited to navigate around them. Tents were pitched in every yard, every house seemed to have a makeshift lean-to attached to one or both sides, and furniture was stacked to the roof of every verandah they passed. Young Leigh thought that he had never seen so many children at once, scrambling, playing, and calling out everywhere. Some pulled extravagantly ugly faces at him as they strode by.

The recruiting officer was red-faced, laconic, and had a perfectly smooth bald head which fascinated young Leigh. He sat behind a desk in an open-fronted tent and looked young Leigh up and down with open disbelief when he quaveringly stated his age, but wrote his name down in the book anyway. Leigh winked encouragingly at his son and the boy tried to smile back. The atmosphere of feverishness made him wish that he could hold his father's hand; the warm security of contact would make this cold fluttery feeling go away. He angled his steps so that he was walking closer to his father.

"What's this?" said Leigh in annoyance, brushing the small hand away. "You're in the army now. You're a soldier, not a milksop. Don't tell me you're starting to miss your mother, a great big boy like you."

"No, Papa—I mean, sir." He swallowed hard. "Of course not."

"Good. Then straighten your back. Hold your head up. Make me proud of you." He went on to describe once again how he had joined the army just the minute he was able to, and what a proud feeling it was to serve his Queen and his country. While he was talking young Leigh gazed about miserably. It seemed that the camp was dismantling, ready to move. The long rows of tents were collapsing, can-

vas rolls piling up in a heap. Horses were stamping their
hind hooves as their bridles and harnesses were buckled
on. There was shouting and the clanging of metal as enormous saucepans and black try-pots were stacked onto a
long cart.

"It looks as though we'll be seeing some action straight
away," said Leigh with relish.

"I say!" called a voice with a soft Scots burr. "I say there!
Yardley! Is that Leigh Yardley?"

Both swung around to see two tall, brawny, red-haired
soldiers advancing from between the heaquarters sheds,
familiar-looking fellows dressed in the uniform of the
Taranaki Volunteers. Their flannel battle dress was decorated with round V.R. buttons, and they wore flat round
caps adorned with braid and black leather leggings. Both
had wide belts and crisscrossed diagonal bands across
their chests.

"It *is* young Yardley, I was right! Cameron here didna
recognise you, but I'd know you anywhere! And this is
your papa! Sorry, sir, not to have picked who you were, but
you've obscured your face a mite since our last acquaintance. Well, how bonny to meet you both. I'm Chester, sir,
no doubt you'd nae recall a detail like that. Conway is
somewhere hereabouts but he's a sergeant now and very
grand."

Young Leigh shook hands shyly, his father with a
grudging courtesy.

"Do you recall who we are now, lad?"

Leigh nodded.

"And how's that bonny mother of yours? Ah, but we
miss her. She knew how to make the best stew on the
whole of the mountainside, and her bread was so grand I
can still taste it. How is she, young fellow? Still as pretty
as ever? She's nae in town with you then, is she?"

"We've enlisted,' said Leigh shortly, noticing his son's
confusion at the mention of his mother. He'd clip his ears
smartly if he started to cry, by the hell he would. Giving
him a warning nudge, he said, "We've become soldiers
now, haven't we, son?"

Chester laughed, showing large yellowish teeth. "How

did you slip in, then? You're nae but a wee lad. Did your father hide you under his coat?"

Leigh said angrily, "Lower your voice! Someone might hear you."

"Ah, but they don't care," said Cameron easily. "They'll take any that's willing, just so long as they're nae Irish. There's been this trouble with the Irish soldiers. You see, they have this idea that the Maoris are too much like themselves to be enemies, with their fish and potatoes and their easy way of life. They've been saying it be murder to shoot them."

"You've got to be joking."

"It's nae joke . . . begorra!" and they both laughed again.

Chester said, "It's the Irish way to be always against the Government. The Maoris say that the missionaries taught them to look up to heaven to pray and while they were busy doing that the Government stole the land from under their feet. The Irish can sympathise with that, so, when it comes to battle, don't want to fight. We heard that though they are short of volunteers they are turning away all the Irish."

"Is that so?" Leigh wasn't interested. "Well, son, we'd best get ourselves settled."

The Seftons were so pleased to have found familiar faces that they did not hear the snub for what it was. Eagerly they offered to help the Yardleys find their commanding officer and their kit issue; and then, once their weapons and cartouche boxes were safely stowed, they insisted on taking them back down into the town for one last look before they began the march out that afternoon. Leigh was disgruntled; he would have preferred to go alone and sup at his old stamping grounds, but young Leigh was delighted. The Sefton boys made excellent guides and pointed out the fortifications that had been added to the town. At a signal from the church bells all the citizens had been instructed to go to one or other of the specially strengthened buildings and stay there until the danger had passed.

"Not that there will be any danger, of course," they added. "There'll nae be a Maori with a drop of fighting blood left in him by the time we've routed them tomorrow, eh, lad?"

"Look at that," said Leigh, pointing to a tight crowd knotted together outside the iron-sided Town Hall. "Who is that old geezer those people are listening to?"

"Some old Quaker, I think," said Cameron. "I forget his name. He's always preaching out against the fighting."

Chester said, "What do you say we lend him an ear for a spell? He's good for a laugh. His ideas make nae sense but he has a fine way of rolling the words over his tongue when he speaks."

In one hand the man shook a shiny black Bible, but the other hand pointed and gesticulated at individuals in the little audience as though he addressed each of them personally. Young Leigh was fascinated by the way the man's white tufted eyebrows jumped and quivered on his tanned brow as he talked.

"And I repeat that it is a damnable sin, yes, a damnable sin in the eyes of God, to shed any blood. God Himself has said so and we should hearken to what God says. To ignore the word of God is to condemn ourselves to the everlasting fires of hell!"

Young Leigh's eyes widened. He had never heard preaching like this before—words so fiery that they burned into his brain.

His father was considerably less impressed. "What about under provocation, old man? What about self-defence?"

The Quaker's head turned slowly towards the source of the taunts. Young Leigh shivered as the flinty eyes focused first on him and then on his father. Truly this man must be a messiah of some kind, or a prophet like Moses, come to save the people from an evil war.

"Provocation?" questioned the Quaker in a thundering indignation. "This is a man who does not know his Bible. In this Holy Book the Lord God says we should turn the other cheek. 'I will be your defence!' saith the Lord. 'There will be no salvation but through me!' "

"Poppycock!" called Leigh, and his son squirmed in embarrassment. "What about these Maoris, then? What would you do if one of those rascals poked a musket barrel into your face, hey? What would your Bible tell you to do then?"

There were murmurs of assent at this.

"I shall tell you exactly what I would do! If my wife and children were murdered by the enemy, yea, even if their blood was spilled before my very eyes, I would still not raise my hand to their murderers."

"Then you are mad!" said Leigh in disgust.

"No!" cried the Quaker. "It is you who are mad. You who don uniforms and take up muskets and venture forth into the land to kill the Maoris. It is you who will suffer the everlasting torments of hell! Yes, I tell you truly . . ."

Young Leigh, pressed close against his father in the crush, felt him grow rigid with anger, then suddenly stoop and pick something up. In the next moment his father's flexed elbow struck him on the side of the head, and he staggered to regain his balance. Tumult sounded in his ears, and when he looked again the Quaker was standing very tall and still and seemed to be glaring directly at him, only this time with a terrible expression on his face and a dripping red blotch in the centre of his brow where a patch of skin had been ripped away.

"Serves him right!" A woman in the front broke the awed silence. "Serves him right for insulting our brave soldiers!" As she spoke she wielded her furled parasol like a whipping stick.

"Quickly, let's go," said Cameron urgently. "They'll all be whaling into him now. The constabulary will come and if we get caught in a street brawl . . ." He whistled. "It'll be nae but the court-martial and triangle for us!"

Obediently the Yardleys hustled after the Sefton brothers. Young Leigh pushed through the gaps forced by his father's much bigger frame. He was feeling physically sick. His father had just thrown a stone and struck a holy man in the face. Struck a holy man while he was talking about God! Young Leigh was no stranger to bullying but he had never realised until now that grownups were capable of similarly vicious acts.

His mother had always told him that grownups were noble and virtuous, excusing his frequent bad behaviour with the reasoning that he would "grow out of it." Now he did not know what to believe and the bewilderment made him giddy. He longed to be able to creep away quietly by himself to sit and think until he felt better.

Twelve hours later he lay on a blanket and stared up at the glittering sky. His body ached with fatigue, but his mind would not rest. The air was filled with the mingled scents of smoke, crushed fern, and sweaty bodies, and sang with the drowsy whine of mosquitoes. Despite the green fern heaped onto the dying fires to discourage them the pests had arrived in their hungry thousands. Slaps and muttered curses disturbed young Leigh's troubled thoughts. As he lay uncomfortably on the cold damp ground he pictured his mother in her big brass bed and his sister in her cot in the room she now had to herself. Skippy would be asleep in his bed on the porch, curled around neatly with nose resting on paws and one ear pricked up the tiniest little bit, listening for rats or for intruders. Even in a deep sleep he was always mindful of his job as watchdog and kept himself alert. Who would be playing with Skippy now? Who would take him for walks? Who would throw a ball for him to fetch?

Overwhelmed by homesickness, Leigh began to weep quietly. He wriggled over gently so that his back was resting against his father's wide back. The feeling of warmth gave him some comfort, but not much. Bleakly he stared into the smoke-blurred darkness. More than anything he wished that he could wake up and find himself safely back in his own bed at home.

The afternoon was a morass of confusion. Soldiers were moving about doing tasks that seemed to make no sense—digging ditches, tying bundles of manuka together, riding up and down on horseback looking grimly determined. Leigh tagged along after his father. All he could remember was that they were in the Fourth Company of Volunteers and their commander was a Captain Watkins. Cameron pointed him out and said that as long as they took care to do exactly what he said they couldn't go wrong. And all that he could understand was that they were going to fight some Maoris who were so completely out of sight behind high wooden fences on the hilltop that Leigh privately wondered how anybody could be sure that they were there.

On the other hand there were any number of Maoris down here mingling with the soldiers. *Kupapas* or "friendlies," the Seftons called them. They looked anything but friendly to young Leigh as they rode about shouting and laughing in a casually insolent manner. They rode like the Maoris in Auckland town, Leigh noticed, with stirrups but no saddle, and with the stirrup irons gripped between their bare toes. Leigh looked at them suspiciously, trying to decide whether they were enemy spies. His back ached from bending over the manuka bundles and he was beginning to feel distinctly hungry and thirsty when suddenly musket fire spat from the palisaded pa. Immediately the bugle sounded, telling the soldiers to take up their arms and make ready, and the next moment Leigh had turned from a thirteen-year-old child into a frightened, bewildered soldier.

Leigh huddled down beside his father, his boots already thick with the yellow clay of the trench bottom. If he looked up he could see the feathery tops of brown fern, and above that the row of pointed tree trunks at the top of the hill. The only sounds were the pattering of musket fire from the Maoris, the occasional wheeling cry of gulls, and from somewhere close by the sigh of breakers. He had not realised that the sea was so near. Their entire march yesterday had been through head-high fern and light bush and Leigh had begun to wonder if they were walking in circles. Now they had been in the trench for over an hour.

From a breastworks nearby the cannon coughed another black ball at the palisades. One of the Maoris in their trench poked up his tattooed face to inspect the damage.

"Ah." He grinned in satisfaction. "Nearly ready, nearly ready. We have a *kokiri* soon, eh? A charge, yes?"

"Stand to your arms!" called Captain Watkins. "Aim high on the palisade. Are you ready? Fire!"

"We're in it now, son! Stand on that powder box so that you can see to aim properly."

He tried to copy his father: he had been determined to follow along and be as good as any of the other men so that his father would be pleased with him. But somehow when it came to translating the resolution into action his body did not respond the way he expected. Obediently he steadied himself on the box and looked towards the pa, his musket barrel sticking out like a pointer to direct his attention. Now that his head was level with the ground he was suddenly overcome with dread. He was so unprotected, so vulnerable. He had the strongest sensation that his head was about to be lopped from his shoulders and there was nothing, nothing that he could do to save himself.

Beside him his father fired his shot and ducked down to reload. After a few seconds he was back again, sliding the musket confidently in his large fleshy hands. "Come on, son!" he shouted, half encouragingly, half in annoyance. "Squeeze that trigger!"

Leigh's fingers fumbled over the tight metal hook. He tried to pull at it but there seemed to be no strength in his fingers. The looming pa seemed to paralyse him. White puffs of smoke flowered on the dark posts and a bullet ploughed crazily through the ground in front of him, kicking up a spray of loose dirt. He leaned against the bank and stared at the scratch it had made in the soil.

"Reload!" called Captain Watkins. "Reload and stand ready!"

Looking up from his tamping rod, Leigh realised that his son was still propped and motionless in the same position. Exasperatedly he grabbed the boy's arm and dragged him down into the trench. "What in hell and hades is the matter with you?" he demanded. "Are you paralysed or what?" When the boy would not look at him but crouched like a sick hen with his head bowed, Leigh grabbed his chin roughly and pulled his face around. "My God!" he said disgustedly. "Crying! Crying like a namby-pamby, parlour-cake, yellow-livered . . ."

"Easy on there! He's nae but a lad!" protested Cameron from farther along the trench.

"Aye, that he is." He let go of the boy's chin so suddenly that young Leigh almost slipped sideways. "He's just a lad and no use for men's business."

"Ready to charge!"

"We'll be going now, son. We soldiers will be getting about our duty," said Leigh contemptuously.

"I tried," pleaded the boy. "I really tried."

His father did not so much as glance in his direction.

"Charge!" yelled Captain Watkins.

Leigh watched his father scramble up the clay bank, his boots scrabbling for footholds. Then he was on his feet and running, stooped over like the wave of other men from the trench, all holding their muskets crosswise and treading with a rapid, bent-legged gait. More white puffs bloomed on the palisades and some of the men stumbled. Leigh crept back onto the powder box. Most of the men were almost at the foot of the serrated wall now. His eyes flicked along the moving row but he could not see the bulky shape of his father. Glancing back along the line, he paused for a second at each man. His father was definitely not there. Crouching awkwardly, the men now scurried towards the cannon-blasted breach at the far end of the palisades.

Suddenly young Leigh cried out, aghast, and before he even realised what was happening he had propelled himself out of the trench and was sprinting across the open space to where his father lay helplessly exposed to enemy bullets. Dashing to turn him over, he noticed that the cloth of his trousers was soggy with blood between knee and groin. It clung to his hand where he touched him and filled his mind with such panic that he became unaware of the zing of bullets or the warning shouts from the men ranged in the trenches behind him. Young Leigh's world contained only the glare of the sun and that fallen body which gasped in perilous danger at his feet.

"I'll soon drag you to safety," he promised. As he bent over his father, something whacked him violently in the chest, knocking all the breath out of him and tumbling him over backwards. Struggling to get up, he wondered why his father had struck him like that when he was only doing his best to help. He could not move; something still pushed at his chest. When he glanced down at his scarlet-splashed shirt he realised what had happened. He died almost instantly.

"I could kill you myself and nae lose a minute's sleep over it," declared Cameron. "A real man would have more sense than to drag a wee bairn into a dirty war and then try to goad him into fighting. Aye, I could kill you myself for what you did to that lad."

Leigh's glazed eyes were turned towards him but he showed no sign of having heard. When Cameron lifted his head and held the water pannier to his lips some of the liquid flowed into his mouth, but when his head was lowered again most of it ran down one side of his chin and puddled on the oilskin stretcher. Cameron wiped it up with a bunched rag.

"You shouldn't talk to him like that," whispered another soldier who was sharing the duty with him.

"Oh, aye. Why not, then?"

"Because he's fading. He's dying, they say. And what a hell of a place to go in, too." The tent smelled of sweat and vomit. Flies circled in the warm air.

"He's nae dying! The surgeon said that he was fine after the amputation."

"But someone told him about his son. Didn't realise who it was, just told him about the brave lad who bought his ticket home while he was trying to rescue one of the wounded. Didn't mean no harm, but it knocked the spirit out of him. He's been fading ever since."

"That was a fine wee lad of his. Like a brother to me, he was. I canna for the life of me understand why his father would bring him to a place like this."

Shrugging, the soldier said, "When he was told about his boy he said, 'All I wanted was to make a man of him.' That's all he said then, and he's said nothing since."

"Only trying to make a man of him . . . aye, he did that an' all," said Cameron. "It'll kill his mother. She's a sweet lass. I warrant she didna know where the bairn was being taken. Poor Mrs. Yardley. He was her only son, too, an' all."

It was such a pathetic little bundle, some muddy clothes folded neatly, a clasp knife and the whistle he had taken on a string around his neck the day of the race meeting. She could remember it bouncing against his chest as he ran out to the gate . . . ran to meet his father.

"We don't usually wrap the things in a flag, like. In fact there ain't usually no things. But we made an exception in 'is case, what with 'im bein' so young an' his father bein' killed as well."

"I beg your pardon?" She had been staring at the clothes and now raised her eyes to his, very slowly. They seemed to float upward by themselves. She was a strikingly pretty woman, past her best, of course, but with those fine bones that people called "aristocratic" and large, dark eyes.

He began to explain again about the flag and how sorry he was but it was plain that she didn't hear him.

A little girl came running in, open-faced and friendly until she saw him, whereupon she suddenly became shy and clung onto the back of her mother's dress, peering around.

"What's that?" she asked at last.

"These are Leigh's things, dear. The kind man brought them for us."

"Isn't he coming home now?"

"No, dear." Her voice was clear and dreamy.

"Why not?"

"His father took him away, and they went to live with Jesus."

"Oh." She thought about it for a few seconds. "Well, I'm glad that he didn't take me! I don't want to see Jesus until I am very, very old!"

When she had skipped out again the woman said, "Please tell me what you know. Please tell me how it happened."

She was so calm that he could scarcely believe it. Her expression, her voice—neither of them seemed natural.

"They both died bravely, extremely bravely. I weren't right there but the other men in their company told me all about it. . . ." He began to describe the events of that afternoon but it was soon obvious that she was not really listening. It was too much for her to take in at once.

Abruptly Juliette left the table where she had been standing and walked to the window. She stood with her eyes closed while the soldier's voice beat in her ears. Her abdomen had begun to contract with pains and she stood with her back to the man so that he would not see her flinch. Childbirth, she realised dully. I had him with these pains and I am losing him in the same way. Oh, Leigh, Leigh, I cared for you with such tender protectiveness and it was all for nothing. You had no life at all and yet it has been taken from you just as you were taken from me.

The soldier cleared his throat. When the woman looked around he saw the unguarded agony in her eyes.

"Such a terrible shame, it were. Such a terrible shame, an' his first day of action an' all."

"His father took him away and murdered him," she said.

Because the soldier had been warned and knew a little of the home situation he said quietly, "His father died too, ma'am."

"Yes, he died." Her voice was throbbing with pain. "He died but he had lived a full life. The boy hadn't even begun his. Do you know what he was like?" she demanded. "A tomcat dragging its young away and killing it! He came and stole him away. Nobody told me what was happening." After an awkward pause she whispered, "I didn't even say goodbye. If he'd been killed in an accident there would be a funeral, his body. I could have said goodbye. This way there's nothing. Nothing at all."

"Please, ma'am," said the soldier, shuffling on his feet. "Please don't be bitter. We're real sorry, but nowt can bring 'im back. It's all in God's hands now."

"In God's judgement, too!" She seemed to grit her teeth for a moment and her eyes stood out, unnaturally bright. Then she relaxed a fraction. "You are right. I shall try not to be bitter." At the mantelshelf she hesitated and turned to him. "Have you any children of your own?"

"Five, ma'am, so far."

"Then you are fortunate. Have you a son of ten or . . . or twelve, by any chance?"

"I have one of nine. Edward, my oldest. Named for the Prince of Wales, he were."

"Then would you be so good as to give him these?" and from the mantelshelf she took three yellow-wrapped packages, each tied with a ribbon bow.

"But . . . oh no, ma'am. I couldn't do that."

"Please do. They were to have been his Christmas gifts. His father took him away a few days before Christmas and I kept the gifts hoping that . . . so that if he came back they would be there waiting for him. Now he never will . . ."

She thrust them into his hands, bursting into tears as she did so. "Please take them and go . . . go quickly, please!"

"I don't know how to thank you . . ."

She shook her head violently. "Please go. I was so terribly afraid that I would never see him again, and now . . ."

Hurriedly he left the room, collected his shako from the maidservant, and walked swiftly up the path to where his horse was tethered at the gate. As he mounted up he could hear her wailing. The noise unnerved him. No matter how often he performed this task he never would get used to it.

Thirty-five

"No doubt you have come here to gloat, Juliette."

Maire sat in her high-backed chair, striking the same pose that Juliette remembered from that long-ago day when she had first seen and been awed by her. She had been casually regal, like a proud animal that fears no other. Over the years she had become more haughty and forbidding. Age had stiffened her while excellent grooming preserved her dramatic style. As always her gown was spotless black, encasing her from chin to wrists. Her hair pulled the skin of her face upward, smoothing out the lines and tightening the chin. But for all that it was an old face, pouched under the eyes and with a mouth bracketed by creases of suffering.

Leigh's death really did shatter her, thought Juliette, recalling the stories she had heard, about how Maire had plunged into such intense mourning that all furniture at Fintona was draped in black, nobody but nuns and priests were admitted to the house, and Maire herself ate only bread and a little milk for more than six months.

"We have not come to gloat but to say goodbye, Mama," Stephen told her. "I have given Mr. McLeay our address and will have any dealings necessary through him."

"Is it really essential that you go away like this?" she asked. Her voice was as conciliatory as she could manage to make it.

"I'm afraid so, Mama. There is no place for Juliette in Auckland society and I will not have my wife and children snubbed. It need not have been so. You always had sufficient influence in this town to have made sure that your daughter-in-law and your grandchildren were accepted,

yet you did nothing but encourage gossip against them.
I've been disappointed with Rose and Jane too, but we
have not come here to find fault, simply to take our leave."

"And you have done so." She rang the bell beside her
chair. "Tawa will see you out."

"Goodbye, Aunt Maire," said Juliette.

Ignoring her, Maire spoke to the Maori woman. "Captain and Mrs. Yardley are leaving now, Tawa."

"Yes, matua. Would you like Dora to read to you now?"

"Send her in, please, Tawa. I could enjoy some *pleasant*
company for what remains of the afternoon."

Stephen laughed. "Goodbye, Mama," he said.

"Are you sure that this is all the luggage you have?"
asked Stephen in mild surprise. "Two crates, one caged
dog, one cabin trunk, and that old workbasket?"

"Quite sure," said Juliette as she locked the door. "And
one of the crates is full of Gladys' things. The Catholic Mission did rather well out of our departure."

"You should have given them the workbasket too. That
thing is far too disgraceful an object for the wife of a prosperous shipowner to be carrying about."

She smiled mysteriously. "That means as much to me as
Clarissa does. I'll never give that away, nor burn it nor sell
it—not that anybody would want to buy it. I agree, it is
tatty, but I have a very special reason for wanting to take
it to San Francisco with us."

"And what might that be?"

"Stephen," she said thoughtfully, "I really think that a
wife should keep a few little secrets from her husband."

"I strongly disagree with that!"

"Really?" She smiled mischievously. "Then you would
prefer that we confess all the little hidden things we have
kept from each other? That you should tell me all about
the ladies you have said sweet things to, and the . . ."

"Stop!" He laughed and swung her up into the carriage.
"We had best be on our way to the wharf or Gladys and the
children will be wondering what has delayed us."

"Let me have one last look at the house. I hate leaving a
place without a long backward glance. Tell me, Stephen, is
it true that in San Francisco the houses are tall and white

and dazzlingly beautiful, and that they are all arranged in rows on hillsides overlooking the harbour?"

"Yes, as a matter of fact, they are."

She said slowly, "I once knew someone whose only dream was to live in a house above the San Francisco Bay. She longed for that so much that she could describe every room in the house down to the last detail."

"What happened to her? Did she achieve her ambition?"

"No, but she had her dream and I rather think that to her it was almost the same thing."

"Perhaps. But I prefer reality and that, my sweet Olivine, is what we are going to enjoy."

Gladys and May waited on the deck of the *Mondrich Princess*. Standing beside them, looking lost, was a diminutive boy with a round girlish face and hair the colour of rich butter.

"I like my little bedroom!" May told her mother. "But it's so tiny and Gladys says she is going to have a bed in there too!"

"That's a c-cabin, and they're not b-b-beds—they're b-bunks!" said the boy.

"He has a funny way of talking," complained May, wrinkling up her nose.

Juliette said quickly, "That is called a stammer, May. It is not funny; more of a nuisance really, like losing your front teeth."

"Yes, yours look f-funny."

"And they'll grow, just as you, young man, will grow out of your stammer. Isn't that so, Stephen?"

"P-P-Papa says," began the boy at the same moment that his father said, "Of course he will."

Juliette looked from one to the other, laughing. "This will never do. All day whenever I have said 'Stephen' you have both rushed to answer. We cannot allow this to go on, can we? Even though Stephen is a perfectly splendid name, one of you will have to change." She knelt to the boy's level. "Papa has had his name for a very long time, so it wouldn't be fair to ask him to change his, would it now? But you, young man, are going to begin a new life in a new country. How would you like to have a new name, too?"

"I want a new name!" insisted May.

"We'll talk about that later," said Juliette. "But right now, would you please help Gladys see that Skippy's cage is loaded aboard safely? Good girl." When they had gone she said, "What do you say to that idea, young man?"

He looked confused. "What n-name do you want m-me to have?"

She took his tiny hands and held them between her gloved ones. "I rather like Daniel myself. Daniel is a brave, noble name. One of the finest names in the whole Bible. What do you think of that?"

He looked back at her steadily with clear brown eyes. "M-m-my mama was called Danielle."

"Yes, she was. Would you like to be named after her?"

"M-Mama would like that. Papa s-s-said I have to re-member her."

"And so you shall, dear. So you shall." She hugged him and looked over the top of his head to Stephen but could not read his expression because her eyes were blurred with tears.

Gently he placed a hand on her cheek. He was close to tears himself. "Thank you, sweet Olivine," he said.

GLOSSARY OF MAORI TERMS

E AHA MAU: What's it to you?

HAKA: war dance performed by warriors

HANGI: earth oven, or feast cooked in earth oven

HUHU: large winged insect with edible grub stage of development

HUIA: bird (now extinct) with greatly prized feathers

KAPAI: good

KAURI: timber tree

KAWAKAWA: timber tree

KINA: spiny sea egg

KOEKOEA: migrating, long-tailed cuckoo

KOKIRI: charge, as in battle

KOWHAI: tree with pretty yellow flowers

KUMARA: sweet potato

KURA: small fresh-water crayfish

MANA: prestige

MANUKA: tea tree, a shrub with tiny leaves

MAORI: native people; the word used as such means "normal"

MAORI (lower-case "m"): maypole swing

MATUA: a term of respect meaning "old mother"

MERE: a flat weapon used for clubbing or splitting the skull of the enemy; if made of greenstone, it would be priceless

MIRO: timber tree

MOKO: a tattoo

MOREPORK: a bird, so named from its cry

MURU: an ancient custom whereby the possessions of someone who has suffered a severe misfortune are plundered by other members of the same tribe

PA: fortified village

PAKEHA: white man

PATAKA: food store on stilts to keep food away from rats
PIPIS: clams
PIU-PIU: grass skirt made of rolled flax strips
POHUTUKAWA: tree with red blossoms that blooms at
   Christmastime
POI: soft ball on string used in women's dancing
PUHA: sow thistle, a little like spinach
RAUPO: reeds
RIMU: timber tree
TANGI: dirge for the dead; a wake
TANIWHA: a fabulous legendary monster
TAPU: sacred
TOHUNGA: native priest, wise man
TOITOI: coarse grass
TUI: a bird called parson bird for white feathers at its
   throat
TUPARA: double-barrelled shotgun
UMU: earth oven
UTU: revenge
WAIPIRO: literally, "stinking water"—whisky
WETA: large wingless long-horned locust
WHARE: a hut

Dear Reader:

If you enjoyed this book, and would like information about future books by this author and other Avon authors, we would be delighted to put you on the mailing list for our ROMANCE NEWSLETTER.

Simply *print* your name and address and send to Avon Books, Room 419, 959 Eighth Ave., N.Y., N.Y. 10019.

We hope to bring you many hours of pleasurable reading!

Sara Reynolds, Editor
Romance Newsletter

Book orders and checks should *only* be sent to Avon Mail Order Dept., 224 W. 57th St., N.Y., N.Y. 10019. Include 50¢ per copy for postage and handling; allow 6-8 weeks for delivery.

THE CAVE DREAMERS

JEANNE WILLIAMS

THE CAVE DREAMERS is a vivid, passionate
novel of the lives and loves of the women
across centuries who share the secret of
"The Cave of Always Summer." From the dawn
of time to the present, the treasured mystery
of the cave is passed and guarded, joining
generation to generation through
their dreams and desires.
83501-0/$7.95

An **AVON** Trade Paperback

Available wherever paperbacks are sold or directly from
the publisher. Include 50¢ per copy for postage and
handling: allow 6—8 weeks for delivery. Avon Books,
Mail Order Dept., 224 W. 57th St., N.Y., N.Y. 10019

Cave Dreamers 5-83

FROM THE MILLION-COPY BESTSELLING AUTHOR OF <u>CASTLES</u>

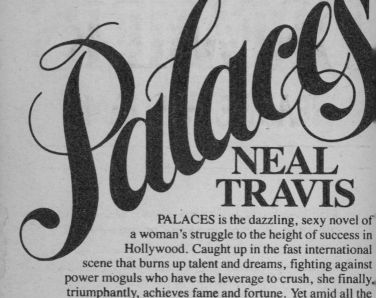

Palaces
NEAL TRAVIS

PALACES is the dazzling, sexy novel of a woman's struggle to the height of success in Hollywood. Caught up in the fast international scene that burns up talent and dreams, fighting against power moguls who have the leverage to crush, she finally, triumphantly, achieves fame and fortune. Yet amid all the glamour and excitement in the celluloid world of illusions, she almost loses the one man whose love is real!

An AVON Paperback   **84517-2/$3.95**

Available wherever paperbacks are sold or directly from the publisher.
Include 50¢ per copy for postage and handling; allow 6–8 weeks for delivery.
Avon Books, Mail Order Dept., 224 W. 57th St., N.Y., N.Y. 10019

Palaces 7-83